P9-CEX-992

ALSO BY STEVEN SPRUILL

Rulers of Darkness

Doubleday

New York London
Toronto
Sydney Auckland

Daughter
of
Darkness

Steven
Spruill

PUBLISHED BY DOUBLEDAY
a division of
Bantam Doubleday Dell Publishing Group, Inc.
1540 Broadway, New York, New York 10036

DOUBLEDAY and the portrayal of an anchor with a
dolphin are trademarks of Doubleday, a division of
Bantam Doubleday Dell Publishing Group, Inc.

Book design by Maria Carella

Library of Congress Cataloging-in-Publication Data
Spruill, Steven G.
Daughter of darkness / Steven Spruill. — 1st ed.
p.   cm.
I. Title.
PS3569.P733D38   1997   96-25040
813'.54—dc20   CIP

ISBN 0-385-48432-1

Printed in the United States of America

June 1997

First Edition

1   3   5   7   9   10   8   6   4   2

I dedicate this novel to my niece,
Lauren Emily Spruill,
a daughter of light

What communion hath light with darkness?

II Corinthians 6:14

1

Dr. Jenn Hluska paused in a hallway of the hospital's pediatrics wing, struck by a vague foreboding. Trying to pin it down, she decided she was just worried about Caroline, poor kid, all alone in Isolation and not doing so well. I'll check on her once more, Jenn thought, and then I'm outta here.

On impulse, she swerved into the doctors' lounge to see who was coming on duty, but the place was deserted, the shift change already over. The air, muggy with body heat, smelled of coffee grounds. On the mirror above the sinks, foggy circles marked where two of her fellow interns must have stood talking as they washed up. The cool glass had condensed that conversation into droplets of water that meandered down and dripped into the sinks. Jenn wished she could decode the plips and plops back into words. She loved being an intern, hated to miss anything, including the fleeting camaraderie of a shift change, but even twenty-four hours wasn't enough to catch all that was going on. She'd do another eight right now, no sweat, but it was against house rules—even the legendary zeal with which hospitals overworked their interns had its limits. Just as well; she could think of worse things, after all, than going home, locking the rest of the world out, and luxuriating in a long, hot shower.

But first, Caroline.

In the anteroom of the Isolation suite, Jenn changed into sterile scrubs then checked the mirror to make sure she'd gotten all her hair tucked up into the surgical cap. Seeing herself like this, wrapped from head to foot in the clean blue armor of her profession, gave her a warm feeling. With the mass of blond hair out of sight and her freckled nose hidden by the mask, she could see no trace of Jenn, youngest intern ever at Adams Memorial. This was Dr. Hrluska, shoulders squared, glad—now that she was a doctor—to be tall, no doubts or fears showing in the cool, green gaze visible above the mask line.

As she stepped through into Caroline's room, Jenn tried to muster some hope, but she knew not much could have changed in the few hours since she'd last checked. Was she overdoing it, getting too involved emotionally? But how could she help it?

Caroline was sitting up in bed, propped against a bank of pillows. Despite her closed eyes, the tension in her face hinted that she was not truly asleep. A lump rose to Jenn's throat. She wanted to hurry to the bedside, gather the girl in her arms and comfort her, but she knew that even her touch would be painful, any movement of the swollen joints more curse than blessing. Such an engaging kid, even in her illness—chestnut hair braided into a pigtail, cheeks rosy with the blood of bursting capillaries. Some might find her face, lengthening toward womanhood, plain—but not if they had seen the wide smile she could bring up even now in her suffering.

Caroline opened her eyes. "Dr. Hrluska," she whispered. "I didn't hear you come in."

"How's it going?"

Caroline made a face, and Jenn knew it was because a shrug, the all-purpose gesture of childhood, would have hurt too much. "How's the soreness today? Better? Worse?"

"About the same, I think. Did you hurt this way too when you had leukemia?"

Jenn nodded.

"But you got better."

"And so will you."

Caroline managed a small version of the smile and Jenn felt a fleeting pressure around her heart. Maybe it wasn't a lie. There was still time. But not much.

"Were you . . . scared sometimes?" Caroline asked.

"You bet I was." Jenn took her hand, hating the barrier of the glove. Only a few microns of latex, helping keep away the infections that could kill now, but how Caroline must long for a true touch. Settling on the edge of the bed, Jenn helped her shift position and adjusted the pillow behind her head. Even these small, careful movements made Caroline wince, driving home how much ground she had lost. One after another, this wretched disease was stealing even the smallest comforts from her. Jenn remembered how it had been, lying week after week in a room like this one. At first, she, too, could rest propped up against pillows, but then the pain in her joints had begun to boil so steadily that real rest was impossible. After much torturous exploration, she'd found a posture that hurt the least, facing the mattress, hunching over her elbows and knees, her forehead pressed against the sheets. If it became necessary, she could show the pose to Caroline—she could do that much.

Easing the back of her hand onto Caroline's forehead, Jenn was alarmed at the feverish burn, so warm it penetrated the glove in an instant. Better increase the acetaminophen level and step it up to five doses a day. Stroking gently down Caroline's arm, Jenn felt for the doughy consistency that would signal rejection of the bone marrow graft. The skin was still resilient, but the thinness, the dwindling cushion of fat and muscle, deepened her fear and frustration. Damn it, why wasn't Caroline getting better? She'd been through the chemo, the marrow transplant, she should be turning the corner. This wasn't twenty years ago, when two thirds of children with acute lymphocytic leukemia died. These days, the expected death rate for kids with ALL was only 5 percent. The rest were either fully cured or went into remission. They weren't supposed to die—not anymore.

And if this is more than leukemia?

A chill passed through Jenn. The even darker affliction that could mask itself as leukemia occurred so rarely she'd been able to avoid thinking about it, but no longer. Two of the three signs *were* present: Caroline had sickened at twelve, just as she entered puberty. And she was not responding to treatment.

Jenn's heart clenched. If this *was* hemophagic leukemia, no one in this hospital, in this whole city, would know it but her. Would she cure Caroline or let her die? When she'd decided on pediatrics, she'd known one day she might have to face this, but not yet, not so soon.

There is one more sign, she thought. Please, God, don't let it be there. Not now. She stood a moment, fighting a sudden, queasy foreboding.

"You look awfully serious, Doctor. What are you thinking about?"

"How thin you are. I think you'd feel better if we could put a pound or two back on you. Don't you like the food they're bringing you?"

Caroline's mouth twisted in distaste.

"What if I could bring you something from outside—pizza, ice cream?"

"No thanks."

"Nothing at all?"

"Uh-uh."

That's enough, Jenn told herself, but knew it was not. "A person can be hungry," she said, "but not know what she wants. Could it be like that?"

"No, Dr. Hrluska. I just don't have any appetite. I'm sorry."

"That's all right." Jenn permitted herself a measure of relief. Back when I was sick, she thought, I'd have said yes. I was hungry all the time, though I didn't realize for what—

She heard someone coming in the hall, the soft tread of athletic shoes, punctuated by a faint tick—Caroline's father, and one of his Nikes must be untied, the lace tapping the floor. Jenn waited, then rose from the bedside and turned to greet him.

"Doctor, how's my girl today?" The cheeriness in his voice didn't make it up to his eyes.

"Hanging in there. I'd like to get her fever down and her weight up, but I'm encouraged about the graft."

"Good . . . good."

Jenn eased back as he hurried to his daughter's bedside, a tall, handsome man, noticeably thinner than when he'd brought Caroline in a month ago. At the start he'd come from his bank dressed in impeccable Brooks Brothers' suits, but lately it was jeans that showed beneath the low hem of the sterile gown. His new thinness, mirroring Caroline's, touched Jenn. He was a good father whose life was being simplified in a terrible way by his daughter's ordeal. Food didn't matter, clothes, the looseness of a shoe, only Caroline.

I've got to get her turned around, Jenn thought.

Turning to leave, she heard the distant rumble of a food cart and decided to wait and see how Caroline actually responded to food when it was under her nose. In minutes, a nurse's aide, capped and gloved, brought in the special tray, everything thoroughly microwaved to make sure it was free of bacteria. When the aide set it on the tray table, Caroline turned her head away.

"C'mon, kiddo," Mr. Osborne said. "You heard what the doctor said about your weight. Down the hatch."

"I don't want to. It hurts when I move my arms."

"I'll help, okay?"

"I'm not a baby and I don't want to be fed."

Jack Osborne's stricken look raised its own reflection in his daughter's face. "Oh, all right," Caroline said.

Jenn had seen enough. Leave the two of them alone now, get out of here, go on home, but something about the tableau held her: Mr. Osborne, tall and dark, raising a plastic tumbler of grape juice toward his daughter's mouth—

Déjà vu swept Jenn, so powerful it startled her. In her mind she saw her father in the dead of night, materializing beside her bed ten years ago—not Dad, but her biological father, Zane. A big man, cat-graceful, with the fine, straight nose of a Roman, sable hair cut short and brushed up, jade eyes simmering in the feeble glow of the room's night light. In her memory, the face bore a look of fatherly adoration. . . .

But that couldn't be how he was, could it?

A sudden sense of loss made her push the memory away.

Turning, she left father and daughter in their cocoon of shared love and pain. In the hall, she stripped off the cap and gloves in vehement tugs.

"Jenn."

Turning, she saw him leaning against the wall, elbows on the wide wooden rail, one foot propped back. He was wearing his usual jeans and leather jacket that, despite his bigness, made her think of James Dean—the old poster Dad continually teased Mom about keeping. Just the sight of him raised her spirits, but she mimicked his blasé tone. "Hugh."

He smiled, showing her he got it. "I would pay money," he said, "for a tape of you pulling that cap off. The way all that hair tumbled down, almost in slow motion, like a golden waterfall on some low-gravity planet. Or a torch as it flares to life—"

"Stop," she laughed. "You're forgiven. Just, please, no more metaphors."

"Similes."

"As if you would know. Didn't you flunk English?"

"Couldn't learn the parts of speech," he agreed equably. The easy modesty was one of the things she loved about him. He'd gotten straight A's at Walt Whitman, one of the top high schools in the Washington area, but she would never have known it if she hadn't caught the "Book Talk" interview on a local cable station. The host, a crusty professor at George Mason U., had asked why Hugh never went to college and Hugh had said his grades were too low, and then the man had held up a fistful of Hugh's high school report cards, dug up who knows how.

"I thought you'd be off duty by now," Hugh said.

"I am. Got to write in a chart, then I'm out of here."

"I've always wanted to hug someone wearing scrubs. May I?" He said it lightly, but it made her wonder how her face must have looked when she'd pulled off the mask. She held out her arms.

Using the propped foot to launch himself fluidly from the wall, he pulled her close, cradling her head against his shoulder. It felt wonderful. The leather of his jacket smelled of clover, and she picked up a trace of fresh mud on his loafers.

"Been lying out in some field again?"

"How'd you know?"

"Never try to fool me, Hugh McCall."

He stood back from her, gazing at her with a serious expression, and she felt suddenly uncomfortable, wondering if he knew, somehow, that she was the one doing the fooling.

"Come on," she said, and led him down the hall. At the nurses' station she pulled Caroline's chart without breaking stride and kept going to her on-call room.

Hugh followed her into the narrow, windowless chamber and plopped down on the cot. Picking up a brown bag on the bed table, he sniffed it. "Supper?"

"Someone else's," Jenn said. "Probably Brad Dietz's."

"That resident who's always hitting on you?"

"They all do that." Seeing Hugh's stricken expression, Jenn laughed. "It's got nothing to do with me. Male residents feel they have to act horny around any female staff or their stethoscopes will shrivel up."

"Nothing to do with you, ri-i-ight."

"Aren't male novelists the same?" she asked innocently.

"No. Our . . . stethoscopes only shrivel if the typesetter brings our hardback in at under three hundred pages."

Jenn scribbled a note about Caroline's bone marrow graft and increased her standing order for acetaminophen. Then she settled next to Hugh on the cot.

He said, "You're not about to get fresh, are you?"

"Maybe."

"What if Brad comes in?"

"He'll run right out again. You look very alpha-male right now."

"I do?"

He sounded surprised. It amazed Jenn how unattuned he seemed to his own intense masculinity. The jeans and leather jacket were not an affectation for him, simply the safest clothes for falling off a motorcycle. He rode the bike so much his thick brown hair always looked a little windblown. Lean-hipped, big-shouldered, at six four he must realize his size was the first thing people saw, but he dealt with it by disarming them with humor and a soft voice, by taking care not to stand too close. He'd never been anything but gentle with her, and yet he had this intriguing bad-boy aura about him. The host on "Book Talk" had failed to get a straight answer on why Hugh had spurned college. Did anyone besides her know it was because he'd decided he'd rather go live with a backwoods uncle and help him run moonshine stills? Knowing his secret was fun— that Hugh McCall had written his first novel to the burble of fermenting corn whiskey as he sat on a stump in some dim, forgotten corner of the Virginia woodlands. The uncle had later been shot dead by a rival, and what, if anything, Hugh had done about it was a secret she did not know, and wasn't sure she wanted to. All he would say is, "I settled my uncle's affairs, left there, and wrote another novel." So there was a gap, and then, at twenty-seven, a year before she'd met him, he'd spent a month in the D.C. jail rather than testify against a Hopi friend who'd "stolen back" some tribal masks from the Smithsonian. It had made the papers—AREA NOVELIST JAILED FOR CONTEMPT. According to the article, Hugh had even managed to win over his jailers with the matter-of-fact way he'd taken his lumps, and by the end they were bringing in his novels to be autographed.

Then, six months ago, he'd shown up at the hospital, looking for a female doctor to interview for medical background in his new novel. Somehow he'd settled on her, a first-year resident—a mere intern, though there were several junior and senior residents and even some attendings who'd have been happy to oblige. She kept wondering what medicine could have to do with his novel, but he never talked about his writing. When it's done, he would say, it will talk for itself. Would people die, she wondered, in the new novel, die horribly as they did in all the others?

Hugh McCall, with warm brown eyes and a crooked, boyish grin, filled his novels with blood—just another piece of the puzzle that, perversely, drew her so. For all his roguish charm, there was a mystery deep inside him, Jenn felt sure, a dark place he had yet to share with her—and that, too, was part of his appeal, for she had her own secret, which she could never share.

All at once Jenn needed to feel him close. She leaned against him and he wrapped an arm around her. At five ten, she fit perfectly beneath the arch of his shoulder. The sinuous weight of his muscles felt good across the nape of her neck. He nuzzled her ear, sending a thrill down her spine. Turning toward him, she found his lips and floated through a long, dreamy kiss. When the blood in her brain began to fizz, she pulled away to breathe. At the same time, she slipped a hand inside his jacket, wiggling her fingers through the gap between his shirt buttons to feel the hard belly beneath. What did he do to keep it so firm? She'd never seen him exercise, but an image came to her now of him sitting on the floor of his Alexandria townhouse, doing situp after situp, until his chest gleamed with sweat. Following her cue, he eased a hand inside her medical coat and blouse and her eyes rolled up with pleasure. He seemed to know just where and how to touch her breast—ah, very nice. The hand withdrew and quickly slipped down to her skirt and under, roaming gently up her thigh. She groaned, her head swimming. She was so aroused she could barely think.

The doorknob rattled, freezing her, stilling Hugh's hand on her breast. Brad's voice came muffled through the door, and Jenn realized someone down the hall had called out to him. With a final, small rattle, the knob spun back and she heard the squeak of his white ducks moving off.

"Dang!" Hugh said. He sat back and blew out a breath.

Jenn could feel her heart pounding. That was too close—Brad Dietz, despite having made it to junior resident, was a total jerk, who never knew when to keep quiet. He'd have spread it all over the ward. But what bothered her even more was that she should have heard him coming. She filed it away, a cheap lesson on the power of distraction. Straightening her clothes, she took a seat on the chair by the bed and gazed at Hugh. He gazed back, and they both burst out laughing at the same time.

He said, "Think maybe we ought to take this show on the road?"

Jenn thought about asking him home to her apartment, ravishing him in her bed, using up some of the night. But after midnight was when he did his writing, and he'd been stalled lately.

"Don't you need to work?" she asked.

He winced. "Too true. I'm stuck on a character. I need to interview a homicide cop. Know any?"

A reflexive wariness filled her. "No," she said.

"How about ex-cops?"

She hesitated, hating to lie to Hugh any more than was absolutely necessary. What could it hurt if he met Merrick? "I do know one of those," she admitted, "but he retired ten years ago."

"No problem. I'm sure he'd remember enough to help me out."

"Let me speak to him, and if he's willing to meet with you, I'll let you know."

"Terrific." Hugh hesitated. "About tonight—I forgot you're just coming off call. You look so fresh . . ."

"It's the coffee. One more cup and I've got brown eyes."

He gave her an enigmatic smile, as if he didn't quite buy it, but surely that was just her paranoia. He said, "How long until you crash?"

Knowing what he was really asking, she did a quick calculation. She was scheduled to present Caroline at Chief of Service rounds tomorrow noon, and to do the best possible job she needed to read up on thymus-derived lymphocyte counts. The journals stacked up in her apartment might be a breeze, or they might be dense.

And she must keep up appearances, always and forever.

"I can't guarantee I wouldn't fall asleep on you," she said.

"Star-crossed lovers."

"At least for tonight."

He got up and leaned over, kissing her. She smelled the clover again, and a hint of male musk, and she wanted him, but she had a lot of experience at passing up what she wanted, so she was careful how she kissed him back.

⁕

Walking down the hall toward her apartment, Jenn regretted her self-control with Hugh. Whatever intellectual rewards the journals might offer would be cold comfort compared to what she could have had. She could still smell Hugh, feel the warmth of his hand on her breast. Tonight would be long without him.

Ah, but I'll be brilliant on rounds.

It didn't exactly cheer her up, but she couldn't pretend it didn't matter, either. She wanted to do well, become the best doctor she was capable of being. More than wanted it, needed it. The blue scrubs *were* armor, and the more constantly and convincingly she wore it the safer she'd be. . . .

That smell!

The nape of Jenn's neck prickled. *Blood?* Slowing, she veered from one side of the hall to the other, sniffing at each apartment door, feeling her stomach plunge as she neared her own. Yes, blood—that dark, gut-tightening smell, like slick glass in a reptile house. Her hand trembled as she unlocked her door. She knew she should not go in, but then the door was somehow open and she was standing in the foyer, unable to move, paralyzed with shock. The blood, a dark, glassy lake of it—so much that, for a moment, she could not focus on the corpse that lay in its center. Horror rose through her in a cold wave as she saw the throat, flayed into ribbons of pink and red. Above it, the face was untouched. Blue eyes, dusky in death, gazed up at her.

Dear God, do I know her?

No.

And then the blood drew her gaze again and the shock faded as Jenn felt the first aching rush of hunger.

2

Merrick Chapman was careful not to let Katie see how much he wanted the injection. With an effort, he kept his eyes off the syringe, but when he heard her thump it to force the bubbles out, the vein in his arm tingled in anticipation.

"Ready?" she asked.

He gave a neutral nod.

As she positioned his arm on the kitchen table, Merrick listened for Gregory upstairs. Nothing. It was years now since he could pick up the faint spill from his son's earphones down here, but there should still be the tap of Gregory's foot as he contemplated his homework to the beat of Nine Inch Nails or the like. Maybe he was between discs, or in one of his Shostakovich moods tonight, but the silence put Merrick on edge. At twelve, Gregory was still too young for the truth, but not too young to start digging for it if he caught Mom shooting up Dad.

"Here goes." Katie's voice had a forced lightness, but he could see in her face the misgivings, the self-doubt. How beautiful she was—the exotic violet of her eyes, her lush mouth, so expressive even when she did not want it to be. He kept his gaze on her as the needle broke through. Coolness flooded his vein, then dispersed. A shadow of weariness passed through him and that was all.

The slightness of his reaction made him uneasy. Hadn't he once felt drained right after a shot? Even breathing had seemed harder for a while. The last few times, he'd barely felt anything.

Was he developing immunity to Fraction Eight?

He felt a quick, sharp dread—

Stop it!

He went through this every time and it was ridiculous. Every year he tired more easily. He was sleeping all night now, he broke into a sweat just from running, would start breathing hard after only ten flights of stairs. In the past year, he had slipped to being barely stronger than he looked—almost as weak as a fit, young normal. All of which proved he *was* aging, even if the only outward sign so far was his graying hair. The wrinkles couldn't be far off, and what mattered most was how he *felt*. At the rate his strength was declining, he'd die within a few more decades.

So quit worrying!

Merrick watched Katie bend the needle over against the table and drop the spent syringe into her medical bag. She stood at the kitchen window, her back to him. The summery brightness of the kitchen stopped at the edge of the curtains, leaving her framed by the darkness outside. A humid breeze, heavy with the haylike scent of autumn leaves, ruffled the curtains and lifted her hair, dark and glossy, from her shoulders. He watched her lean forward into the breeze and brace her hands on the lip of the sink as though a weight had settled over her. His heart ached for her. Rising, he enfolded her from behind, crossing her arms under his, burying his face in her soft, dark hair.

"You make me so happy," he murmured.

"I do, don't I." She nestled back against him. "It's just that I . . ." She trailed off.

"I really do want it this way," he assured her softly, "and you're saving the life of a wonderful young woman."

"You're who's saving her."

"All I do is trade blood with her. You figured it all out."

"Sometimes I wish I hadn't."

"You can't mean that," he said, dismayed. "It was brilliant. Only a few people have heard of progeria and no one knows about me and my kind, yet somehow, you connected the two diseases."

"What you have is not a disease."

"But it is, Katie. Hold a mirror up to progeria and I'm its reflection, everything in reverse. I *saw* Rebecca when she came to your ward ten years ago. She was aging on fast forward, nine years old, but she looked eighty—and part of me envied her because for so long I had been frozen in time, while all I loved died around me. You found a way to save us both."

"I found a way to kill you," Katie said tightly. "That's what aging is, Merrick. A polite word for dying."

He wished he'd kept his mouth shut. When was he going to accept that he'd never find the right words to comfort Katie at these moments? Every month it was the same. On the day of the shot, her somber mood would begin before breakfast, when she drew 30 cc of his blood. Later, in the outpatient clinic, she'd no doubt hide her feelings from Rebecca as she drew an equal amount of blood from her. But at some point she'd cry. He always knew, because the rims of her eyes would be tinged with red when she came home that evening. Probably the tears came when Katie was safely alone in her lab, extracting Fraction Eight from Rebecca's blood and checking the sample she'd taken from him to make sure he had not begun to develop antigens which would cause Rebecca to reject his blood. Injecting his blood into Rebecca would be the easy part for Katie, allowing her to feel like the healer she was.

But then she had to return to him for the final act, so odious to her.

At least it was over now. By tomorrow, Katie would feel better, knowing she had a month before Rebecca's blood would again deteriorate to a toxic level of Fraction Eight; a month before his blood would, conversely, recover enough to repeat its temporary cleansing of Rebecca's.

For him, what counted was that, for two or three weeks of that month, his body—beneath the surface at least—would age.

Merrick hugged Katie closer. "To be able to stay with the woman I love—believe me, I have never been happier in my life."

"Don't say that. It's bad luck." She rapped on the Formica beside the sink, then knocked the hard pine of the kitchen table.

"I can't believe you did that, an educated woman, a doctor—"

"Whose mother was born in the bayous, don't forget." Katie waggled the horns of her little and index fingers at him.

"Your mother has a Ph.D. and I've never seen her knock wood."

"She's sneaky about it. But just watch her when she comes up next month."

"She's coming here?" Merrick pretended to sound aggrieved.

"For my forty-fourth."

"What—birthday? Impossible."

Katie rewarded him with a quick smile. It did seem impossible. Only the faint wrinkles beginning to etch the corners of her eyes gave the slightest hint. She had the fine, straight posture of a woman who'd like to be taller than five and a half feet. Hiking the stairs at Georgetown Hospital and other exercises she ad-libbed on the fly had kept her slim as a schoolgirl. The thought that he really might be able to gaze into those enchanting violet eyes for the next thirty or forty years, that he might not have to move on, roused a still-new joy in him.

"Did you mean it," she asked, "about me making you happy?"

"Did I say that?"

She made a face at him.

"When you pout like that I want to kiss you."

"I'm not pouting."

"Come here, Doctor, and let me cover your pouty lips with kisses."

"God, if you guys are going to be gross, I'm leaving."

Merrick turned in surprise. Gregory stood in the kitchen doorway, his lanky body canted several different ways at once with that endearing awkwardness only kids on the verge of their teens seemed able to manage. But not so awkward I heard him coming, Merrick thought.

"Don't tell me you're still hungry," Katie said.

"Is any of that pizza from last week left?" Gregory headed to the refrigerator and foraged in its depths. Watching him filled Merrick with gladness. So much like Katie, he was—same offbeat sense of humor, same violet eyes. Already taller, but lithe like her. And *my* brown hair, Merrick thought, then remembered his hair was gray now. What would Gregory be like at thirty? forty? *I'll get to see it! For the first time, I'll be a friend of my son, the man.*

With a little squawk of triumph, Gregory withdrew a wedge-shaped lump of tinfoil and headed back out of the kitchen.

"That's got an extra topping by now," Katie called after him. "Penicillin."

"You guys just go on with whatever you were doing," Gregory called back, and then he was gone, bounding upstairs—this time making plenty of noise.

"Where were we?" Katie asked.

"You were going to let me kiss your pouty lips."

"You'll have to catch me first."

Merrick chased her around the table, holding back just enough, admiring her athletic grace, enjoying her laughter and shrieks as he snagged, then let slip the tail of her blouse. She stopped and faced him, grinning, on the other side of the table. "What are you getting me for my birthday?"

"Slippery-soled shoes."

The phone rang. He picked up.

"Merrick, it's me. I'm in my apartment. I need help."

The terror in Jenn's voice tightened the skin on his scalp. Never happier in his life, but in an instant, he knew that was about to change. "I'll be right there," he said.

As he hung up, he tried to keep the alarm from his face, but Katie had already seen it.

"Who?"

"Jenn. She's in trouble."

Katie's face paled. "Oh, Merrick. She hasn't—"

"I don't know." He headed for the door.

"Be careful," she whispered behind him.

Racing up the stairwell to the seventh floor, Merrick ignored the burn in his legs. When he was almost to Jenn's door, it opened and he saw first her, then the body, the torn throat. He flung an arm up to cover his eyes, but too late, as the hunger raged to life in him. The slick of blood seized him with a gravity so fierce he could not back away. So fresh, still shiny, that wonderful smell! He stared at it, horrified, and yet drawn, fighting the urge to fall to his knees and lap the blood from the floor. Here was his nightmare, the thing he'd feared most for Jenn, and—even now—he, too, could not escape the pull of blood.

Hurrying to him, Jenn drew him into a hug. "Merrick, thank God you're here."

"Oh, Jenn, no."

She stepped back, as if slapped. "It wasn't *me*. *I* didn't do that."

He saw in her face she was telling the truth. Relief swept him. "I'm sorry, I'm *sorry*." He held out his hands to her. She took them and said it was all right, but her stiffness told him she was still indignant. He understood: ever since the change she had fought this thing, had never lost; he'd just insulted her pride.

But pride was a danger to them. It made the wall they had built against their own bloodthirsty natures seem thicker than it was.

"Merrick, I'm scared." Jenn glanced fearfully at the body, then away. "I can't make any sense out of this."

I'm scared too, Merrick thought. He could feel it, now—a new fear, tying an icy knot in his throat. This was too much like what had happened ten years ago, the bloody corpse Zane had flung like a gauntlet at his feet. Zane was dead, it was inconceivable he could be alive, and yet, *someone* had done this.

Someone who thinks like my son.

The coldness in Merrick's throat spread down into his chest, a suffocating feeling of dread. He fought it off. He must be calm now, and rational. There had to be some other explanation and he must find it.

He drew Jenn with him deeper into the apartment, as far from the corpse as they could get. Keeping his back to the dead woman, he made sure he blocked Jenn's view. "Tell me everything you know," he said.

"I worked a triple shift. I was gone for twenty-four hours. When I got home, she was there."

"The door?"

"Locked, just as I'd left it."

"Know her?"

"Never seen her before. And there's no purse, no ID on her. I have absolutely no idea who she could be."

"You searched the apartment?"

"Of course. No one is here. As far as I can tell, nothing was touched."

"Leave any windows open?"

"No, and none were."

"How long since you found her?"

"About an hour."

Merrick's fear eased a little. "At least it's not a setup. Whoever did this wouldn't give you that much time before he rang the police down on you."

"What are we going to do?"

"I have to look at her again now, and I want you to help me, do you understand?"

Jenn frowned. "You're afraid you might drink?"

"The blood is still quite fresh. Surely you want it too."

She flushed. "I didn't take any. I . . . I *did* think of it, though. I mean, she was dead when I found her. For a minute, all I could think was that her blood had already drained out, that it was no use to her anymore, and what difference would it make? But then I realized it might compromise me, weaken me."

Might? She was scaring him again. She should not have let herself even think about it. "I'm glad you didn't take any," he said.

The green eyes, so like her father's, warmed in a way Zane's could not have. "You won't drink either," she said confidently.

"All the same, I want you to be ready to pull me off."

"What if you're too strong?"

"I'm not. Not anymore."

Returning to the corpse, he crouched, conscious of Jenn's hand on his shoulder. The desire to lunge at the torn throat swept through him, far stronger than he'd have expected.

He studied her, lying there, arms to the sides, palms up, feet together. Bodies did not fall that way. Hers had not been carelessly dropped. The palms-up hands seemed to be saying, I surrender. Come to me. Nothing sexual in it—he'd seen the leavings of necrophiles, the nakedness, the ghastly poses, too many times to be mistaken. This woman was fully dressed, the hem of her skirt chastely at the knee.

No, the invitation here was to come and drink.

Steeling himself, Merrick studied the ravaged throat. No knife had done this. The throat had been stripped down by human teeth—in a frenzy, perhaps, but one guided by instinctive knowledge of how best to drain not just the carotids and jugulars, but the rich network of capillaries that serviced the trachea and esophagus. Merrick's heart sank.

Zane? he wondered again. No, it just couldn't be.

But still, one of us.

He stood and stumbled backward a step, feeling Jenn's hands steady him, turning toward her as he found his footing. He was sweating—welcome enough as another sign the injections were working, but now it unnerved him, driving home his deterioration. I'm too far gone for this, he thought.

So you'll just have to roll back the clock for the next few hours.

"Do you think it was a hemophage?" she asked.

"Has to be."

"Then we can't call the police."

Merrick was surprised to find himself weighing it. Ten years ago, he would have agreed. He knew the police. They would tell themselves this woman had been killed by a psycho, a vicious maniac who thought he was a vampire. But some would wonder if there wasn't something more—especially those who had been around ten years ago when Zane had left the body so much like this one at the National Cathedral. Then, the medical examiner had found a few drops of Zane's blood, and it had been a very near thing. The murders had never been solved; interest had died away, but he knew the matter was filed, not forgotten. If the police see this woman, Merrick thought, they'll blow the dust off those old files and pick up the trails I worked so hard to bury. This time they might make it all the way.

But would that be so bad?

"Merrick? Don't tell me you're actually considering it."

The alarm in Jenn's voice caught him. Even if his own survival instinct was fading, along with so much else, hers was not.

"Of all of us," he said, "you are the only one with clean hands, the only one who does not deserve to die."

"You don't know that." She stared at him. "Maybe there are others of us who don't kill. And if we're discovered, think how many normals would die. They'd panic. Even after they learned how to detect us, for every phage they managed to bury, thousands of them would die—far more than now."

He went to her window and looked out across Washington. The night sky glowed with the lights of the city he had once protected. Some trick of the humidity tainted the glow red, as though the capital were sinking beneath a mist of its own blood. Jenn was right. It was one thing for him to choose mortality and quite another to risk condemning thousands of others to death. And what could the police do? Any cop who got close to the creature who had done this would be damn unlucky.

"Poor woman," Jenn said.

He turned from the window, afraid she was looking at the body, but she had covered her face with both hands.

"She must have family," Jenn went on, "maybe a husband or boyfriend. By tomorrow, they'll be worried about her, then scared, then terrified. We can't call the police, but we can't just take her out and bury her somewhere. How long would her people go on looking, never finding her, never having peace again?"

"Let's take this one step at a time. Before we do anything else, we've got to clean up this blood." Merrick glanced at the red lake, and saw with relief that its surface had dulled, and with it, his desire. "It's starting to dry out—I think we'll be all right now."

"I'll get a mop and some buckets."

When the floor around the corpse was dry, Merrick lifted the body and Jenn cleaned beneath it. The dead woman was light, as though the blood had contained everything of substance in her. He felt the old sorrow he'd tried to leave behind when, ten years ago, he'd ended his long career in police work. It was hard to grasp that there was no longer anyone inside this woman. The eyes still had a faint sheen. For a second, he saw Zane reflected in them, and the skin between his shoulder blades rippled with dread—but no, it was his own face, captured there in the dead eyes.

What is your name? Merrick silently asked the corpse. I want to return you to your loved ones, but I have to know your name.

Setting her down again, he rolled her to one side and pulled her dress away from the nape of her neck, searching the stained fabric, the Rorschach blot of dried blood. No laundry marks. Had the killer removed them along with her purse?

Or was the dress too new?

The label, also darkened with blood, was still readable. *Nordstrom.* He let himself hope. "That rug in your bedroom," he said to Jenn. "It's about six by eight, right?"

"Right."

She brought it to him and he wrapped the dead woman up in it. "You'd better be the one to carry her down," he said. "If you run into anyone, a woman will arouse less suspicion. I'll bring my car around. The trunk should be plenty big if we bend her a little."

"Where are we going?"

"The Pentagon City mall."

Jenn gave him a searching look. "Why won't you tell me what we're going to do?"

"I don't yet know if it will work." True enough, but not the real truth, and when she seemed to accept it, he felt a pang of guilt.

Leaving Jenn in the car to protect the body, Merrick walked from the parking garage into the second-floor Nordstrom entrance. As he recalled, women's clothing was here and on the floor above, a dozen different nooks, each carrying its own segment, from casual to business to designer dresses. The dead woman's dress was a "casual"—top floor. He took the escalator, rising between columns of dark, burnished wood, trying not to think of Zane, dead for years, and yet conjured to life in his memory by that ghastly—and seductive—ripped throat. . . .

Merrick shook the image off, as soothing piano music began to percolate up from some lower level of the store. He tried to imagine his own fingers flowing over the keys, but his tight grip on the escalator's handrail loosened only slightly.

What if, somehow, it *is* Zane?

Merrick's stomach twisted, pulling him into a slight stoop against the incline of the escalator. The thought was unbearable. He could not face Zane again—and not just because he could no longer win. He had used himself up the last time, had lost the moral strength, as important as the physical.

It's *not* him, Merrick told himself.

With an effort, he focused again on his plan: dresses, so many, would one like the victim's still be here? Wending his way between the circular racks, he looked for the floral pattern, the soft pinks and greens that had clothed her before the blood had poured out—

There!

Picking the dress from the rack, he made his way to the counter, hoping to find a face he knew.

"Lieutenant!"

It was Linnie, small and dark-haired, with porcelain skin, wearing a smile that, on another night, could have sold him his own coat. "Long time no see," she said.

"Too long. I'm glad you're here." He held up the dress. "Any chance you sold one of these recently in a size six?"

Linnie's face crinkled in a frown of concentration. "Nope. But let me see what I can find out." She turned to the tiny screen of her computer and tapped a few keys. "A date would help."

"Try the past three weeks."

" 'Kay." Linnie tapped some more. "Here we go. Wanda sold one just a week ago, size six." She hesitated, looking up at him. "This is police business, right?"

"Right." *But with luck they'll never know.*

"Emmy Rittenhouse, 1215 North Fort Meyer Drive."

"Thanks, Linnie."

"Don't mention it. Doesn't your wife have a birthday coming up? Cathy—no, Katie?"

Merrick nodded, impressed all over again—Linnie hadn't even looked at the computer screen. He promised to bring Katie in, then hurried back to the car. Jenn seemed content with his thumbs-up. He drove them in silence the mile to Emmy Rittenhouse's address, a hilltop apartment building that would have looked out over the Iwo Jima Memorial and the Potomac toward Washington if not for a larger apartment building in between. Pulling into the small parking lot, Merrick stopped the car. "You have her scent?"

"I'll never forget it," Jenn said.

"We need her car."

Jenn gazed at him in the near darkness. "I see."

Pleased at her quickness, Merrick also felt a chill of foreboding. So quick, but would she stay strong enough never to use what she was learning tonight? He said, "I'll walk with you."

He stayed a step or two behind to keep from breaking her concentration as she walked up and down the rows of cars. She stopped beside an aging Saab, looking not at it but up at the apartment building. Bending to the door handle, she quickly straightened again. "This is it."

"Get inside."

"It's locked."

Moving up beside her, Merrick inserted the tips of his fingers in the top of the door crease and bore down. It was harder than he expected, but the locking bolt snapped and the door popped open.

"Oh," Jenn said. "Right."

His fingers hurt. How strange that such a small, simple thing could give him pain now. Sliding into the seat, he felt beneath the dash and pulled the wires down and out to where Jenn could see them. "Watch me," he said. "I hope you'll never need to do this, but you might some day." Peeling the insulation with a fingernail, he crossed the wires. The engine stuttered to life.

"Pretty slick," she said.

Getting out, he motioned her into the driver's seat. "Meet me down the hill. There's a dark stretch alongside the Netherlands Carillon, where the grove of trees is. We'll transfer the body there and then you follow me."

She nodded.

After they'd put Emmy into the backseat of her car, Merrick led the way out of the city, along the George Washington Parkway. Below on his right, he caught glimpses of the Potomac River—but the road wasn't high enough yet, the bluff not steep enough. As he drove, he kept the Saab in his rearview mirror, pleased at Jenn's nerve, her show of calm, and at the same time afraid for her. His mind kept circling back to two questions. First, why? Why had a phage singled out Jenn for this bizarre and horrifying contact?

The other question was who? The only answer that could have made sense was impossible. Dear God, it *had* to be impossible.

Then why is it the precise thing Zane would do if he were alive? He would come back for her, try and take her from me.

And I can't stop him.

Merrick felt a raw pulse of panic in his hands, like a boot heel grinding into his palms. He blew out a long, forceful breath, but his lungs still felt full of pent-up air.

With a start, he realized the bluffs were high and steep enough now. As he pulled over to the shoulder, Jenn drew up behind him. Walking back to the idling Saab, he nodded at Jenn to get out.

"We can't be seen now," he told her.

"I understand."

When she had turned away to watch the parkway, Merrick pulled Emmy into the front seat and positioned her behind the wheel, then got out. With an elbow, he smashed at the windshield. Nothing happened, and he felt a fleeting embarrassment at his weakness, even though Jenn had not seen. It took several blows to get the safety glass to bend inward and fracture, and several more to break it apart into shards. His elbow throbbed as he slid into the car again. He was conscious of the continual hum of cars going past, more than he'd like, but not too many—Jenn should be able to handle each driver in turn.

Did she realize he could no longer manage it himself, could no longer reach out mentally, attune himself to the blood flow across a normal's retinas and squeeze down the capillaries where his image fell? Why hadn't he told her? He'd known it for months, since that uncomfortable moment on the subway when a pesky bail bondsman he'd known years ago had stepped into his car and he'd tried to edit himself from the man's vision. Unfazed, the pest had come straight to him and started yakking. Since then, further failed attempts had confirmed it: the part of his brain that had once effortlessly projected Influence had sunk into permanent numbness. Fine with him—yet another sign the Fraction Eight was working. He simply hadn't gotten around to telling Jenn, that was all, and now was hardly the moment.

Merrick gathered himself, hating what he was about to do. Grasping Emmy by the hair, he pulled her head forward through the shattered glass and jammed her throat several times against the shards. Sickened, he pulled her back. Turning the wheel to point toward the drop-off, he got out and unscrewed the lid of the gas tank. According to the Saab's gauge, the tank was more than half full. From his own trunk, he took a rag and the quart of oil he always kept in reserve. Dousing the rag, he stuffed it into the opening of the Saab's gas tank, then lit it. If it didn't burn away completely, a good forensic team might know what it meant, but even if they decided murder, there was now an alternative explanation for the ripped throat. Quickly, he reached across Emmy's body and slipped the shift lever into drive. The car rolled forward, gathering speed, then plunged over the edge and down the steep bluff. He waited, listening to the screech of metal, the snapping of branches, until he heard the dull thump of the explosion. An orange glare shimmered back up the slope toward him.

Turning, he saw that Jenn was already getting into his car. He slid into the driver's side and pulled back onto the parkway. His collar was drenched with sweat and his elbow throbbed. Why must he feel so miserable, so *unclean?* With any luck, he had saved Emmy's family from the anguish of knowing she had been murdered, and certainly from the slow torment of searching but never finding her. Their grief would be as quick and clean as grief could ever be. They would never know the horror that had stalked and killed their Emmy.

And to do it, he had used a favorite trick of those he used to hunt. To remain undiscovered and unsuspected, phages often hid their murders with faked car crashes, as he had just done. Zane must have worked the deception many times. And now I've put the idea in Jenn's head, Merrick thought, I've shown her how to do it, just as surely as if I'd been Zane, deliberately raising her as a killer. I even felt clever as I pushed Emmy's car over the edge of the cliff.

Merrick suppressed a groan. He had not felt as much like his own kind in five hundred years, and it was not a good feeling. Mindful of Jenn beside him, he resisted an urge to pound the steering wheel. How he hated it, this eternal, unshakable attraction to blood. It chilled him to think that tonight someone had deliberately aroused it in his granddaughter. But the careful arrangement of Emmy's body made it clear; she had not merely been left in Jenn's foyer, she had been *presented*, just as a lion will lay fresh kill at the feet of its cub to awaken its killer instinct.

Zane, is it you?

"Who could have done this?" Jenn murmured.

The dread rose in Merrick again, the fear he'd felt as that other face had peered back from the dead woman's eyes like a final image engraved by death. "If I didn't know it was impossible," he said, "I would say your father is back."

3

Startled, Jenn looked at Merrick. "I can't imagine my own father leaving a corpse on my doorstep."

"That's because you didn't know him."

His reply cut her, but she didn't reply, aware that Merrick's obtuseness was partly her own fault. Quite right, she hadn't known her father, and how could Merrick guess she'd have liked to? In his anguished but rigid disapproval of Zane, he probably couldn't imagine her feeling anything different. Zane *was* a murderer—appalling, yes—but also her father, who had both given and saved her life, and she remembered just enough from her few moments with him to feel he might even have loved her, and if he had, he could not have been entirely evil.

But somehow she'd never been able to say any of this to Merrick, and certainly couldn't now, when it might provoke an argument, or worse, push him back into the silence he usually kept about Zane. Locking his own son in the vault to die must have torn Merrick to his core, which was probably why he never wanted to talk about Zane. So it had to be significant that he'd just mentioned Zane, and all she wanted right now was to know why.

An ambulance siren, very faint, rose and fell behind them, then died away. Jenn hoped for the sake of the rescue workers that the flames had performed their final mercies on Emmy's body.

"Why does the corpse make you think of Zane?" she asked.

"When you opened your door and saw her lying there, what did you feel?"

"Shock . . . horror."

"And then?"

Desire. Jenn did not want to say it. "I see. You mean the body was a sort of gift."

"Not a gift. A temptation. Zane would despise the life you're living. He'd want you to give up, stop fighting your nature. He'd know how a fresh kill would excite you."

"But wouldn't he try to persuade me first—come to me, get to know me a little?" Hearing the wistfulness in her own voice, Jenn wished she could take the words back. Merrick glanced at her and she knew he had heard it too.

"Have you forgotten what I've told you about him?" Merrick asked. "He was not the type to get to know anyone, Jenn. He lived a willfully solitary life, interested in only one thing—killing. He was a predator, far beyond what he needed to survive, utterly without conscience. In five hundred years he probably killed more people than even the longest-lived of us, which would make him the worst one-on-one murderer in history—"

Jenn recoiled inwardly—how harsh Merrick's view of Zane was. With an effort, she kept her voice and expression mild.

"Yes, you've made that very clear and I haven't forgotten, but surely that isn't all there was to him. Do you know for a fact he never had friends, fell in love, maybe even . . . wanted to have children?"

"I can't imagine him doing any of those things."

"But you can't *know* he didn't—how could you? For hundreds of years, the only time you got near him was when you hunted him."

Merrick said nothing. His lips made a tight line and she could tell his jaw was clenched.

"I'm sorry to push you," she said. "I can see that it hurts you to talk about him. But do you know what that tells me? That, despite everything, *you* loved him."

He shot her an exasperated look. "What does it matter? He's dead."

"You're absolutely sure of that, even after tonight?"

"Where I put him, escape was impossible. That was ten years ago, which means he's been dead at least eight."

"But if he *did* somehow get out—"

"He'd have come after both of us long before now."

Jenn tried to find a flaw in his logic and could not. She felt a strange mixture of disappointment and relief. How long had she fantasized about Zane—about what she would say and do if she could only have an hour with him? But fantasies were one thing and real life another. A mysterious father lost in time was safe, a living Zane anything but.

"You asked me who could have done this," Merrick said, "but if either of us might know, it's more likely you."

"But I have no idea," she protested. "You and Zane were the only two phages who ever knew I existed. How could another one find out? The only thing I can think of is that one could have seen us feed."

"I doubt that."

"How then? No one could know I don't sleep. At the hospital, I do my tired intern act whenever I remember to. I can't think of anything else. Except when we're feeding, I look and act just like any normal."

Merrick took a breath as if to disagree, then said nothing.

"What?" she said. "Come on, if I've got a neon sign flashing in the middle of my forehead or something, I need to know it."

"It wouldn't be anything obvious."

"Then what?"

"It's possible he would pick up on your physical beauty, your vibrancy. You're intensely attractive, Jenn. You radiate good health—you almost glow."

She felt herself flush. "Might you be a wee bit prejudiced?"

"No doubt, but it's also the truth. Nature designed us to be attractive to our prey."

Jenn felt a cold prickle at the nape of her neck. "I wish you wouldn't talk like that. I don't care what nature did, we're not predators—not you and me."

Merrick was silent.

She shivered. A predator *was* out there somewhere, and had set his sights on her. Not a normal man, but one immensely stronger and more dangerous to her. The reality was starting to sink in, and it terrified her. "Another phage watching me, knowing about me. I don't like it."

"What we have to do now is turn the tables, give you a shot at detecting him."

"I'm listening."

"You already know part of what to look for: above average height, top physical condition, an overall attractiveness."

Jenn found herself thinking of Hugh. *No, that's absurd.*

"The other signs will be more subtle. I used to observe the eyes. When someone has lived a few hundred years, there is a certain look. It may come across as impatience. You might be talking to him about something you think is unique and complicated, and you get the sense he'd like you to finish."

"Because he's heard it all before and is bored with it."

"In essence, yes. Sometimes it will be a sense of distance, a feeling he is looking through you, barely seeing you. Or you might become aware of an uncommon stillness in him. Normals generally look around a bit when they talk; their gaze moves, if only back and forth between your two eyes. Look for other small oddities. Over the years, I picked up initially on several phages just because of the slowness with which they blinked."

Listening to him, imagining the long, dark history behind his words, Jenn felt her fear deepening, scooping into the hollow of her stomach. Suddenly, he was not Grandfather but the one phages had called *assassin*—a renegade, hunter of hunters, feared by his own kind for hundreds of years. A more accurate term might have been executioner, but he'd been more than that, too. Reeve of a dozen shires in medieval England, later working on a score of modern police forces in turn, all over the world, using those positions to gather the information he needed to hunt down and bury phages. How could she reconcile that long, violent era with the Merrick of now, who lived tranquilly with Katie? She had never doubted he loathed killing and yet he had killed, over and over. His reason—that thousands more would die if he did not kill—did not entirely explain the mystery.

Jenn loved him dearly, but would she ever really know him?

She had trouble even grasping his age. He still looked young, so straight and tall she could barely keep in mind he was her grandfather, much less someone far, far older. In normal humans, the first signs of aging usually showed up in the hair, and this was true for Merrick, too. The Fraction Eight injections had turned his from brown to gray but the handsome face was still unlined and everyone assumed his hair color was premature. He tried to hide his physique with loose, professorial clothes, but in full stride, his pantleg would fall across the sculpted calf of a ballet dancer, or a sleeve would creep up his forearm, revealing the corded muscles that could once tear a car door off. Only now, in the weight of his words, could she glimpse the Merrick inside the youthful body, an ancient who had observed humanity for so long—both normals and phages—that he could tell predator from prey by the way they blinked.

I'm glad he's on my side, she thought, but the fear remained, and if anything, his frightening history made her feel more vulnerable. Merrick had made many enemies among phages. Zane had been the most formidable, but there must be numerous others who hated him—and feared him as well, not knowing how his powers had diminished.

But no phage would be terrified of her—a mere cub. And what better way to strike back at the hated "assassin," than to bury his granddaughter?

Jenn tried to swallow, but her throat locked.

Merrick glanced at her. "Are you all right?"

"I'm scared," she admitted.

"I'd be worried if you weren't."

"What you said about recognizing phages applies mostly to older ones, but what if the one who's after me is young?"

"I doubt that. To have detected what you are, he'd need a lot of experience."

"If he's that seasoned, what hope do *I* have of detecting *him*?"

"You're very smart, intuitive. And you've got me. I'm no longer up to facing another phage physically, but I know a lot that might help you."

"As always." She reached over and covered his hand on the wheel. The tight, straining tendons, the almost feverish heat in his skin, deepened her unease. He was upset, of course—they both were. But where was this fierce physical tension coming from? She had the sudden conviction that he was hiding more than unease, a fear bordering on dread. Why?

Her mind went back to Zane, and suddenly she realized there had, in fact, been a flaw in Merrick's logic: if Zane had, somehow, escaped the tomb, he would *not* have come back much earlier. He'd have been too terrified.

Jenn's mouth went dry. He wouldn't know Merrick was deliberately weakening himself, she thought. It might take him years to screw up enough courage to come back here.

And then Jenn realized that Merrick knew this too. It was why he was so tense.

A sudden nervous excitement throbbed in the hollow of her stomach. She was afraid—near panic at the thought her father might really be alive—but fascinated, too. His fear and hatred of Merrick would make him more dangerous than any other phage who might be stalking her. But only if his hate also extended to her. . . .

Jenn's mind spun. She was getting ahead of herself. All she knew for sure was that it *could* logically be Zane, but it was still a very long shot for one very simple reason: *how could he have escaped the tomb?*

The car entered a long curve, pressing her against the door, and she realized Merrick had turned off the parkway onto the entrance ramp to Rosslyn. He was heading for Key Bridge and the city. "You're taking me home?" she asked.

"Yes."

"Wouldn't it be better if I went with you to the vault?"

He gave her a single, sharp glance, and that was enough.

"Merrick—"

"There's no chance he's alive."

"Then why are you going to the vault?"

"I don't know that I am."

"You've never lied to me."

"And I'm not lying now. I . . . I don't know if I *can* go back there."

"All the more reason to take me with you. I'll help you, be there with you." Even as she said it, she knew it might be untrue. She was terrified. If the tomb was empty, she might be too shocked, too overwhelmed by her own fears—and her even more dangerous hopes—to be any use at all to Merrick.

But I have to know, she thought.

At the end of the long exit loop, the light was red. Jenn watched the traffic from Arlington stream over the graceful stone arches of the Key Bridge toward Georgetown. It seemed slightly unreal, everything a bit suspect. For ten years, she had never questioned that her father was dead, never imagined she might actually see him again in anything but her imagination, but now there was a chance, however small, that he was alive, and suddenly she was terrified. That Zane would kill her?

That he harbored no love for her after all?

Both! she thought—and didn't know which was worse.

"You *do* think he could have gotten out," she said.

"How?" Merrick asked in a strained voice. "Jenn, I knew what I was doing when I built that vault. The outer wall is a foot of reinforced concrete that's been curing for forty years and is hard as granite by now. The soil surrounding the vault is hardpan clay. I installed a platinum iridium door originally made for a walk-in safe. Inside the vault is a commons area surrounded by individual cells. I locked Zane in one of those. There is no keyhole on the inside of the cell door; it locks from the outside, a four-inch turnbolt that slides into a steel frame around the door. No one ever escaped that vault, so how could Zane?"

"Are you trying to convince me, or yourself?"

"I can't imagine how he could have done it."

"There's only one way to be sure, isn't there?"

"Jenn, you can't know what you're letting yourself in for. His body will be a ghastly sight."

"He was my father."

"Your father is James Hrluska."

"You know what I'm saying."

"You are nothing like him. And you owe him nothing."

"Except my life."

An anguished groan escaped Merrick, and she realized she had twisted the knife that had no doubt been buried in him from the moment he first stood by her bedside and realized what she was. Let a child die in innocence, or give her blood? She might have to face the same choice with Caroline, and there could be no harder one. Only human blood would cure hemophagic leukemia, but it would also awaken the genes that would force the child to take blood every few weeks from then on to survive. Those same genes unleashed a lust to kill that only the strongest will could resist. If Merrick had given her blood, it was more than likely she'd have become a vicious killer. She could not really blame him for deciding not to—especially since he hadn't known then that she was his own flesh and blood—his granddaughter. Merrick had decided he must not intervene.

And then Zane had done it for him.

"I'm sorry," she said. "I don't want to hurt you—that's the last thing I would ever want. But it was Zane who saved me. He's not just my father, he gave me life again when it was almost gone."

Horns began to blare behind them. Merrick pulled through the now-green light and, instead of turning toward Washington, navigated the winding street up through the business district of Rosslyn to Route 50.

Her heart began to beat faster. She said, "We both need to go back there. We should have done it years ago."

Merrick shook his head firmly. She could feel his dread mixing with the dark excitement in her gut. In all likelihood, Zane would be there, dead, and it *would* be ghastly. But she needed to see, to put him to rest in her mind in a way she had not yet done.

And if he isn't there?

Jenn pressed a hand to her face, thumb and finger hard against her eyelids. Fear and excitement, locked together, danced around madly in her brain, almost blocking out Merrick's voice.

"I'm sorry," she said. "What?"

"How did you know I was going there?"

"I didn't."

He grunted, and she realized it was a failed attempt to laugh.

"You want me with you," she said. "You know you do."

"No."

"But you need me."

"Yes."

They said nothing more as Route 50 carried them through Arlington and Falls Church, beyond the beltway, into the Virginia countryside. The road dwindled finally to two lanes. A few miles later, Merrick turned onto the country road Jenn remembered from ten years ago, when she'd sat in the backseat, every part of her focused on her father, who lay in the trunk of the car at her back, bound with thick wire.

Merrick turned off onto a dirt road—hardly a road at all, just twin ruts. Tall weeds shone in the headlights, brushing the sides of the car as they bumped along. Ahead, Jenn saw the forest, a dark wall of trees so dense it seemed there would be no room for the car to enter, but they squeezed through. Moths fluttered in the low beams; Jenn waited for Merrick to turn the headlights off entirely, then realized he could no longer see in the dark well enough to do that. He slowed and she saw a small tree ahead, fallen across the trail. Stopping the car, Merrick stared out at the barrier. His will seemed to have drained from him.

"I'll get it," Jenn said. Hopping out, she grabbed the trunk of the tree and lifted. A section long enough to clear the way broke out with a rotten crunch. She pitched it through a gap in the trees and got in again. Merrick drove forward, following the ruts until they petered out. Wordlessly, he got out and retrieved a flashlight from the trunk.

She followed him into the dense growth. An owl hooted and she jumped, then fought down a prickly laugh. The beam of the flashlight caught glowing green eyes ahead. Merrick doused the light long enough for the deer to crash away through the undergrowth. As he moved ahead again, his steps began to drag; she resisted the urge to push ahead of him. She knew the way now, she was sure.

"There," he whispered, and in the beam of his light she saw the four oaks that anchored the corners of the clearing. A few fledgling maples, not present ten years ago, blurred what had been the edges of the rough square. Her dread sharpened. This was where she had stood that night when Merrick and Katie had thought she was still back in the car. Right here, frozen in terror as the earth opened and swallowed her father and grandfather. Only one had returned.

The memory vanished, shoved out by another: *smaller, thinner, she rode on a man's shoulders. The night was moonless, dark. She had not felt so alive in a long time; the fever and aching joints of only a few days before had vanished, but she was hungry—very hungry. Reaching an apartment building, the man climbed, carrying her straight up the wall. How could he cling like this? It was magic! A glance down pulled a dizzied gasp from her. Don't worry, the man murmured. We won't fall. Soon you'll be able to do this too. I'll teach you.*

She laughed breathlessly. Could he really be her father? He seemed to know so much about her. And he had brought her the special medicine that had cured her. Not even Katie had been able to do that . . .

Merrick uttered a formless sound and Jenn realized he had found the trapdoor under the dead leaves. Beneath would be the vault door itself. On his knees now, Merrick rummaged through the carpet of dead leaves, found the ring, pulled the trapdoor open. Jenn reached him as he finished dialing the combination. The door lowered into a darkness pierced down the middle by the white well of the flashlight beam. Suddenly the beam spun and dropped, dying in a crunch of glass.

"God bloody damn!" Merrick gasped.

"It's all right," she said. "I'll be able to see. Just tell me where to look."

"I have to come," he said.

"Follow me in, then."

Jenn's stomach squirmed as she descended into the small, concrete anteroom. As her eyes adjusted, the darkness flared to infrared, revealing a door. When she opened it, dry, parchment-scented air swept her face. Taking Merrick's hand, she led him through. Inside, two rows of cots stretched to the far end of the vault, two rows of withered bodies. They looked like ancient pharaohs—stick arms and legs, leathery faces crowned with long, white manes. Their dulled eyes stared past her at the ceiling. Jenn swallowed, sickened and horrified. How long had they lived after Merrick had locked them in here? Consciousness had probably lingered for at least a year, and it might have taken another year for the final release of death. For the second time tonight, she found herself afraid of Merrick . . .

Jenn reminded herself that the vault—forced separation from the blood of prey—had been Merrick's only hope of stopping these killers, and that the lives of these ghastly creatures had been far crueler than their deaths. How many people had each of them killed?

Looking up, Jenn saw that Merrick was groping along one of the walls, feeling the doors. His hand found the turnbolt, and she realized he could see a little, that he had not yet lost all his visual edge. He whispered something—*I'm sorry*—and she realized he was not here, but back in the past, at that terrible moment when his hand had turned the bolt the other way.

Tears of sympathy flooded her eyes.

Merrick pulled the door open and stared inside. Falling to his knees, he cried, "God help us!"

4

He's alive! Paralyzed with shock, Jenn stared at Merrick. She must get to him, help him, but her legs would not move. Frozen, she stared at the yawning door of the cell. This was all wrong—if Zane was alive, he'd have come to her, told her he loved her, not the torn throat, her doorstep baited with blood.

Could this be a dream?

Jenn touched her face, pushing a cheek in with her fingertip. The sensation felt real but couldn't dreams seem very real sometimes? So long since she'd slept, she could scarcely remember dreaming, but what if she *had* somehow dozed off? This *would* be the nightmare, this monstrous place, waiting ten years to gape open and swallow her.

Merrick groaned, and it broke her paralysis. *He'll go mad!*

Hurrying to his side, she tried to pull him up, but his body stayed rigid, hands clenched between his knees, eyes staring into the dark hole of the cell. She could not look yet. Moving between him and the cell, she took Merrick's face in her hands. What she saw terrified her—peeled, bulging eyes, his mouth so twisted with dread she hardly recognized him.

Despite the dark, his pupils had constricted to pinpoints—no way could he be seeing anything now.

Turning, she edged into the cell. Empty—he was not wrong. The bed along one wall trailed sheets and a blanket in muddled disarray. There was nothing else in the narrow space. As she turned back toward Merrick, she saw something on the inside of the door—long silvery scratches that ran along the steel from top to bottom. An image struck her of her father's hooked hands raking the door in a frenzy. Sick with horror, she stumbled out and crouched before her grandfather. "Merrick. *Merrick!*"

He seemed unable to hear her.

She slapped him. "Stop it, you're scaring me."

At last his pupils dilated and his eyes focused on her.

"It's all right," she said.

"No."

She pulled him to her, hugged him, alarmed at the catatonic rigidity of his body. It had taken everything he had to seal his own son away in this place. And now to find it was for nothing.

"Sandeman!" Merrick cried suddenly. Pulling free of her, he ran to the door at the end of the commons area and flung it open. Hurrying after him, Jenn found him sitting on the floor beside a corpse less withered than the others. Dead for only seven or eight years, perhaps. The face looked oddly gentle, scholarly—or maybe it was the effect of the room, the mountains of books all around, stacked neatly against the walls.

Her mind jittered backward a few seconds and she realized Merrick had not touched the deadbolt. "This cell wasn't locked!" she said.

"He was my friend."

She stared at him, trying to grasp it.

"He asked to be here," Merrick explained. "He wanted to stop killing, but couldn't. He tried to feed the way we do, but as soon as he saw the blood . . ."

Yes, Jenn thought. That's the worst moment.

"He must have let Zane out," she said.

"Damn it, no!"

Jenn put a hand on Merrick's shoulder. "Sorry, I'm not thinking straight. There'd still be the main door."

"Zane could get through that on his own. There's a dial on the inside, in case the door closed, somehow, when I was in here."

"But the combination—"

"Zane was an expert. With his hearing, he could have memorized the sound of the tumblers as I brought him in. Sandeman had no expertise with safes, which is why I didn't have to lock his cell. Only if he had let Zane out could the safe door have been opened, and Sandeman would never betray me by letting him out. He helped me capture Zane—if it weren't for him, Zane would have buried me behind your house that night."

"My house?"

Merrick, gazing at Sandeman, seemed not to hear. In her memory, she saw her darkened front yard, Merrick lying still on the grass and Zane bending over him, binding him with cable. Jenn shivered, feeling again the cool wooden floor against her bare feet. I was standing at my bedroom window, she thought, looking down at them. My father was tying him up, but then he stopped and wandered away, almost like he was sleepwalking. There was blood on Merrick's chest.

Wrenching free of the memory, Jenn studied the dead face, trying to place Sandeman in that gruesome scene, ten years ago. She couldn't, but maybe he'd been out of sight.

She thought again of the ghastly scratches inside Zane's door. What if Sandeman heard him clawing, maybe even screaming in his frenzy? That would be hard to take.

"He'd never betray me," Merrick said again.

"Maybe one of the phages in the commons still had enough strength to crawl to Zane's door and let him out."

"No. Most of them were dead when I put Zane in here and the others were far beyond moving. I never put any phage in the commons area until they were too weak to move—and then only if I needed their cells for new captives. And besides, they're all here. If any besides

Sandeman had been alive, he'd have taken them out with him, just to spite me."

Or because he couldn't stand to see them caged here, Jenn thought. She squeezed Merrick's shoulder. "We're both half in shock. We'll figure out how he escaped later."

Reaching up, Merrick grasped her hand for a second. Then, with infinite gentleness, he picked up Sandeman's body and arranged it on the bed. Laying one of Sandeman's withered hands on his chest, he slipped a book into the stiff fingers. Still looking down at his dead friend, he said, "I have to go after Zane."

Jenn looked at him, alarmed. Was he totally addled? "You can't," she said. "The Fraction Eight injections—you're no match for him now."

"He doesn't know that. If he did, he'd have killed me after he first got out. My guess is he ran, somewhere far away. But now he's back. He's still afraid of me, so he wants to get at me through you. I can no longer beat him physically, but maybe I can scare him off."

"And if he calls your bluff?" Jenn said. "No, I have to handle this."

"You? He'll destroy your life, or he'll bury you."

Jenn felt a flash of anger. "Kill his own daughter? I don't believe it."

Merrick shook his head. "You don't understand. This isn't about you. It's about taking you away from me."

Jenn looked away, stung. Was it really so impossible that Zane had come back because he wanted to be with her, because he felt something for her; surely even a murderer could love his own daughter?

* * *

Zane felt himself freeze like a scared rabbit as his father emerged from the vault. The leaves of the sumac bush seemed suddenly too sparse to hide him; he should have found a better place, further away—fifty yards wouldn't be enough if the wind changed or Merrick happened to look his way. The trees weren't very thick around the clearing, giving the old devil numerous lines of sight. Night was like day to him—no phage was more powerful, more skilled at detection. . . .

Stop it. You're all right—as long as you keep still.

Easing the pent-up air from his lungs, Zane began to breathe again. A cloud slid off the moon and Merrick's hair gleamed in the sudden deluge of light. Zane wished it were truly a sign of frailty, that silvery hair, but knew it was not. Merrick had done it at least three times before, bleaching his hair, then dyeing it gray, to make the normals around him think he was aging so he could have a few extra years with one wife or another. *How nice for you, Father, that you have cute tricks to help you feel complacent, but how do you feel now that you've seen my empty cell?* Studying Merrick for any sign of agitation or alarm, Zane saw none and felt cheated. Of course, at this distance he really couldn't make out Father's expression—and he had no desire to be closer. Surely, at the very least, the old man must be confused, shocked. . . .

Zane stopped thinking about him as Jenn emerged. The sight of her made his heart swell. So beautiful, so radiant she needed no moon to glow. She had grown tall—an inch or two under six feet. The corn silk hair had thickened and darkened to the honeyed hue of a lion's coat. The last time she'd been a thin child. Now she was a woman with shoulders, and long, sleekly muscled legs. *My daughter!*

Gazing raptly at her, Zane wondered, as he had so many times, at her power over him. Why was he so enchanted with her? With all the women he had visited in the night, he must have sired other children, many, but he'd never given it a thought until that night ten years ago when he'd discovered Jenn. Were any of his other children phages? Probably not, with the gene so recessive. He had nothing to give a normal child. That must be why he'd never given it any thought. But Jenn, ah, Jenn—he could give her the world.

The one Merrick was taking from her.

And she could give him something, too. Someone to be close to. *How much I've missed.*

As Zane thought of the lost years, bitterness rose in his throat. To find her like that, a girl of twelve, to feel his heart begin to open, only to have Merrick tear him from her and throw him in the vault—galling! And now she had grown from girl to woman without him. *I should have been* there, Zane thought, to see each little change in her, to marvel at her transformation from frail girl to powerful phage; to guide her into her new life.

You *could* have been there.

Zane winced. How that thought gnawed at him. After all, he'd gotten loose within weeks, while Jenn was still young. Weeks, but an eternity when you were waiting to die, when you knew it might be a year before you could even slip into the uneasy rest of unconsciousness. How many times had he paced off that noxious ten feet, back and forth like the leopard in its cage, pushing off the walls, peeling away the minutes one by one, feeling as if he might suffocate, wishing he could. Getting hungrier and hungrier for blood, knowing he would eventually starve for it, but that he'd go insane first.

It had nearly broken him.

Scrambling up into the light and air, he could think of only one thing—to get far away, as fast as possible. I couldn't have stayed, he told himself. And even if I could, what was the use? The minute I started coming around Jenn, Father is so fey he'd have picked it up, even if she didn't tell him. And if I'd tried to snatch her and run, he'd have followed me to the ends of the earth.

Zane saw that Jenn and Merrick were walking away. She put a hand on Merrick's shoulder; the little gesture made Zane's teeth clench. At the edge of the clearing, almost into the trees, Merrick stopped and turned.

He senses me!

Fear swept Zane again. He fought the urge to back further into the bush. He must not move, mustn't even blink. He held his breath, terrified, as Merrick's gaze swept toward him.

And past.

Finally, Merrick and Jenn stepped into the trees, and Zane continued to keep perfectly still, waiting for the fear to thaw so he could move again. Disgusting, how scared he was. It had been good living without the terror, feeling secure because he knew Merrick considered him buried and dead. Ten years of no running, the easy life in San Francisco, had made him forget how bad feeling afraid could be. Sitting here now, waiting for the strength to come back into him, he was almost sorry he'd stumbled across the old article in *USA Today*. If he hadn't overheard that guy two weeks ago at the bar of the Fairmont bragging about stocking up on Krugerrands—and even then, it had taken a fluke of circumstance. A small fortune in gold, Zane thought, but the crazy bastard didn't keep it in a safe. Finally I got so desperate to find the gold I started pulling open kitchen drawers, and, amazingly, there she was, smiling up at me!

Zane pulled the article from inside his jacket, unfolding it with loving care. The headline beneath her picture read MED STUDENT RESCUES TODDLER. The article was three years old, so the guy had probably looked at Jenn hundreds of times since using the paper to line the drawer. The odd way the paper had been folded showed that he'd deliberately put her picture facing up, so that each time he opened the drawer, he could glance through the corkscrews and grating boards and see the pretty face. He misses her now, Zane thought. He can't figure out why someone would break in and steal nothing but the lining of his kitchen drawer. He doesn't know that she's rarer, more precious than a fortune in gold.

Zane gazed at the photo. She'd been nineteen when it was taken, and you could still see traces of the child she had been, which was why he'd recognized her so quickly. But there were also intriguing changes, a firming of the jaw, something powerful emerging in the eyes. And pain, too. A question that only he could see: *Who am I? I need someone to tell me.*

I will tell you, Zane thought.

The distant, low growl of Merrick's car engine floated through the trees. Zane rose and stepped from the thicket, rolling his head on his shoulders, relaxing the bunched muscles of his neck. He refolded the clipping—the priceless photo of his daughter and the horrifying, glorifying account of her heroism—and slipped it back into his jacket. How close she came to destroying us all, Zane thought with a chill.

He went to the clearing and stood at the entrance to the vault, now buried under the leaves again. Being so close made the muscles in his legs stiffen and tremble, as though he were standing at the edge of a cliff. His stomach churned with a dread so fierce it dizzied him, but he held himself in place until fury burned away his fear. Old man, he thought, you've had my daughter ten years, and what have you taught her? Only the worst, the most dangerous of errors. The same insanity you tried to program into me.

Well, your time is up. It's my time now.

And if she rejects me?

Zane shook his head fiercely, but remembered the loving way she'd just put her hand on Father's shoulder. What if they were too close, Jenn and Merrick? What if he couldn't break that bond?

Would he be able to take the next step? Wouldn't a wolf brainwashed to think she is a sheep be better off dead?

5

As Merrick drove away from her apartment building, Jenn realized she was more afraid than she'd thought. She had a sudden, powerful urge to run from the lobby and flag him down, tell him she'd changed her mind about staying with him and Katie tonight. Crossing her arms, she held herself in place. I'd be putting them in danger, she thought. There'd be nothing Merrick could do—and if Zane realizes that, it could be the end for Merrick.

No, I have to try and keep the two apart.

Merrick glanced back and she gave him a reassuring wave, and then he was gone and she stood, acutely conscious she was alone. The thought of going up to her apartment oppressed her. It would still smell to her of blood; she would see Emmy Rittenhouse's body every time she looked at the foyer. Every sound would play on her nerves, and worst, she would still be alone.

Hugh—yes!

She glanced at her watch. Nearly midnight, but that was no problem. Right about now he'd just be cranking it up on his writing. . . .

But what if Zane saw her go there?

The thought chilled her. Might he be watching her? Staring out at Connecticut Avenue, she searched the dark, shiny windows of parked cars.

But *would* she see him?

A creepy paranoia swept her, prickling at the roots of her eyes. Don't do this to yourself, she thought. Remember what Merrick said: *I know it won't be easy, Jenn, but try to put Zane from your mind. If he knew he could kill me, that is what he'd do, but corrupting you would be almost as sweet to him. He may come to you when he's sure I'm not around, may tell you he loves you, but remember that he can't—there's no love in him. The most important thing is not to let him separate you from the life you've chosen. Stay yourself, keep to your routines, go on living life your way as much as possible. That's the best way to fight him.*

Right, Jenn thought dryly, just go on living my life. She remembered saying the same thing only a few weeks ago to a patient with cancer. Now she would find out just how much harder it was to do than to say. She nerved herself up. I go to Hugh's house a couple of nights a week, she thought. So I'm going now. If I don't, I'm cutting myself off from the man I want to be with.

Starting out the door, Jenn remembered she was supposed to present Caroline at Chief of Service rounds tomorrow. The notion had a curious lack of substance, as though it did not really apply to her. She shook herself mentally—*Come on, blow it at rounds, and you'll plant doubts in the minds of the head of pediatrics, your chief resident, and whatever attendings show up. Nothing could cut you off quicker from the life you want to lead.*

She did some quick planning: Chief of Service rounds weren't until noon tomorrow but once she hit the ward at seven she'd have no further chance to prepare. Sometime tonight she needed to read up on thymus-derived lymphocyte counts. She didn't have to do it here, though. She could take the journals along to Hugh's and read them there. They were stacked on the table in her dining alcove.

At her apartment door, she paused. *What if Zane is in there again—this time waiting for me?* Despite everything, the thought raised a nervous excitement in her. Stepping inside, she breathed through her mouth to avoid any lingering fragrance of Emmy's blood. Hurrying to the table, she picked up the journal articles. At the door, she paused and looked back. The apartment seemed unnaturally vivid; the Persian rugs Merrick had given her glowed with molten reds and golds, and the outlines of the camelback couch and brass end tables seemed sharp enough to cut. Just to the side of the couch, the cream paint of the wall shimmered as if about to boil, sending a nervous charge across her skin.

"Father?" she whispered.

No answer. The paint flattened into inertness.

He couldn't hide that way, she thought. Not from me.

Exasperated at the way she had spooked herself, she firmly shut the door.

As she drove her old MG through the night toward Hugh's place, the nerves in her neck began to crawl. Keeping five miles an hour below the speed limit, she checked her rearview mirror over and over. Everyone kept rushing forward to pass her; she could detect no car hanging back. But if Zane *could* hide himself from her, he could also hide the car he was driving. According to Merrick, phages usually could not Influence each other, but she was inexperienced, and Zane wasn't just any phage.

But if he'd really been there in my apartment, Jenn thought, he'd have answered me.

I called him Father.

She winced. Merrick had warned her Zane would exploit the slightest sympathy she might feel. But was that really all her father wanted—to use her? Might Merrick, even with his vastly superior knowledge, be wrong? Truth was, it was all assumption, wasn't it? They didn't even know for sure Zane was the one who had left the corpse on her doorstep. She could think of no other explanation, but that didn't mean there wasn't one.

A soft chiming caught Jenn's attention. To her left she saw the Washington Marina sliding by and realized the sound came from tackle and rigging tapping against aluminum masts. The beauty of the scene held her as she passed, boats and slices of moonlight riding the sinuous black ripples of the harbor together. Then the marina gave way to the dark groves of trees that flanked the final access to Alexandria. She'd had enough of trees tonight and was glad when the first gas stations, shops, and hotels of Old Town began to roll by. The commercial district had been kept tastefully low to the ground and, wherever possible, harmonious with the old houses, shops, and taverns that still endured along the way. Imagining the ancient cobblestones that lay beneath the asphalt, she wished she could have seen this street a hundred and fifty years ago, as Merrick had.

Hugh's townhouse was antique brown brick, with a small, roofed stoop in front and a bricked-in courtyard in back. Hidden away on quiet Fayette Street, several blocks off the main drag, it was part of a genteel old neighborhood that could as easily have graced New Orleans or Savannah. His place even had the luxury of a parking space in the rear, next to the garbage cans. The narrow alley leading back to it was plenty wide enough for her MG, and Hugh had left just enough room beside his Harley for the little car. The rear gate was locked; as she walked back up the alley to the front stoop, eagerness swelled in her, and she cautioned herself to act natural. Hugh was perceptive, and if he picked up her anxiety and agitation, he'd demand an explanation.

When she reached the front door, it was already open. Hugh stood with arms spread in the small foyer. His face had a fresh-scrubbed look; kissing him, she smelled pine soap. Unable to hold back, she hugged him so hard he overbalanced and backed them into the ancient, elongated bell from Thailand he'd slung from a brace of posts in the entry. Keeping an arm around her, he waltzed her through the dining alcove and down three steps to the little sunken living room. She loved this room with its curious mix of antique cast-iron fireplace and modern cathedral ceiling. He'd used the extra wall space to hang a gorgeous medieval tapestry that looked authentic but had to be fake. Inhaling the fragrance of the burning oak logs, she purged her nostrils of the last traces of blood. "Kind of balmy tonight for a fire, isn't it?"

"Fires take time to build. You have to fuss with them, get the kindling just right. And when you get it going, you have this little feeling of accomplishment."

Seeing his laptop sitting on the leather couch across from the fireplace, she understood. Only the bottom half of the screen was filled with text, which meant it was the opening of a chapter, and he hadn't even scrolled down yet. "Still stuck?" she asked.

He nodded glumly, running his hand back along his head, pulling his hair down tight. When he released it, it sprang up as if he'd taken a jolt of electricity. His brown eyes smoldered with exasperation and his clothes were rumpled, as though the laptop had dragged him down on the floor and wrestled him. The wonder was, even mussed and rumpled like this, he was very handsome.

"Knowing how to write is easy," he said with a dark scowl. "It's knowing *what* to write that's hard."

She drifted toward the couch, but he beat her there and shut off the computer. She said, "The devil is in the details, eh?"

"And Satan is in the segues."

"Need some inspiration?"

"That's rubbish," he groused. "People think writers just sit around waiting for the muse to come sit on their shoulder and whisper deathless prose in their ears, dictate whole passages that will sing with the voice of angels . . ."

He trailed off as he noticed she was undoing the top button on her blouse. She could not believe she was doing this. Did she think it would make her fears about Zane go away? *Yes!—for a while, anyway.* But Hugh was in a bleak mood. What if he didn't want to right now? She'd be mortified. . . .

Hugh cleared his throat. "Which is not to say that inspiration is entirely without place in the life of a novelist."

Relieved at the avidness in his eyes, she finished with the buttons as he settled beside her and watched. Slipping a hand under either side of the blouse, he fit his fingers into the grooves between her ribs. His hands were warm and felt nice. Easing them up, he spread his thumbs back to catch the crease under each breast. A sweet intimacy flowed from the gentle gesture. His tongue circled the edge of an aureole before finding the nipple, drawing it into hardness, and she smothered a moan in the tangle of his hair.

"Jenn, you're so beautiful," he murmured, "so good, so precious to me."

The loving words took her past arousal to all that she adored about him, large and small—his tenderness with her, his lack of glibness at moments like these, and his genuineness all the time; the way he kept the bird feeder outside his window full; the fact that his humor was never cruel; his courtesy to strangers, the unobtrusive dignity he kept about him even when they were ready to cut loose and be animals with each other. And the way he made her feel about herself with his gaze, words, and touch—worthy of admiration, good all the way through instead of just on the surface.

His hands trembled as he undid her belt, and this obvious sign of his desire inflamed her own lust. He slid her skirt down and descended with it, until he was kissing where the waist of her panties had just been. Pulling him up, she ripped down the front of his shirt and heard his buttons skittering away across the floor. Then she got his belt undone and worked at his jeans, holding her breath as his tongue caressed hers. She felt his hands on her rump and, kicking away his pants, joined herself to him, exploring the hard planes of his ribs with the sensitized insides of her thighs, then locking her ankles behind him. His hard chest swelled against her as he finally took a breath.

"It's so good to hold you," he whispered.

She saw the flames in the fireplace dancing behind him, and then the fire inside her began to build, a wonderful warmth that spread up her belly and into her breasts, driving back the coldness of her fear and anxiety about Zane. As he rocked inside her, Hugh's body became slick, releasing the smell of his cologne, something called Green Water she'd bought him for his birthday. It made her want to bite him, taste his tanned skin. She circled her hands behind him, into the hollows under his shoulder blades, pulling him closer still. The fire rose inside her, filling her throat until she wanted to shout with pleasure. He slowed, drawing it out, and she heard herself saying his name over and over, "Hugh, Hugh, Hugh-h-h-h!" and then it was happening, the exquisite spasms going on until she did shout.

For a long time, he held her to him, one hand cupping the nape of her neck now. His fingers, twined into her hair, massaged the tight muscles at the base of her skull. It felt wonderful. "When I'm touching you," he said, "I feel like nothing bad could ever happen."

"Me too."

Rolling at last to the side, he let his arms flop, making no effort to hide the part of him that was still tense. She wanted to touch it, and, overcoming her sudden shyness, she did. It was very hot, and she knew her hand would smell of him later, and was glad.

Turning his head, he gazed at her. "Are you okay?"

"What do you mean?"

"You were afraid when you came in. Something's bothering you. Why don't you tell me about it?"

For a moment she was surprised. *How did he know?* And then she realized that, however he knew, she *did* want to talk about it.

But it was a bad idea.

"I . . . can't."

"Okay." Getting up, he pulled his jeans and shirt back on, then began crawling around the floor.

"What are you doing?"

"Looking for my buttons."

He did not sound angry or hurt, but he didn't sound droll either, and she could feel him withdrawing, just that little bit. If there was anything worse than being alone, it was being alone while someone you loved was in the same room with you.

But Hugh had no idea how hard this was. Not since she was twelve, before the leukemia, had she let herself open up to anyone. That was the first thing she'd realized when the change had come over her—that she must seal away what she had become. Not only must, *wanted* to. It was easy, because she was so ashamed. She drank blood, damn it, and if anyone knew, they would be horrified and disgusted by her. So she must never do or say anything even to hint at it. Not to the kids at school, Mom or Dad, the boys—and later men—she had dated. No one.

And not Hugh—*especially* not Hugh.

But was her secret really at stake here?

Eagerness swelled in her as she saw it might not be. If she didn't give Hugh any reason to think she and her father were anything but normal, surely there should be room to talk about Zane's return. Her mind raced ahead, partitioning what she could say from what she couldn't, reshaping it so she could keep to the truth as much as possible. Because the idea was not simply to confide in Hugh but to get his help. God, how wonderful that would be!

"You have to promise not to tell anyone," she said, "not ever."

Hugh stopped picking up buttons and looked at her. "Tell them what?"

"Promise."

Rising from the floor, he sat beside her again. "I won't tell anyone."

He waited expectantly, but she still could not make the words come out. They seemed stuck in her throat. What if she slipped, and Hugh got a whiff of her real self? It could end up endangering their relationship—and possibly much more.

But now she'd committed herself, so she must say something. "You remember my father?"

"James?" Hugh smiled. "How could I forget? I'm still looking for a way to fit his method for growing huge zucchini into a novel—"

"James is . . . not my father."

Hugh raised an eyebrow, but that was all.

His muted reaction encouraged her. This wasn't so bad. She said, "I mean, he is my father in the all-important sense of having raised me, but not in the trivial sense of having *fathered* me."

"You don't sound as if you think it's trivial."

She swallowed. "Don't I?"

Hugh studied her. "Does James know you're not his daughter?"

"No."

Hugh settled back on the couch. "Ahhhhh."

He still did not seem too shocked. This was under control, it was all right. Jenn studied her next words, turning them over in her mind before saying them. "My biological father came through town very briefly almost twenty-three years ago, and I was born nine months later."

"When did you find this out?"

"Ten years ago." Jenn wondered if giving him the time frame was going too far. No, surely that bit of the truth couldn't hurt.

Hugh's face furrowed in confusion. "You learned it when you were only *twelve?* How? Surely your mother didn't tell you."

"No. She has no idea that I know." *Because she doesn't know it herself.* "I learned it from my father. He came through town again, briefly, and paid a call on me when Mom and Dad weren't around." Jenn's anxiety began to rise. She must rein herself in. She had never been drunk, but had seen drunks in ER spilling their life stories, and that was the way this felt inside, slippery and out of control.

Hugh cocked his head. "So this guy comes to town and says, 'Hi, Jenn, you're my daughter.' How do you know it isn't bull?"

"You should see the two of us together." It sounded weak. This was what happened when you started to spin stories. She wasn't even sure, apart from the deep green of her eyes, if she resembled Zane. Her memories of him were not that solid.

"So-o-o-o-o," Hugh said, "may I presume this guy has now come back to town yet again?"

"Yes."

"And is threatening to tell your dad?"

"No. He just makes me nervous, that's all. He's . . . not a good guy."

"What do you mean?"

Jenn groped for words that would tell him how she felt without telling him too much. "I think he may be some kind of criminal." She had a brief awareness of Hugh's pulse speeding up before she cut herself off, shaken. Don't do that, she thought. You don't read people like that—and especially not Hugh.

"A thief?" he asked.

"Worse. Much worse."

He gazed at her with dread fascination. His sudden intensity made her uncomfortable.

"Are we talking about murder?"

She said nothing, then realized her silence was all the confirmation Hugh needed. His hands went to his temples, as if he'd felt a sudden pain there. "Are you afraid of him?"

"A little, yes." *More than a little. But that's not all I feel. If it were, this would be easy—all I'd have to do is run like hell from Zane.*

"Want to move in with me for a while?" Hugh said.

"No—thanks." She groaned inwardly. Now she had Hugh thinking of protecting her, a bad idea. "I'm sure he wouldn't hurt me. It just upset me to see him again, that's all."

"What are you going to do?"

"I don't know."

He took her hand, held it in both of his, and she realized his hands felt warm because hers were so cold. Was that how he'd known she was upset? She couldn't believe she'd said so much. It should have been second nature to keep it all to herself, but he'd seen right through her somehow. She remembered what Merrick had said about the ability of older phages to read people. A chill went through her, and then she put the thought from her mind. Absurd. Next she'd have herself believing it was Hugh who'd left the body on her doorstep.

"I'm all right," she said. "I'm fine. He just came through to see me. I'm sure he doesn't want trouble. He'll be on his way again—I get the feeling he never stays anywhere for long."

"Still, maybe I should talk to the guy."

"No. I can handle this." But could she?

"You sure?"

"I'm sure." Jenn made a point of looking at her watch. "Damn, I have to go."

"Why?"

Because I've already said too much, and if I stay, I'm afraid I'll really go too far. She remembered the journal articles—still on her car seat. "I haven't boned up for Chief of Service rounds tomorrow," she said. Getting up, she took a step toward the door. With a resigned look, he walked her there and kissed her good night. Wanting desperately to stay with him, she made herself smile and walk out.

When she got home, she crept around the apartment, listening for any sounds of movement. She poked into the corners and under the table, kicked into the shallow closet. Nothing. The faint smell of Emmy's blood was all but wiped out, thank goodness, by the fragrance of Hugh's sweat on her skin.

Taking the journals to her bedroom, she sat on her bed and read for two hours. It should have taken one, but her eyes kept skipping between the lines, sliding along the white into inner spaces she had not visited in ten years. When she was satisfied she knew enough about lymphocyte counts, she pushed the journals aside. Restless, she wandered out to the kitchen, around the apartment, then back to her bedroom. Standing at her bookcase, she ran a finger along the spines of her books, not sure what she was looking for until the finger stopped, like a divining rod finding water. She pulled the book out—*The Secret Princess,* in which a young peasant girl finds out she's really the king's daughter. Her favorite story when she was a kid . . .

What is it?

Turning out the lights, she sat against her bedstead, listening to the silence of the building seep through her apartment.

And then she had it.

Feeling a strange, almost guilty delight, she cradled the book against her chest, closed her eyes, and gave herself over to the memory she'd just found: she had shown this book to Zane in her bedroom that night, after the hospital had discharged her and she was back home. He'd slipped soundlessly into the house while her parents had slept in the next room. Had she been afraid? She could not remember that. What she remembered, what had popped into her mind like a lost and forbidden treasure, was the talk she'd had with him. He asked me about the pictures on my walls, she thought, and my doll collection. Then, seeing all my books, he asked what my favorite was, and of course I pointed to this one. He asked me to tell him what it was about, and I did.

And then, he told me he was my father: *I am like the king in this book. After you were conceived, but before you were born, I was forced to flee from here or be killed. It is still dangerous for me here, but I have come back for you.*

Jenn savored the words, carried in her unconscious all these years: I have come back for you. For *you.*

And now, once again, he had come back—a killer, a ruler of darkness, and she was scared, yes, but she was also glad.

And that was what scared her most.

⌧

After Jenn left, Hugh sat staring at his word processor, seeing nothing on the screen. Jenn's father is a murderer, he thought.

A murderer not in jail, who has not been caught.

Feeling a dark excitement, he typed the word on his screen—*murderer.* Then other words—*ten years ago!!!!*

Hugh groaned. He never used exclamation points.

He was getting too excited about this. It might mean nothing.

I should be ashamed, he thought. When I started to fall for Jenn, I promised myself I wouldn't use her. And tonight? Those questions I asked her were for me, not her. I could tell she was afraid, I should have insisted she move in with me.

He got up and went to the foyer, as if it weren't too late to stop her from leaving, to keep her here. Angry, he kicked the gong. It gave a low, shuddering tone, not nearly enough noise to repay the pain in his toe. What would Jenn think if she knew his first words to her had been a lie, that he hadn't given a damn about interviewing a woman intern, that the meeting he'd set up with her hadn't had anything at all to do with research for a novel? That it hadn't even been her he was interested in, but Merrick, who might hold the key to both his past and his future. That he'd found out she was close to Merrick and decided to mine her for information about the man who'd hunted the vampire killer ten years ago, not for any novel but for a reason that was desperately more important.

But I *do* love her, he thought.

Returning to the living room, he stirred the crumbling logs on his grate. Sparks flew up and a few tongues of flame licked the charred logs then subsided again. Stalking through his house, he found himself in the spare bedroom he had intended to use as an office. It contained a perfectly good desk he never used, a small closet full of supplies such as paper clips and typewriter ribbons from before he'd gotten the laptop.

The file in one corner was now the only important thing in the room.

Unlocking its top drawer, Hugh pulled out the *Washington Post* clippings from ten years ago: VAMPIRE KILLER TERRORIZES NATION'S CAPITAL. He'd highlighted all the quotes from homicide lieutenant Merrick Chapman in yellow—masterful non-answers to reporters' questions, fascinating despite, or perhaps because of, their utter lack of actual substance, especially when you considered the bottom line: Merrick had never caught the killer. The gruesome murders had stopped abruptly, and after that the stories had gradually petered out.

Did Jenn know that one of Merrick's colleagues on the force during the murders thought he might have deliberately bungled the investigation? I still don't know how she's connected to all this, he thought. All I know is what I knew from the start, that when I staked out Merrick's house ten nights in a row, I saw her come and go six of those nights. So now we're together, and I fell for her, and I'm still going to use her if I can.

I *have* to.

Hugh felt the headache returning, a few dull stabs at the base of his skull that would quickly grow to more if he did not do something. And the first thing he must do was stop thinking about this. Thinking, banging his head against the mystery of the murders, was what caused the headaches—they came at no other time. But how would he ever solve it, if his brain wouldn't allow him to think about it?

Deeply frustrated, he put the clippings back, then found the bottle of Tylenol III in the bathroom medicine cabinet, and gulped down three tablets. After a few minutes the codeine went to work and the pain eased a little.

Lying down on the cool tiles of the bathroom floor, he tried to relax and empty his mind. But tonight it wasn't so easy, not easy at all, because it was the most important thing in his life, this terrifying unanswered question, and Jenn had just brought it into a new, sharper focus: *The murders ten years ago—was the killer Jenn's father? Or was it me?*

6

Dropping her notes on the lectern, Jenn sat on the chair behind it and gazed out at the empty amphitheater, trying to focus on her presentation. It worried her that she felt no nervousness about it. In a few minutes, doctors would begin ambling into the rising tiers of seats—most, her fellow interns, but a few with real power over her future—and all she could think of was Zane, as if her hopes and fears about him had scorched a path in her mind no other fires could burn through.

She watched the two doors at the rear of the amphitheater. What if Zane walked through one? Not impossible. To know where she lived, he must have been watching her—might even be in this room with her now. Merrick had said her father would hate the life she was living. The thought that he might be here, hiding himself, watching her with disapproval or even malevolence, filled her with turmoil. She did not want him watching her, she wanted him to come out of the shadows, tell her what he wanted, why he had come back, what he felt about her.

At the same time, she was terrified at what might happen if he did.

A couple of interns came through one of the doors and shuffled

down the aisle like sleepwalkers. As soon as they sat down, they'd probably *be* asleep. One waved at her and she lifted a hand. Within minutes,
the amphitheater began to fill up, and as doctors kept flowing down the
aisles and into the curving rows of seats, a nerve in her stomach started to
twang after all. What were all these people doing here? She couldn't
remember ever seeing such a crowd at Chief of Service rounds. Except for
a few gaps, they covered the rising tiers to the back wall. The throng of
fellow interns down in front, she expected—they more or less had to
attend. The smaller packs of senior residents out to the side weren't too
much of a threat either, but those attendings finding seats in the upper
reaches—it would take only one or two who wanted to show off at her
expense. . . .

And here came Fortis Wayne—on time, for once! Jenn's anxiety
deepened as she watched the chief of pediatrics descend the aisle and turn
in at a row midway back in the center section. Though he was small
enough to slip down the row easily, the other doctors each rose as he
passed them. The middle seat had been left empty for him; settling into
it, he crouched forward and scanned the room like a scrawny spider surrounded by a web full of future meals. And I'm today's blue plate special,
Jenn thought, feeling another pulse in her stomach. How did a guy like
Wayne ever end up head of pediatrics? Apparently, he was good with
newborns, but she couldn't imagine children or adolescents feeling com-
fortable with him. You didn't have to be Mr. Rogers to take care of kids,
but Dr. Wayne plain looked scary. A lot of it was his eyes. They stared
out at you from under their hoods of bone with frosty calculation. His
face was top-heavy with forehead, an effect he emphasized by slicking his
black hair straight back to expose pale triangles of flesh on either side. He
did have a good mouth, nicely shaped and always turned up a little at the
corners. The word was not to watch his mouth, though, because you'd
think everything was fine and then you'd be twice as shocked when he
ripped into you.

What made him so prickly? He had a stammer, but only intermit-
tently, and it was oddly selective—he could flawlessly rattle off words like
laryngopharyngectomy or cineroentgenofluorography, but "good job" or

"nice call," seemed to give him more trouble. She'd heard that, in private, he liked to encourage his residents to confide in him, then nail them when they admitted to imperfections. . . .

Knock it off! Jenn could not believe she was so anxious. With the horrors of the vault and her fears about Zane, she'd been sure nothing about this presentation today could scare her. But it seemed there was adrenaline left in her after all.

The murmur fell away as Dr. Wayne stared around the auditorium. Turning back to the front, he nodded at her. "Okay, Dr.—" he consulted his clipboard—"Hrluska. What kind of name is that?"

She took her place at the lectern. "Bohemian—before it got a little scrambled at Ellis Island."

Wayne gave her a cool smile. "Bohemian. I wasn't ah-ah-aware they'd seceded from the Czech Republic."

Jenn swallowed the urge to tell him the name went back to the twelfth century when Bohemia was its own country. What difference did her name make? She had none of Dad's blood in her veins anyway, and would, in a few decades, have to lose Jenn Hrluska and become some other fresh-faced young woman—

Jenn's heart seized as she saw a tall man slip into the back of the auditorium and then she recognized him as just one of the attendings in neurology.

Christ, you've got to forget Zane—at least for the next hour!

"I believe you are pre-ahhhh-senting the case of Caroline Osborne today?"

"Yes, sir."

Wayne flicked a hand and she realized he was telling her to begin. "Caroline is a twelve-year-old Caucasian female brought into ER six weeks ago by her father, who had noticed blood on her toothbrush. Her mother died two years ago at this hospital from a primary brain tumor diagnosed as a high-grade ependymoma. Caroline has no siblings. I was in ER when Caroline was brought in, and I conducted the initial exam. Her presenting symptoms were paleness, low-grade fever, swollen and bleeding gums, fatigue, lymphadenopathy, and sternal tenderness. Physical exam revealed a swollen spleen. Based on the symptoms and exam, I ordered a stat blood workup including, of course, CBC and differential. Her white count at that time was forty thousand and she was anemic. As soon as the lab work came back, I admitted Caroline to the adolescent ward with a tentative diagnosis of acute lymphocytic leukemia."

Pausing for a breath, Jenn felt her confidence edging back. Despite her nervous stomach, her voice seemed reasonably clear and strong. "I called in a consult from hematology," she went on, "and Dr. Blandon set up a course of chemotherapy, which brought Caroline's white count down to twenty thousand. In her second week of hospitalization, her fever ran between 101 and 103, despite acetaminophen q4h. A week after termination of chemo, the white count began to rise again. Dr. Blandon found a match from her father and performed a marrow transplant a little over two weeks ago on October 3. To date there has been no sign of Graft vs Host disease, but despite the absence of rejection Caroline's condition has continued to slowly deteriorate. If I could have the blood work slide . . ."

Jenn waited while her medical student, Lila Degeneris, flicked on the overhead projector. Lila neglected to also dial down the lights in the amphitheater, which left the blood work numbers looking pale. Not wanting to embarrass her, Jenn started to talk about the chart anyway, but Dr. Wayne held up a hand.

"I think your num-numbers could use a transfusion."

Dutiful laughter rippled around the room. Penetrating the glare of the projector, Jenn brought Lila out of silhouette and found eye contact. The med student jumped guiltily and hurried to the bank of rheostats, plunging the room into near darkness.

If Zane is outside, this is when he'll slip in. Watching the two doors in the rear, Jenn said, "This workup was done yesterday. Ah . . . as you can see, Caroline is now thrombocytopenic and her white count has increased to seventy thousand. She . . . was short of breath this morning, and a physical exam revealed enlargement of both the liver and spleen sufficient to compress the lungs. You will also note . . . you'll note that the thymus-derived lymphocyte count indicates a dangerously low level of cell-mediated immunity." The squares of light at the back of the auditorium remained unbroken, and Jenn struggled to regain her concentration. "I called in another hematology consult—this morning, that is—with Dr. Blandon and Dr. Agnusson. Dr. Agnusson, an attending in hematology, will comment further in a few moments."

"Dr. Herl-luska," Fortis Wayne said.

Here it comes. "Sir?"

"To what do you attribute your patient's failure to respond to this very aggressive treatment you've bih-been pursuing—not only her failure to respond but the fact that she is getting worse?"

The word "aggressive" cued Jenn that he might really mean *too* aggressive, but in what sense? Did he think the chemo course had been too severe? It *had* been severe, but it had to be to suppress Caroline's immune responses so her body wouldn't reject the graft. Chemo was one of the most powerful weapons against leukemia, and protocols now were much more refined than a few years ago. Even so, Wayne quarreled periodically with hematology about the protocols. She could hand his question off to Dr. Agnusson, but that might seem weak-kneed. She said, "Caroline's failure to respond so far may be related to her age. Peak incidence of ALL is between age three and seven, and the highest cure rate also falls within this range. At twelve, Caroline's prognosis is not as good as for a younger child, and her condition was already fairly advanced when she was admitted, due to her failure to report feeling sick to her father."

"How do you know she failed to report it?"

"By talking with Caroline. She did not want to worry her father, who had, two years before, lost his wife to cancer."

"Are you saying this girl knew she had cancer?"

"No sir, just that she feared it and knew that any serious sickness would terrify her father. Caroline was brought in only when her father walked past the bathroom as she was brushing her teeth and saw blood on her toothbrush."

"You should have mentioned that in your summary."

I did, didn't I? Jenn thought, but said nothing.

Wayne fussed with his clipboard as if looking at his notes. "So it's not yuh-your fault Caroline is doing poorly?"

"I'd be glad if someone could show me it is my fault."

Wayne stared at her. "Would you?"

"Yes, sir, because then I could do something about it."

One of the senior residents off to the side clapped once, then froze as Wayne's head swiveled sharply toward him. In the near darkness of the amphitheater, Jenn saw a hundred ghostly faces peering at her, as if she had suddenly become a curiosity beyond imagining. One of the attendings near the back leaned to the woman in the next chair and whispered, and Jenn's hearing sharpened, bringing his words to her: "You say she's twenty-*two*?"

Wayne settled back, eyeing her again. "So who is going to-to bail out our young intern in her quest for knowledge?"

"Have you looked for chromosomal abnormalities?" asked a woman in the back.

"What good would that do?" someone else asked. "Even if she shows irregularities, there isn't any vehicle for correcting genetic defects."

"This *is* a teaching hospital," the woman replied tartly.

Ask me about thymus-derived lymphocyte counts.

"Why did you go for the marrow transplant so soon, when your patient was obviously still reeling from the chemo?"

Jenn saw it was Brad Dietz, the junior resident who'd almost barged in on her and Hugh in the on-call room yesterday. She heard a few groans and someone whispered, "What a suck-up."

She knew she could pass the ball to Agnusson now, but she said, "Caroline's disease is advanced enough that we felt she might never be stronger."

Agnusson stepped to her side. "If I may, Dr. Hrluska."

She moved over, relieved, and listened while Agnusson and Wayne had a suddenly genteel discussion of chemo and marrow transplants. Someone threw her a question on disseminated intravascular coagulation.

She had not put DIC on her reading list because Caroline showed no signs of it, but she found herself calling up a passable answer from somewhere.

Then, abruptly, Dr. Wayne was standing. "That's all we have time for today," he said. "Thank you for coming over, Dr. Agnusson. Next week Dr. Coates, also currently on adolescent, will be presenting a case of metastasized choriocarcinoma."

Taking their cue from Wayne's abrupt dismissal, everyone got up and headed for the exits. Jenn walked off the stage feeling deflated. She hadn't expected applause, and she knew Wayne wasn't high on praise, but still his utter failure to acknowledge her stung. A hundred hours a week she threw herself into Adams Memorial, and while she didn't feel physical fatigue the way the other interns did, she did suffer the constant emotional strain. And if Zane was truly back, that strain was, at the very least, going to increase sharply. She loved being a doctor, but—with or without Zane—if the next eight months were as brutal as the first four, it would be the toughest year of her life, worse in some ways even than her leukemia ten years ago. Back then, strangely, she had been sad for her parents but hadn't thought to be sad for herself. Now sadness was an everyday thing. Each time she lost one of the kids on the wards it tore at her insides. So far, three preemies, hopelessly early, had died under her hands as she worked frantically to resuscitate them. She'd watched children with AIDS languish on the ward because their parents had abandoned them and they had nowhere else to go; she'd held a severely deformed infant with heart defects and DO NOT RESUSCITATE on its chart, cradling it in her arms as it turned blue from the effort to breathe and then died.

And even this presentation today had been painful. Caroline did not have the unwitting craving to drink human blood that would indicate hemophagia, thank God, but she *was* in bad shape. I've done everything I know and still she's going downhill. No one helped me today, no real ideas, and then Wayne stalks out like Caroline is my fault.

Just what is it that I love so much about this life?

The thought, coming from nowhere, made her uneasy. It was what Zane might ask, if he had, somehow, been in the amphitheater and seen her taking the heat today. I *do* love medicine, she thought, and I'm not going to let him—or anything—change that.

Picking up her pace, she headed into the "gerbil run"—the name generations of interns had given the glassed-in archway that spanned south parking and connected the older, main body of Adams Memorial to psychiatry and the pediatrics wing. A surprisingly hot October sun beat down through the glass, dropping a dense black shadow that hugged her feet. She checked her watch—one o'clock. Getting ready for the presentation had put her behind. She had blood to draw, IVs to start; she needed to track down the lab results on her sickle-cell patient, get a neuro consult on the kid in 506 who was becoming clumsy in the hands, and she had a mountain of progress notes to catch up on—

"Jenn!"

Turning, she saw Lila hurrying to catch up and slowed to accommodate the med student's short legs. Lila barely came up to her shoulder and the twenty extra pounds she was carrying slowed her more. A flush darkened her Mediterranean skin and her curly hair glistened where it met her forehead. Despite being smart and eager to learn, Lila seemed always in a sweat about something. I need to get her to relax a little, Jenn thought.

"Sorry about that," Lila huffed.

"About what?"

"Forgetting the lights."

"No problem."

"I thought you did great."

Warmed, Jenn patted Lila's shoulder.

"She's right. You were stupendous." Brad Dietz, moving up on them with his long, easy stride. Damn, and just when she was starting to get back into a decent mood.

"No thanks to you," she said.

"Hey, I threw you a real softie and you handled it great."

"Right."

Jenn was aware of Lila's gaze flicking back and forth between the two of them, and then, of something else: Brad's breath—what was that odd chalky scent? Jenn looked into his eyes. The pupils were dilated, but your pupils could expand just because you liked what you were seeing, which Brad had lately been making all too plain he did.

"I like your eyes too," Brad said, and she realized she'd been gazing into his.

She said, "Lila, would you excuse us please?"

"Uh, sure. See you on the ward?"

"Five minutes."

Brad watched Lila scurry off. "What a tub."

"Too bad your own tub is so shallow."

"Hey, give me a break. They can't all be gorgeous, like you." He gazed at her without a trace of self-consciousness, taking it for granted she'd be grateful for his flattery. What made him so confident? He had a certain preppie good looks, sure; the thick blond hair, the sleek body that had probably excelled on the Harvard squash courts. But she couldn't be less interested.

Brad said, "I've got two box seats at Ford's Theater tonight."

"Good—just enough room for you and your ego."

"Jenn, Jenn," he murmured reproachfully. "If you'd give me a chance, you wouldn't be sorry."

She sniffed his blood. It smelled too sweet, almost sugary. He's on something, she thought, then remembered rumors that someone had been raiding the meds closet at the main nurses' station on pediatrics. Was that someone Brad?

Read him.

The idea repulsed her. It was against her principles—

But so was an intern treating patients while using. Listening for the faint hiss of Brad's blood, she picked up its rapid, staccato rhythm and realized his pulse was racing. *Amphetamines?* All at once, she was furious at him, for being so stupid, for endangering himself, and for bringing every intern and resident on the ward under suspicion. Grabbing his arm, she pulled him over to the glass wall of the corridor, away from the hurrying staff traffic.

"Oooh," Brad said, "I love it when you're rough."

"What are you on?"

His face went serious. "What are you talking about?"

"Come on, Brad, it's obvious."

"This isn't funny, Jenn."

"I couldn't agree more. Are you aware the nursing staff will be watching all of us very closely? They take it personally when someone raids their meds, and interns are always the prime suspects. I'm sure Liz Marsh would like nothing better than to catch herself a snotty young pup of a doctor. I hope for your sake it's not you."

"Liz Marsh," Brad said contemptuously.

"You think a director of nursing can't touch you because your father chairs the hospital board? She catches you and you can be gone tomorrow."

Brad paled. "You're the one who sounds high," he snapped. "You don't want to go out with me, just say so, but don't make wild accusations, hear?" He pointed a finger in her face, and she resisted the impulse to grab it and give it a twist. He was scared, she could tell. She remembered what Katie had confided to her about her own bout with amphetamines during her internship year—a grim story Katie hadn't even shared with Merrick. How the little pills gave you a quick physical lift, a surge of confidence, the conviction you could do anything. But as you came to need higher and higher doses, the drug would turn on you. You'd begin to feel irritated, your hands would tremble uncontrollably; you'd have trouble sleeping. Brad must know all this but thought he wouldn't let it get that far, because amphetamines made you confident even when you shouldn't be. He's a pain in the neck, Jenn thought, but he's also in trouble, a fellow resident.

"Brad, if you need help—"

"Forget it," he snapped. "And remember what I said." He slid a few steps away along the glass, then hurried off, throwing a final scared glance over his shoulder, as if she were some kind of witch. She realized it had been a mistake to confront him. When he calmed down he might start wondering how she had known his little secret. It was a long jump from wondering to *she's not a normal human,* but how dangerous to nudge a normal even one step in that direction.

We could *be unmasked.*

A ripple of fear passed through her. With her own secret to protect, she should have let Brad think he was keeping his. But she had too much to do to worry about that now. She decided to get Lila to draw the blood and start IV lines, which would free her for the sickle-cell case, and then some charting.

Her plan bogged down almost at once, as she watched Lila trying to stick the first patient.

"I just can't get it." Lila's voice brimmed with frustration.

Containing her own frustration, Jenn moved to help her. The kid, an obese fourteen-year-old, had gone pale with the attempt to remain tough, and Jenn could see tears at the corners of his eyes.

"Let me give it a try," she said, taking the needle from Lila, who stepped back with a grateful nod. Bending over the kid's arm, Jenn focused on the pale, meaty flesh, feeling the usual low excitement as she sensed the vein. Fortunately, she could always find enough control to get her through drawing bloods or setting lines, something that both pleased and puzzled her. The role of doctor seemed to protect her somehow. People wondered if male doctors became aroused when they did breast exams, but she could now believe they did not. There was some kind of mystical contract deep inside you to protect and never harm, weird but powerful—and very good. Still, it would be nice when she became an R-2 and could let the new crop of interns draw the blood. Later still, she could settle in as an attending, where she'd be even further removed from the process, simply writing the order and letting an intern or a lab tech do the sticking. . . .

A tremor of uncertainty passed through her and she wondered if her future was really so sure. A week ago she wouldn't have questioned it, but if Merrick was right, Zane would try to knock her life off course—or worse. No! she thought, desperately. Merrick is wrong. Ten years ago, Zane told me he'd come back for me—for *me,* not to destroy me.

She listened for the vein, homing on the sibilant whisper of blood, then eased the needle through the cushion of fat. The instant dark blood began to spurt into the tube, she looked away, releasing the rubber tourniquet and laying it aside. Her throat crawled with thirst, and she could feel her teeth clenching, but that was normal. "Here," she said, and Lila moved forward to take the still-filling tube from her.

"Amazing!" Lila said. "I don't know how you do that."

And let's hope you never find out. "It comes with practice. You'll get better."

Lila glanced at her Felix the Cat watch. "Damn! I'm supposed to be at the library. We've got exams next week and I'm in a study group."

So much for handing off some work to Lila, Jenn thought. But that's all right. Work is exactly what I need right now. "No problem," she said, "as soon as you finish this."

"Thanks! See you tomorrow."

After Lila left, the day became a blur of new admissions, more blood work, chart notes, and consults. At four, Jenn had cleared most of the jam away and it was time for her to be leaving, too. The thought made her anxious. What would she find when she went home tonight? Another corpse?

Or maybe Zane would come to her.

Not tonight, Jenn thought. I've had enough excitement for one day.

But she found herself hurrying now. *If I could just talk to him . . .*

Passing the nurses' station, she lifted a hand in automatic farewell, then realized the area behind the counter was empty. Not uncommon, with the ward so full, but something wasn't quite right. Stopping, she gave the alcove her full attention.

The meds closet.

Jenn stared at the door in the back of the station. It was open half an inch. The blade of light showing through the crack must be what had tripped the alarm in her subconscious. The meds closet was off limits to everyone but the charge nurse. It was supposed to be kept locked at all times when no one was in the station. Maybe the charge nurse was in the closet.

Or maybe it was the thief.

Brad?

Jenn knew she should keep on walking, but what if Brad *was* in there, popping amphetamines, and later tonight, full of godlike confidence, he made a mistake and one of the kids died for it?

Slipping behind the counter, she put her eye to the crack in the door, but it was too narrow to see inside. The hinges gave a muted squeak as she eased the door open. The short entryway of the L-shaped closet was empty. Stepping around the corner, she saw that there was no one in the long part of the L either. The rows of white plastic containers seemed undisturbed, though she could smell capsule gelatin and the faint, bitter odor of painkillers.

Behind her, the hinges creaked again, followed by a stealthy footstep—*a trap!*

Clamping down on her panic, Jenn hurried to the end of the closet and turned just as Liz Marsh, director of nursing, rounded the corner. Reaching out mentally, Jenn constricted the capillaries of Marsh's retinas precisely where her image fell. The nurse's gaze slid blindly across her, triggering a roller-coaster plunge in her stomach, even though she knew her image wasn't registering. Right now, Marsh's brain was filling in the blood-deprived blank zone with surrounding context, just as it did for the two permanent blind spots where the optic nerves exited each eye. Still, it was unnerving to see Marsh seeming to stare straight at her. The closet was so narrow that two people would have to turn sideways to pass each other. If she moves two steps deeper, Jenn thought, I won't be able to avoid her. She'll bump right into me, and then I've had it.

Leave! Agonized, Jenn tried to project the message into Marsh's brain, but the woman just stood there frowning. Her squarish face, with its hard-etched wrinkles and the smart but aloof eyes, had intimidated plenty of nurses and its share of young doctors, too. Jenn found it terrifying now. Liz Marsh, with her no-nonsense reputation built on a fifteen-year reign as director of nursing, might be the one person at Adams Memorial who could swear a resident had made herself invisible and be believed.

With a perplexed shake of her head, Marsh turned and left the closet.

Jenn hurried after her, slipping past within inches before Marsh could turn and ease the door back into its nearly closed position.

As Jenn found refuge in the stairwell, relief transformed her fear into a rush of euphoria. Close—too close—but she'd gotten away with it!

She raced down five flights of steps and emerged into the parking lot. The setting sun threw long, slanting lines of light and shadow across the lot. She stood, savoring the rosy band of sky above the west wing of the hospital until her heartbeat returned to normal. When she got to her MG, she sat for a moment in the cozy, protected nest of the driver's seat, sobering again as she thought about her narrow escape. What would she have done if Liz Marsh *had* accidentally touched her?

Kill her. You'd have had no choice.

Jenn pounded the steering wheel. *Get out of my mind, Zane!*

But as she pulled slowly from the parking lot, she knew there was only one person in her mind, herself—and that, in the few hours between yesterday and today, that self had started to change.

7

I have to tell Katie about Zane, Merrick thought. Tonight, now.

How he dreaded it. Rising from the piano, he wandered to a wall of the music room, pressing his palms and forehead into the cool paint. He loved this room, his favorite, a snug, windowless haven in the heart of the house where he and Katie had spent countless hours listening to Rachmaninoff and Mozart, or sitting together at her old upright to hammer out chopsticks and other ditties from her high school days. Sometimes, when he could feel the life fading from him, the centuries of blood and death weighing him down, he would come in here alone and touch the walls like this. It comforted him to imagine the gentler memories sealed with the cushioning layers of wallpaper beneath the paint. He would like, some time, to clean away the paint and burrow down through those layers to find what each inhabitant of this house before him had found beautiful. Their lives, brief as fireflies, were what he craved for himself now—just his own twenty or thirty summers and winters with Katie.

Don't let it end so soon, please.

He listened to Katie on the phone in the next room, giving instructions to the night technician in her lab at Georgetown Hospital. Her voice was light, free of worry, and in a minute she would come in here and he would destroy that.

Correction: Zane would. *Damn you, why'd you have to come back?*

Pulling away from the wall, Merrick returned to the piano seat and settled backward on it so he could face the little sofa and beyond it the door. He heard the phone click down; she came in smiling at him, then sobering. "What is it? What's wrong?"

"Come in and have a seat."

He saw her shoulders stiffen as she sat on the sofa's edge, facing him.

"Are you finally going to tell me about last night?" she asked. "Jenn *is* in trouble, isn't she?"

"We're all in trouble."

He told her about the body on Jenn's doorstep, about going to Zane's tomb and finding it empty. As he spoke, he saw the blood drain from her face.

"Oh, Merrick, *no!*"

He knelt, pulling her to him. She hugged him back, but he could feel her trembling. Sorry, so sorry; he closed his eyes, trying to draw her fear into himself. Ten years ago she had suffered terrors beyond endurance, ending with that last hellish night, when she had looked up from the bottom of her own freshly dug grave to see Zane bouncing Gregory on his knee, one hand on her baby's neck, ready to snap it in an instant.

She had thought all that was over, and now he was telling her it wasn't, that Zane was back. My own son, he thought. My responsibility and I failed.

"He'll kill you," she whispered, still clinging to him.

"No . . ." Love for her overwhelmed him and for a moment he was unsure of his voice. All she'd suffered, and yet her first thought was for him. "If he knew he could kill me, I'd already be dead."

She pulled back, keeping hold of his hands. A small hope dawned in her face as she worked through what he'd said. His hope was smaller. To Katie and everyone around him, he still looked young, except for the silver hair. Zane will ignore that, Merrick thought, since I've faked turning gray before. But who knows what other sign he might detect, some small evidence of decline too slight for me or those around me to have noticed? He must have taken a look at me by now from a distance, probably several. So far, he has seen what he expects to. But a closer look, a single shake of his preconceptions, and we could all die.

Katie said, "If he's still afraid of you, why did he leave a body? That's how it started last time, that body at the cathedral, to taunt you."

"This is different. He was giving Jenn a gift, the best gift he could imagine."

"A dead body?"

"No. Fresh blood, in its original container."

Katie shuddered. "You frighten me when you talk that way."

"If we're going to survive, you have to understand how he thinks."

"How who thinks?"

Gregory! A shock ran up Merrick's spine. *How much did he hear?*

Katie's expression smoothed out as she turned to her son. "Hiya, sport."

"Hi, Mom, hi, Dad. How who thinks? Come on, you guys. You were talking about me, weren't you?"

"Nope," Merrick said. "Believe it or not, we occasionally discuss less important subjects."

Gregory gave him a skeptical squint, and Merrick marveled at how much like his mother's it was. "Son, are you wearing my sweatshirt again?"

"It almost fits me now."

The flutter of pride in his voice kept Merrick from pointing out that the shirt hung halfway to his knees. He found himself thinking that Gregory's roughening alto would, any day now, drop to bass.

"I need to go over to Shelley's, all right?"

Katie started to shake her head.

"You *need?*" Merrick said quickly.

"She's got the new *Mirage* CD-ROM," he said, as if it explained everything. "Supposed to be awesome. C'mon, I've done my math and science."

"Are her parents there?"

Gregory flushed a little. "Sure."

"Be back by ten."

"You got it."

He bounded out. Reading Katie's expression, Merrick was afraid she was about to run after him.

"I can't believe you let him go," she said.

"He'll be fine. Shelley is only two doors down."

"But if Zane—"

"He won't. Look, he's *scared* of me. If he wasn't, yes, Gregory would be in danger. Zane would probably forget about Jenn and kill you and Gregory to make me suffer—"

"Merrick, stop . . ." Katie looked terrified.

He patted her shoulder. "The point is, he *is* afraid, so he has to settle for getting at me some other way. Jenn is perfect. He thinks I took her from him. As long as he's trying to woo her, he'll have to consider her feelings. He knows she spends a lot of time over here with the three of us. So even if he thought he might get past me to hurt you or Gregory, he'll fear it would turn Jenn against him. That's why I think we're safe, at least for now."

"What about later? If Zane decides to go after Gregory, he won't even be on guard. Maybe we should tell him. Maybe it's time we told him everything."

The suggestion startled Merrick, then filled him with dismay, which quickly turned to a familiar, queasy fear. *Son, I drink blood.* Good Christ, he couldn't imagine Gregory being anything but repulsed and horrified. Surely Katie must see that?

No, it wouldn't help—and it was impossible, not now, not for a long time.

He forced his voice to calmness. "Telling Gregory his father is a 'vampire' will solve nothing. It will only create a whole new set of problems."

Katie touched his hand. "He'd still love you."

"That isn't the point."

"Isn't it?"

"Katie, think back to the fear you felt when you learned what I am and multiply that by the difference between your age and Gregory's."

"I don't remember being all that scared."

"Because you've had ten years to forget how hard it hit you, ten years in which none of your initial fears have been confirmed. Your comfort with me now comes from time—years of it. Plus you were an adult, not a vulnerable child full of childish fears which life hasn't yet laid to rest. And even so, I believe I just heard you say, 'You frighten me when you talk like that.'"

She gave him a somber, reflective look.

"Even if Gregory could handle the fear," Merrick said, "he's too young to carry a burden like that around with him. Adolescents want desperately to be part of the group—that's what the next few years are going to be all about for him. I don't want him to have to deal, at the same time, with knowing he's the son of a freak, much less that the next year or so might turn him into a freak himself."

"Merrick . . ." She pressed her hands to her mouth.

"I know it's hard," he said gently, "but try not to be afraid. I don't think Zane will move against us now, and possibly not at all. It's Jenn we have to worry about."

Katie took a deep breath, then nodded. "Poor Jenn. This is the last thing she needs."

"I doubt he'll make much headway with her," Merrick said.

Katie gave him a thoughtful look. "I'm not so sure you're right. What I remember mostly is being terrified. But he has an odd grace, too. A strange, dark . . . beauty, almost. I can imagine him acting gentle, being quite persuasive. James Hrluska thinks he's Jenn's father, and so does Jenn's mother, but Jenn knows better. In her own mind she's an adoptee, and that can raise a lot of complicated emotions, strange divisions of loyalty. Even when the 'stepfather' is as good as hers, there can be buried longings, glowing fantasies about the missing 'true' father."

Merrick couldn't help but feel the rightness of what she was saying. And Jenn's initial responses had not been everything he could have hoped. He *had* sensed ambivalence in her.

"But she's strong," Katie said. "I'm sure she'll resist him."

"I wish I were."

Katie said nothing, and the uncertainty in her face made his heart sink. "We have to be ready to help her," he said.

"How?" When he did not answer, Katie's eyes widened. "You're thinking of quitting the injections."

"No," he said quickly.

"Maybe you should."

He stood, filled with turmoil. The thought of going back on his decision to live out a normal life span and die filled him with dread. He did not want to return, even temporarily, to what he'd been. He wanted to be with Katie to the end, to die with her. "If I stopped taking Fraction Eight," he said, "could you, as a hematologist, guarantee that, once my cells recovered all their functions, they wouldn't immediately produce immunity to it?"

"No, how could I?"

He knew she did not want him to grow old and die with her, was helping him do it only because it was what *he* so desperately wanted. She'd be willing to accept the pain of growing old while he did not, of uprooting her home and medical practice every few years so his perpetual youthfulness could go undetected, of enduring the cool glances of people who thought a young man could not love an older woman; of coming to hate what she saw in the mirror.

He could not let that happen.

"We have no idea how long it would take me to get back to what I was," he said. "Or even if I could get back. Maybe the aging is permanent. And I can't risk becoming immune to Fraction Eight. I've had a thousand years; all I want is thirty or forty more with you."

Her eyes brimmed with tears, and he knew if he took her in his arms again, she'd lose it, and that she didn't want to, so he could only stand, looking at her.

"If it's what you want," she said.

"It is *all* I want. But I *do* think Fraction Eight might be the answer. Remember, ten years ago, your original intention was to use it as a weapon against Zane—"

"Not exactly. I was trying to save one of my patients with a long-shot experiment."

"Okay, but when you tried Fraction Eight on Zane's blood from his victim it was because you were desperate for a way to attack him and nothing else you'd tried would faze those cells. It can be a weapon, Katie. You said yourself, aging me is another word for killing me."

"You're saying increase the concentration?"

"Yes."

Katie looked thoughtful. "Even if you're right, I see two problems. First, how do I get enough blood to achieve such a concentrated potency? We're talking two or three pints. Rebecca can spare only a few ounces a month and I just drew from her. So I'd have to find other patients." She chewed at her lip. "Progeria is very rare, but if I look far enough we could do it. I could put the word out to my friends in teaching hospitals around the country that I'm screening subjects for a study of progeria. But there's still one other problem. Ten years ago, when I tried to inject Zane, he moved so fast I didn't even see him swat the syringe out of my hand."

"He won't be too fast for another phage," Merrick said. "Jenn isn't as strong as Zane, but she's probably as quick, maybe quicker."

"You're right." For the first time, Katie began to look hopeful. "I'll spread word I'm paying a hundred bucks to each patient who will let me draw a pint of blood. I'll fly around and collect the samples. If I push it, we might have enough blood within a week. It doesn't take long to separate the Fraction Eight—a few hours."

The excitement in her voice buoyed Merrick. "All right," he said. *Even if it doesn't work, at least we're fighting back.*

"Anybody home?"

Jenn's voice, floating in from the parlor, startled him. A few years ago, he'd have heard her light tread on the front stoop, her key turning in the lock. Even a week ago, he'd have been glad to find that he could no longer hear it. But now . . . if he could just turn the clock back until he'd dealt with Zane, then be sure of making it run forward again.

"Back here," Katie called out.

Catching the door frame on either side, Jenn leaned in and eyed them. Merrick waved her in. She was still dressed in the white slacks and blouse she wore to the hospital. She surprised him by collapsing on the couch, almost as if she were tired.

"What a day," she said.

"How did it go at Chief of Service rounds?" Katie asked.

"All right, I guess."

"That's not what I heard. Nels Agnusson called me and said you were terrific."

Jenn brightened. "He did?"

"Absolutely. He said you had all your dogs in a row. I didn't have the heart to tell him it was ducks."

Jenn laughed. "He speaks very good English, but when he gets into idioms, he kind of loses his way. During the marrow extraction on Caroline, I heard him tell his resident to hand him the picking-cotton canister."

Merrick chafed under their banter, wanting to ask Jenn if anything had happened—anything important—and then he reminded himself that this *was* important. She was doing just as he'd advised, refusing to let Zane dominate her thinking. He made himself come up with a few questions of his own about rounds, her patient Caroline, her day on the ward. As they talked, he saw that she was holding something back. Unable to resist any longer, he asked, "Any contact?"

The green eyes, so like her father's, focused somewhere between fear and excitement. "Nothing," she said. "Sometimes I think I sense him nearby, but it's probably just nerves. Do you think he'd come to the hospital?"

It made him think of walking into Jenn's room ten years ago, seeing Zane standing behind James and Ann Hrluska, unseen by them and Jenn. "It's possible," he said. "He could use Influence to hide himself from the people around you. If he does that, be careful not to give any sign that you see him when others can't—it'll be harder than you think."

"I'm ready for Zane," she said.

She didn't look nearly as sure as she sounded. It disheartened him. If Katie *could* find enough progeria donors to extract a killing or wounding dose of Fraction Eight, Jenn was the only one capable of injecting Zane. Could she stab a deadly needle into her own father?

The phone next to the sofa rang. Katie picked up, then handed it to Jenn. "Your mother," she said.

Jenn took the phone eagerly, but as she listened, her expression clouded into worry. "I'll be right there," she said. Hanging up, she looked at Katie. "James fainted," she said. "It only lasted a few seconds and Mom says he seems all right now, but she wants to drive him to the ER and he's refusing. For a meek little guy, he can be stubborn."

"He should be checked out," Katie said.

"Absolutely. I'll head over there right now."

Alarms went off in Merrick's mind. Fainting was the result of changes in blood flow—which is exactly what phages caused when they used Influence. Zane wouldn't even have to be inside the Hrluska house to do it. But why . . .

Because James Hrluska is the number-one obstacle to Jenn's thinking of him as her father.

"I'll come with you," Merrick said.

"No thanks." Jenn said it a little too quickly, and he realized she was thinking the same thing he was. *And she's afraid for me.* Watching her hurry out, Merrick felt a galling impotence.

Turning back to Katie, he saw she'd read him. He hated for her to see him like this, helpless and weak.

"You're still stronger than him up here," she said softly, tapping her head. "That's how we're going to beat him."

He said, "Did you hear what she called her father?"

Katie raised an eyebrow. "Dad—she usually calls him Dad."

"Then why did she just call him James?"

8

Jenn felt the muscles in her neck and back tighten with anxiety as she drove deeper into the Virginia countryside. In her rearview mirror, she could see the lights of Fairfax City dwindling to an orange glow on the horizon behind her. Just a few more turns up through some wooded hills to Mason Road and she'd be there.

Would Zane be there too? Had he used Influence on James—
Dad.

Jenn shook her head, chagrined. She could not believe she'd actually called him James in front of Merrick, who could not have missed it. But, really, there was no confusion in her mind. Zane was her father—technically, but James was, first, last, and always, her dad.

She must not slip up like that again.

The MG's engine rose in pitch as it climbed through the turns. What if Zane *was* up here? Conflicting emotions pulled her back and forth. It angered her that he might harm someone she loved, but if this *was* his doing, she was also relieved that his touch had been so light. Zane could kill so easily, in a way that could never be proven, without even coming into the house. For him, making Dad faint might be an act of mercy and restraint, but why do it at all?

Is he trying to call me out here?

The thought both chilled and excited her. She tried putting herself into Zane's mind. He'd probably assume Merrick had warned her not to have any contact with him; that if he simply called and asked her to meet, she wouldn't, and if he approached her cold, she'd run. So he might think he needed a way to hook her—but not too hard. This would fit. Zane would expect that if he made James faint, Mom would call her daughter the M.D.

What he would *not* expect, Jenn thought, was that I'd be at Merrick's when the call came.

She winced. She had wounded Merrick's pride when she'd refused to let him come. *But I had to. He can't risk facing off with Zane, surely he understands.* Still, she admired his courage—or was it simply the persistence of memory, a millennium of being more powerful than any other phage?

Slowing for the turn onto Mason Road, Jenn wished her engine were quieter. Usually, she liked its mouthiness—half the fun of driving the old car was its ferocious growl as it ate up the highway. But tonight it meant her folks would probably hear her pull into the driveway, and she wouldn't have a chance to quietly check around outside before coming in.

Peering ahead, Jenn scanned her parents' house, the sixth out of eight before the road ended in a cul-de-sac. The long front yard was empty and she could see no one in the shadows on this side of the house. Her mind boiled, making it hard to think. What was she missing? Zane's car—if he was here, he must have driven and he'd want to hide the car. She scanned the other side of the road, never cleared because the developer had gone bankrupt. There had been a temporary dirt road back in there, but she could pick up no glint of metal in the gaps between trees. . . .

Of course you can't. Zane gave Merrick the slip for five hundred years, and you think you're going to catch him in a mistake tonight?

Parking at the top of the driveway, Jenn grabbed her medical bag.

Easing the car door shut, she saw the front curtains part. Mom gave her a little wave, and she waved back, swallowing her frustration. Nothing to do now but go in.

Mom held the door open for her and pulled her inside. "Your father is in the living room. I told him to sit and stay that way."

"And he listened?"

Mom rolled her eyes, then hurried into the living room ahead of her. As she followed, Jenn cast quick looks around—straight through into the kitchen, at the dining room off to the side, up the stairway. No sign of Zane, but would she be able to see him if he were in here? As she crossed into the living room, the dark zone at the top of the stairs licked at the nape of her neck.

Mom had taken up a position behind Dad; as he tried to rise from his easy chair, she held him down with a hand on the shoulder.

"Come on, dear," he complained, but stayed seated.

The image lingered for Jenn as she greeted him—Dad straining to rise, Mom holding him down so easily. So much of their marriage was encoded in that one little transaction. Dad could be stubborn, but Mom was the strong one. She was, what, forty-five now, but still slim and youthful enough to wear her blond hair long. Last year, giving in to a growing nearsightedness, she'd bought some stylish, oversized glasses, which took a few candle power off the startling blue of her eyes but left the oval beauty of her face undisturbed. Though she would deny it, she looked more like an actress than a bank teller.

Dad, on the other hand, looked every one of his forty-nine years, and more. His brown hair was riddled with gray and on top you could see his scalp. A small second chin was creeping in, keeping pace with the rounding belly. The ghost of the handsome young man in his college photos still flickered in him from time to time, but he did little to keep it alive. If Mom regretted the passing of that younger, thinner man, she never gave any sign of it.

"I didn't know interns had their own medical bags," Dad said.

"Katie gave it to me when I graduated. This is the first time I've taken it out of the car."

"Well, I'm sorry to disappoint you, but it's totally unnecessary."

"Dr. Hrluska will decide that," Mom said with more than a trace of pride.

Dad grunted, but Jenn could see he liked the sound of "doctor," too. *And so do I.* "Here, give me your arm." She slipped the blood pressure cuff over his soft biceps, pumped it up, and listened to his pulse with her stethoscope as the air bled from the cuff. One-twenty over seventy—a bit low on the diastole, but well within normal. His color looked fine now, no trace of paleness beneath his fading gardener's tan. He was wearing a roomy green T-shirt so it couldn't have been too tight a collar.

"Did you feel any shortness of breath before you passed out?"

"I didn't really pass out—"

"Yes you did, dear."

"I just got a little fuzzy there for a few seconds, and now your mother wants to make a federal case out of it."

"Shortness of breath?" Jenn repeated.

"Nope."

"Any pain?"

He shook his head.

She went through the rest of it—tightness in the chest, vertigo, medications, and so on. All negative. She felt his forehead—no fever— then quickly probed the rest of his head, looking for bumps.

"You were doing dishes, right? Any chance you locked your knees?"

"No, I walk around when I dry dishes, and your mother doesn't let me goose step."

Smiling, Jenn thought, that's something I might have said. Have I acquired his sense of humor? It was not something she'd ever thought about before.

"How about work?" she asked. "Any unusual pressures or tensions there?"

Dad's face sobered. "Well, now that you mention it, yes. They moved the water cooler."

Mom cuffed his bald spot. "Be serious."

"Y'all are just making a mountain out of a molehill."

Jenn felt some of the tension drain from her. She didn't know whether to be relieved or disappointed. She didn't want Zane messing with Dad, but if he was *not* why Dad had fainted, she'd be uneasy until she found the medical reason.

And you wanted to see Zane.

He might still be around—she hadn't ruled it out yet. She'd need to search the house, and then outside.

"What do you think?" Mom asked.

"I want him to drop by the clinic tomorrow for blood work and an EKG, but I admit I'm stumped. His vital signs are good now."

"See?" Dad said triumphantly.

The worry in Mom's face eased a bit. "Well . . ."

"We were saving dessert until after the dishes," Dad said. "How about a piece of pound cake?"

"Sounds good."

Dad's face lit with such pleasure that she felt a twinge of guilt. Clearly, he'd expected her to say no. "I'll just run up to my room," she said, "and wash up." *And see if you have an unexpected guest up there.*

Jenn's hands ached with nervousness as she mounted the steps; what if she did find Zane? They couldn't talk here. Would he try to embrace her? Or would they just stand, staring at each other. Either way, it would be surreal.

But if he was here, she wanted to know, had to know.

Quickly, she checked all the rooms, not bothering with the lights. She couldn't see him anywhere, not in the closets or under the beds. He could still be outside though. How could she check before she left?

In her room, she went into the bathroom and sat on the edge of the tub, feeling confused. She wanted to see Zane, but also didn't. She had a creeping feeling of being disloyal to Dad. The pleasure on his face when she'd agreed to stay for dessert nagged at her. I've been neglecting them lately, she thought.

But she had so little free time now, and what there was she spent mostly with Hugh, or at Katie and Merrick's. And it took almost an hour to drive out here.

But where was the old pull? Before the leukemia, there had been no secret she and Mom couldn't share. Then, in a few weeks, Jenny the girl had become Jenn, a hemophage, someone who could be her whole self only around Merrick. If it hadn't been for him, the gulf between her and her parents would have been worse. Merrick had taught her how to keep it all together, to confine the new and terrifying part of herself to those few hours after midnight twice a month when he took her out to feed. Everyone had secrets, he'd assured her, things about themselves they didn't want others to know. Her classmates all felt different and alone at times, too—maybe not as much as she did, but she was still human, still needed and deserved friends. He'd kept her from withdrawing, isolating herself. Because of his encouragement, she'd hung out at the mall with her girlfriends, played "Veronica" to Ian Blake's "Archie" in the school play, gone to the prom with Davey Price—and shared it all with Mom. At graduation, smiling into Katie's camera, feeling the arms of her parents around her, she'd been so filled with love she'd thought she would burst. Going off to Boston U, she'd missed them terribly, walking the campus late at night that first year, her eyes filled with tears of purest homesickness. Every weekend she could, she'd managed to come home. Then, gradually, starting with her second year, she'd missed them less. And now it seemed she could do without them for weeks. Maybe it was normal, but it saddened her.

Jenn flushed the toilet and went back downstairs. Sitting down at the kitchen table, hearing its loose leg squeak, she remembered mealtimes when she was a kid: At breakfast, Dad used to say, "put me in a piece of toast," and then Mom and I would tease him about it and he'd get very annoyed. And at supper, Mom would ask me how school went, and I'd say okay. Then Dad would say, "What did you do?" and I'd say, "Nothing," and then they'd grill me until I found something to tell them. I didn't realize how much fun we were having, how nice it was. And now it seems almost like it all happened to someone else.

Dad set the cake on the table and started cutting her a piece.

"Not so big," she said.

"Come on, you're so thin you'll blow away."

Nibbling, Jenn wondered what Dad would think if she told him she weighed nearly a hundred and seventy, her muscles were so dense. Did he really have no clue, even subconsciously, of what she'd become?

And Mom . . .

Jenn tried to suppress the taboo images, but they came anyway: her mother and father sleeping side by side while a man crept up the stairs—no, much more than a man, tall and powerful, beautiful as Lucifer. Zane standing by the bed, deepening James's slumber into unconsciousness, leaving Ann in a dreamlike state perhaps, as he used her body. A rape, though Zane had spared Mom any cruelty in the act. He'd even unknowingly left her with a child she could love without reservation.

But a more remote, lonely coupling was hard to imagine.

"How about another slice?" Dad said.

"No, I'm stuffed, really. In fact, I think I'll take a turn or two around the house to walk it off." She pushed back from the table, pleased by her sudden inspiration.

"I'll go with you," James said.

"No!" She smiled to soften it. "I think you'd better take it easy, just for tonight. Doctor's orders. I'll be right back." Before he could argue, she got up and slipped out the back door.

She stood a moment, nervous again, inspecting the tangled shapes in the back garden—a dozen tomato plants, still tall but starting to wither. A light breeze fluttered the vines, making the leaves dance in the milky light of the half moon. Drawing in the cool, humid air, she smelled the churned earth where Dad had, a few weeks ago, dug up this year's little crop of potatoes. Crickets chirped in the garden and beyond, a sweet, lazy sound.

Striking out around the corner of the house, she listened, trying to hear if Zane might be circling away ahead of her. She hurried around the front corner of the house, then slowed when she saw no dark shape heading away. She looked up at the roof. He could be up there, on the other side of the peak. The siding would be too slick to climb, but he could have scaled the brick chimney.

"Jenn?"

Mom, calling out a window.

Reluctantly, she headed back. Returning to the warmth of the kitchen, she felt let down. If Zane was out there, he was keeping away.

Could it be that he was afraid, too?

No, surely not. He was a phage in his prime, powerful, invulnerable. What could he have to fear from her?

The TV was going in the living room now, a canned laugh track, depressing in its banality. She realized Mom had come into the kitchen and was eyeing her, one hand tucked behind her back.

"What?" Jenn asked.

"Guess what I discovered the other day?"

"Why men can pat each other on the rump but can't hug each other?"

"Oh, I've known that for ages," Mom laughed. "You'll learn it too, as time goes by." She swept the hidden hand from behind her back. It took a second for the little red book in it to snap into focus.

"My diary!"

"I was cleaning out some of your old things for Goodwill and I found it in a drawer. Here, you can sit at the table while I go check on your dad."

Jenn sank into the chair Mom pulled out. Summoning the combination from memory, she unlocked it, opened it at random, and began to read: *I asked Jimmy W. to sit with me at lunch, and he turned red as a beet. He's really cute, but he seems to think girls are poison. Guess I'll just have to wait until he grows up too.* Reading the date, Jenn smiled. She had been eleven when she'd penned those words.

Paging forward, she found the first entries from when she was in the hospital. The neat penmanship had started to slant and wobble. *March 7: My joints ache so much. My doctor says it's normal and she'll give me more painkiller. Dr. O'Keefe is so beautiful. Her name is Katie and she has dark hair. Her eyes are pretty even though she doesn't wear mascara, because it would get on the microscope. . . .*

March 27: Finally someone told me the truth. Detective Chapman—his first name is Merrick, which I think is neat. He's the policeman who comes around to do magic tricks for the kids. I think he and Katie have a thing. I always thought it would be Katie who told me, and I know she wanted to, but she just couldn't, and now it turns out to be Merrick. I asked him if I was dying and he just looked at me, real sad, and said yes. I got the strangest feeling that he understood me exactly . . .

The entry trailed off, the last one. Jenn closed the book with a sense of loss. Her life, the good and the bad, was no longer something she could dare write down. Slipping her diary into her medical bag, she joined her parents in the living room.

⁂

In the darkness outside, Zane pressed an ear to the curtained kitchen window. No sound from the kitchen, but he could hear the television going in another room, some witless cartoon show. Straightening, he backed away from the window, maddened by the indignity he was forced to endure just to be close to his daughter. When she'd come out, he'd come so close to letting her find him—

But no, not until he was sure she wasn't playing the bait in Merrick's trap.

She belonged out here with him in the darkness they were born to rule, not inside that flimsy burrow, where fear of the night whimpered from every lit bulb. Hunger for her clawed at him—to hear her voice, to have her gaze at him with the affection she was now squandering on the man inside. How could the dolt even imagine that anyone so magnificent as Jenn could have come from him? Zane swallowed a groan of fury and anguish. *I have to wake you up, daughter. How can I win you? I need you with me. You* are *magnificent—but you could be so much more with me to help you. We're the same flesh and blood; I understand you as no one else will.*

If you can just understand me . . .

Laughter leaked through the window—Jenn's mixed with the impostor's, and Zane felt his teeth bare in rage. He'd counted on her feelings for Hrluska to lure her out here, but having to endure their camaraderie through the wall was harder to stomach than he'd feared. *Do I have to* play it this way? I could wait until she leaves, then just pop a blood vessel in Hrluska's brain.

A savage pleasure filled him at the thought of the silly bastard falling over dead. And then what? Ann was still beautiful, desirable. He could strike up a relationship with her—that would be hard, but he could do it. Of course, he'd have to wait while she mourned. How long? A few weeks wouldn't be enough. Months would be more like it, after which he'd have to contrive a way to meet Ann, court her, marry her. Even then, he would officially be only Jenn's stepfather. And could he really stand everyday domesticity? He'd have to take a job or explain how he got his money. He'd be locked into one geographic area, which would mean he'd have to be even more careful than usual when he fed.

And how would Jenn react to all this? As soon as he moved in on Ann, Jenn would suspect Hrluska's cerebrovascular accident had been no accident.

No, Zane thought. I mustn't kill him—at least not yet. And living with Ann and Jenn together is only fantasy—couldn't happen. With Merrick around, I could never come into society even if I wanted to. It's too late anyway to make up that kind of family. Jenn is an adult now. So just stick to the plan, show her how wrong Merrick is and get her away from him.

And then, Zane thought, I'll make her my equal, my companion. We'll hunt together. We'll . . . *talk.*

Zane ached with longing. He must make it happen.

Hrluska laughed again, a genial pudding of sound that could only have come from a man who had never suffered real pain. Frustration raged in Zane. *I want to kill him, just let me kill him now!*

Reaching mentally into the house, he once again found the steady pulse of James Hrluska's blood . . .

<hr />

Jenn studied her father. "How are you feeling now?" she asked.

He leaned forward in the chair and flexed his biceps like a weight lifter, turning his roly-poly arms this way and that. She grinned and then broke down laughing with him. Mom shook her head, but had to smile.

Returning his attention to the TV, Dad chuckled again. "Get a load of this. Bart Simpson is on jury duty, and he . . ."

Jenn saw Dad's eyes flutter and roll up in his head. Alarmed, she sprang to his side and caught him as he sagged sideways in the chair. He gasped a deep breath, clawing at her arm, then his eyes focused again. "What?" he said thickly.

"You fainted again."

"Did not," he said indignantly.

Conscious of her mother hovering over them, Jenn laid two fingers along the carotid artery in Dad's throat.

"Is he all right?" Mom cried.

"Sh-h-h—I need to take his pulse now." Jenn felt Dad's heartbeat race suddenly, then drop back to a slow, even beat. Again it raced, eight fast beats, then eight slow. Eight fast, eight slow—

Jenn froze, stunned, as she realized what was happening. Zane *was* doing this—nothing else could explain such a rhythm.

He'll kill him!

Terrified, Jenn thought of running outside, finding Zane, attacking him, then caught herself. He was too strong for her, and Dad was still awake, still all right—

She realized his pulse was steady again and her terror eased. *Maybe Zane is only trying to signal me.*

I have to answer him back, but without making Mom or Dad suspicious.

Her mind was blank. Come *on!*

And then she had it.

"This is my fault," she said. "I should have warned you off the cake. Eating draws blood away from the brain—not a good idea after you've fainted. Just to be sure that's all it is, I'm going to talk to a blood expert—"

"Dr. O'Keefe?" Mom asked.

"No, this guy specializes in blood flow, not hematology. He's been around a long time and knows everything there is to know about circulation. I've been wanting to meet him anyway, so I'll just arrange to get together. I'll do it as soon as I leave tonight." Jenn prayed desperately that Zane was listening, reading the double meaning in the words.

"If you really think it's necessary," Dad said.

Forcing herself to look calm, Jenn nodded and kept her fingers on his pulse. Answer me . . . *Father, please!* For several seconds she felt no change. Then the pulse speeded and slowed, speeded and slowed, and she felt her own heart begin to race.

9

I*'m about to see my father!* Jenn's heart pounded. The room around her was a blur, as though she were plunging head over heels down a steep slope. This is *wrong!* she thought. How can I want this so much?

He saved your life.

But it was more than that, a crazy conviction—buried for many years and now rising up—that he was her father in some sense other than biology. But how could that make any sense?

She realized her parents were looking at her oddly. She wanted to run out now, before Zane changed his mind—but no, Mom and Dad would find that strange. First she had to reassure them on their own crisis.

Pills, she thought.

Picking up her medical bag, she found a small plastic bottle of generic acetaminophen. It was unlikely Dad or Mom would know it was a common aspirin substitute. "Your blood pressure's a bit low," she told James. "That can cause fainting. I want you to take one of these capsules now, and then one every morning and evening until they're gone. That should keep you from having any more problems." *That, and me asking Zane to stay away from you.*

James accepted the bottle with a satisfied expression.

Okay, good, what next?

She had another inspiration. "Make sure he sits tight," she said to Mom, "while I get him a glass of water."

In the kitchen, she let the water run while she used the phone to dial her home number. As her machine picked up, she hit "*" to skip the message, then punched in the three-digit code the hospital used for paging through to her. Hanging up, she prayed it would work. All her answering machine had to do was relay the page back here to her beeper, but "here" was pretty far out in the country. It would all depend on whether this house was close enough to a cellular relay station. She'd know in a minute.

Filling the glass, she hurried back to the living room. As she handed it to James, her beeper went off. *Yes!* Pulling her pager from her belt, she pretended to consult the readout. Since she'd called in from her parents' house, the caller ID had bounced back their phone number as the one to call. Making sure neither of them could see the number, she said, "It's the hospital. I'd better call in."

"You go right ahead," James said. "I'm fine."

Using the phone by his chair, she dialed her own number again. "This is Dr. Hrluska," she said over the babble of her own taped voice. "Yes. Yes. I understand." Covering the mouthpiece, she looked at Dad. "Are you sure you're okay?"

"You bet."

Over his shoulder, Mom nodded at her and made shooing motions.

"I'll be there as soon as I can," she said into the phone. "Meanwhile, start a D5 drip and get a blood workup."

Hanging up, she made a rueful face. "Sorry."

"Go," Dad said. "But drive carefully—no speeding."

Mom walked her to the door. "Thanks for coming out."

"Sure. A good night's sleep and he should be fine. See if you can get him to turn in now, and I'll call you in the morning."

Mom hugged her; Jenn was so eager to go that she had to stop herself from shrugging free at once. Instead, she gave her mother an extra squeeze, then whispered an impulsive, "I love you."

"I love you too, Jenny."

Hurrying up the long driveway, Jenn resisted the urge to look around her. Where was Zane? Behind the hedge that divided the lot from next door's? On the roof behind her, or maybe walking noiselessly along right beside her? He was close by, she could feel it, sense his gaze like a hot breeze on her skin. Waiting until she heard the front door close behind her, she murmured, "I have to make them think I've left. Meet me in the woods across the road in fifteen minutes."

He gave no answer.

As soon as she'd driven around the corner, Jenn pulled over and got out, loping back through the trees. She felt keyed up, so hyperconscious that her feet seemed to have eyes, propelling her over the cluttered, uneven ground in smooth silence. When she drew even with her house, she settled beside a large oak and watched the lot, searching for any flicker of movement around its perimeter. The light in the master bedroom upstairs winked out. A long moon-shadow of the house stretched toward her, laying down a channel of blackness through the front lawn. Nothing moved. Time seemed to have slowed to a crawl. Half an hour dragged by, her excitement fading until a glum disappointment settled over her. Had he not heard her? Her low murmur had sounded plenty loud to her— she'd have been able to hear it a hundred feet away. Maybe he'd decided not to come. But why?

She started to rise, then thought, I'll give him five more minutes.

And then a warning breath whispered along her skin, raising goose bumps. Springing up, she spun toward him, frightened, then saw that he was still quite far off, fifty feet back into the trees. He stopped, as if arrested by her sudden movement. When she kept still, he came toward her again, closing the gap to twenty feet. Watching him come, she stared avidly, feeling caught up in a dream. He wore a long greatcoat that flared behind him with each stride. At ten feet, he stopped. So tall, his hair longer than she remembered, thick and straight. The part in it looked odd, and she realized it was on the right. Was he left-handed? He does look like me, she thought. The same eyes, mouth, and chin, but his hair is so dark, like Merrick's.

"Jenn." His voice was deep and husky, as though he rarely used it. He gazed at her, and in his eyes she saw the love she had always fantasized but never dared believe. Tears rimmed her eyes.

"Zane," she said. In her fantasies, she had always called him Father, but now something stopped her.

"You heard me coming," he said admiringly.

"No. I felt it, like someone looking at me."

"As if I were a normal."

"No, a different feeling than that."

"Good." He gazed at her. "You don't know how I've longed to see you. May I come a little closer? I won't touch you." When she said nothing, he stepped closer and studied her. "So beautiful. . . . Your eyes! They were blue, but now they're green, like mine."

"Yours were blue, too," she said. "Before the leukemia."

He looked surprised.

"Merrick told me once," she said.

Zane turned his head away slightly, giving her a skeptical sidelong glance. "I don't remember."

Jenn felt a sudden sense of unreality. Why was she talking to him about his eyes? "What you did to my father tonight—"

"He is *not* your father."

Careful!

"All right, but I love him. I want you to leave him alone."

"I did him no harm."

"You could have slipped, gone too far."

"I don't slip."

"Don't go near him again, or my mother either."

Zane's eyes glittered, and a world of blood and death yawned open to her, but then he smiled with a warmth that blunted her alarm. "You give orders like a queen. You're quite brave, aren't you?"

"No. I'm scared."

"But that's precisely what gives bravery its meaning. We're here, you and I, even though we're both very afraid. That makes us brave."

She wondered what he meant. Surely he was not afraid of her—

Merrick. He thinks Merrick might have shadowed me here tonight, that this could be a trap. Jenn realized suddenly what a risk she was taking. Each word she said—or didn't say—could undo not just her, but Katie, Merrick, and Gregory. Merrick was not here, and what would Zane conclude? Probably just that she hadn't told Merrick she was coming here. But even that held danger. Now he might think he could cut the two of them apart. *He'll exploit the slightest sympathy you may feel.*

"You look troubled," Zane said.

She felt a chill, remembering what Merrick had said about the ability of older phages to read people. "This is not an everyday occurrence for me."

Zane smiled. "Nor for me." He sobered, and his eyes became intense. "I should have come back long ago. Even if he had buried me again. A month with you, a week, would have been worth it."

Jenn, despite herself, felt her heart opening to him. Could she believe him?

"How did you get out of the vault?" she asked. "I saw your cell. You couldn't have escaped without help."

"But here I am."

"Did Sandeman help you, or was it some other way?"

"I don't want to talk about the vault."

She heard his fear in the tightness of his voice. For a second, she could see him hurling himself at the door of his cell, again and again. She shuddered in sympathy for him. "Why did you come back here?"

"To be with my daughter."

"Then why not just knock on my door? Why kill an innocent woman? Did you really think that would draw me to you?"

"Innocent? She ate a big steak just before she died. Someone else killed the animal for her, and a restaurant cooked a piece of it, and then she ate it."

"Cattle aren't people."

"And normals aren't the same as us. If that woman was innocent, so am I. Or we are both guilty. The point is, you are no more like them than they are like the cattle they kill and eat. When you saw that woman, saw the blood, you wanted it, you know you did."

"But I didn't touch it."

"Only because my father has twisted you so badly you can't see the truth when it lies at your feet."

"The truth," she said, "is that I'm a human being. The only difference between me and most people is that I have a genetic defect to overcome."

"A defect?" Zane cried. "Jenn, you are a lord of this planet! Look at me." He pulled a big knife from inside his greatcoat and, before she could move, slashed his wrist. She gasped; blood spurted, then trickled, as the wound quickly closed. "Is this a defect? This is how I fed you that first night I found you in the hospital. Alone in the dark of night, in the last minutes of your life." He slashed again, spraying the ground with blood. "This is how I kept you alive until I could go out and make a kill. Cutting myself again and again so you could drink. You owe your life to me."

Jenn felt suddenly anxious. It was true, but she wanted him to say no more.

"If it had been up to Merrick," Zane said, "you would not be here now. He stood by your hospital bed week after week—to make *sure* you died, so he wouldn't have to hunt you down and bury you later. That is what he does, Jenn. He buries us."

Jenn felt a rising anger. "He didn't know I was his granddaughter."

"So what? You were a child, dying, and he knew what you needed but wouldn't give it to you. He's more vicious than you or I could ever be, because he kills his own kind. He hunted me for five hundred years—his own son—"

"I know all this, and it's not the way you make it sound."

Zane shook his head reproachfully. There was a sudden, luminous sadness in his eyes. "Do you know why he was able to bury me ten years ago?"

No! Don't ask me that. "Because he was stronger."

Zane drew a deep breath, expelled it, as if battling to keep his patience. "He'd been stronger than me for five hundred years, but he'd never buried me."

"Because he didn't want to. Did you ever think of that?"

Zane smiled coldly. "Oh, he wanted to. But that night I *had* him, trussed up with wire, lying beside the grave I'd dug. I was about to roll him in, to save myself and all the others of his own kind he would destroy. And you know why."

Jenn turned away to keep him from seeing the tears that scalded her eyes. The memory turned inside her like broken glass:

Jenny is drifting, as if in her sleep, across the field toward Zane and Merrick. She can see Zane sitting beside the grave, holding Gregory on his lap. And there at the grave's edge lies Merrick, bound in thick cable. She can't see Katie. Is she down in the grave? Merrick and Zane begin to shout at each other. She realizes they are arguing over her. Zane accuses Merrick of letting her die. And then she cries, "Maybe he should have."

They turn in surprise to look at her. "No," Merrick says. "I was wrong. No matter who you were or what you might one day become, I should have saved you. And now it's too late. But always remember that I love you very much."

"He doesn't," Zane says. "He's only saying that to—"

"Stop it, both of you!" Jenny screams. She turns and runs.

Zane cries out her name; glancing back, she sees him leap up, spilling Gregory from his lap. "Wait!" he pleads, but she keeps running. Stumbling, she falls, and then she hears the gunshots, BOOM-BOOM-BOOM, and her father lies on the ground, shot in the head with the gun Katie has pulled from Merrick's ankle holster. Within seconds, the wounds in his brain will heal, but it will take several minutes more for his disrupted mind to regain control of his body. Enough time for Katie to free Merrick . . .

Jenn groaned, pushing the memory away at last. Zane was still gazing at her, but she couldn't meet his eyes. A formless grief filled her. She felt Zane's hand on her shoulder; let it rest there for a second, then shrugged it away. "I wish neither of you had ever heard of me."

"Don't say that."

"I don't want to be caught between you," she said hotly. "Not again."

"And you shouldn't be," Zane said soothingly. "You can leave him."

"No."

"Oh, Jenn, how can I make you see it? Merrick has brainwashed you, tried to pervert you the way he perverted himself. You can never be like them, never be one of them. You're a wolf trying to live with the sheep."

"I am a human being, a doctor. I don't kill people, I save them."

"That is not your nature," Zane said softly. "That's how you fight your nature."

"If that's my choice—"

"We have no choice." Zane's voice was suddenly bleak. "I know you want to love them, but you can't, you mustn't."

Hearing the sadness in his voice, she wondered. Had Zane tried to love normals?

She wanted to ask him, longed to know, but first she had to make him understand. "I'll never do what you want."

His expression turned grim. "I *will* save you," he said. "Whatever it takes. It might hurt, but in the end you'll thank me. Just remember, whatever happens, that I do it because I love you."

She looked away, caught between dread and a longing she found impossible to suppress. "If you hurt anyone I love . . ."

But he was gone, vanished into the darkness.

1 0

As dawn neared, Jenn sat on the concrete slab of her balcony, looking out at a world that seemed to have tilted under her. Hugging her drawn-up knees, afraid, very afraid of Zane, she at the same time felt drawn back toward him. Had it really been love in his eyes, or was she clinging to girlhood fantasies? If truly he loved her, how could he threaten her? *It might hurt, but in the end you'll thank me.* What might hurt? Would he go after James—really go after him this time? Or Mom, Katie, Gregory—no one she cared about would be safe from him.

Or did he mean he'd hurt me literally—physically?

The idea of pain, maybe even her death, should terrify her, and yet she seemed to be having trouble taking it seriously. Since the leukemia, she'd never been sick, never hurt. I've started to feel invulnerable, she thought, but I'm not—not to him. He almost buried Merrick. What chance would I have? And if all he wants is to hurt Merrick, that would all but kill me.

Jenn realized with a start that the Washington skyline had turned from black to a dusky olive color. Almost dawn. She was shivering—

sometime during the night, the concrete had turned cold against her rump, and the chill had now begun to eat through the soles of her shoes. Bands of soreness throbbed along her back where it pressed against the bars of the railing. I've got to pull myself together, she thought, and get ready for work.

In a minute.

Her mind was so full of Zane it was hard to think about anything else. I should be angry, she thought. Telling me he intends to change my life—what right does he have?

I want to see him again.

Jenn groaned, exasperated. What was it in him that drew her so? He'd seemed so sad and alone. That tantalizing hint at the end, her powerful impression he'd been speaking from painful experience when he'd told her she couldn't love normals. He has tried it himself, she thought. And his failures have made him bitter. It was so at odds with what Merrick had told her—*there is no love in him.*

Merrick could be wrong; she wanted him to be wrong.

If she rejected Zane now, she would never know.

But if I help him . . .

The idea excited her. She got up, and the ache faded from her back. Leaning on the rail, she looked south, watching the rooftops of downtown Washington brighten to a dusky rose as the darkness shrank back. Ten years ago, she thought, Zane came to bury Merrick, but then he discovered me. I threw him off course—so far off he ended up buried himself. And now he's back, even though he must be terrified of Merrick. Surely he wouldn't risk a prolonged and horrible death just for a chance at hurting Merrick. He *needs* me. He might not even understand it himself, but maybe what he really wants is for me to help him change, give up killing, join the human race.

Might. Maybe.

But if I could do it. . . .

A thrill went through her. Zane coming in from the cold with her, maybe even reconciling with *his* father—

She heard the faint, distant bells of the National Cathedral chime the half hour. Six-thirty? *Damn!* she thought. I *have* to get to work! Hurrying inside, Jenn jumped in and out of the shower, pulled on fresh whites, and ran down the seven flights to the apartment's rear parking lot. By gunning the MG through two yellow lights, she made it downtown in eight minutes and stepped onto the pediatrics ward at 7:05, only five minutes late. There was just time for a quick check on Caroline before walking rounds. As she pulled on scrubs, cap, and gloves, she thought: I must be careful. Merrick tried with Zane and failed.

But then I'm his daughter. I'm not threatening to him the way Merrick was.

As Jenn stepped through into Caroline's room, one look at the child pushed Zane from her thoughts. Alarmed, she moved quickly to the bedside. Caroline's skin had taken on a bluish cast and her breathing was labored.

"Morning. How's my favorite patient?" She tried to force cheer into her voice.

Caroline gazed up at her with dulled, feverish eyes. "You say that . . . to everyone, hunh."

"Nope," Jenn said truthfully. "Look's like you're having a little trouble catching your breath."

"It's so *warm.*"

"Is that fever bugging you again?"

"Mmhmh."

Glancing at the chart, Jenn saw the ominous upward turn on the temperature graph. Caroline coughed, a mild, dry sound that struck fear into Jenn. Hearing a rustle behind her, Jenn turned as Lila Degeneris hurried in.

"Thought I saw you. . . ." Lila's gaze settled on Caroline and her eyes widened above the mask. "Hi, there," she said. It sounded more like, oh no.

Jenn drew Lila back toward the door. "Who was on call last night?"

"Ah-h-m, Brad. He's at the nurses' station right now chafing for rounds to start so he can hand everything off and go home."

Jenn seethed. Brad must not even have stuck his head into Caroline's room last night. There was no chart note from him, and no request for lab work. "Lila, I need an immediate blood gas and sputum sample on Caroline. Forget rounds, I'll tell them what you're doing." Turning to Caroline, Jenn spoke louder. "Dr. Degeneris will be right back, and then I'll be around again a few minutes later, okay?"

" 'Kay."

Jenn motioned Lila into the hall.

"What is it?" Lila whispered. "She looks awful."

"I'm afraid it might be PCP."

Lila winced, and Jenn was glad she grasped the danger. *Pneumocystis carinii* was a common bacterium that could be found in the lungs of healthy people. But the complete chemotherapeutic suppression of Caroline's immune system, necessary to keep her body from instantly rejecting the marrow transplant from her father, had left her as defenseless against infection as an AIDS patient.

"While you draw blood," Jenn said, "I'm going to get her started on Sulfamethoprim and oxygen, and we'll work in an aerosol of pentamidine."

"Like Brad should have done last night."

Jenn gave a noncommittal grunt, uncomfortable with bad-mouthing Brad to his back. But just wait until she could get him alone. "We have to have those lab results, stat. If the techs give you trouble, come straight to me."

"Right."

Jenn checked the chart for any history of allergic reaction to sulfa drugs. Finding none, she wrote the orders for meds and oxygen, then found Brad, not in the nurses' station but at the coffee machine in the doctors' lounge. He looked tired, absolutely whipped. His blond hair stuck up in back; normally glossy and well groomed, it looked greasy. Dark circles hung like inverted rainbows under his eyes. Some of her anger cooled. "Rough night?" she asked.

He groaned. "I think I'm getting the flu."

"Is that why you didn't go in Caroline's room?"

He nodded. "With her vulnerability to infection . . ."

The last of Jenn's anger drained away, leaving her feeling vaguely cheated. This was a hell of a mess, but if Brad really had the flu, then he had done the right thing—almost. "Did you check for nursing notes on her?"

He stared at her. "What's the matter?"

"I think she may have pneumonia."

"Christ!" He sounded genuinely upset.

"Her breathing is labored and she's coughing and cyanotic. She should have been put on oxygen at once, Brad."

"Well, in night lighting that might be hard to see. And you know how bad Barb's eyes are getting. Damn it, she's just too old for the night shift."

"Right now, *you* look too old."

"Damn straight."

Perversely, Jenn was glad to see the fatigue in him. Maybe their little confrontation yesterday had scared him into backing off the amphetamines and this wasn't flu but withdrawal. "Well," she said, "you're almost out of here. Time for rounds, and then you'd better get straight home to bed."

As she reached the door, Brad caught up with her and wordlessly handed her a cup of coffee. She hesitated.

"Don't worry," he said. "I just washed my hands, and I only touched the bottom of the cup." Sensing it was a peace offering, she accepted it and took a few swallows. Caffeine could have no more effect on her than the flu virus, but she pounded coffee and Cokes with the other interns anyway, because it's what they all did, and the more like them she looked, the safer she felt.

The two other interns on today were waiting with the charge nurse at the station; Dave Bledsoe, the second-year resident in charge, was late, as usual. When they finally got underway and reached Caroline's room, Jenn was relieved to see that her color was better. The mask clearly was helping, but her breathing was still a bit strained. Jenn presented her treatment plan for Caroline. Dave told her to wait for the blood gases, then decide whether the respirator would be necessary.

As they finished rounds, Jenn made herself put Caroline from her mind and think about Lila. She was responsible for Lila's training on the ward, and dealing with the lab could be a challenge. Techs, jaded by constant requests to run tests immediately, could be hard to push, especially by a third-year med student. So she needed to be ready to give Lila some backup and a little coaching.

After rounds came the intake conference in the meeting room next to the nurses' station. As Jenn passed the station, one of the nurses hailed her, pointing to the phone.

Jenn punched the flashing button and picked up. "Hrluska."

"Hey, Jenn."

"Hugh." His voice raised an instant warmth in her. "How's it going, big boy?"

"Good. But I'll be a lot better when I give you a big champagne hug tonight."

For a second, Jenn drew a total blank. "Your book party!"

"I'm going to ignore your flabbergasted tone and assume nothing so earthshaking could have slipped your mind."

"Omni Shoreham, Suite 100, right?"

"Right."

"It didn't slip my mind. I just totally forgot."

Hugh's laugh was genuine. "Well, healing the sick does take priority."

Jenn felt a sudden pressure in her throat. A *party?* With all that had been happening, how could she possibly go to a party? What if Zane tried to get in touch with her again tonight? "Can you give me the starting time again?"

"Around eight. I could pick you up—"

"No, better not. One of my patients is crumping on me, and I may be a bit late. You need to be there on time for your adoring public. I'll meet you there."

"No problem, I understand. Is it Caroline?"

"Afraid so."

"Damn. Are *you* okay?"

"Sure. I'm a trained physician, hard as nails."

"I'll save extra hugs for you."

"Good."

"Oh, one other thing: any chance you could bring Merrick along? I'd love to meet him, and I really need to talk to an ex-homicide guy."

"I'll see," Jenn said. "If things aren't too crazy here, and I get a chance to get in touch with him."

"Thanks. Sorry to call you at work, but I kept getting your machine last night. Guess you were really zonked."

Jenn summoned a dim memory of the phone ringing several times. She'd heard it through the glass of the balcony door but had been so obsessed with Zane that it hadn't really registered. "Uh, yeah."

"You sure you're okay? Maybe being an intern is finally catching up with you, and if it is, you should go home and hit the sack after you're done with Caroline."

"No way. I'm fine, and I wouldn't miss your big night for anything."

"I'm mad about you, do you know that?"

His low voice, very serious, gave her a tender feeling. She kissed the phone and hung up smiling, but quickly sobered. What had Hugh meant, her internship *finally* catching up with her? She'd been careful to act tired around him after coming off shift, to tell him she'd slept like the dead, the little white lies so necessary to her life. Apparently they hadn't been convincing.

Troubled, she joined the intake conference in the meeting room. Brad had admitted three people from ER last night, and she was assigned a sixteen-year-old anorectic. At least Brad had found the sense, despite his flu, to put the girl on a fluid and nutrient IV. Now that her dehydration and electrolyte imbalance had been treated with the IV fluids, what she needed most was a psychiatrist. Jenn made six calls over the next two hours, trying to get the girl transferred to MHU, but the beds were all full.

Just after one o'clock, Lila flagged her down with the lab results for Caroline. Her face was grim. "You called it," she said. "Her oxygen saturation is way down. And the sputum is loaded with *Pneumocystis.*"

Jenn scanned the blood gas printout. It was borderline for putting Caroline on a respirator. Damn! The respirator was a serious step, because of the dependency and further loss of lung function that often followed. But if Caroline could get enough oxygen no other way . . . Jenn decided to wait a few hours, give the antibiotics, oxygen by mask, and the pentamidine aerosol a chance to kick in. "You got these pretty fast," she said approvingly to Lila. "Did the lab give you any trouble?"

"Not after I told the tech you'd have lunch with him."

Jenn gaped.

"But only when you get time. I made that very clear."

"Oh well, that's all right, since I'll never get time. But just for that, you get to stick my patient in 34. She's anorectic and it looks like we've got her for the next few days. We need a chem 20 on her, and a urinalysis. Listen to her heart, too. If you hear anything abnormal, let me know and we'll call in cardiology for an EKG."

"Gotcha." Lila turned half away, then back. "Oh, I almost forgot— Dr. Wayne wants to see you."

"What?"

"He was just looking for you in the doctors' lounge."

"Lila, you don't 'almost forget' it when the head of peds wants to see someone."

"Sorry. I guess I was just preoccupied with Caroline."

Fortis Wayne's office was across the parking lot from peds, in the older, center of the hospital. Jenn hurried through the "gerbil run" to the main building. His office had a large anteroom, choked with dark green plants that seemed to have been selected for their huge leaves. Evelyn, Dr. Wayne's secretary and receptionist, and as sweet as he was sour, waved her over to the counter. "Oh, there you are, Dr. Hrluska. Let me page him."

"What's this about?"

Evelyn shrugged and rolled her eyes, but Jenn got the impression she *did* know—and that it wasn't good. As she searched her mind, Wayne bustled past, waving her through, and to a seat in front of his mammoth desk. The dark paneling and bookcases along the walls, the deep green carpet, made her feel as if she were in a posh men's club from a Cary

Grant movie. The only hint of Dr. Wayne's specialty was a squared-off array of crayon drawings sealed beneath the glass that protected his desk.

Tipping back, Wayne laced his hands behind his head and contemplated her. "How's it going, Doctor?"

"Fine," Jenn said.

"No problems on the ward?"

"Nothing *but* problems." Jenn felt her smile congeal as Wayne did not return it.

"Sometimes it can seem over . . . ver-whelming."

She got the feeling he was prompting her. "Sure, but I like the challenges."

"They can wear you down."

"I suppose."

He snorted and leaned forward. "You suppose."

Her scalp prickled. What was he fishing for?

Reaching into a pocket of his lab coat, Wayne flipped some capsules onto the table. "Know what these are?"

Leaning forward, Jenn picked up one of the capsules and rolled it over, looking for printing.

"Methylphenidate," Wayne said.

"Ritalin?"

"Very good, Doctor. You got that ver-very fast. Our main tool against attention deficit hyperactivity in kids, which also just happens to be an amphetamine."

A thrill of fear went through Jenn. So *that's* what this was about.

"These came from yuh-your locker," Wayne said. "You had quite a cache squirreled away in there."

Brad! Jenn's face flamed with outrage. With an effort, she kept her voice calm. "Dr. Wayne, if you say you found those in my locker, then you did, but I did not put them there."

"Is that so?"

"Yes, sir, it is."

"We had to cut the luh-lock off, and I presume anyone else would have to do the same. Have you given anyone else a key to your pah-uh-padlock?"

"No, sir, but it wouldn't be that hard to get."

"How so?"

"I keep it in a pocket of my lab coat. I take the coat off and put on scrubs whenever I go into Caroline's room. Anyone could slip the key from my pocket then."

"Isn't that rather careless?"

"Yes, I now see that it is."

"So you are not stealing amphetamines from the drug closet and using them."

"Absolutely not."

Wayne turned sideways in his chair, eyeing her. In profile, the slight curve of lip that everyone thought was a smile seemed exaggerated. But his face was utterly empty of warmth. Jenn's stomach throbbed with alarm. "Dr. Wayne, who told you to look in my locker?"

"What makes you think any-y-yone told me? I've been getting reports about you from, you know, several quarters. How energetic you are, how you often stay after shift, how you never seem tired."

"I wasn't aware those virtues might be held against me."

"Don't get smart with me, young lady. Virtue does not come out of a drug closet."

"Was it Dr. Dietz?"

Wayne stared at her, and from his hesitation, Jenn knew she was right. "Because you should know," she went on, "that I confronted him yesterday about whether he was using amphetamines."

"On what basis?"

Because I could smell it, hear it in his pulse . . . Damn! "He seemed very charged up and a little . . . inappropriate. And I noticed that his pupils were dilated."

"Let's stick to the matter at hand, shall we? Are you will-uh-willing to give the lab a sample of blood?"

Jenn felt herself freezing with alarm. This was it, what Merrick had warned her about so many times. *We must not be discovered.* Dared she say no? It would be like admitting guilt.

"Come on, Dr. Herl-luska, if you're in-n-innocent as you say, you have nothing to fear from a blood test."

Jenn wanted to shout with frustration. She had *everything* to fear, and not because Brad had probably laced her coffee with Ritalin. Phage blood was not normal, and no one must see hers under a microscope. But what could she do? Even this little bit of hesitation was dangerous. "If I take a blood test, I want my accuser to take one as well."

"That is not your decision."

"Just because Brad's father chairs the hospital board—"

Wayne slapped his desk, his face instantly red. "That's ee-ee-nough, Doctor! Will you or won't you take a blood test?"

Jenn struggled to remain calm. "Of course I will. And when the results come in, I'll expect your apology."

Wayne gaped at her, pop-eyed. "Will you now? Will you!" He went on staring at her, his fingers drumming the desk, and hope welled in her that he was going to back down, but then he picked up the phone and called the lab. Service chiefs had no trouble getting techs up at once, and within minutes, before she could fully think through her plan, a young tech named Edwina, with a round, pretty face and the hard-nosed air of a drill sergeant, was slipping the needle into her arm. Almost at once, Jenn could feel the skin around the needle trying to push it back out and close the small puncture wound. She felt almost sick with fear. Edwina was sure to notice—

But then the small tube was full and the tech withdrew the needle, put a ball of cotton on the injection site, and slapped a Band-Aid over it. "Keep pressure on that for a few minutes," she ordered, as if Jenn knew nothing about drawing blood. At least the cotton would hide the fact that the wound had already vanished. As Edwina turned to go, Jenn rose, too. "If there's nothing else, I need to get back to the ward."

Wayne flipped the back of one hand in dismissal. Jenn hurried through the anteroom. The tech was just in front of her, the corridor empty. Jenn resisted the impulse to strike now, take her blood back at once. Instead, she noiselessly followed Edwina back into the main corridor, through the gerbil run to the annex, using Influence to pinch off her image in any eye that looked her way. Stepping onto the elevator with Edwina, Jenn backed into an empty corner, praying the cage would not fill up with people on the way down.

When Edwina reached the lab, Jenn followed her in, just one step behind, breathless with tension. She mustn't slip. As the tech moved toward the tox screening equipment, Jenn dilated her jugulars, just a touch. Edwina's knees buckled, then caught. "Whew!" she said. Wiping her forehead, she set her kit with the test tube on a counter—*No, don't sit down!* Edwina leaned on the back of a chair, letting her head hang. *Low blood sugar,* Jenn thought, trying to will the idea into the woman's brain. It should be the first thing a hematology technician would think.

Edwina straightened and headed out of the lab again.

Jenn grabbed the tube of her own blood and followed her to the door, watched her head down the hall toward the snack room. I've got a minute or two, Jenn thought, while she hits the vending machines. Food isn't allowed in the lab but a candy bar won't take long. Grabbing an empty test tube and syringe from Edwina's kit, Jenn headed deeper into the lab, toward the hum of the CBC analyzer. A middle-aged brunette whose name tag said Trish sat at the machine, watching the CRT screen as a blood sample worked its way through the small tubes on the surface of the analyzer.

Trish, I need 10 cc of your blood, all right?

A firm touch to the jugulars and Trish slumped back unconscious, jaw gaping open, as the blood dumped from her brain. Jenn pushed the sleeve of Trish's lab coat up her arm, so worried she felt only the dimmest flicker of desire to drink as she dilated the vein in the crook of the arm and slipped the needle in. Blood poured into the tube. When it was full, Jenn forced herself to keep pressure on the puncture site while the seconds crawled by. She listened to the space behind her, concentrating on the lab door. Any second now, that door would open and Edwina would walk back in. Lifting the cotton ball, Jenn watched a single drop of blood ooze out. Footsteps approached—*No more time!*

Jenn transferred the label from the tube containing her own blood to the new tube, then jerked Trish's sleeve back down. Running back to Edwina's station, she slid Trish's blood into the kit just as Edwina walked in. Jenn had to dodge to avoid her. Catching the door before it swung shut, she escaped into the hall and leaned for a second against the wall, pressing a hand against her chest, trying to ease the hammering of her heart.

You mustn't be seen here.

Hurrying to the stairwell, Jenn ran up to peds, feeling safe only when she stepped onto the ward. Safe for the moment. What if Trish has AIDS? Jenn thought. She looked clean as a kindergarten teacher, but what if she's using drugs herself?

That will still be better than what will happen if these people ever got a good close look at phage blood. At least this way I've got a chance.

In the doctors' lounge, Jenn emptied the tube with her blood into the toilet and flushed it away.

The next hour was a blur. A cold anxiety enveloped her, making it hard to concentrate as she showed Lila how to start a Foley catheter, checked an asthmatic child in ER, and then looked in on Caroline again, who seemed no better but at least no worse. At four o'clock, Jenn sat in the conference room, staring at a stack of charts, trying to force her mind to focus so she could catch up the notes. The door opened and Dr. Fortis Wayne entered, his face grim. Jenn stared up at him, feeling paralyzed, unable to speak.

"Dr. Hrluska, I have the results of your blood test."

She nodded.

"Everything came back normal," Wayne said. "No amphetamines."

He seemed to be waiting for her to say something. What did he expect, that she'd gush all over him with gratitude?

Wayne cleared his throat. "I'm sure you understand, I have to follow up on such a serious allegation. I would be der-derel-lict in my duty otherwise."

Still she said nothing, furious at him now for what he had put her through.

"If you ever reach a position like mine," he said gruffly, "maybe you'll understand." Turning on his heel, he stalked out.

Jenn shoved the charts aside. The anger drained out of her, replaced by depression. She felt betrayed. Zane had warned her she could not be like normals, never be one of them. Physically, he was right enough, but she had felt certain that, in the most important sense, he was wrong. She lived her life with normals, worked with them, treated them, was in love with one of them. Zane was wrong—she would never have questioned it.

Until now.

11

By the time Jenn could get away from the hospital, it was almost ten and Hugh's book party was in full swing. She walked in, determined to enjoy herself. She would put her father, Fortis Wayne, Caroline, and everything else from her mind and have fun, damn it!

But first she needed to get the feel of it, warm herself up.

Finding a corner that gave her a good view of the suite's main room, she sipped champagne and watched. People were packed wall to wall for one purpose, to honor Hugh McCall for his latest novel, *Parentheses*. The massed body heat had prompted someone to draw back the curtains and slide the high windows open a few inches; night shone black against the glass, throwing the brightly lit scene into vivid relief. Hugh sat against one wall, surrounded by his editor, agent, and publicist and book types from the Washington media. She had known he was a rising star, but seeing this, it really struck her. He's going to be famous, she thought, feeling a sense of wonder.

And he's in love with *me*!

The mob around Hugh opened for a second and she gave him a

quick once-over. He was more dressed down than the rest of the crowd, but that was what everyone expected of a writer, and he did look author-like in his loose-fitting brick-brown jacket, dark green T-shirt, and soft khakis. He had managed to rein in his hair, but it was drying out now, fluffing back into the James Dean wildness she preferred. For a man who liked to be alone, he was making a good show of being in his element, smiling, shaking hands, signing book after book from a dwindling pile on the coffee table in front of him. At Hugh's shoulder, she recognized the handsome Irish mug of Robert Moran, who looked more like a retired prizefighter than a U.S. representative and former mayor of Alexandria. And next she spotted Gordon Peterson, the much-admired news anchor for the local CBS affiliate. Hearing a familiar voice, deep and richly modulated, she tracked it to Robert Aubry Davis of WETA, Washington's premier classical music station. She'd never met Hugh's publisher or editor, nor anyone else from the New York contingent, but fancied she could pick out some of them from their tweedy clothes and trendy hair-cuts. What a tribute to Hugh that they'd all come—she felt thrilled for him.

An image flared in her mind, brief and vivid as a strobe flash, of herself pinned to the ground by a seething mass of normals. Champagne spilled along her wrist. I could have been unmasked! she thought. Damn Fortis Wayne!

Take it easy. Everything worked out fine.

Hugh leaned into a gap between the people who encircled him, finding her with his gaze. He showed her his hands, encumbered by a copy of his book and a tumbler brimming with bourbon, then motioned her over with a backward pull of his head; she waved and mouthed, *I'm fine.* But she wasn't. The thought of being caught up in the crush of people around Hugh was making her spine crawl.

She set her glass on an end table. Why bother with champagne when it couldn't give her the buzz everyone else in the room seemed to be enjoying? To keep up appearances, of course. But it would be so nice not to have to, to be able to lay aside all affectations, large and small—the drinking coffee because other doctors did, the acting tired at the end of long shifts, the pretense that she slept at night. Hey, everybody—I have an announcement. I sat on my balcony all last night, thinking about dear old—very old—Dad, who looks twenty-five and has probably killed at least ten thousand of you, one at a time, over the past five centuries.

Knock it off!

Jenn picked up a copy of Hugh's novel from the stack. A very simple jacket—just the word *Parentheses*, Hugh's name, and the two curved lines of the title, all in a deep red that stood out against the glossy black background. Opening to the flyleaf, she read the e.e. cummings quote from which Hugh had taken the title:

*for life's not a paragraph
and death i think is no parenthesis*

Suddenly she saw the two other words embedded in the title, *parent theses*. But there was nothing about parents in the novel, at least nothing obvious. She'd made the connection because of her own life, her new theory about her father—that, unconsciously, he wanted her to save him. Could he be here in this room now? The thought sent a tingle along her spine, and then she realized that he wouldn't want to be seen by so many people—and it would be too taxing to hide himself from them. It's a good thing he's not here, Jenn thought. He'd see me standing off by myself in a room full of normals and think he'd made his point.

"You must be Dr. Hrluska."

Jenn turned. The man was handsome, with wavy salt-and-pepper hair, lush eyebrows, and a warm smile. Late forties, Jenn guessed, but he might be older. "I'm Robert Thielman," he said. "Hugh's agent."

"Jenn." She hid her surprise. Hugh had told her his agent was sixty, but no way did this man look it. She shook the offered hand, conscious of a direct curiosity in his eyes, feeling flattered. According to Hugh, Thielman was near the top of that small circle of elite New York literary agents—men and women, mostly unknown to the public, who lunched with the publishers, chief editors, and heads of the great houses.

"Champagne?" Robert asked.

She found herself nodding, though she'd just set a nearly full glass down. He slid with practiced skill through the crowd at the bar and returned, holding out a glass. She took a ritual sip. "Hugh's so excited," she said.

"He has reason to be. *Parentheses* is terrific."

"All that blood, though."

"A dark novel," Robert agreed. "Where does Hugh get it, I wonder? He really makes you *feel* it, doesn't he? Dr. Trevor's fear as he wakens from the nightmares that might not be nightmares. Hugh makes you identify with him and puts that pressure right there in your own throat."

Jenn was impressed by how aptly he had captured the mood of the novel, in just sentences. Hugh had told her tales of Robert persuading publishers to hand over millions to his top authors, sometimes before they had written a word, and now she could believe it. He had presence. There was a controlled sizzle in his eyes, a worldly insouciance in the way he held himself. If he said the world was flat, you might believe him.

"*Parentheses* is good," Jenn agreed. "I think it's his best yet—of course, he hasn't let me see the one he's writing now. But something tells me it'll be dark and scary, too. Why do people want to read about blood and gore; murder?"

Robert tilted his head back and eyed her as if he found the question disappointing. "Why would a nice, intelligent young woman want to spend her life surrounded by the illness and death of young people?"

The question gave her a shock. She understood the urge to kill as few humans could. It was the curse of her existence. She could not fathom why some normals found murder fascinating—and knew she should not be discussing it with a man as perceptive as this one.

"I'm not in pediatrics to see death," she said. "I'm there to fight it." *And to remind myself every day that I'm a healer, not a killer.*

As if aware of her discomfort, Robert smoothly changed tacks, asking her what sorts of novels she liked to read, and a moment later, Hugh broke free and sallied up with a grin. Robert wordlessly took the book and bourbon from him, and Hugh knew at once what to do with his freed hands. Jenn hugged him back, feeling good for the first time that evening.

Pressing his cheek to hers, he whispered into her ear, "I'm so glad you came."

"This is great," she murmured back.

"Without you here, it wouldn't mean anything."

"I'm very proud of you."

Hugh squeezed her and stepped back, accepting the bourbon from Robert.

"Mr. McCall?"

Hugh made space to admit a fourth person into their little circle. The woman was beautiful in a slightly off-kilter way, with a long throat and glossy, black hair that curved inward to her shoulders. Her jaw was close to being square but added character rather than blockiness to her face. All of a sudden, Jenn recognized her—Christiana Clark from "DomeWatch," a TV show in which reporters discussed the latest Capitol Hill doings. Christiana was a regular, and not just because the camera adored her. She was highly informed and personable. Jenn remembered Hugh roping her into watching "DomeWatch" one Sunday afternoon when Christiana had been on, and she had marveled at the woman's animation, the almost exaggerated expressiveness of her mouth and hands, which would have come across badly on most women but, somehow, not on her. She had a genuine warmth and sparkle that spilled over onto the other "talking heads" on the show, helping them to come alive, too. Christiana always looked a knockout on "DomeWatch," and Jenn admired her taste tonight—a short-waisted jacket, very soft-looking, in a broad blue and black plaid, complemented by a black skirt short enough to show off delicately molded knees.

"You're Christiana Clark," Hugh said.

She smiled. "That's right."

Hugh stuck his hand out and Christiana shook it. After he introduced Jenn and Robert, he said, "I love you on 'DomeWatch.'"

"I love your novels," Christiana replied. "It must be exciting to be such a good writer."

"Thanks. Tonight, yes. But most of the time, you just sit there in front of the word processor trying to force out the next few sentences."

"But that could be exciting, too—exploring inner space, discovering the characters and their ideas, the hopes and fears inside yourself."

"When it's working," Hugh said.

"Come on now, you must love it, or you'd do something with a regular paycheck."

"You've got me there," Hugh agreed.

Jenn began to take notice. This was not, somehow, just polite conversation. Christiana had some deeper agenda.

"Actually," Hugh said, "I *do* love it, though I'm never sure why."

A wistful look came over Christiana's face. "I've been thinking of writing a novel."

Glancing at Robert, Jenn saw that his expression could have been a model for the Sphinx. She suppressed a smile.

"You should," Hugh said. "With all the inside stuff you know, you could write the great Washington novel."

"No, I couldn't begin to write as well as you do."

"Hey, what you do for the *Times* isn't that different."

"Could I talk with you about it, maybe get some pointers?"

"How about later, when the crowd has thinned out some. My publisher will kill me if I don't mingle and sign books."

"Fine," Christiana said. "See you in a bit."

After she moved off, Jenn said, "What a beautiful woman."

"I hadn't noticed," Hugh said.

Jenn and Robert burst out laughing. "What kind of pointers are you going to give her?" Jenn teased.

"Never start a novel with 'It was a dark and stormy night.'"

Later, when the party was winding down, Christiana circled back to ask if Hugh was ready.

"You bet," he said. "Mind if Jenn sits in?"

"Of course not."

"Thanks," Jenn said, "but I need to check in at the hospital. You guys go ahead. I'll catch you afterward, Hugh."

Jenn waited until Christiana had led Hugh off into another room, then felt relieved to slip out into the empty hallway. Part of her had enjoyed the past hour, meeting Hugh's publishing friends. And Christiana was interesting, her candle power up close, somehow not quite what it was on camera. *She* seems a little depressed, too, Jenn thought—

Not that *I'm* depressed.

A group from the suite poured into the hall, drinks in hand, and she found herself moving off toward the elevator. She'd had enough of people for the moment. What she longed for now was a little silence, some space. Getting off in the lobby, Jenn found her way through a closed garden café to the promenade at the rear of the hotel, a long patio tiled in octagonal saltillo that glowed softly under mock gaslights. Beyond the promenade, the hillside dropped away into the dark expanse of Rock Creek Park. A mist, scented in damp bark and autumn leaves, rolled up from the crowns of the trees. The evening was mild, almost warm, one of those pleasant echoes of summer common to Washington Octobers. She strode toward the end of the promenade, filling her lungs with the fragrant air, savoring the peace. She *did* need to call the hospital, check on Caroline, but she could do that in a few minutes.

After a couple of turns up and down the promenade, Jenn toyed with going down into the park, finding a path that would lead her to the creek. Instead she turned onto a sidewalk that led around the end of the hotel back up toward Connecticut Avenue. Halfway along the side of the building, she heard soft footfalls behind her. Glancing over her shoulder, she saw a jogger laboring up the path toward her. It struck her that a lot of women would be afraid—was this really an innocent jogger, or did he have some ferocious criminal intent? How different did it make her, not having the fear?

Very different, kiddo.

She shook her head, frustrated that she could not seem to shake her feelings of alienation. That jerk Fortis Wayne had dug into something real, something deeper than she liked to admit, and she was going to have to work to cover it back up.

Jenn moved aside to give the jogger room to pass.

Then felt his arm snake around her chest. The blade of a knife pressed her throat.

"Keep quiet, bitch, or I'll cut your throat."

What was that on his breath—*peanut butter?* Oh, this was too stupid—

In the next instant she realized she was in trouble. The blade was so close she might not be able to push it away before he could cut her throat. And if he managed to do that, he would learn a secret no normal must ever know. She'd have no choice but to kill him.

Angry that a man like this could even exist, she made herself respond as he no doubt expected. "Don't hurt me," she whispered. "I'll do whatever you want."

The pressure of the blade eased. As the arm around her chest started to move down, she grabbed the wrist of his knife hand and pushed the blade away from her throat. Twisting his wrist—*watch it!*—she heard bones snap. The sound excited her; she felt her control slipping and then lost it completely. Keeping hold of the shattered wrist, she grabbed his ankle and swung him into the air, spinning him in a half circle, then releasing him. He sailed through the air, way down the path. Hitting on a shoulder, he rolled over and over, his body flopping with the sudden looseness of a corpse as it came to rest. He wasn't moving. He lay stock still. Appalled, she stared at him. Dear God, she thought, I've killed him!

Christiana stood at the window of the suite's bedroom, gazing out as Hugh talked—something about not needing an agent until she'd gotten a publisher interested. But she didn't care about the words, the advice, only him. She was acutely conscious that the few other people who'd been having private parlays in here had cleared out, that she was alone with this brilliant hunk, and she was both excited and nervous.

It was ridiculous. I interviewed Rabin, she thought, a day before he was assassinated. I talk to senators all the time. Bill Clinton calls me by my first name.

She found Hugh's reflection in the glass. He was so compelling. Not just his height, his rugged build, those smoldering brown eyes. His gaze was direct and warm, giving you the feeling he was interested in you as a person, even while you were leading him to talk about himself. And there was humor in his eyes. Here, on his big night, he wasn't taking it all too seriously.

But in one way he plainly was odd—here they were, alone, and he hadn't taken one step toward her or tried the slightest flirtation. Was he really such a straight arrow? Was he so totally infatuated with Jenn? Well, why not? Christiana thought. She's beautiful. Men all over the room were noticing her. I could be attracted to her myself, if I went that way. . . .

God, had she really thought that? Was she so bored, so desperate for change? What was Jenn's last name? Hrluska—*Dr.* Jenn Hrluska, so she was as accomplished as she was gorgeous.

Something familiar about her, Christiana thought. I've seen her somewhere. A while ago. Television? No. But somewhere. . . .

Never mind—it'll come to me.

She realized Hugh was asking her a question—was there an hour or two a day she could set aside for writing on a regular basis? She told him about her busy schedule, the words coming automatically, boring her. What was *wrong* with her? Most people would be overjoyed to have her success—national television, easy access to the great and powerful, a six-figure salary.

Boring, all boring.

She'd had more fun as a cub reporter on the crime beat at the *Times*. Astonishing. Back then she'd thought she hated it. She'd schemed like crazy to get away from stakeouts and bloody bodies.

Something outside beyond the glass drew Christiana's eye. Down below, on the sidewalk that skirted the hotel, a man and woman were standing very close at the fading edge of a pool of light. Christiana froze as she realized the man's arm was across the woman's throat. What was that—a knife?

She saw the woman turn and pick the man up by his hand and leg, spinning him, throwing him through the air. Before Christiana could gasp, the man sailed maybe thirty feet and sprawled out flat, lying still. She stared, stunned. Was he dead? No, now he was getting up, limping away, bent over, his wrist tucked into his stomach.

Suddenly, the woman looked straight up at her—*Dr. Hrluska!* Startled, Christiana turned away from the window. A chill crawled up her spine. *Why did she look up here? It was almost as if she knew I was watching her . . .*

Damn! No one could be that strong.

All of a sudden, Christiana knew where she had seen Jenn Hrluska before.

12

I'm drunk, Hugh thought, or close to it. That annoyed him. He would now have to put effort into acting sober. Drinking was one thing, even being drunk—though this was his first time since high school, but being so drunk you actually looked drunk was flat-out stupid and he despised it. Might as well wear a sign that said, "Duh."

Where was Jenn?

He looked around the room. Most everyone had left, except for his editor, Gil Faber, on his hands and knees probing the carpet for a lost contact lens, Christiana Clark, talking to Robert, a reporter from the *Washington Times,* observably drunk and still going for it. The other five or six people in the room he did not know.

No Jenn.

Surely she wouldn't take off without at least saying good night.

Settling back in the thronelike wicker peacock chair, Hugh watched Christiana and Robert. Robert was talking now, and Christiana was pay-ing rapt attention, which should be enough to charm any man, but Robert looked as near uncomfortable as he ever permitted himself. As if sensing it, Christiana edged back from him. Perceptive woman, Ms. Clark.

And beautiful, yes, he certainly had noticed.

Christiana and Robert stood together a moment longer, looking around and past each other. Hugh had the sudden impression Christiana was killing time. *Waiting to talk to me again?* The idea was making him feel a bit randy.

Catching movement at the corner of his eye, he swung his head around. Jenn steadied up in his vision, gazing down at him with those wonderful, green eyes. "Hey, big guy."

Gathering himself, he managed to stand up smoothly. He gave his tongue a few experimental flips behind closed lips. On the verge of asking where she'd been, he was saved by a last-second glimmer of wisdom. Instead, he said, "That gentleman on his hands and knees, who is our host, has informed me that this suite is mine for the night. After these people leave, we could cuddle around the fire."

"There is no fire," she said, "which is just as well, because there is no fireplace."

"I was speaking metaphorically."

"Oh, Hugh, I'm sorry. I'd love to stay, but I can't. I just got beeped."

Suddenly he could see the strain in her face. "Nothing serious, I hope."

"It's Caroline again—still. She's been fighting pneumonia, and now I have to go in and put her on a respirator. I'll have to watch her. I may be there all night."

The worry in her voice sent a pulse of sobriety through him. "I'm sorry."

"Me too. Tonight is so special for you, and I wanted to share it as much as I could." She bit her lip. "Damn this goddamn pneumonia. And damn leukemia, too!"

"Come on, she'll pull through. With you in her corner, she's got to."

Jenn gave him a wan smile. "I'll think of you," she said in a lowered voice. "I'll wish I was in that big bed with you."

"Me too, but since you won't be, I believe I'll just drive on home."

She gazed into his eyes, as if looking through to the muzzy innards of his brain. "I don't think that's a good idea."

"I'm perfectly fine."

"For most purposes, yes, but not for driving."

"I can stand on one foot and recite 'The Raven' backward. Raven the."

She laughed, and for a second the strain was gone from her face. "Promise you'll stay here tonight. I don't want to have to worry about you."

"If you'll promise to introduce me to Merrick in the next two days."

She winced. "I forgot to ask him tonight. It was so hectic at the hospital . . ."

"Maybe you could hook us up tomorrow."

"I'll try. But you might do better to just walk into one of the district police stations. I'm sure any detective would be glad to talk to a famous author."

She's evading me, Hugh thought. I noticed her in the first place because she kept going into Merrick's house. And now she's trying to keep us apart. Why? And why do I keep letting her?

But he already knew the answer, didn't he? The truth was, he didn't really need Jenn to get to Merrick. He could have gone up to Merrick months ago, presented himself as a writer, and used some pretext to ask about the murders ten years ago, but deep inside he'd known he wasn't ready to ask those questions. That he was afraid of the answers he might get.

Christiana leaned around Jenn. "Good night, Hugh."

"Night, Christiana."

"Thanks for the tips. Again—congratulations! Dr. Hrluska, it was nice to meet you." Christiana gave Jenn's upper arm a quick double squeeze and Hugh had the oddest impression she was probing her muscle.

"Likewise," Jenn said, turning. Christiana gave her a nervous smile and then she was gone, except for a lingering jasmine scent. She was very tense, Hugh thought.

"You *will* sleep here tonight?" Jenn said.

He nodded.

She pulled his head forward and kissed him hard on the lips, and he felt not passion in her, but a strange desperation. He wanted to hold on to her, ask her what was wrong, but a kid with leukemia was wrong enough. He waved her on her way.

As soon as she was out the door, disappointment began to take hold. He'd counted on being with Jenn tonight, holding her close after everyone was gone. He could almost feel the smoothness of her hips beneath his hands, taste the salty sweetness of her tongue.

He noticed that the last guests were starting to drift out, too. The drunk reporter, the people he didn't know, and then his editor. He found the presence of mind to thank Gil for the party. Robert lingered a moment. "You were a hit tonight, my friend. And I'm glad I got a chance to meet Jenn. She's an extraordinary young woman."

"I've never known anyone like her. She's . . . magnificent." A lump rose in Hugh's throat, the booze, making him sentimental—more than usual.

"Marry her," Robert said. He looked entirely serious.

Hugh thought again about how he and Jenn had met, why he had sought her out, and felt suddenly unworthy of her. "Nothing would make me happier," he said. "But I can't ask her—not yet."

"Novelists," Robert said with a mixture of affection and exasperation, but he didn't push it, and Hugh was glad.

He offered his hand to Robert. "Thanks for coming down."

"Wouldn't have missed it." Robert held on an extra beat and then he, too, was gone.

Alone, Hugh gazed around the empty suite, at the empty wine and champagne bottles lined up along the bar, at the empty places where stacks of his novel had been, at the empty Jack Daniel's at the foot of the peacock chair. Wandering through the suite, he found the master bedroom and stared at the king-sized bed that would feel empty even after he crawled into it. Yes, he'd promised Jenn he'd sleep here tonight, but first he wanted to feel some wind on his face.

Down in the parking lot, he spent ten sour-mashed minutes trying to remember where he'd parked. When he finally located his Harley, chained to a grate, the key to the padlock slipped from his fingers and vanished into the sewer. Seething, he stomped in circles around the bike, chanting "fuck" under his breath until it occurred to him that he looked and sounded like a giant chicken.

All right, bolt cutters.

Where in hell was he going to find them this time of night? A boozy inspiration struck him—the hotel health club!

Closed, of course.

But he found a security guard who, for a hundred bucks and the promise of a free autographed novel, went in and got him the bolt cutters the attendant used to cut forgetful guests' padlocks off their lockers.

Chopping the padlock off gave Hugh a savage pleasure. He slipped the cutters into the saddlebag—a hundred bucks was "own" not "rent." As he started the bike, husky overtones in the engine noise reminded him that the muffler was slowly going bad. The extra noise fit his grouchy mood, but he resisted the urge to rev up to full throttle and give a thundering wake-up raspberry to everyone in the hotel. Easing out of the parking lot, he headed down Connecticut Avenue to the park entrance. The bike plowed through the stagnant midnight air, conjuring the illusion of a breeze. He throttled up until the damp air scoured his face, but he still felt thickheaded. Leaning into the curves of the road that wound south through Rock Creek Park, he imagined smashing up, being carried into the emergency room of Adams Memorial Hospital, IVs dripping into him, Jenn bending over him, terrified and distraught. "Oh, Hugh, I'm so sorry I didn't stay with you. Speak to me. . . ."

I'm pathetic, Hugh thought with a pained grin.

The park road straightened and broadened into four lanes, sweeping him under the long, massive overhang of the Kennedy Center. On his right, the Potomac gleamed like spilled mercury in the moonlight. Passing between the winged, golden horses that guarded Memorial Bridge, he scanned the black hillside on the far bank, finding the wavering apostrophe of flame above Arlington Cemetery. The sadness it usually made him feel was deepened, tonight, by the bourbon, and he averted his eyes.

Upriver, he glimpsed a few darkened boats anchored in the broad bend that swept Georgetown, and then he was in Virginia, the Potomac behind him. Picking up Route 50, he sped past Fort Myer into Arlington and then through Falls Church and into the countryside.

I love her so much it hurts, he thought. I want her to take care of that kid, but I want her with me, too. Tonight of all nights.

Still drunk, yessir.

Humidity slicked his face now, as though he'd been sweating, but he drove on, letting the speed creep up to sixty, then seventy, feeling the road throb into his hands, up his arms. Following a string of impulses that seemed almost to prompt him, he veered off onto a side road, then another. The second road began to look familiar. Had he ever been on it before? No.

Not that he remembered.

Somehow, though, he knew there would be another road up ahead, not even a road, really, but two tire lanes through the tall grass. Slowing the bike, he followed the sweep of his headlight to its margin, watching the weedy roadside . . .

There!

Hugh stopped the bike, and sat, idling, feeling a sudden turmoil low in his gut. Bent weeds marked the twin paths of car tires. The headlight picked up the course of the overgrown lane until it vanished into a wall of trees about fifty yards away. A dull throb started up in Hugh's head, too soon for a hangover. I *know* this place, he thought. That's why I drove here.

Easing the throttle around, he bounced along one of the tire tracks and into the woods. The trees closed in on either side, a dense tunnel of blackness around the narrow beam of his headlight. The lane grew so bumpy he had trouble, even at a crawl, controlling the bike. Parking it, he pulled his flashlight from the saddlebag and continued through the trees on foot, shining the light around, not sure what he was doing. A strange compulsion gripped him—he had to see more. The beam picked out a thick, ancient oak, with a black lightning burn down the trunk. He knew he had seen it before, this very tree, with its scarred bark. But when?

Uncle Tydus!

And then he knew where he was. Tydus had been looking for undeveloped woods, an out-of-the-way place with no evidence of human activity, so he could put up another still. He told me to go scout him a place, Hugh thought. It was just before he was shot . . .

Ten years ago!

A blade of pain slid down through Hugh's head from above one ear and cutting to his jaw on the other side. Gasping, he staggered off the path and sat against a tree. He held his head between his hands, pressing gently, trying to think of nothing, to empty his mind of both thought and pain. Gradually the throbbing eased.

This memory wasn't just from ten years ago, it was from the blank days—

Christ!

Half-blinded by a new ax-stroke of pain, Hugh breathed deeply, and thought about floating on a rubber raft on a vast, smooth sea. The sun was on his face. It was warm . . .

He felt his back melting into the tree trunk. The grass was soft under him. He could feel the bourbon in him, washing through his veins in sleepy waves. Crickets began to chirp around him, a sweet, lulling sound. As long as he listened to it and didn't try to remember, he'd be all right. . . .

For a while, he was nowhere, then he had a dim awareness of lying on his side, knees doubled up, on the backseat of a car. He tried to open his eyes but the lids resisted, sticking together. One arm was numb, pinned beneath him, the other stretched along his side. He tried to lift his head, but it was too heavy. The effort caused his unpinned arm to slide off his body and over the edge of the seat. His palm slapped down not on the floor of the car but on something soft. Dread oozed through him as he realized it was flesh, someone's thigh, downy smooth, but too cool.

He snatched his hand back. No, he thought. No, please.

With a huge effort, he lifted himself enough to slide his other arm forward, freeing it of the weight of his body. The fingers of that hand prickled to life and, in the burn of returning circulation, he realized there was something in that hand. He did not want to know what. He lay for a moment, eyes stuck shut, paralyzed with foreboding. Tears seeped under his lids, and the lashes loosened and pulled apart, and he was looking at the woman's shoulder and head, cocked up against the back door. She stared at him, her pupils so wide he could not tell the color of her eyes. Blood collared her neck and covered the top of her white T-shirt like a crimson nun's collar. Suddenly, he knew what lay within the curl of his other hand—the butt of a knife. Cold terror choked him. I killed her, he thought. I was out of my head . . .

Nauseous, he released the knife and clapped the hand against his mouth, then jerked it away again, staring at the sticky film of blood, horror-stricken as he realized his face was covered with it. A scream pushed at the paralyzed muscles of his throat—

Hugh awoke, open-mouthed, wheezing out a ghost scream. The car and dead woman were gone, but his heart went on pounding in terror. For a moment he had no idea where he was, then reality knit back together and he remembered the book party, riding his Harley through the night, finding this woods.

He felt only a small relief. The dream again.

Pushing up, he staggered to his bike and got on, driven by the need to get away from this place. Back on the road, he gulped the air that pounded his face, trying to shake off the clinging fog of the dream. That's all it was, he told himself. A dream. It never happened. I could not have done something so horrible.

⁕

Sometime around midnight, on the edge of a restless doze, it struck Merrick that Jenn had made contact with Zane.

He sat up in bed, the tendrils of sleep falling away, and tried to nail down the intuition. She had sounded fine the morning after checking on her father. Low blood pressure, she'd said, nothing serious. He'd read the implicit subtext—*it wasn't Zane*—and felt reassured. Then, tonight, she'd called as she was leaving the hospital to tell him everything was still all right. She'd sounded a little depressed—a patient in trouble, she'd said, and he didn't doubt it.

So what was bothering him?

All the things she had not said. Usually she'd chat with him a while, especially when she was feeling low. She had not said more than a few sentences.

Merrick sighed. A thousand years of reading people, but he could still miss things.

Getting out of bed, he went silently down the hall to Gregory's room and opened the door. The boy lay sprawled across the bed, earphones on, mouth gaping in sleep. Merrick went to him and eased the volume down, then removed the earphones. He slipped Gregory's shoes off and covered him with a blanket. Lingering a moment, he gazed down at his sleeping son, his heart brimming with a love so deep it scared him. He remembered Katie's phone call from Kansas City: *make sure he doesn't sleep in his clothes.* Ah, well, letting Gregory get away with a few things was the higher duty of a father.

Merrick turned out the light and padded down to the kitchen, taking a slice of pizza from the fridge. It had not yet gotten fully cold. *And don't you two eat pizza every night. Take him out to dinner and try to get some salad into him.*

Merrick took a bite, barely tasting it, knowing the emptiness he was trying to fill was not in his stomach. Only a day, and he missed Katie. Time meant so much more to him now. When he lay on his deathbed, what would he give to have this day back to spend with Katie?

Merrick shook off the morbid thought. When the time came, he must remember that he'd had her longer and more fully than any of the others. Besides, she was safer in Kansas City—and she might have located a boy with progeria.

The pizza turned heavy in Merrick's throat. He tried not to think about what would happen if they managed to concentrate a megadose of Fraction Eight. It would fall to Jenn to drive the needle into her father.

Even if she was fast enough, could she find the iron will to kill her own father?

My son.

Merrick's eyes stung as he remembered Zane at Gregory's age, a kid who had suddenly started doing battle with his cowlicks, who turned pink when the girls teased him. A boy still grieving the loss of his mother to the coughing disease. We were living just outside Shiring then, Merrick thought. We had a few friends in the village, mostly his mother's, but all we really had after she died was each other. I never anticipated he might get sick—that after so many normal children, this one might be like me.

Closing his eyes, Merrick saw back through the centuries. A memory came to him of sitting at a broad wooden table with his son, roast venison hot in his mouth. The main tavern in Shiring. He could almost feel the fresh straw under his feet, smell the earthy mixture of smoke, roast meat, and body odor. The constant, low babble in the tavern gave way to peals of laughter at a table near the fireplace, where a fat man and his two daughters were eating bread and pottage.

"See that girl over there, Da?" Zane said. "She keeps looking at me."

"Over where?"

Zane made a self-conscious sideward motion of his head. "There, by the fire. That last table."

"The one with crossed eyes and yellow hair?"

"No-o-o-o. The other one, with black hair and . . ."

"Yes?" Merrick thought he knew, but he wondered with amusement if his son would say it.

"You know." Zane's voice cracked, but Merrick was careful not to smile.

"Big breasts?"

Zane flushed scarlet but nodded.

"Why would she be watching you?"

"I don't know."

"Maybe she likes you." Merrick cuffed him on the shoulder.

Zane grinned and made a silly face, still mostly boy, but Merrick knew he was feeling the beginnings of something else, both thrilling and scary.

"Shall I go ask her if she likes you?"

Zane choked on a mouthful of venison and Merrick slapped him on the back until he got his breath again.

Zane leaned close. "What do you think she'd do if she knew I liked her?"

"What would you like her to do?"

"I don't know."

"Are you sure?"

Zane blushed again. "You'll laugh."

"No I won't. What is it? You'd like to kiss her?"

Zane laughed in what might be relief. "Kiss her? I've kissed girls."

"Have you now."

"Last year Mary, the hooper's girl, she gave me a piece of cheese to kiss her behind the mill."

"Was it fun?"

"No, Da. But maybe we were doing it wrong."

"So you'd like to give it another try with that girl over there, would you?"

Zane looked at her, and the excitement on his face almost made Merrick laugh.

Then Zane sobered and looked down. "I saw you kissing Mam once."

Panged, Merrick gave his son's shoulder a squeeze. "Your mother and I . . . we were . . ." He was unable to go on.

"I know. And now she's gone." Zane's voice was low with bitterness. "Will you marry someone else?"

Merrick looked into the fire. "It's too soon to even think about it."

"But later?"

All at once he understood what might be behind his son's question. "Love is what makes life worth living," he said.

"I wish I had never loved Mam." Zane's voice was a whisper now, as if the muscles of his own throat were trying to strangle him. His eyes shone.

Merrick hid his dismay. "You mustn't say that. I know it hurts you that Mam is gone. But it's best for you now to put away that pain."

"If I hadn't loved her, I wouldn't hurt so much."

"And all those nights when she told you stories about the animals in the forest, and the little people who live under the earth? When she taught you to juggle and showed you how to whistle with a blade of grass? All those hugs and the kisses on top of your head? You could talk to her about anything. Would you really go back and throw all that away?"

Zane gazed at him. "It's gone anyway."

"But you had it, and you'll have it again. You'll be a man soon, and you'll love a woman as a man does. You'll marry her and be with her and do things together. You'll be able to talk to her beside the fire, about everything that matters to you. You'll know there's someone who cares what happens to you, who will be happy when you are happy, and help you when you're sad. It will be the best thing there is, better even than Mam."

Zane glanced at the black-haired girl. "And if my wife dies too?"

"It will be terrible, but not as terrible as if you never had her." Merrick watched Zane struggle silently with life's painful and sublime equation. He wished he could put into Zane his own sureness that love plus loss equals go out and love again. He wished he could tell Zane how he knew this—that Mam was not his first wife but his sixth, that Zane had twenty half brothers and sisters spread back over four centuries, two of them still alive in the South of France, bent over with age now. But that could not be. Zane's world had gone hard and frightening enough without the boy having to face the darkness in his own father. Dear Son, Merrick thought, I know better than any man alive how hard it is to lose someone you love. But if it had become too hard, you would not exist. And I would not be able to sit here beside you now, with my heart so full, wishing I could hug you without embarrassing you.

Zane took in a deep breath and let it out, and the pain in his face sank from sight. He looked at the tankard in front of Merrick. "Could I have some of your ale, Da?"

It was something he'd been asking since he was seven or eight, but had never gotten. Without hesitation, Merrick shoved the tankard over to him.

Zane's eyes widened with delight. He picked the ale up eagerly and took a deep swallow. His eyes reddened and he squirmed on the bench, his face screwing into an expression so appalled that Merrick struggled not to laugh. When Zane could speak again, he said, "Damn, that's good!"

And then we laughed together, Merrick thought. We laughed so hard we cried. He stared at the half-eaten slice of pizza. Returning it to the fridge, he washed his hands and tidied up the kitchen, just as if his face were not wet with tears.

13

By the time Jenn got Caroline on the respirator and stabilized, it was nearly 3 A.M. Driving the nearly empty streets home, she let her mind go back to what had happened outside the hotel. An aftershock of alarm rippled through her. She had almost killed that man.

Maybe I should have.

She was astonished at how easily the thought came. She knew she had no right to set herself up as judge, jury, and executioner, but was letting him go really so much better? Women she would never meet would be at risk, women who could not break the sick bastard's wrist while trying to be gentle, or throw him the length of a volleyball court.

What I wanted to do was tear his throat open.

Jenn shuddered. *What am I?*

She parked in the lot behind her apartment and looked up at her bedroom window seven stories above. Was it dark? Why was she doing this? *Zane.* But he would hardly need to put on the lights, would he?

As she reached her apartment door, her nerves sharpened, and she glanced up and down the hall, listening. At 3 A.M., the building was silent, except for a steady, distant murmur in the air ducts. Dropping all mental barriers brought her only one additional sound—the busy whisper of cockroach feet along the acoustic tile overhead, which she quickly suppressed. Bending, she examined the lock. No scratches, but nor had there been any the night she'd found the body.

Unlocking the door, she stepped into the foyer. The smell of blood was all but gone from the floorboards; no fresh corpse. But a faint tingling persisted along her spine.

"Zane," she said, "are you in here?"

No answer.

"If you're here, show yourself. I need to talk to you."

Nothing. But her uneasiness persisted, and now she felt a little anger, too. She didn't want him watching her, staying aloof. She wanted to see him, damn it.

She made a thorough search of the apartment, then remembered that would do no good if he was, somehow, able to use Influence to blind even another phage. Turning on all the lights, she grabbed the broom from her kitchenette and crept around the apartment, swinging the bristles back and forth ahead of her, missing no place where Zane might be hiding—even the ceiling over door lintels and other fixtures that might give him enough purchase to perch above her. If he was in here, he'd have to move when she got close, and in the near-total silence, she'd hear him.

Maybe.

As she carefully quartered the apartment, she heard no whisper of other feet, no thump of someone dropping down. She saved her bedroom for last. Nothing.

I'm alone, she thought, and felt both relief and disappointment.

I do need to talk to someone, she thought.

Merrick.

Her hand was on the phone before she realized he would be asleep. She envied him. To sleep, to escape for a little while, was the most precious thing she could imagine.

But then I've been given what most people would long for—immunity from illness, physical strength, boundless energy, a life that will go on and on . . .

All I have to do is keep drinking blood every two weeks.

"Zane?" she said again, though she was certain now that he wasn't here. It was the oddest feeling, but it was as if she needed him—was disappointed he wasn't here. Merrick is asleep, she thought, no longer really one of us. Why couldn't you have been a father to me, Zane? I need a father who knows what I am and understands how I feel.

Pulling off her clothes, Jenn slipped into the green robe Katie had gotten her last Christmas. She was acutely conscious of her vitality, of the silky tides of air that rolled effortlessly through her lungs. How horrible for poor Caroline to fight for every breath. With the tube of the respirator down her throat, her color had improved almost at once. All the same, it was an ominous step. A respirator was quick to create dependency, weakening the lungs by the very act of supporting them. If pneumonia were Caroline's only problem, the respirator would tide her over until the Sulfamethoprim and pentamidine could suppress the *Pneumocystis.* But what if she never comes off the machine? She can't even speak now with that awful tube down her throat. What if I never hear her voice again?

Jenn sat on the edge of the bed, bouncing a little, trying to throw off the bleak feeling, the tension that knotted her neck and shoulders. She needed to do something, get her mind off Caroline and off the man outside the hotel.

I could go see Hugh, she thought. As always, the thought of being with him gave her an instant lift. Hugh would be sleeping off the bourbon, but that didn't matter. All she really needed was to slide into bed, pull his arm across her, just lie there for what was left of the night, and feel his close warmth. The hospital could beep her at the hotel as easily as here.

Shrugging out of the robe, she went to the shower and fiddled with the knobs until the stream of water was quite hot. If she was going to lie in bed with Hugh, she needed to get the smell of cigarette smoke out of her hair. She'd never seen so many people smoking as at Hugh's party—

must be the New Yorkers. Lighting up was rare at Washington gatherings. Why does *anyone* do it? Jenn wondered as she stepped under the shower head.

The hot water felt good beating against her face, streaming through her hair, cleaning away not just the residue of smoke, but some of the clammy unease that had clung to her since Fortis Wayne had made her take the blood test. Turning, she let the warm blast pound the tension from her neck and shoulders. She worked some coconut shampoo into her hair. The scent brought back warm memories of the beach two months ago, that sunny August weekend with Hugh, the first time they'd made love—

Something moved at the corner of her eye.

Whirling, she froze in shock. A man—outside the shower! He was naked! Her shock turned to outrage. Throwing the door back, she started to yell, then felt her breath leave her as she realized who it was. "Brad!" she said, stunned.

His eyes were unfocused, half closed, his mouth gaping open. He weaved on his feet like a drunk about to fall down. Her mind slipped and slid, trying to grasp what was happening.

How did he get in here?

And then another scent penetrated the smell of coconut—*blood!* It streamed from crescent-shaped gashes on Brad's wrists and spattered on the floor. The wonderful smell of it expanded, filling her head, inflaming her. She *wanted* it.

Brad started to fall. Grabbing him, she dragged him into the shower with her, letting him sag down as she brought one wrist to her mouth and began to suck—

NO!

With a fierce effort, she dropped his wrist and jumped from the shower. Tourniquet—she must stop the bleeding. Grabbing a towel, she tore it into strips and turned back to Brad. The shower was still on, rinsing his blood into a swirling orange tide along the tiles. Moaning, she shut the water off and tied a strip of towel around one of his slashed wrists, then the other. Her hands shook so badly she could barely control them. The taste, already on her lips, was driving her mad with desire.

He's your patient!

As she twisted the second strip tight, a hand grabbed her arm from behind and lifted her away from Brad. She stiffened, too startled to scream. The hand spun her around.

Zane!

She stared at him, stunned.

"What are you doing?"

"I have to save him." Her voice sounded faint, far away.

Zane's gaze burned into her. "Drink," he said. "You know you want to."

"No!"

"He deserves it."

"I can't."

"He'll die anyway—I won't let you save him. Will you let his blood go to waste?"

"Get out of here," she gasped.

Zane shook his head.

Jenn realized suddenly that she was naked. She started to grab for a towel, and then a flicker of uncertainty crossed Zane's face and she knew that he had realized it too. A desperate idea struck her. She thrust her breasts toward him. "Is this what you came for? To see your daughter like this?"

Zane paled. He backed away a step.

"Go ahead," she cried. "Look! I can't stop you."

He turned his head aside. "Cover yourself."

"Look! You *know* you want to!"

Zane backed away another step, still averting his eyes. "Stop this."

"Bastard! Pervert!"

He ran. In seconds, she heard the door open and close.

Relief flooded her, then vanished as she turned back to Brad and saw that one of the tourniquets had slipped loose. She wound it tight again, then pulled the wrist to her mouth before she knew what she was doing. Lunging up, she wet a washrag and jammed it into her mouth, feeling her teeth grind savagely as her throat convulsed around the trickle of water. Turning her back on Brad, she fled to her bedroom and snatched up the phone, then let the receiver fall. How would she explain Brad being in her apartment, naked, with his wrists slashed?

If you call emergency, you'll have lost your chance. You don't have to save him. Zane is right. He tried to destroy you. You can drink his blood, then take him out and bury him. No one will ever know—

"Stop it!"

She called Merrick. The phone rang only once before he picked up. His voice sounded very alert, and she realized he had not been sleeping after all.

"I have to feed," she said.

"Jenn. It's not time yet. Another week—"

"Now, tonight. Have you set something up?"

"Yes." There was a pause. "You've seen Zane."

She gave a thin laugh. "Oh yes." Quickly, she told him about Brad. "I've stopped the bleeding. I'm about to call 911—"

"No—you've got to get him away from your apartment first."

He's right, Jenn thought, startled by her own lapse in thinking. If they come here, they'll wonder why Brad would try to commit suicide in my apartment, maybe even suspect I did this to him. Brad couldn't set them straight—Zane probably put him under before bringing him here to cut his wrists. If Brad wakes up here, he'll have more questions than anyone. Good thing I called Merrick . . . *now snap out of it!*

"I understand," she said. "I've stabilized him enough so that I could drive him back to his apartment and then call the ambulance."

"Good, but make sure you let no one see the two of you while you're getting him home."

"Of course," she said, then realized it was a fair reminder, as rattled as she must sound.

"When the ambulance comes," Merrick said, "tell them you got a call from Brad and he didn't sound good, so you went over there."

"Right. But, Merrick, I mean it—I really have to feed." Her throat crawled with need. She felt humiliated by her desperation, her weakening control, scared she might go back to Brad, and this time she would not be able to stop herself from drinking. *Please don't question me.*

"I understand," he said. "As soon as the ambulance has taken Brad away, get back to your place. I'll be there waiting for you and we'll go out. Be strong now. You can handle this—you *will* handle it."

"Yes." She swallowed, feeling calmer, stronger. But the thirst was powerful, too.

"I think Zane can keep me from seeing him," Jenn said.

Merrick glanced at her, his face an eerie mask in the green glow of the dashboard lights. Nothing looked or felt quite right. She was feverish with the need for blood. Merrick had said the house was about a half hour away, in a rural part of southern Maryland. She wished he would drive faster. Didn't he realize that every second she had to wait was an agony?

Merrick said, "I've never heard of a phage who could hide himself from other phages simply by Influencing the capillaries in the eyes, the way we do with normals. The parts of your brain that project Influence would be stimulated if Zane did that around you, let alone if he tried to do it *to* you. It would be as obvious as a shout."

"He's been at the hospital," Jenn snapped, "and I never saw him." Her irritation startled her. It came from her hunger, she realized, the frustration of not being able to satisfy her craving.

"What makes you think he was at the hospital?"

"He knew Brad had set me up with Dr. Wayne."

"What?"

She realized she hadn't told Merrick about being forced to take the blood test. His expression turned grim as he listened.

"To know about the blood test," she said, "Zane must have been hanging around the hospital, watching me. But I never saw or felt him."

"He could have heard someone talking about it afterward," Merrick said. "The nurses' station or doctors' lounge when you weren't even in the hospital."

Jenn realized he was right. By now, everyone on peds probably knew she'd been forced to take a blood test, and that Brad was the one who'd set her up.

"When Brad was in your apartment," Merrick said, "did he seem at all aware of what was going on?"

"No. While I was waiting at his place for the ambulance, he came around enough to recognize me. But he was really confused. He had no idea how his wrists had been cut."

Merrick nodded. "Zane would put him under, probably before he even got inside his apartment. Did the ambulance people seem satisfied with why you were at Brad's?"

"I kept it as vague as I could. I said Brad had called me and that he didn't sound too good so I went over."

"You didn't tell them he was specifically threatening suicide?"

"No. But don't think I wasn't tempted."

"It could ruin his career."

"Who cares?" Merrick looked sharply at her, and she said, "Give me a break—he tried to ruin *my* career."

"You're glad Zane did that to him?"

She looked out the window at the dark countryside. "No."

"It took great strength not to drink his blood. I'm proud of you."

"I wanted to," Jenn said.

"But you didn't."

"I don't like Brad," she said, "but I wouldn't wish what happened to him on my worst enemy. He lost a lot of blood. He'll need at least a couple of days in the hospital, and when he can't explain how his wrists were cut, they may even put him on a locked ward." She realized she did feel sorry for Brad. He'd have a lot of explaining and persuading to do before Fortis Wayne would let him back on the ward, and how could he explain it when he didn't even know how it had happened.

Merrick slapped the steering wheel. "*Damn* Zane. He knew exactly what he was doing to you. Why can't he leave you alone?"

"Because he wants me with him."

"He wants you away from me."

"If he has no feelings for me as his daughter," she said hotly, "why did he back away when he realized I was naked? He was embarrassed, ashamed, so upset that he ran from me."

Merrick said nothing. Her anger cooled, and she thought, I've embarrassed him. But where is his answer?

Merrick slowed the car and doused the headlights, pulling off the road behind a stand of sumac bushes. "We have to walk through these trees," he said, "a few hundred yards will bring us into their backyard. They have a dog, but you'll have no trouble putting it to sleep. The lock on the back door will be no challenge. Are you ready?"

"Let's go." Eagerness filled her.

He hesitated. "You're very hungry now, which means you must be twice as careful. If you lose control, I'm no longer strong enough to hold you back."

"I'll be fine," she said. *Let's go, let's do it!*

But Merrick did not move. "Bill and Michelle McDonough," he said distinctly. "They've been married ten months. She volunteers at a homeless shelter, and he works with Cub Scouts. They have no children yet, but there are people who need them."

"I understand," Jenn said.

She followed Merrick through the woods, so alert, so hypersensitized she could almost feel the moonlight sliding along her arms. She became aware of a small, dozing pulse ahead, felt it pick up, suddenly. *The dog!* Before she could reach out, it barked, once, and then she dilated its jugulars just enough to knock it out. A moment later, Merrick stepped ahead of her into the backyard. As he started for the door, she caught his arm and pointed to an upstairs window, open a few inches. He nodded and she hurried to the wall, fitting her fingers into the mortar creases, scrambling up noiselessly. She remembered that first time again, on Zane's shoulders. *Soon you'll be able to do this too. I'll teach you.*

But Zane hadn't taught her, Merrick had, maybe at the very same moment Zane had been trying, in desperation, to claw through the steel door of his tomb.

Reaching the window, Jenn paused and let her senses probe into the house. At once she picked up the rhythms of their pulses—much too fast to be asleep. A cold alarm pierced her. Had the dog wakened them? Were they already dialing the police?

"Oh, Bill," the woman moaned. "Yes, Bill."

Jenn grinned in relief. The dog might have wakened them, but they were anything but alarmed. She tested the window. It was new, and slipped up noiselessly. She followed the grunts and moans through a narrow hallway. *Put them to sleep. Do it now.* But she did not. The master bedroom was quaintly small, half taken up by the king-sized bed. They were being very quiet now, touching each other's bodies, every sense focused on each other. Averting her eyes, Jenn stood inside the doorway, embarrassed and a little aroused at the sound of their kissing. Their intimacy touched her, and she was glad, because it would give her something to cling to in the dangerous moments ahead.

The woman climaxed with a few moans and the man shouted as he came. She let them lie a few minutes, then dilated their jugulars, just a few deft, mental touches to dump blood from their brains, leaving them sprawled naked on the covers, lost in a deep postcoital sleep.

Starting downstairs to let Merrick in, Jenn heard a faint sound at the bedroom window. There he was, peering in at her, hanging by his fingertips on the sill. He looked rather pleased with himself, and she felt a rush of affection for him. Once the most powerful of phages, how he must hate to let his decline show. This was the side of him she wished she would see more often when they fed.

Helping him in, she turned back to the unconscious couple. Anticipation filled her; the muscles in her throat tightened as she dilated the large vein behind the ankles of both people. Merrick handed her the transfusion packs. Inserting the needles, she averted her eyes from the provocative spill of blood into the tubes. But there was no way to entirely stop what was coming. As her pack grew heavy in her hand, she felt her lips pulling back from her teeth and was powerless to stop it. The edges of her vision reddened. She longed to fall on the man, to tear his throat open with her teeth and drink her fill—

No, stop it!

In desperation, she looked to Merrick. He had turned away from the woman's ankle, his face twisted with the effort of control. "Breathe," he whispered.

Jenn pulled a deep breath and her head cleared a little.

And then the packs were full.

Back in the woods, she ran ahead of Merrick, sailing over fallen limbs, driven by her hunger. Nothing else mattered but getting to the car, where it would be safe to drink. Breaking from the woods, she lunged into the passenger seat, holding the hot blood against her chest. A moment later, Merrick slid in beside her. As soon as they were moving, she opened the transfusion pack, and put it to her mouth. The first gulp was exquisite. A firestorm of ecstasy flooded her veins, *I love it, God help me!* Greedily she drank the rest. As the rush of well-being spread through her, she became conscious of the faintest sounds—the chirr of crickets beyond the sealed windows, the muted snick snick of oiled pistons. The thin glow of the moon swelled to a dazzling radiance in the car. I may play racquetball up there someday! Jenn thought. I may practice medicine on another planet. Who knows what the twenty-ninth century will be like?

I will—so long as I go on feeding!

Turning to Merrick, she saw that he was still holding back. "Afraid to drink and drive?"

He smiled, but she could sense his depression. She tried not to resent the pall he cast. He'd had his thousand years and was weary of it. She understood; she just wished he could understand her. We did nothing wrong, she thought. Those people back there will wake up fine in the morning. I'd have asked permission if I could, but they won't miss a pint, and if any other phage had visited them tonight, they'd be dead now. What about my patients—Caroline, the others? Would they be better off if I died an agonizing death from blood deprivation? Surely I give back more than I take. I didn't ask to be born with the gene.

Why must I feel so guilty?

14

Jenn passed the few hours until dawn pacing around her apartment. Taking a slightly different path each time, she worked on silence, on sensing the grain of the parquet with her feet so she could glide over the stress points and find the firm places that would not creak. At the same time, she paged through her old diary, using only her peripheral vision to steer her back and forth between kitchenette and living room, through to the bathroom and out to the bedroom.

She felt strong, invincible.

That was the best part of a feeding, the way your mind fed off the intense well-being of your body. This must be how amphetamines felt to a normal, except no side effects, no distortion of judgment—her sense of physical power was objectively accurate and, while the feeding had made her keener mentally, she had no illusions that her thinking was infallible.

What was happening inside her right now? As a doctor of medicine, she would love to know. Katie, in studying those samples of Zane's blood ten years ago, had theorized that phages might have specialized tissue in their stomachs which transformed the blood of a feeding into the remarkable energy barrier around Zane's blood cells—a barrier impervious to all chemical reagents and even to the huge dose of radiation thrown at it by an electron microscope, making the cells impossible to analyze. The only thing Katie had found to penetrate that barrier was a specific fraction of blood from her patient with progeria, the disease that caused accelerated aging. What a fascinating symmetry—rare humans who aged too fast and others who barely aged at all.

Katie kept quiet about what she found, Jenn thought, but the normals almost got another shot at us, thanks to Brad and Fortis Wayne.

February 12: Yesterday, Mom and I went to the bookstore and I got this book, The Secret Princess, *and I read it last night under the covers with the flashlight. It was great. I feel just like that girl who didn't know her father was a king, but always felt she was more than a commoner. Wouldn't it be wonderful if I really were a princess? Of course, I'd bring Mom and Daddy to the castle with me, and my father the king would be grateful to them for taking care of me, and would make them rich and happy, and we'd all be to-gether. . . .*

The scrawled sentiments brought a sad smile to Jenn's face. I was prescient, she thought, but I didn't have it quite right.

Putting the diary back in the drawer, Jenn changed into her white ducks and blouse and left for work early. She wanted to give herself plenty of time before rounds for Caroline, just in case. She was basically optimistic, though. Four hours on the respirator should have started to make a difference.

But when she reached Caroline's room, her hopes faded. The bluish tinge had not left the girl's skin—if anything it was worse. Despite the steady clicks and sighs of the respirator, Caroline clearly was still not drawing enough oxygen through the congested tissues of her lungs. Beneath her closed eyelids, the humps of her corneas were rolled up and unmoving. In fact, there was no movement in her at all, except for the forced rise and fall of her chest. Her utter stillness made Jenn's heart sink. Gone were Caroline's restless fidgets, the uncomfortable squirming caused by the constant pain in her joints. To lie this still, she must have sunk into unconsciousness.

Jenn tried to take her pulse; the beat was so feeble she could barely feel it, so she used Influence to get a better reading. The rhythm was fast and thready. She did not need to page through the chart for the latest blood gas figures.

You're losing her.

Fiercely, she resisted the thought. Losing wasn't the same as lost— the pneumonia might still yield to the powerful drugs. "I'm here, Caroline," she said. "I won't give up, and you mustn't either."

The bumps under the girl's eyelids crept down, and Jenn realized the pupils would be focused on her if the lids were open. It was eerie— Caroline clearly was unconscious, but on some level still responding to her. Jenn forced warmth and confidence into her voice: "I'm going to call your dad. He'll be right here at your bedside. Don't give up, sweetheart, don't give up."

Caroline's eyes, beneath their lids, held a second longer, then rolled back up. Jenn felt a desperate urgency to do something—something more. If only she could transfer to the girl some of the strength and vitality she was feeling now. Frustrated, she did what she could, making sure the sheathed wires of the heart monitor weren't tangled and that the dextrose IV was secure in Caroline's arm. Then she went to the nurses' station and called Jack Osborne. His receptionist said he was not in the office, so she dialed his home and he answered at once, his voice thin with fear. Her throat tightened in sympathy. "Mr. Osborne, this is Dr. Hrluska. I wanted to let you know that I've suspended normal visiting hours for you. You're free to be with Caroline as much as you like."

"Is she—"

"She's hanging in there. Just remember to scrub and take the normal precautions."

" 'Hanging in there'—what does that mean, exactly?"

Jenn groped for words of reassurance, then realized that would not be fair. "I'm not encouraged right now," she said, "but things could turn around."

"Doctor, you have to save her. She's all I've got."

"I'm doing my best. Don't give up hope—I haven't."

"I'll be right in," he said and hung up.

For a moment, Jenn stood at the station, too depressed to move. With an effort, she rallied herself. She was doing everything possible for Caroline, and she had other patients. Rounds would begin in just a few minutes, and she'd have to cram any new admissions assigned to her into a morning schedule that was already too full. On top of that, there was a teaching conference on anorexia at noon, which she was supposed to attend.

And I have to go see Brad, she realized.

That prospect made her feel even more depressed. Even if Zane had made sure Brad never saw him last night, Influence couldn't blot out hearing or touch. Brad had been in no shape to make it into her apartment without help. Despite his befuddlement, he might have been dimly aware of Zane's hands on his arms, someone steadying him as he walked in, a grip he could feel but not see. She had to make sure he did not remember any of those things.

Phoning the medical floor, Jenn learned that Brad had been transferred to the Mental Health Unit. God, should she be relieved or alarmed? They might have put him there simply to keep him from trying again. Or he might have started saying "crazy" things about an invisible man cutting his wrists. She needed to know.

When finally she got a break, it was almost two. She hurried through the gerbil run into the main building, and from there to the annex that housed psychiatry. Ringing the bell, she waited almost a minute for an orderly to come unlock the door. As she stepped through into the short entry hall, she felt a qualm in her stomach. She hated this place—the locked doors, the wire mesh on the windows, the constant, obvious watchfulness of the staff. She followed the orderly through the entry hall into the large commons area. A patient and another orderly were playing Ping-Pong at a table near the center, neither of them moving much, sending the ball back and forth with torpid clacks. Two patients stood at the pool table, studying the arrangement of the balls with the disinterested patience of the depressed. Others sat in the islands of chairs scattered around the commons, reading magazines or gazing into space. Though it was still day, everything had the jaundiced tint of artificial light, since the patient rooms which ringed the commons cut it off from any windows. The warm air itself seemed anxious.

Jenn followed the orderly to the glassed-in nurses' station that surveyed the ward like an airport's control tower. A stout young nurse with big shoulders and an intent face sat at the counter, writing chart notes. Her name tag read Rilla Rhodes, RN. Jenn introduced herself and asked about Brad.

"Dr. Hrluska," Rilla said reflectively. "Oh yes—you brought Dr. Dietz in last night, didn't you?"

"That's right. We work together."

Rilla shook her head grimly. "Four units of blood got him back on the beam physically, but he's pretty confused."

"Really?"

"Sleeps a lot. When he's awake, he can't remember the past two days. He claims to have no idea how his wrists got cut."

Jenn felt so relieved she almost smiled. "Does he seem depressed?"

"Oh, sure, but you'd expect that, wouldn't you, with a suicide attempt."

"Would you mind if I had a look at his chart?"

The nurse looked uncomfortable. "I don't know. If you had been called in on a medical consult, but you being a friend of his, I really shouldn't even be talking about it."

"May I visit him for a few moments?"

"Sure. He's in Room 31. But don't be surprised if he doesn't say much. He ought to be grateful, you saving his life and all, but A, he can't remember and B, suicides aren't always glad when someone bails them out."

"I understand." On the way to Brad's room, Jenn's relief faded a little. Something was odd here. It made sense that Brad, as dazed as he'd been, wouldn't remember last night, but two days?

The shades in Brad's room had been drawn, steeping everything in gloom. The only light came from the bathroom door, which stood open an inch; Jenn's retinas adjusted at once, taking up the available light and turning the room bright as day. Brad gazed toward her.

"Hi, it's Jenn."

He shifted in his bed, revealing wrists thick with bandages. As she moved closer, she was chilled by his empty expression.

"How are you feeling, Brad?"

He groaned and turned away.

"They say you can't remember the past couple of days."

"I'm finished," he mumbled. "They'll never take me back on peds after this." He rolled his head back toward her. "I didn't try to kill myself. I wouldn't do that."

No, you certainly wouldn't. The wrists you tried to cut, professionally, were mine. "If you didn't do it, who did?"

"They tell me you found me."

"You called," she said. "You didn't sound too good, so I came over."

"I didn't sound too good? What do you mean?"

Jenn shrugged.

"Did you see anyone else when you came?"

"Nope. Just you." Tuning into his blood flow, she tried to feel her way past the raw pulse at his wrists and throat. The familiar veins and arteries of the brain stem came to her quickly, but the blood vessels of the brain itself, screened by constant neural "noise," were beyond Influence and hard, even, to detect. For a moment, she could not find her way through the noise, and then she caught the murmur of blood in the brain itself. There seemed to be a disruption in it, an odd ripple in the circling flow of blood, as though someone had placed a rock in the middle of a shallow stream, changing the pattern and sound of the current. The temperature in the room seemed to drop suddenly, raising goose bumps on Jenn's arms.

Had Zane done this?

The thought both chilled and awed her. According to Merrick,

Zane *did* have the ability to project Influence beyond the brain stem into the brain itself. That's how he almost beat Merrick ten years ago, increasing blood flow in a capillary in Merrick's temporal area, which caused him to be overwhelmed by a memory. Like those experiments where they stimulate neurons with tiny electrodes and people relive memories, only Zane was using Influence instead of an electrode. Merrick said he lost all sense of what was going on around him—Zane got him almost tied up in cable before he was able to break free.

And now Brad, but something more permanent. Jenn's awe deepened. What power Zane must have, what control to be able not just to locate the source of Brad's immediate memories but to exert Influence there. It made sense that blood flow would concentrate at the sites of the most recent neural activity. Zane must have detected that flow and struck there, squeezing the capillaries down until the neurons in each microscopic area died from lack of blood. Jenn shuddered, feeling not just the majesty but the cruelty of what Zane had done. He'd given Brad a stroke. The doctors here had missed the diagnosis, but it was easy to understand why. The listlessness and forgetfulness of a temporal lobe stroke were also key symptoms of depression. And since Brad showed no aphasia or paralysis, none of the impairment common to a broader stroke affecting the brain's speech or motor areas, his doctors had seen what they expected to see in a suicide: depression.

"Tell them," Brad whispered. "You know me. Tell them I'd never try to kill myself."

Jenn could not meet his gaze. "I have to go."

He gave a bitter laugh. "That's right. I almost forgot that, too—how much you hate me."

"I don't hate you, Brad."

But he had closed his eyes.

The pettiness of it brought back all her resentment. She wished she had never met him. Even in his sick bed, with his wrists slashed and no memory of why, Brad Dietz was dangerous. She could feel it. His overall memory was unaffected. As soon as he could pull himself together and convince them he wasn't suicidal, he'd be out of here, and he'd take his paranoia about her with him. He could end up trying to point the finger at her again, and this time the charge wouldn't be drug use but attempted murder.

Zane was right. I should have let him die.

She tried to reject the thought, but it clung with frightening force. *Zane is changing me.* She felt a surge of panic. *I'm not like this . . .*

But I am.

Jenn looked away from Brad, afraid suddenly of what she might do. The urge to kill him was planted in her, fused with her genes. All Zane had done was pass it on to her genetically—and all she had to do now was stop fighting it. It was there last night, every time she fed—the urge to kill. Could biochemicals be so much more powerful than rational thought? She had willed herself not to kill, but her will seemed so weak— and growing weaker.

Jenn left Brad's room without saying good-bye, afraid even to look at him again.

⟡

She stayed at the hospital until nearly seven, finding things to do well after she'd finished her duties. Throwing herself into work seemed to lighten her mood, even though she felt so gloomy about Caroline. There was no change in her—still unconscious and cyanotic, but holding on. Before Jenn left, she made the night intern promise to keep close watch and call her at once if there was any change.

In the parking lot, she stood a moment, dragging the cool air into her lungs, as if Caroline's battle to breathe had infected her. At seven no trace of daylight was left, but the dark sky had a touch of very deep green in it, one of the rarer colors of darkness and quite beautiful. In contrast, the cars gleamed coldly under the lights of the parking lot.

"Jenn—over here."

Following the voice, she saw Hugh sitting astride his Harley, one arm outstretched to lean on her car. At once, her spirits lifted. They hadn't agreed to meet but he was just what she needed. With a wave, she hurried to him. He leaned toward her for a kiss. Conscious of the windows of the hospital rising behind her, she made it a quick one.

"Want to take a ride?" he asked.

"Where to?"

"Not far. I want to show you something."

He seemed subdued. She wondered if he might be miffed at her for not staying with him at the hotel. No, that wasn't like him.

"What about my car?"

"I'll bring you back." He produced her helmet from one of the bike's saddlebags. "Come on. How bad could it be? You'll get to hug me on the way."

"What makes you think anyone would want to hug you?" she said, but she drew the helmet down over her hair and slid onto the bike behind Hugh. Wrapping her arms around him, she leaned her head against his back and savored the hard feel of him beneath the leather jacket. The bike throbbed to life, the old muffler giving out an animal growl as Hugh wheeled around corners and sped along back streets. When he reached Wisconsin Avenue, he turned south, and she decided he was heading for Georgetown, but then he slowed and turned in at the National Cathedral and at once she felt uneasy. This was where, ten years ago, it had all started, the heart-rending duel to the death between Zane and Merrick that had not ended in death after all. What could Hugh want to show her here?

He coasted to a stop on the south drive near the front of the cathedral. The twin towers of Peter and Paul soared up above her, the stone glowing like white gold in the spotlights at their base. Above them, the black sky roiled with the green undertones she had seen earlier, making her think of a sea awash in oil. Dizzied, she looked down again as Hugh pulled free and got off the bike. He stood gazing at the foot of the south tower, and her foreboding deepened. She was sorry she'd come. Sliding off the bike, she stood beside him. "What is it, Hugh?"

"One night ten years ago," he said, "during a fierce windstorm, a priest came out and took a turn around the cathedral to make sure the stained glass windows were all right. The wind was so savage it blew his hat into that box elder bush, right there behind the flank of the tower. He chased it down, and when he bent to pick it up, he saw a body lying under the bush." Hugh was watching her closely as he talked. She felt almost nauseous.

"Do you know about that murder, Jenn?"

With an effort, she hid her consternation, the sudden fear boiling in her stomach. Of course she knew, but how could Hugh wonder that, knowing she'd have been only twelve? He'd have been only eighteen himself, the year he'd taken up with his moonshining uncle. What was it to him, this old horror, this sickening piece of everything she feared most? The victim was a woman, she thought. The grand-niece of the British ambassador. She'd gone jogging, and Zane killed her.

But what do I say to Hugh?

Anxiety vibrated through her; she kept it from her face. "You brought me here to talk about a murder?"

He gazed at her. "You do know about it, don't you?"

"Hugh, what is this? You're acting strangely. I'm not sure I like it."

His face softened. "I'm sorry. But this is important to me."

"What makes you think I'd know anything about this murder?"

Hugh took off his helmet, dropped it in the grass, and pulled a hand along his hair. She knew she was frustrating him, but he was scaring her. "When we talked about your father the other night," he said, "you mentioned that he came through town ten years ago—that's when you found out he was your father, because he told you. You also said he was a murderer—"

"Wait. I didn't say that."

"Not exactly, but you implied it."

Jenn's stomach churned. She should never have talked about Zane— But how had Hugh made the connection?

"What are you implying—that my father is the killer? That's crazy, straight out of nowhere."

"Not if your real father revealed himself to you while you were in the hospital and you then confided that to Merrick Chapman."

"Merrick." Her heart sank.

"Yes. He was the homicide lieutenant in charge of that case, and he kept coming around to see you in the hospital, didn't he, right while he was investigating the murder?"

"Hugh!" She tried to act indignant, but now she was terrified. Why had he been digging into this? "Merrick didn't come around to see just me, he visited the pediatric ward of the hospital regularly as part of a police outreach program. He did magic tricks for the sick kids. I just happened to be one of them."

"But you've been friends with him ever since."

"Sure. So what? He's a kind and caring man. He helped me through a difficult time, so I've kept in touch with him."

"When did your father approach you?"

"After I got out of the hospital—quite a bit later," she lied without hesitation. "So I couldn't have confided anything about my father to Merrick during the investigation even if he and I were as close then as you're assuming. Hugh, you're interrogating me, and I don't like it. What's this all about? Why do you care?"

"Jenn, I need your help, and I don't think you're being totally honest with me. You've more than just kept in touch with Merrick. His wife and he put you through medical school. You go to their house at least a couple of times a week. In fact, you have a key to their front door."

Suddenly, anger swept away her fear. "You've been *spying* on me? And you accuse me of not being honest—"

He sank into a squat, arms along his knees, staring at the ground. "I'm sorry," he said in a low voice. "I'm ashamed of what I've done, but I'm fighting for my life."

She saw tears in his eyes, and it melted her anger. Kneeling beside him, she took his arms and drew him up again. "Hugh, what is it? Tell me."

He swallowed and looked past her at the cathedral. The fear in his face raised a fresh dread in her. "I didn't just bring you here to grill you," he said, "but to come clean myself, and ask for your forgiveness."

"Maybe you should have started with that."

"Yes." He took a deep breath. "All right. When I came to the hospital saying I wanted to interview a doctor, that was bull. I wanted to meet you specifically, because I'd been watching Merrick's house and I'd seen you coming and going a lot."

Jenn suppressed a groan. This was disaster. Had he seen them go out to feed, followed them maybe? She wanted to run away now, before he could say anything else. But she said, "Why were you watching Merrick's house?"

"I was really spying on Merrick, not you, but when I saw how much you were with him, I decided I needed to meet you, too. I thought maybe you could help me get to him. But that was before I started falling for you—which happened almost at once. As soon as I realized it, I gave up any thought of using you to find out about Merrick. But when you talked about your father the other night, I realized you might know more than I thought, and it wasn't just your odd connection to Merrick anymore—"

"Know more about *what?*"

He hesitated, looking away. "Those murders ten years ago. The one here and the other two attributed to the same killer. I've studied them, learned everything I could. The killer was never caught."

"But why would you need me to introduce you to Merrick? Why not just go up and introduce yourself and say you're a writer and you want to ask him about the murders ten years ago?"

Hugh gave a threadbare laugh. "I could have, and I should have— long ago. The fact is, you were a way of stalling. I was having trouble screwing up my nerve to approach Merrick, and when I saw you coming and going there, I got interested in you."

"Why would you be scared of Merrick?" she asked, dreading the answer.

"Not of Merrick, of what he might tell me."

"About the murders?"

"Yes. I . . . I'm afraid the killer might be me."

"Hugh!" She stared at him, astonished, not knowing whether to laugh in relief or weep for him. How long had he tormented himself with this absurd notion? "How could you kill someone and not know it?" she said. "If you've made such a study of these murders, you must know where you were when they happened, what you were doing."

"No. The week when the three murders happened is gone from my mind. The whole week is a blank."

She stared at him, afraid again. "You lost an entire week of your life?"

"Yes. I was working with my uncle Tydus. It was just before he was shot. Maybe he could have told me where I was, what I was doing that week, but he's dead. I was with him. He'd sent me out to find a new site for a still, and then nothing for a week. When my memory picks up again, I'm standing in the door of his cabin, looking at his corpse. For all I know I, not one of his rivals, killed him."

She took his hands. They were very cold. "Hugh, no. You are not a murderer. I have never been so sure of anything. Just because you have a blank period in your memory—"

"There's more," he said flatly. "I dream about the murdered women. And sometimes it happens when I'm awake, which means it's not really a dream but a memory—"

"Or a hallucination."

He gave her a wan smile. "I'd give anything if I could know you are right."

"You're not crazy, and you're not a killer either."

He closed his eyes. "I'm in a car with one of them, and the knife is in my hand. It happened again last night. It was so real, her lying there, blood all over her shirt. And on me." He broke off with a shudder.

She pulled him to her, holding him, torn between the desire to help him and her own fear. She had the answer he needed. She knew who had done the murders, but he would not be content if she merely told him it was Zane. He would investigate, probe, try to prove it for himself. He was smart and resourceful with the most powerful of motivations. If he got to the truth, it would affect much more than just his life and hers. Right now, to stay hidden, most phages fed carefully, only when they needed to, hiding behind missing person statistics or covering their tracks the way Merrick had covered Zane's the other night, with faked auto accidents, fires, and the like. If anything happened to drag phages into the open, the careful harvesting would be replaced by a bloodbath. Panic would spread around the world. Thousands, hundreds of thousands, would die.

No, however much it hurt her to see Hugh suffer like this, she must keep quiet.

Hugh looked at her again. "Jenn, do you forgive me?"

"Of course," she said. She hugged him to her, feeling ashamed, knowing it was she who should ask for forgiveness. "I wish I could help you," she said softly. "You're not a murderer, Hugh. I know you too well. Have faith in yourself. There's some other reason for these dreams, maybe nothing at all. Those novels you write—maybe they overstimulate your imagination . . ."

"The novels don't cause the imagination," Hugh said. "The imagination, the *dreams,* cause the novels."

"Hugh . . ." Jenn stopped, startled, as she saw Zane over Hugh's shoulder, walking toward them up the slope on the other side of the south drive. She held Hugh to her, terrified he might turn around. Zane crossed the road and walked noiselessly up to them. She stared at him, frozen in fear for Hugh. He circled behind her. What was he doing—looking at Hugh's face? Hugh did not react, and she realized Zane was using Influence to remove his image. An instant later, Hugh went utterly limp and sagged against her. Panic welled up in her, and then she realized his breathing and blood flow were still normal. Clinging to him, holding him up, she said, "What are you *doing?*"

Zane moved back into her field of vision, and she saw that his eyes were wide with shock. "Is this man your lover?"

"No," she said.

He stared at her. "Don't lie to me. I can see it in your face. You've got to get rid of him—"

"Go to hell!"

Zane's eyes closed for a moment. When he opened them again, they held a fierce urgency. "Jenn, please, *listen.* This man is a great danger to you. Get rid of him, or I'll have to do it for you."

15

Christiana Clark was bursting with anticipation. It was a feeling she'd not had for some time and she intended to relish it. Spreading the notes and tapes she'd accumulated about Jenn across her big coffee table, she kicked off her high heels, skinned away her pantyhose, and wriggled her toes with relief. She settled cross-legged on the floor and leaned back against the padded flank of the sofa. The first chill sip of Château Ste. Michelle chardonnay tasted wonderful. Two swallows more, and the velvety, oaken tang of the wine began to soothe away the ring of tension at the top of her throat. Beyond the coffee table, the picture window overlooking the Potomac delivered her cherished view of the Kennedy Center and Watergate. The setting sun was giving the white walls of the concert hall and opera house a bloody glow.

Ignoring the stuff she'd gathered today, Christiana instead picked up the *USA Today* article from three years ago and peered at the photo. It raised an eerie tingle between her shoulder blades. Jenn Hrluska had been nineteen then, but there was something so knowing in her eyes. That gaze—direct, almost challenging—and the mouth caught your eye, too, so composed for someone barely a woman. That's why she had looked familiar at Hugh McCall's party, this photo. Christiana was impressed with herself. Pure happenstance that she'd seen this photo to begin with, probably either lying around the *Times* newsroom or somewhere on the road. But pulling it from memory three years later was pretty sharp. Of course, if, while talking with Hugh, she hadn't looked out the window and seen what Jenn had done, it wouldn't have become so important to remember. And I'd probably sleep a lot better tonight, she thought.

But who wants to sleep better? I'm hooked.

She spread on the table the photocopy she'd retrieved from the microfilm reader. MED STUDENT RESCUES TODDLER. *Ten minutes under the ice without coming up for air.* A sudden rash of goose bumps made Christiana shiver. When she'd first read it, she could remember thinking, "Wow, amazing!" She also remembered thinking there had to be more to the story than the *USA Today* reporter had uncovered in his shallow take. But at the time she'd been so heavily on the make for a spot on "DomeWatch," she'd just let it slide.

That was before she'd seen pretty Dr. Hrluska sail a grown man like a paper airplane.

She scanned the article. It described how the cold had actually helped save the toddler, triggering a spooky neurological reaction called the mammalian diving reflex, which had been discovered in earlier cases of infants and children revived after being submerged in cold water. Evidently the reflex worked by putting the deeply unconscious child into a sort of cryogenic shut-down in which the brain and vital organs could survive for perhaps half an hour on residual oxygen. But Jenn, diving into frigid water after that child, had been an adult, and anything but unconscious. Okay, you might find air between the ice and water, but what about the cold? If you fell into freezing water, you'd grow numb and go under in a minute.

Maybe the witnesses were wrong and it had been less than ten minutes. Or there was a freak warmer current that had enabled her to keep moving. Maybe, maybe. Maybe she'd thrown that mugger thirty feet because she'd had a world-class surge of adrenaline or he had light bones, or gravity had taken a sudden vacation.

"No, I don't think so," Christiana said aloud.

Then what?

Looking up, Christiana watched the Kennedy Center fade to gray, then blaze white as its floodlights lit. She ignored the tape recorder at a bottom corner of her vision, not quite ready to push "play." She'd done well in only a day, finding one of the doctor's classmates from middle school and a close friend from her high school. Her excuse for prying had worked like a charm. Neither woman had had any trouble believing Jenn would be included in a "Where Are They Now?" article on exceptional children. And the doctor was impressive, no question about it. Hrluska had sped through Thomas Jefferson, Arlington's high school for brainy science types, in two years. Straight A's, and she'd managed to find time for sports and parties, too, though only fourteen at graduation. A very mature fourteen, both physically and mentally, from what the interviewee had said.

But that was the least of it.

Christiana pushed "play" and out came the husky voice of Elaine Breslin, who'd gotten more talkative with each cup of black coffee as the two of them sat at a white table in Breslin's retro-modern kitchen: "You never thought of Jenn being younger than you," Breslin said. "She was tall and well filled out, smart of course, and not the giggly type at all. TJ takes a certain number of kids who are streaking, age-wise—Jenn wasn't even the youngest when I was there. But she had the poise, the look of an upperclassman almost from the day she walked in."

Listening now, Christiana could hear even more plainly the respect in Breslin's voice. And this was not a woman who impressed easily. Elaine's house, in the richest part of McLean, had been a marvel, probably six bedrooms, pool out back, and no sign of a husband. Only three years out of college herself, and Elaine was running her own consulting firm. What would it have been like to go to a school like Jefferson, where you were already among the anointed, instead of overcrowded Midwood in decaying Brooklyn? With a start like Elaine's and Jenn's, Christiana thought, I could have been Harvard instead of Kingsborough.

But then I wouldn't have had to spend three years monitoring the police band and trying to push my way past flatfoots at crime scenes. My most exciting three years ever.

"She was good-looking then?" Christiana heard herself ask.

"Good-looking? Hey, I'm not exactly Phil Graham in drag, but if I'd looked that good, I'd have been hard to live with, you know? Jenn was very easy to live with. She wasn't nicey-nice, but she was pleasant to everybody. . . . Well, almost everybody."

"Tell me about that."

"Well, there was this guy, Bobby Sequist. He was a stud—people think all smart guys are pencil-necks with taped glasses and factory-fresh blue jeans, but I can tell you they're not. Bobby was big, broad-shoul-dered, a star fullback, and a whiz at chemistry. A lot of us had our eye on him, but from the day Jenn came, he set his sights on her. He tried every way he knew to get Jenn to tumble, but she kept putting him off politely. Looking back, maybe she felt uncomfortable being just fourteen, which other people kept forgetting. At the time, the rest of us were green with envy, couldn't understand it at all. Then one day I guess Bobby got frustrated and annoyed at being put off. We were in the hall milling around between classes. I had become friends with Jenn by this time and we were talking. Over her shoulder, I see Bobby slipping up behind her. He has this intent look. When he's right behind her, he reaches around and gives her breast a squeeze—I couldn't believe it! A second later, Jenn's arm blurs and the next thing I know, Bobby's lying on the floor, holding his arm and writhing. Somehow, Jenn's broken both bones of his forearm. She was really upset, trying to help him up, apologizing, whereas I'm like, 'Serves you right, creep.' Needless to say, Bobby never looks at Jenn again."

"You say Jenn's arm blurred?"

"I never saw anyone move so fast in my life, before or since. It was uncanny."

Listening to the tape hiss silently, Christiana felt the same flutter in her stomach she'd felt the first time.

"Ever see her do anything else like that?"

"No. The girls' wrestling coach tried to get her to join the team, but she wouldn't. In gym class, she stayed away from things like weights. But you should have seen her run. She was fast and smooth, really well coordinated. I think she had second best time on the forty-meter dash, and she looked like she was just loping along."

"Second best?"

"Yeah. Believe it or not, I was the best."

Because she liked you.

"What was her home life like, do you know?"

"Not really. I sort of remember her mom from when we had the class play and she helped out with the costumes. A pretty woman, blond like Jenn. The two of them seemed close." Another pause. "But there *was* this sad quality to Jenn sometimes, as though she had a secret burden, something she carried around with her and never let anyone see. I'd tell my troubles to her, never the other way around. If I tried to get into her stuff, she'd let me in a little, then start me laughing about something else.

"Only later would I realize I never did find out what was bugging her. If anything. I mean, why would she be sad? She had everything going for her. And from what I hear, she's really kept it going, a doctor and all. Did you know she saved a kid from drowning three years ago?"

"Yes."

"When I read about that, I thought it was so great, so . . . *Jenn*. A genuine hero."

There was no irony, and only the slightest envy in Breslin's voice. Christiana shut the tape recorder off. Bright, beautiful, nice, an M.D., and a hero. Was Dr. Jenn Hrluska something else, too? The offspring of some ultra-secret experiment in selective breeding, maybe. Or pumped up on steroids and mind-sharpening drugs, or . . .

Christiana's imagination failed her. High school in two years, college in three. Tall and well developed at thirteen. Brilliant. Strong—*very* strong, and very fast. Highly resistant to cold. Possibly able to hold her breath for *ten* minutes. . . .

Christiana felt a low, pleasant buzz of excitement. What was she dealing with here? She didn't know yet, but she was going to find out.

⚜

Merrick was playing the eighth invention of J. S. Bach, savoring its simplicity and the way the near perfect two-part round fitted together, when he became aware of someone behind him. Not a sound, but that peculiar itch at the roots of his eyes he'd used to get, and still would if he'd just fed. Then he caught a faint whiff of her, the familiar, fresh-cut apple smell, and he finished the piece. "Can you tell me where the round breaks down?" he asked without turning.

"Measure eight," Jenn answered behind him. "Bach had to cheat a little or it would have sounded wrong. 'Row, Row, Row Your Boat,' it's not."

"Are you teasing me?" Merrick swiveled around on the bench, smiling.

"Only a little."

"Measure eight, correct. Very good for someone who can barely carry a tune."

She shrugged. "It's audible math—you can't miss it. That would have been Bach's real genius. He should have become a mathematician and left the composing to Fred Handel."

It was how they'd used to joust, a pleasant game they'd discovered years ago, and Merrick wanted to carry this one on a little further, but he could see she was upset. She'd come for a reason. He said, "It's good to see you."

She came over and gave him a peck, then sat on the couch, facing him. "Where are Gregory and Katie?"

"Gregory's in his bedroom on the phone with one of his feminine admirers and Katie's in St. Louis. A symposium." No point in telling her what Katie was really doing. If she succeeded in bringing back enough progeria blood for a concentrated dose of Fraction Eight, then there'd be the time to share that burden with Jenn, not before.

"Miss her?" Jenn asked.

"You bet. But let's talk about you. Something's bothering you. Have you seen Zane again?"

She nodded. "But before I tell you about that, there's something more. I don't know how to start."

He waited, filled with foreboding. What could be more than Zane coming at her again?

"I should have told you this before . . ."

All of a sudden, looking at her face, he was struck by an intuition. "You're in love!"

Her eyes widened. "How do you *do* that?"

He stared at her, still flabbergasted, then jumped from the bench as delight took him over. He'd been hoping for this for years. Loving a normal, more than anything he could ever say or do, would save her, as it had saved him. And with Zane back, she needed all the salvation she could find. "This is wonderful," he said. "Who is he? When can I meet him?"

"Slow down, Merrick."

He'd been about to hug her; instead he settled on the piano bench.

"His name is Hugh McCall," she said.

"The novelist!"

"Yes. But listen: Hugh and I were at the National Cathedral today, and that's when I saw Zane."

Merrick's heart went cold. "At the *cathedral?*"

"Yes. I don't know what Zane was trying to do, but he seemed surprised when he saw Hugh's face—surprised and afraid. It was almost as if he already knew Hugh, and never expected to find us together. But it doesn't make sense. Why would he know Hugh, unless he'd seen us together earlier—in which case he wouldn't be surprised."

Merrick was baffled, too.

"As soon as he saw Hugh," Jenn said, "he put him under. I guess he did it so he could speak to me without being heard. So he could make his threat—'This man is a great danger to you,' or words to that effect. Then he threatened that I must get rid of Hugh or he would. And before I could get any more out of him, he took off. Fortunately, Hugh had only been out a couple of seconds and didn't even realize it."

"What were you doing at the cathedral in the first place?"

"Hugh took me there. He's obsessed with the murders ten years ago, but not because of Zane. He has some notion that he may have done them."

"What?" Merrick listened with consternation as she told him about Hugh's missing week, his murderous dreams, memories of being in a car with the corpse. "Is there any doubt in your mind," she asked, "that my father did those killings?"

"None." He saw her relief in the way her shoulders relaxed.

"That's what I thought. I just wish there was some way to tell Hugh that."

"But you know you can't."

"Oh, I hate this!"

Merrick went to her, knowing the time for the hug had come. He held her, patting her back, searching for words to soothe her and finding none.

"How could Hugh possibly be a danger to me?" Jenn said, her voice muffled against his shoulder.

"Maybe Zane's afraid you'll slip up and reveal yourself to him. As I've told you, he does consider it dangerous to form attachments to normals—our 'prey,' as he thinks of them. He despised me for doing it. If only he had let himself love or even like one, things could have been so different."

Jenn pulled back and gave him a questioning look. "You've said this before, that Zane couldn't love, but how can you be so sure? Maybe he did love a normal."

"Not that I'm aware—not after I gave him blood and he became a phage."

"What about other phages?"

"That I don't know."

Jenn continued to study him. "And what about you?"

"Sandeman was my friend, even after I started burying other phages."

"What sorts of things did you and he do? Where did you go?"

"Restaurants."

She laughed. "Restaurants!"

"Sandeman loved to eat out. We also discussed books, philosophy. We went to plays. But this was only every few years. We also went years without seeing each other."

"Why?"

"He was Russian by birth and lived mostly there, in various cities, where there was never a shortage of bad guys for him to prey on—first under the Tsars and then under Stalin. I lived mostly in Britain and Europe. Before the trains, it was a very long ride between us, coach or horseback."

"If you liked him so much, why didn't you just settle near him?"

"Because we'd have been working the same kill zone. You have to remember, in the early years of our friendship, I was a killer as surely as Sandeman. I managed to avoid it much of the time by staying close to the current war, which in those days was never far away in England and Scotland. I'd walk the battlefields after dark, find those who were in pain and dying. . . ." Merrick paused, pulled down by what he was saying. Jenn was gazing at him with a mixture of sympathy and dread that made him uncomfortable. "My point is," he said, "that it's hard to have a relationship with another phage. Certain realities tend to keep our paths from crossing. We're so rare that we're generally born and raised apart from each other. Looking like healthy normal humans, we don't recognize each other if we pass in the street. If I used Influence around another phage, that would trip the alarm, but how often would that happen by chance?"

Jenn's expression had turned wistful. "It's sad, don't you think? Lions have prides and we don't even know each other."

"Lions have their own society because they don't mind spooking the zebras—it's how they hunt. If you must compare us to animals, leopards are a better example. They depend, as phages do, on stealth, and they, like phages, are loners."

"So we have no society? Not even small groups, in secret?"

Merrick hesitated. For years he'd been dreading this question, but it came as no surprise that she'd finally asked it. *And if you have to lie to keep her from danger, then you have become a danger, too.* "Before Zane was born," he said, "before I began to hunt other phages, some of us who had managed to identify each other would meet every so often at remote castles, protected places in the woods."

Jenn perked up. "Really? What would you do when you met?"

"Talk, socialize. There was music, we showed each other our paintings, our manuscripts, gave each other an audience—the applause and admiration we dared not seek from normals. Fame of any kind is a curse to us, following us when we move, but we gave each other small doses of it within our circle. We also met to bring each other up to date on what was happening in our current home countries. Sometimes one or another of us had formed temporary relationships with unwitting normals, people with extraordinary talent who became, in a sense, protégés. For example, one of our group was a gifted painter who, because of the things he said to Cézanne and his contemporaries, helped found Impressionism."

"And you," Jenn said. "You planted the idea of blood transfusion, after you'd discovered how to do it."

"That was well after I'd begun hunting other phages. Even if I'd still been with the group, they'd have disapproved of my sharing the idea of transfusion, because it was science. All of us foresaw hundreds of years ago that scientific applications would eventually be a threat to us, and that is now a fact—especially video cameras, which we can't blind with Influence."

"It sounds like your phage friends were good people," Jenn said wistfully.

"We were all killers."

"But enlightened enough to give something back for what you took. After you started hunting phages, did you go after any of the group?"

"No, my dear." Merrick looked at her, dismayed. *Does she think I have no heart at all?*

"I didn't mean to offend you."

"No, I should have told you these things before, and helped you to understand."

"Were there women in the group?"

"A few. As you know, you are rare among the rare."

Her expression turned almost mischievous. "Did you ever pair off with a female phage during your gatherings?"

Merrick saw Arlana in his mind—Arlana, wearing her prized gown of Chinese silk, which she had to keep hidden when she returned to an Edinburgh as yet unaware of such fabrics. He remembered them sitting, alone except for each other, in the great hall of the castle. The Marquis de Lucientes had taken his other guests on a midnight ride on the magnificent stallions he had found in Arabia. Merrick knew he should have gone with them, but Arlana had waved him over to the fire, and without thinking he had joined her. . . .

She was sitting on an ottoman made of Damascus leather dyed in alternate wedges of black and cadmium yellow. He took one of the wooden benches a few feet away, drawn by her beauty, but determined not to let it fully into his awareness. The fire danced in reflection along the emerald-colored silk, where her thigh drew it tight. He could not seem to tear his gaze from it. He felt his blood surging down and was powerless to stop it.

"You flatter me," she said.

Looking up, he found her smiling at him, the full lips curved so subtly he could not be sure if she was amused or aroused. A mass of dark red hair spilled onto her shoulders. Her face was a perfect oval, her skin a flawless cream. He could smell the hot silk, the carnal heat of her skin, could imagine the fullness of her breasts against his hands.

She said, "How long since you've had a woman?"

He managed a smile. "Do you think I would feel this only if I had been without for a long time? You do your own attractiveness an injustice."

"But you are going to reject me."

He revised his estimate of her age upward. He had been under the impression she was around two hundred, but she was far too good at reading voice to be so young.

"I'm a fool," he confessed, hoping it would end the conversation.

She shifted on the ottoman, and tongues of reflected flames toured her flat midriff; his fingertips ached to brush the satiny fabric, feel her soft firmness beneath. She studied him. "They tell me you marry normals."

"That's right."

"And that you come here only when you've had to leave one."

He said nothing.

"Your last wife is still alive?"

He thought of Kendra, a thousand miles away, in the cottage in South Wales at the edge of the big lake. She would be asleep now, her gray hair tangled, mouth open in a soft snore. The wrinkles under her jaw, which she kept covered with a neckpiece all day, would be exposed now to the night. His heart twisted in mourning. Did she dream of him, her "dead" husband? He hoped not.

Arlana sighed. "The rumors are true, then. You have left but you are being faithful. Are you Catholic?"

"I practice no religion."

"Then why?"

"My wife is alone in her bed. . . ." His throat locked.

"Yes, I see," Arlana said softly. "But I must tell you, your loyalty to her only makes me desire you all the more."

Without wanting to, he read the blood surging in her nipples and the exquisite folds between her thighs. It was too much to bear. He rose. "I'm afraid you must excuse me."

She gazed up at him, her eyes moist. "You are so beautiful," she said. "When she dies, and you have mourned your last, come find me."

"I will," he said.

But he didn't.

"I'm sorry," Jenn said. "I didn't mean to embarrass you."

He waved a pardoning hand, still half caught in the memory.

She studied him. "You look so sad. Were you remembering one of your wives?"

"Yes," he admitted, impressed. How perceptive she was already. Now if she could only read with equal skill the realities in Zane's face.

"It must have been very hard for you," she said softly. "Falling in love with a normal, knowing you must leave her. When the time came, how did you find the strength to go?"

He knew she was thinking of Hugh now, wondering what she would do when her time came.

"The years of love can outweigh the pain of leaving," he said.

"Yes, but afterward, how could you stand the loneliness, knowing someone you loved was still there, still alive, and all you had to do was go back to her?"

"It was hard," Merrick said. "But I had no choice as time moved on and I didn't age. Going back would have meant being unmasked, not just to my wife but to her community. I would have become Merrick the warlock, Merrick, spawn of the devil, who eats babies and causes cows to abort. My wife would have been forced either to renounce me or be hunted down with me. The only way I could save her would be to kill her friends, whom fear had turned into enemies."

Her eyes turned distant. "Such pain," she murmured.

"Don't think like that," he said. "All love involves pain."

"I think now I understand," Jenn said, "why you want to grow old and die with Katie."

The flatness of her voice worried him. "You're young," he said. "You and Hugh are just beginning. Don't try and guess the future. Forget about pain. When the time comes, you'll be able to take it. But without love, life isn't worth living."

She managed a smile for him. "You are a hopeless romantic, do you know that?"

He could not think what to say. In some strange way, the conversation had gotten beyond him. She seemed so tense, gloomy. She's worried about Hugh, he thought. Not her future, but right now. She's afraid of what Zane might do to him. "I think Hugh is safe, for now," he said. "If Zane knows you love him, he won't risk alienating you at this point—"

"It's not only that," Jenn said.

"Then what?"

"The way Zane reacted to him. Fear, Merrick, not some generalized worry about the theoretical danger of loving normals, but real fear. I could see it in his eyes. I keep thinking about Hugh's horrible dreams, the memories. His missing a week out of his life—that's fact, and what I keep wondering is might he be missing more?"

"I don't follow."

Jenn's hands were tightly clamped together now, her fingers interlaced and twisting against each other. "He's a good man, I know that. I couldn't be wrong about that, I just couldn't, but that only makes it more possible."

All at once, Merrick understood. "You're afraid he might be a phage?"

She hesitated, then nodded.

Merrick got up, troubled, and began to pace as he tried to think it through. "Forgive me for asking this, but have you slept with him?"

She nodded again.

"I mean *slept*, as in he was asleep."

"How could I be sure?"

"By reading his pulse."

"Couldn't he control his own blood flow?"

"Probably." Merrick felt thickheaded. "Have you seen him bleed?"

"No, but that proves nothing."

"Let me get this straight. The blank periods—what are you saying, that he might be a phage and not know it? That he's a split personality?"

"Listen, during my rotation on psychiatry, I had a patient who was three different people, and none of them knew each other. Half the time I thought he was faking, but the longer I was with him, the more convinced I became. The theory is that immense pressure causes the split. Hugh is a good and decent man. If he also had a powerful compulsion to kill and drink blood—if he had our gene, it would be terrifying to him. Those first few months after the change were certainly terrifying to me. I thought I might go crazy under the burden of what I had become, but I had you to help me every step of the way—"

"Wait," Merrick said. "If Hugh is a phage, he had the leukemia. He'd remember that, and it's something that can be checked and verified—"

"Not necessarily," Jenn said. "He might have gotten blood before he became ill enough to be hospitalized. There'd be no record on that, and it might be just one more thing he won't let himself remember. You haven't seen him, Merrick. He's tall, very handsome, magnificent. He could be one of us and not know it. He could be going out at night to kill, and that's where these memories and 'dreams' are coming from. He could be fighting it with denial. He may be dragging out the span between kills, and that could weaken him enough to sleep, for example."

Listening to her, Merrick heard anxiety, and something else, something she was trying to hide from him, and maybe even from herself. Excitement? His heart sank. She could be right about Hugh.

But what was worse, a part of her *wanted* to be right about him.

16

Christiana felt excited as she opened the small top drawer of her jewelry case and removed her lock picks. Holding them gave her a buzz, as though they'd closed a circuit between her fingers. She remembered the last time she'd used them, ten years ago, when they'd gotten her into that high-priced call girl's apartment in Manhattan. There, in a hollow bedpost, she'd found the pictures and negatives the woman had been using to blackmail the mayor. Then, in the deal of a lifetime, she'd quietly taken them to the mayor, and in gratitude, he'd given her an exclusive on his plans to run for governor—which, thanks to her he now was free to do. That scoop had gotten her off the crime beat at the *Times.* No more all-night stakeouts, eating those horrible orange crackers pasted together by peanut butter, no more "no comments" from press-shy police lieutenants. The day she'd joined the political desk, she'd almost thrown the picks away. How odd that she hadn't. Sometimes the back part of your brain knew things the front didn't.

Did she still have the touch?

What kind of lock would Dr. Hrluska's door have?

I'd better practice, first, Christiana thought. At the door to her own apartment, she studied first the lock, then the array of picks. Maybe this thin one with the curved tip? Fanning the others back, she slipped it in. Her fingers turned sweaty as memories of those other times flamed up— the Domingo Bar and Grill at 4 A.M., when she'd failed to find any gambling markers. The warehouse off Tenth Avenue, where she'd done better, two hundred stolen TV sets in mix-and-match factory cartons. On the crime beat, to get the story you often had to make the story. Politicians were a piece of cake and so much duller.

The pick met resistance and she wiggled it, then heard in her mind the voice of Elvis Dicipio, detective first class: *Don't hold on too tight. You squeeze its skinny little lungs and it'll go dead on you. Just give it a twitch, then let it twitch back.* A sweet guy, Elvis, darkly handsome and a good dresser, but a terrible kisser and wantonly dumb about anything not having to do with the Knicks or robbery/homicide.

Relaxing her grip, Christiana gave the pick a gentle push. It jammed on some angle deep within the lock and wouldn't turn. She had to yank to get it out. Trying another pick, this time she closed her eyes. At once, her sense of touch sharpened. She could feel the complex inner caverns of the lock now, the tiny stalactites and stalagmites of tempered steel that blocked her way. Worming the pick through them, she raised it and turned it at the same time and the deadbolt slid open. With a feeling of triumph, Christiana pulled the pick out. It was like riding a bicycle, you never forgot.

A nerve twanged deep in Christiana's stomach. Dear God, was she really going to do this? So much risk. If she got caught, the *Times* would probably fire her. No more "DomeWatch." A huge scandal, probably make the national media.

But thinking of the danger was only pumping her up. She hadn't been this excited since the thing with the mayor.

All the same, Dr. Hrluska might be dangerous—and not just to muggers.

She'll never know I was there.

As Christiana drove from Rosslyn across Roosevelt Bridge and into the city, she went over her plan. Knowing if Jenn was at home would be easy—just look for the little MG in the parking lot, tag number 386dh. If it wasn't there, go up and in. If it was, wait until tomorrow.

But once she was in, then what?

Christiana thought of the favorite places people had for hiding things. Bagged in the freezer, taped to the backs of drawers, down inside heating vents, the back of the toilet, inside books. Every one obvious, but all of them together took time. She'd been in the call girl's place almost an hour before finding the hollow in the bedpost. Soaked with sweat, Christiana remembered, but *I was so intensely* alive.

All right, *what* should I be looking for?

This was harder: birth certificate, medical records—Jenn being a doctor, she might keep copies of tests on herself at home. Letters, particularly personal ones. Photos.

The biggest prize of all would be a diary.

Hrluska's high school classmate had said she'd had the feeling Jenn carried around a secret burden, something she didn't share with anyone. Everyone needed to talk to someone, and if Jenn didn't, there was a chance she had written it all down. So first the night table drawer, then bookcases.

Stopping for a light, Christiana slid the tape recorder across the seat and pushed play. Out came the voice of Tisha Dedrick, who'd attended middle school with Jenn and was now an English teacher.

"When Jenny came back from the leukemia, she was different." A high, prissy voice. Christiana could imagine Miss Dedrick's students mimicking it behind her back.

"How so?"

"Well, partly it was physical. Before she got sick, she was rather thin and frail. I remember her hair was very blond, fine as corn silk. She wasn't short exactly, but there was no bigness to her. She had narrow shoulders. She looked like Alice, you know, in the Lewis Carroll book."

"Alice in Wonderland."

"And that's exactly what middle school is—all of us wondering if boys would ever be interested in us, if we'd ever grow up, wondering what high school would be like. For a while there, we were all wondering if we'd ever see Jenny again. She was out more than three months, and the reports got worse and worse. Then, suddenly, she was back. She looked about the same, but she had more energy, it seemed. She certainly wasn't convalescing the way you'd expect. And within weeks, as I remember, her shoulders broadened and her hair darkened and thickened. All of a sudden, she could swing a bat, and she became the star forward of our soccer team—"

"How about mentally? Any difference there?"

Christiana bit at her lip. This was where she'd almost cut off what was to be the most important part of the interview. Always wait until they stop talking, she reminded herself. Basic interviewing 101, but she'd been impatient with Tisha Dedrick's fussy pace.

"Certainly brighter than average," Tisha answered. "A's and B's, and maybe it could have been better if she hadn't spent so much time reading comic books. She loved comics. After she came back, she was much more focused. She'd always been quick, but now she was super sharp. She almost beat me out for valedictorian, and I wouldn't have given her much chance of that before she got sick."

"Yeah, right," Christiana said now, as she'd wanted to during the interview. Tisha should have realized Christiana Clark, ace reporter, would have already looked at the yearbook and would know that Jenn *had* beaten her out for valedictorian.

"But one other thing about her, physically," Tisha said. "After she came back from the hospital, her eyes were green."

"They weren't green when she went in?"

"They were blue. I'm almost sure of that."

Christiana felt a chill, though she'd played this part of the tape several times now. She heard herself say, "Could she have begun to wear contact lenses?"

"It's possible. I don't see how else it could have happened. That was what the other girls decided, but she never admitted or denied it."

"Maybe she was worried the other girls would think she was being vain?"

"Maybe. But usually, if you look real close, you can see if someone is wearing contacts—you know, that little edge that shows up around the iris. I looked for it whenever I got the chance, but I never could see it. I never could."

Christiana shut the recorder off. Most of what Tisha had to say could easily be explained—middle school was puberty time, and all girls had a growth spurt of some kind, even if it was only a few inches. And maybe the illness had made Jenn resolve to be more serious, to throw away the comic books and bear down on the textbooks.

But could leukemia—could *anything*—make a person's eyes change color?

Christiana turned into the parking lot of Jenn's apartment, feeling her heart beat down to her fingers as they squeezed the steering wheel. She drove up and down the rows of cars on tenterhooks now that she was so close. There was the red MG, license 386dh, damn! Jenn was in.

Christiana parked her car well away from the doctor's, but keeping it in view. It was only eight-thirty. Maybe Hrluska would go out for a date with her hunky novelist boyfriend, or get called in by the hospital.

Maybe she would come down and troll for muggers.

An hour, Christiana thought. I'll wait an hour.

She had an odd longing for some of the orange crackers with peanut butter.

⁂

Jenn sat slumped on the camelback couch in her living room, tormenting herself. Could her theory about Hugh being a phage and not knowing it be possible?

Have you seen him sleep—and been sure?

Have you ever seen him sick?

Have you ever seen him bleed?

Sleep could be the result of blood deprivation. If Hugh had split into two personalities, and the normal one was being able to hang on to control most of the time, he would get less blood than he needed. That would permit him to sleep. In fact, he did not seem to need much sleep.

She had never seen him sick. At the cathedral, Zane had put Hugh under for a few seconds with Influence, but if anyone could do that to another phage, it would be Zane.

The key test was how Hugh would bleed.

She had never seen him cut, but if he *was* a phage, any flesh wound would heal almost at once, even if he'd missed several feedings. She knew that because of an appalling story Merrick had told her once. When he was young, still reeling emotionally, he'd tried several times to stop feeding. His longest attempt, lasting nearly six months, had aged him severely, stooping his shoulders and causing his face to become heavily wrinkled. Finally he'd become so desperate he'd started slashing at his own arms in an effort to get blood. The wounds had healed at once, before he could get more than a few tastes. Unable to stand the agony of withdrawal any longer, he'd started to feed again and his body had quickly regained its youth.

If Hugh was a phage, a cut would prove it.

So what do I do? Jenn thought. Cut Hugh and say oops, sorry?

Suppose she could think of a way, and Hugh saw himself heal at once. Could the shock of it break down the wall he'd built between his two selves? Victims of split personality built those walls because they could not bear the reality of their other self or selves. If there was such a wall inside him and she tore it down, Hugh would not thank her. More likely he'd lash out at her—which might be what Zane had meant when he'd warned her Hugh was dangerous to her. Why would Zane say that about a normal? But a phage, older and more experienced, could more than hurt her, he could bury her.

But Hugh loves me.

The Hugh you *know* loves you.

And that was the other risk. Even if Hugh did not lash out at her for making him see his other self, once the barrier was down, that murdering self might swallow forever the one she knew and loved.

And if he's not a phage, and you live with him for twenty years, and then you have to leave him, what will that do to you?

Jenn groaned. I want him the way he's always been—*and* I want him for a thousand years.

She felt mired in indecision. She couldn't move. She knew she'd rather have him as he was, with all her doubts, than risk losing him altogether—and maybe herself as well.

So stop thinking about it, before you drive yourself crazy.

She got up and went to the kitchenette, standing at the refrigerator. She was not hungry, not thirsty. She had caught up on her reading. Hugh had said he was going to try to get some writing done tonight, if he could, and she was afraid to see him right now anyway.

Caroline!

Jenn felt a pang that she could have forgotten her. There had been no call from the night orderly, and that was a good sign. Maybe Caroline had turned the corner.

Jenn reached for her pager to make sure it was on full charge. It wasn't there. She groped along her belt, then hurried back to the couch, pulling up the cushions. Gone! She felt a rush of anxiety. The night orderly might have paged her after all. Had she left the blasted thing at the hospital? No, she never took it off her belt at work. Maybe it had slipped off at Merrick's when she'd been sitting on the couch in the music room.

Hurrying to the pass-through counter between the kitchenette and dining alcove, she picked up the phone, then froze as she heard the bolt in her apartment door slide back. The hairs on her arms stood up. Before she could move, the door opened and Zane stepped into the foyer.

She stared at him, shocked. A second passed before she could find her voice. "Ha . . . have you ever heard of knocking?"

He looked embarrassed. "Sorry. I've gotten into the habit of making as little noise as possible. Learned it from my father, as a matter of fact."

As her shock faded, a fierce nervousness took hold. The last time he'd come here, he'd dragged Brad in with him. But now he'd come alone, hands empty. He looked as nervous as she felt, and she realized it was only the second time she'd seen him indoors. He would avoid being inside, she thought, because he could too easily be trapped. Coming to me like this is a big step for him.

The knowledge eased some of her tension. Suddenly, she was glad he had come. She could ask him to explain about Hugh. "We need to talk," she said.

"Yes."

"Sit down." She gestured to the dining room table. Pulling out a chair, he settled gingerly, as if ready to spring up again. His hair was neatly brushed up from the high forehead. He wore charcoal slacks and a dark sport coat with a subtle, pebbled pattern. His shirt was black silk, with a mandarin collar. She noticed that his shoes were a soft leather, expensive-looking, but unpolished. He was not a man who willingly reflected light.

"Would you like some coffee?"

He shook his head, and at the same time said, "Yes."

She laughed, and then he did too. "Just a minute." She busied her hands with the familiar ritual of laying the filter, scooping from the tin, pouring the water. The machine began to crackle, and she sat across the table from him while the rich aroma of hazelnut filled the room. "What did you mean," she asked, "when you said Hugh was dangerous to me?"

He hesitated. "I'm sorry about that. I shouldn't have spoken to you that way. I meant only that you can't love a normal. They grow old, they die, and you are alone again."

He's lying, she thought. But the lie made her wonder. Here it was again, the hint that Zane had tried to love and failed. This could be the opening she needed to let her try to help him.

"Do you speak from experience?" she asked.

"Yes."

"A woman?"

He looked uncomfortable now, but gave a slight nod.

"Who was she?"

"I'd really rather not talk about her, but I wouldn't wish the pain it brought me on anyone, and most especially on the daughter that I love."

The words warmed her, she could not help it. Was he aware how powerful they were to her? "If only I could be sure you mean that."

He gazed at her, and she imagined she could see it in his eyes. "What must I do to convince you?"

"Could you leave me be?"

He looked stung. "Is that what you want?"

"Could you?"

"Jenn, you are asking me to let you be lost."

"I'm not the one who is lost."

He opened his mouth, but no words came out.

"What happened between you and your father?" she asked.

His face hardened. "So long ago," he murmured. "Do we have to talk about that?"

"There isn't much you want to talk about, is there?"

Zane sighed. "He couldn't accept what I was, just as he couldn't accept himself. He made me leave him—drove me away, in fact."

"*Why?*"

"You know why. Because I killed."

"Killed, in general, or someone in particular?"

Zane eyed her. "Father has never told you?"

"Only that you kept killing, though he'd done everything he could to help you to stop. Was there something specific that set him off."

"Why are you so curious about it?"

"I'm curious about you, all right? Tell me, please."

Zane cleared his throat. "I killed someone in order to help him. Instead, he was enraged. He buried me, but the grave was too shallow. He underestimated my strength, and I escaped."

"Or maybe he wanted you to escape."

Zane leaned forward, his eyes intense. "Oh no. He wanted to *destroy* me, his own flesh and blood."

"Who did you kill?"

Zane looked away. "His wife. The one after my mother. He'd had his twenty years with her and had left her, but wouldn't let himself love any other woman. He was putting himself through a lot of grief, and meanwhile, she had remarried. I killed her to free him. I didn't even drink her blood. Father and I had been apart for years, by then, but I had stayed close without him knowing it. After I killed the woman, he came after me. The old boy is a hell of a tracker, I can tell you that, and I wasn't much of a challenge back then—hadn't had the sense to get clear of Britain. I was up in the Scottish lowlands, hiding in some woods near Dunblane. I'll never forget his face. I was on a path and he leapt down from a tree in front of me. Such rage in his eyes, such hatred!"

Zane's eyes had gone glassy, and Jenn realized with a shock that he was afraid, the memory so powerful that it could terrify him even after hundreds of years. She could not condone what he had done, and yet, somehow, she understood it. I should not understand, she thought. I should be horrified.

Against her will, she felt her hand reaching out across the table toward him.

And then the apartment door slammed open and Merrick burst in. Zane leapt up with a cry of terror and ran deeper into the apartment. Jenn followed, afraid for him, making it to her bedroom just as he leapt through the window in a shower of glass and dropped out of sight toward the parking lot, seven stories below.

"Father!" she screamed.

17

After half an hour of waiting in the parking lot to see if Hrluska would leave, Christiana felt her patience crumbling. She beat out the rhythm to *Bolero* on the steering wheel—endless repetitions—until the pads of her fingers started to hurt. She dialed the radio to WTOP and listened to "Today on the Hill," and the national news, turning it off when they lapsed into a lurid account of today's execution by lethal injection of a death row inmate in Virginia. Using the balconies as markers, she counted the stories on the apartment building—ten—then composed in her head a fantasy "DomeWatch"-style report of Senator Barbara Boxer beating Senator Alphonse "Gus" D'Amato at mud wrestling.

She checked her watch—an hour gone now.

What am I doing? Sitting here, watching a red MG go from zero to zero, hoping she'll come out and drive it away so I can break into her apartment.

This is nuts.

She reached for the ignition, then pulled her hand back, as she already had half a dozen times. Thing was, there *was* more to this, her instincts told her that. Even now, with the stories she'd gathered on Hrluska starting to fade like a mirage, there was still that stunning moment she'd seen with her own eyes. A man thrown a good thirty feet, and he was at least the doctor's height and much bulkier. Weighed a hundred-eighty pounds minimum, and she'd thrown him the length of a house.

On the other hand, weren't there stories of mothers at an accident lifting a half-ton car off a child pinned under the wreck? Jenn had been attacked with a knife, in fear for her life. Panic burns hot. *I was way high above her,* Christiana thought, *and it was dark down there. Maybe it was only twenty feet, or ten.*

What about blue eyes turning green?

Right, and the woman who claimed that lied about beating Jenn out for valedictorian.

Ten minutes under the ice . . .

Who could keep accurate time when they're standing beside a frozen lake, terrified that a child is drowning?

Reaching for the key again, Christiana heard the crash of breaking glass above and to her left. As her head swung toward the apartment, she picked up a dark shape hurtling down the side of the building. For a second, her mind refused to accept the flailing form for what it was—

A man—

Too startled even to scream, she watched, horrified, as he crashed into the pavement at the edge of the parking lot.

She flung her car door open and stood, but her legs went soft, she couldn't move. Staring up, she saw light pouring from the shattered window, high above. With a sick feeling she looked at the man again, knowing he must be dead. God, he'd be red paste, arms bending the wrong way, head pulped. If she went over, she'd throw up.

The dark shape on the pavement moved, and her breath caught.

The man stood and looked straight at her.

Then, without moving a muscle, he vanished.

Christiana, who never in her life had fainted, fainted.

As he got up, Zane felt the startled gaze of a normal on him. His whole body rang with pain, but he couldn't think about that now. In an instant, he found her—there, standing in the open car door. Homing on her retinas, he found his image and pinched off the capillaries that fed it. Though he hadn't touched her jugular veins, the woman slid down, catching her chin on the open door and flopping back into the car.

She saw it all, he thought. *I've got to kill her.*

Father—no time!

Looking up at Jenn's window, he saw Father lean out and look down at him—*Run!* A fresh panic surged through him and he dashed a few steps the wrong way, then remembered his escape route and sprinted around the back of the apartment building. No time even to look over his shoulder—by now Merrick would have sprung down onto the pavement and would be chasing him, and the old bastard was *fast.* Plunging into the small park behind Jenn's apartment, Zane ran through the trees, barely feeling a spark of pain in his cheek as a thorny branch raked open the skin. A few drops of blood sprayed and the wound closed. Up and out the other side of the park, then left, behind the 7-Eleven, and down the alley that serviced the back entrances of a line of shops. Lifting the manhole at the end of the alley, he ignored the rungs set into the concrete and dropped twenty feet straight down the shaft. He crouched there, shin-deep in stinking water, and held absolutely still. The water gurgled past his feet, cold and slimy, but he welcomed its sound, which might be enough to keep Merrick from hearing the hiss of his racing blood. As his eyes switched to infrared, Zane saw a rat staring at him from a niche in the concrete wall farther down the tunnel. He waved an arm at it, but it did not move. This sewer was its turf.

Zane tried to fight off his despair. *Damn* Father, running him off like a gutless dog, less brave than that rat down the tunnel. But what was he to do? Stay and fight? Go into the ground again? The rat doesn't know what it's looking at, Zane thought, but I know my father only too well. Even if I could have taken him one-on-one, Jenn would have made it two-on-one. She'd side with him, no question. And that would have hurt.

Galled, Zane closed his eyes so he wouldn't have to see the brazen rat. Listening to the ground above him, he shifted one hand, planting it against the concrete of the shaft so he could pick up any vibration near the manhole cover above. Minutes crawled by and he heard no sound, felt no vibration. He began to hope. Merrick had taken a wrong turn. I got away, he thought with relief. The one thing I'm better at than he is.

He remained still. The danger wasn't past—he must wait here, silent, until he was sure Merrick was nowhere above. Then he would find his way to the next storm drain, two blocks down, and crawl out.

As his panic subsided, he thought again of the woman in the car. She saw me fall and get up again. What if she tells the police? He felt a fresh anxiety. Could he find her later? He'd gotten only the vaguest impression of her—dark hair to her shoulders, which probably meant a younger women. A small, white car, probably Japanese. That was all. He'd been too far away and too terrified to register more.

No, he'd never be able to track her down. She would go to the police . . .

And say what?

"Officer, I saw a man fall seven stories, jump up, and disappear right in front of my eyes."

Zane almost smiled, but the fact that she would not be able to convince anyone in authority didn't remove all danger. *She* would believe. Fortunately, normals were mentally weak. They had a great capacity to waver, to begin to doubt even their own eyes. One brush with the "impossible" could get written off—a hallucination, her imagination. But he must make sure she never saw him again.

Filing the woman away in the back of his mind, Zane thought about Jenn. She had been reaching out to touch him just before Merrick had burst in. Remembering it, he choked back a groan. So close—he'd come so close. Now Merrick would really be on alert, close to Jenn, never letting her forget for a moment what a devil her father was.

It would be dangerous even to get near her again.

I have to make her leave town. Get her away from him, or I'll never have a chance. Yes, leave Washington and Merrick wouldn't be able to follow—not without leaving his precious Katie and his son.

But how? She'll never willingly walk away from her internship or from him.

Unless I can make it so she has no choice.

Zane listened to the gurgle of filthy water around his feet, waiting for an idea. He could feel it, just beyond his grasp.

Her enemy—Dietz!

If she murders Dr. Dietz, she'll have to leave.

He knew just how to make it happen.

Jenn sat down on her bed, stunned and shaken. She was glad Merrick was still alive.

And furious at him.

He turned back from the window. "He's run away. He's gone."

"Do you know how lucky that makes you?" she said hotly.

"Yes."

"What in the hell did you think you were doing, breaking in like that?"

"Trying to save your life."

"We were just talking. We were going to have a cup of coffee, damn it."

"A cup of coffee." Merrick shook his head. "Have you heard the expression 'When you sup with the devil, use a long spoon?'"

"He's not the devil. He's human, like you and me. He's my father. Without Zane we wouldn't be having this conversation—or any other."

"I thank him for that."

"But you ask me to disown him."

Merrick's shoulders slumped. He suddenly looked forlorn.

Her anger cooled. "I'm sorry I shouted at you."

"I guess I deserved it, or you wouldn't have done it." He sat beside her and stared at the shattered window. "I don't know what to say anymore. I feel sure that Zane will do you terrible harm, but what you say is also true."

"He told me why you hate him."

Merrick stiffened, as though she'd knifed him. "Gweneth." He took a breath, and when he spoke again, his voice was subdued. "Zane's mother died when he was eleven. He never got over it. That pain, more than anything I tried to teach him, is what shaped him. I didn't remarry until Zane and I weren't together anymore. But he knew, and he hated Gweneth. In his mind, she was an impostor, stealing his dead mother's place."

"If you weren't together anymore, how do you know this?"

"I know him."

"But if you're right, why didn't he kill Gweneth while you and she were still together?"

"Because I was there to protect her. The reason he and I weren't together anymore was that I'd told him I couldn't let him go on killing innocents, that I'd bury him if he continued. So he ran away."

"Would you have?"

Merrick closed his eyes. "I don't know. Probably. What else could I do? Every young woman he killed was my doing, too. I had made him what he was, I had failed to change him, and I was the only one who could stop him. But instead, I warned him. I let him live."

"He didn't run very far. He still wanted to be near you."

Merrick gave her a sharp look. "He said that?"

"In so many words. And I believe it."

"It's possible. Despite everything, we . . . had loved each other very much." Merrick's voice was heavy with an old pain. His eyes went distant, staring through the broken glass at the night, and she knew he was looking into a time far past, a different kind of darkness. "By the time I left Gweneth," he murmured, "Zane and I had been apart nearly twenty-five years. I still thought about him, but I'd long since come to believe he was gone far away and forever. I had no idea he'd been hanging around in the near shadows all that time. If only I could go back, start over."

"What would you do? Bury him instead of warning him? Or maybe you wouldn't have given him blood in the first place."

He paled, and she regretted the barb, but before she could say more, he said, "I'd give him blood, just as I would have done for you, if I'd known you were my granddaughter. He was my son and he was dying. I was sure I could teach him to control himself. Where I went wrong with Zane was later. When he started killing innocents, and I couldn't get him to stop. Then I *should* have buried him."

Jenn felt a chill. This was the part of him that frightened her. If she had not learned to control her urge to kill, would he have buried her? Had he watched her those first few years for signs of a slip? Had all his kindness, his loving help, hidden another Merrick who could have buried her without mercy? It wasn't a fair question, because he'd have been showing mercy to the hundreds, the thousands she would have killed. But they were strangers. She was Jenn, his granddaughter. But he can't hurt you now, she reminded herself.

And you mustn't think this way. You owe him everything.

Almost.

The rest, you owe Zane.

"I was willing to let Zane go," Merrick said. "When I didn't know who he'd kill. For twenty-five years I never let myself think much about it. How many women died in those twenty-five years? But, see, I didn't love those women. It took Gweneth's death to show me how wrong I'd been."

"And because you couldn't forgive yourself, you couldn't forgive him."

"She was my *wife*."

"Zane said she'd remarried."

"Only because I had been forced by time to leave her. She thought she was a widow."

"So then why couldn't you, too, let yourself heal and go on?"

Merrick gave her a look of such weary forbearance that, for a second, she thought she could see a thousand years in his eyes, all of it spent struggling against his own murderous desires.

He said, "How convenient for me if I could marry a woman, and after twenty years, leave her and marry another. That's not love, that is infidelity. I loved Gweneth. After I left her, I kept track of her life.

Sometimes, at night, I slipped into her cottage and watched her sleep in the arms of her new husband. He was a gentle man, one of the village bakers. He made good bread—I tried some once. I was glad for Gweneth."

"So you went on loving her from a distance—just as Zane did you. When you were watching her, he was watching you. He saw your self-denial. He killed her to free you."

Merrick stared. "You believe that?"

"That's what he told me, and, yes, I believe him. From your view-point, it was a terrible thing, but he wasn't reasoning from your view-point."

Merrick continued to stare at her. "And you? What is your view-point?"

"He was wrong to kill her—of course he was."

"Thank heaven for that, at least."

She shook her head. "Doesn't it matter at all to you why he did it?"

At first, Merrick didn't answer. "Even if Zane loved me then, we've since been enemies for five hundred years. That makes it a bit late for understanding, don't you think? Do you really believe that Zane and I could just have a chat, work out our differences? Maybe when I came in, you should have grabbed him and said, 'Don't run, he can't hurt you. Let's all just sit down and have some coffee and we'll talk. One lump or two?'" Merrick gave a bitter laugh. "I'd have been dead before the sugar could dissolve."

"Merrick!" she said.

He went to the window. "I'm sorry," he said. "You already know how I feel about this, and it's past time for me to shut up. You're a grown woman, and how you respond to him is your decision. As for me, I have to fight him. I hope you can understand that."

"I understand it. But don't. He hasn't come back for you, I'm convinced of that. If you show your face to him again, you might not be so lucky, and I couldn't stand to lose you."

"I guess we should call someone and arrange to get this window fixed."

She realized the visit was over. "Before we do that, one last question."

He turned. "Jenn—"

"Why did you come over, when I had just been at your place?"

He looked startled, then reached into his coat pocket and pulled out her beeper. "This thing was down in the sofa in the music room. I found it when it went off."

"It went off?" Jumping up, Jenn took it from him, feeling a sudden coldness in her chest. The number in the screen was the hospital's, Five East—her floor.

Snatching up the phone beside her bed, she dialed. When the night nurse picked up, she said, "This is Dr. Hrluska. Is it Caroline?"

"Afraid so," the nurse said. "You'd better hurry."

18

Christiana gazed through teary, half-closed eyes at the radiant circle of light. She seemed to be floating toward it. Am I dying? she wondered. I'm not scared. Then it's true, what they say!

Joy, pure and exhilarating as a rainbow, began to flow through her . . .

But what was that around the light?

It looked like . . . gray cloth.

She realized her legs were chilly and then that she was not floating, but lying on her back, her body on a slant. The circle of light contracted a little and suddenly she could make out small, round ridges in it.

That is the dome light of my car, she thought.

And then it all came rushing back—waiting for Jenn, the man crashing down into the pavement, then springing to his feet—

"Oh, Christ, I fainted."

She tried to sit up. Her head spun; waiting a second, she grabbed the steering wheel and slowly pulled herself upright. Her chin hurt. Fingering it, she felt a scabbed-over cut. How had that happened? Must have hit it when she passed out. How long had she been unconscious? She looked at her watch—almost ten. She'd gotten here, what, at eight-thirty, waited an hour and had been about to leave, and then . . .

Nine-thirty to ten, she'd been out almost half an hour! No one fainted for that long—the blow to her jaw must have done it.

He didn't just get up, he vanished.

In a spurt of fear, she yanked the door shut, cutting off the dome light. Jamming the lock down, she stared at the place where the man had fallen. He should have been dead, smashed on the pavement, but instead he'd gotten up, looked straight at her, then dissolved into thin air.

What next? The police?

They'll never believe me, she realized at once. They'll think I've lost my mind . . .

Have I?

The new, uglier fear slithered through her. Craziness, God no, please not that. She had never in her life had such sensations. If she had only imagined this, then everything that seemed clear in her life might, from here on, be unsure, clouded. I'm a reporter, she thought. I deal in facts—reality. I have to know what's real and what isn't. If I can't, I'm not me anymore. I'm not anyone.

She sat, staring at the spot where she thought the man had fallen. If you're a reporter, she told herself, then go check it out.

Getting out of the car made her woozy, forcing her to hang on to the door for a minute. Maybe she ought to go to the emergency room . . .

But if there *was* any evidence, it might not be here when she got back.

After a few deep breaths, she felt better. She walked to the side of the apartment building, where the man had—or had not—crashed down. Broken glass glinted—a huge spill of it at the edge of the parking lot, scattered in a rough circle right where she'd seen the man hit.

I have not lost my mind.

She felt better for only a few seconds before the weight of this being *real* landed on her. How could someone fall seven stories and leap up unhurt? What kind of man could vanish like that?

Was it a man?

Christiana's scalp crawled. It might be better if she *had* imagined this—not madness, nothing could be worse than that, but maybe an understandable, permissible, one-time-only delirium. Had the man—or whatever it was—known she'd seen him? Clearly, he had not wanted her to. What if he were to come after her now? She felt a quick rush of fright—

But wait: if the creature had wanted to harm her, he'd had the chance as she lay unconscious. But he had let her be. An image flickered in her mind of the face that had stared at her for that second: rugged, handsome, the tall, lithe body of a dark angel. I never believed in angels, she thought, and felt a quickening lift. She had seen something amazing—if not an angel, maybe the reality behind the myth.

Whatever it was, she must know.

Christiana looked around, eager, suddenly, to know if anyone else had seen this, but the parking lot was deserted. In half an hour, no one had even come to clean up the glass. She herself had seen it only because she'd happened to be outside watching and had heard the glass break. Inside the building, the sound would be less, and even if some tenants had heard it and looked out, they'd have seen only the litter of glass—the manlike creature had disappeared almost at once.

Looking up, Christiana searched for the broken window. After a minute, she saw it, dark now, a rectangle of soft black that stood out from the faint sheen of reflection on the surrounding windows. She counted balconies again—the broken window was on the seventh floor. Her heart began to pound. Hrluska's apartment, she'd bet on it.

Turning, she looked for Jenn's red MG. It was gone, the parking space empty now.

Hurrying into the lobby, Christiana checked the mailboxes. Hrluska—714!

She pushed the elevator button over and over. When the doors opened, a man stepped off with only a glance at her jaw. She waited impatiently as the elevator crawled up to seven, then walked down the deserted hallway until she found 714. Her excitement grew—from the outside, the broken window was in the middle of the building, and 714 was exactly halfway down the hall.

Remembering the picks in her pocket, she had them in her hand before fear hit again, a cold vapor that filled her stomach. Just because the doctor's car was gone, didn't mean no one was inside. Someone could be in there, waiting—another one like she'd seen fall. Fear spread through her, making her shiver. I have a good career, she thought. I have "DomeWatch."

I've had it for four years, the same thing over and over.

Pressing an ear to the door, she listened. Silence. She might never get such a chance again. Strike while the iron is hot—that was how she'd used to be, when she'd first become a reporter, before all the pancake makeup and scripted talk. Whether or not this turned out to be the reality behind the angel myth, it could turn out to be the story to end all stories, and if she didn't have the guts, then she could forget about having an interesting life again and stay a talking head until they got bored with her and rolled her backstage to gather dust with the other props.

Stooping, she slipped a pick into the lock and worked it, splitting her worry between the sensations in her fingertips and the silence of the hallway. If someone came, she must be ready to flee. She gave up on the first pick and chose another, trying to let her hand relax. Feel it, fe-e-e-l it—*there!* The bolt slid back and the door receded an inch. Remembering the way she'd used to do it, she stood and knocked, letting that push the door in and open. "Hello? Anybody home?"

No answer. The apartment was dark. Steeling herself, she stepped inside, found the switch, and turned on the lights, pulling the door shut behind her. "Hello," she said again, louder.

Nothing.

Her pulse hammered in her throat. She was so afraid she was almost dizzy. She took in the foyer and living room with a quick sweep. Ordinary-looking place, old-fashioned sofa, a few lamps, and a leather recliner. The red carpet looked like a real Persian. It was huge. How did an intern get money for that—or for an MG for that matter? Christiana made a mental note to check out Dr. Hrluska's parents. Inhaling, she smelled hazelnut coffee. She moved to the kitchenette. A full pot, still warm, sat in the coffeemaker. Neat kitchen, no dishes in the sink. Two chairs were pulled back from the table, disturbing the room's pin-neatness.

Keep moving!

Christiana hurried back into the bedroom, feeling the drop in temperature as she entered and flipped on a light. The broken window gaped at her, black with the night sky, white curtains ruffling at its edges. The bed was rumpled at the foot, as though someone had just sat there. Chair in the corner, closet with six or seven dresses and some suits and, at the other end, jeans. Remembering her mental preparation while driving over, Christiana went to the bed table and pulled open its single drawer.

The diary was there!

With a quick, fierce pleasure, Christiana lifted it out, then hesitated. Look at it here, or take it out? It resisted opening. Seeing the combination lock, she made a quick decision. Her picks were no good on this; she'd have to break it. Better to take it, then. Maybe the doctor would think the man who had leapt from her window had stolen it.

Christiana made a quick pass through the other traditional hiding places and found nothing, no photos or envelopes taped to the backs of dresser drawers, nothing bagged in the freezer or toilet tank.

You've got what you hoped for. Time to go.

Christiana slipped back into the hall. The urge to keep going and race home with her prize was almost overpowering, but she made herself stoop again and insert the pick. It went more quickly now that her fingertips knew the lock. The bolt slid home and she hurried toward the elevator, then hesitated. What if the doors opened in the lobby and she found herself facing Hrluska? Heading to the stairs instead, she tucked the diary into her jacket. Once back in the safety of her car, she let out a huge sigh of relief.

Driving home, she felt more alive than she had in a long time. She still had it—the guts, the sheer nerve, to seize the moment. And what a moment this might be. With luck, in the small, red book beside her was the Jenn Hrluska that only Jenn Hrluska knew, the one who could stay under the ice for ten minutes and toss a man like a horseshoe. The woman was too smart, probably, to hold on to anything, diary, or otherwise, that could directly reveal her. But it would almost surely be there between the lines for someone who knew how to look. If I'm lucky, Christiana thought, I may even find a glimpse of the creature that jumped from her window.

And the more I know, the easier it will be to prove.

Hurrying toward Caroline's room, Jenn fought a feeling close to panic. I can't lose her, she thought. Not my Caroline. In the anteroom, she changed quickly, then hesitated, circling her mask with a gloved fingertip, sealing its rim more tightly to her face, stalling because she was terrified to go in. She could hear the beep of the heart monitor—too slow, far too slow, and the inexorable rhythm of the respirator.

And Caroline's father saying, "Come on, baby, hold on."

Jenn stepped into the room. The night intern wasn't there, but the second-year resident Dave Bledsoe was. He stood back from Mr. Osborne, heavy and solid as a post, his eyes impassive above the mask. Jenn hurried to the bedside. A glance at the monitor showed her that Caroline was dying. This time there could be no question. Her blood pressure had sunk to eighty-five over fifty. Her skin was a dusky blue white. Her father was talking, keeping up a constant, reassuring murmur there was no chance his daughter could hear. Jenn felt her hands clenching in desperation, but what could she do? Caroline was already on the respirator. Every tube, every line with any hope of helping her, was already placed, every medication given, every monitor on.

Jack Osborne glanced at her, his face hard with fear, then said, "Caroline, honey, your doctor's here." In a lower voice, he said, "Can't you please help her?"

Jenn glanced quickly at Dave, who minimally shook his head. She tried to answer Osborne, but ended up shaking her own head.

"If you want to hold her hand," Dave said, "it would be fine."

Osborne swallowed hard. His eyes shone suddenly. But he took his daughter's hand in both of his. "It's me, honey. Your daddy."

Jenn stood frozen, feeling helpless.

Osborne bent over his daughter and took her in his arms. Thinking of infection, Jenn took a step toward him, but Dave caught her arm and again shook his head.

The blood pressure monitor began to signal, and then the cardiac alarm went off, a steady, high whine. A glance at the flat line on the scope told Jenn Caroline's heart had stopped.

Jenn tore her arm free, but Dave grabbed it again. "I need to start external massage," she whispered urgently. "We have to call a code."

"No."

Jenn wanted to scream at him, punch him, but she fought to control herself, holding up both hands to show she was all right. When he released her, she went to Caroline, found her hand dangling through from between her father's back and arm as he hugged her. Taking it, she gave it a squeeze. Jack Osborne must have felt her behind him, because he nudged her away—ever so slightly, but it cut her to the quick.

"I'm sorry," she said, backing off. He did not acknowledge her. His body shook with sobs. Dave motioned toward the door with his head. Crushed, Jenn stumbled out.

She glimpsed herself in the mirror in the anteroom tearing off a mask darkened with tears. Then a vivid, frozen snapshot of the trash bin, filled with discarded latex gloves, her own tumbling down on top.

The stairs, silent and airless, letting her down in a free fall where she could see her feet descending but could feel nothing. She burst into the chill air of the parking lot and screamed. A man getting out of his car straightened and stared at her.

She wanted to kill him.

She ran from the lot into the alley where they parked out-of-service ambulances. Brief impression of a steel bumper buckling under her kick, but still no real feeling.

Walking down Sixteenth Street, with Rock Creek Park drawing her on her right. But if she ran into someone down there, she *would* kill him, stupid flimsy people, so she stayed on the sidewalk, found herself thinking about what Zane had said:

You can't love a normal.

19

Jenn waited with cold amusement for Dr. Fortis Wayne to acknowledge her. There he sat, enthroned behind that mammoth desk, peering at a letter, ignoring her so he could feel important. But he was more aware of her than he pretended—she could sense his blood gathering in his loins, and it disgusted her. How adolescent, having the hots for one of his interns. Or maybe there was something arousing in the letter—she mustn't start thinking she could read minds, only blood flow. . . .

And you shouldn't be doing that much.

Jenn stopped her scan of Dr. Wayne's blood, surprised at herself for having invaded his privacy. How could he help how his body responded to her? He was responsible only for how he acted toward her. Which was bad enough—

Worry about how you are acting.

Recognizing the chiding voice inside her as Merrick's, Jenn wished she could shut it up, just this once. You are how you act, he had certainly drummed that into her. Act like a phage and you're a phage. Act like a normal, and you're a normal. Well, she'd been acting like a normal, and what pain it was bringing her. Half the night she'd cried for Caroline and now had no tears left, only this aching place in her chest. I knew she might die, but I didn't grasp it emotionally. I survived leukemia, and I just felt she would too, had to, and she didn't. I did everything I could, and she died anyway. I hate feeling this way. I can stand losing a preemie that's only been in the world a few seconds, but I *loved* Caroline.

I shouldn't have let myself.

But if I learn not to care, what kind of doctor will I be?

Jenn felt as if she were being sucked up in a tornado, everything she had believed torn loose to swirl around her, and where would it all come down? Not just Caroline, but her parents and Hugh, too? Suddenly she felt afraid of her love for him. She'd let herself go with him, as with Caroline, because it had felt right; love was magical, so she'd let her feeling for Hugh grow until it had filled her like a constant warm light, a solid link to the world of normals. But last night, stalking the streets in fury over losing Caroline, she had begun to hope Hugh McCall was not a normal, even though it might mean he was a killer, because if he wasn't a phage she would some day have to lose him, and how could she bear it? She wanted a love with no deception that could last a hundred years, five hundred. Was that so much to ask? Twenty years was nothing, an eye blink, and if she went on loving normals, how many broken hearts would it take to make her into a Zane? Last night, she'd imagined that Hugh *was* a phage and had felt that it might even be good. They would go on the hunt together—not the careful, measured sipping as with Merrick, but a real hunt. Such images her mind had thrown up: Hugh, who had been so kind and gentle with her, severing the throat of a faceless normal who was going to die in a few years or decades anyway. Hugh drawing her with him to the pumping wound. And then I lay down the burden, Jenn thought, of caring for anything so easily snatched away. She shivered with dread but also with desire.

"Are you chi-chilly?"

She realized Dr. Wayne had put down his letter and was eyeing her.

"No, I'm fine." With an effort, she pulled herself back to what she must do now, the first step, just an exploration, nothing more now. "Thank you for seeing me on such short notice."

His hand twitched, as if shooing off a fly. "I presume it's something urgent."

"Yes. I need to take leave."

His arched eyebrows shot up, and the perpetual semi-smile in-grained at the corners of his mouth deepened in a way only a few days ago she would have found ominous. Now it didn't scare her. Somehow, she'd taken away his power to frighten her. It felt good.

"Impossible," he said.

"You haven't even heard my reasons."

"I can-can't imagine any reason good enough for a first-year resident to take a va-a-acation after only four months on service."

"I didn't say vacation, I said leave."

"Are you ill?"

Yes, she thought, but shook her head. "I need a week or so to think things over." *A week of not caring about anyone who can die. To decide if I can bear that again. A week just for myself.*

Wayne got up and sat on the corner of his desk, one leg dangling off the edge, the other foot planted on the floor. "Surely you aren't still upset about that blood test?"

"Wouldn't you be if you were in my place?"

His eyes widened, as if he found the idea of putting himself in her place incredible. "It was necessary. I can't have interns stealing drugs. They were, after all, found in your locker."

"As if I would be so stupid."

Wayne snorted. "You'd be sur-surprised how stupid I have seen in-terns be. Really, Doctor, you must de-ee-velop a thicker skin if you are to succeed in the practice of medicine. It is not for the fay-faint of heart. Now if that's all—"

"It is not all. I need a week of leave, without any penalty on my record, effective immediately."

Wayne sprang up from the corner of the desk. "Immediately!" he sputtered. "That *is* impossible. I'm already short-handed because of Dr. Dietz—"

"If you'd seen a little sooner that he, not I, was the one with the drug problem maybe he wouldn't be on the psychiatric ward right now and I wouldn't be asking for leave."

"Don't be im-m-mpudent. Just because, in hindsight—"

"*Not* hindsight. I warned you the day you ordered me to take a blood test that Brad was using amphetamines and that he planted the Ritalin in my locker to throw suspicion my way. You ignored me. Though my blood test proved you were wrong about me, you continued to ignore what I had said about Brad, and now you've been proven wrong about him, too. I wonder what the chairman of our hospital board would think if he knew that one of his clinical directors ignored all warning signs and let his son deteriorate to the point of suicide."

Wayne stared at her with a shocked expression. "Are you threatening me?"

"I'm pointing out to you possible consequences of your mistakes in judgment."

"And if I doh-don't grant you immediate leave, you'll go running off to Brad's father."

"Whether or not you give me leave, I will not tell Brad's father anything, unless he asks."

Wayne tried to keep his face set, but she caught a flicker of relief. Then she dropped the other shoe: "Since I did save his son's life, I imagine he will be talking to me, and if he starts asking me questions, I will answer."

Dr. Wayne gave her a smile devoid of warmth. "But if I let you go on leave, your ans-s-swers might be different."

"Either way, I won't lie." *Except about what really happened to Brad.* "But if I'm on leave, that means no beeper, no being called in to the hospital. I'll be harder for anyone to reach, that's a simple fact, and it includes you as surely as it does Brad's father, so will you please stop trying to make it sound like blackmail."

Wayne stared at her with a mixture of anger and admiration. "By

God, you're smooth for being hardly more than a girl. But it *is* blackmail, and I won't . . . uh . . ."

Jenn was barely aware of pushing him, just a touch of Influence to dilate his jugular veins and shift blood away from his brain. He plopped back on the corner of the desk again and swayed. Rising, she caught him by the shoulder. "Are you all right?"

"Dizzy," he mumbled.

"Here, let me help you." Grasping his upper arms, she lifted him, steered him around to his chair, and eased him down into it. "Would you like a glass of water?"

He gave a wobbly nod.

What are you *do*ing! she thought as she hurried into his bathroom and drew a paper cup of water from the sink. Back at his side, she cradled the back of his head while holding the cup to his lips. Some of the water dribbled down his chin and onto his collar. "Looks like maybe you need to take a little leave, too," she said.

"Wha . . . ?"

Realizing he was too far gone, she tightened up the jugulars and dilated the carotid arteries a bit. At once, he roused himself. She stepped back. He fussed at his collar, frowning. "What happened?"

"You almost fainted," she said. "We were discussing my request for leave, and suddenly you became very pale."

"Oh yes. As I said, I really can't . . ." His eyes lost focus as she drained some blood from his brain again, this time with better control. He gazed at her with sleepy passivity, and she realized he was where she wanted him, still conscious but without any train of thought, his mind empty and vulnerable to suggestion.

She pulled from her pocket the leave form she had filled out. "I want you to check off 'approved' on this and sign it."

"Yes," he said serenely, but made no move.

She put the paper before him, took a pen from his desk, and checked 'approved,' then handed the pen to him. "It will be best for both of us. Now sign it."

"Yes," he said again with more conviction, and this time he did it.

She thanked him and hurried out with the slip, releasing her hold on his blood only when she was in the hall and moving away from his office. She could feel her own heart pounding with exhilaration. It was so easy! she thought. Dr. Fortis Wayne, the bogeyman, terror of the interns, and I had him under my control. He was down deep, handing his breathing tube to the fishies. What will he think when it sinks in what he did? He let me tell him what to do, and he won't understand that. He'll know something happened to his mind and that will scare him.

He might even be a little scared of me, now.

A passing nurse gave her an odd look and she realized she was grinning. Fortis Wayne, scared of her—she loved it. *Still think I'm barely more than a girl, you randy old goat? I'm a lot more, and you'd better hope you never find out how much.*

And *I'd* better hope you don't either, she thought, sobering.

Back on pediatrics, she found Dave Bledsoe in the break room looking at some lab results. When she handed him the leave slip, he frowned. "What the hell! You can't take leave now. We can't spare you."

"Take that up with Dr. Wayne. I'm out of here."

"Wait a minute. What's the idea of going over my head? There's a chain of command here . . ." Bledsoe trailed off, and she realized that something in the way she was looking at him had cautioned him. *I'm still rolling. I've still got the power.*

He said, "I get it—you're shook up about Caroline."

"Aren't you?"

He hesitated. "Not really. I'm sorry she died, but we did all we could, and that includes you. You've got to put it out of your mind and move on."

"Do I?"

"Jenn, we all lose patients. Your mistake was letting yourself get so emotionally involved."

"You're right." She turned and opened the door.

"Wait, damn it! When are you coming back?"

"When I've made sense out of a few things."

"That's not good enough!"

She turned back to him. "So fire me." A sense of unreality swept her, as though she were suddenly detached from herself, watching a stranger speak through her mouth.

Dave grimaced. "No one's firing you. I'm just a goddamned second-year resident. Only Dr. Wayne can fire you—"

"Fine. You have his signature on the leave slip. If you have a problem with this, go see him."

Dave stared at her. "Christ," he groaned. "Don't burn out on me, Jenn. You're the best intern on this ward. We need you."

She felt the sharp edge inside her soften, but only a little. "Dave, look, I may be back tomorrow apologizing for all this, but right now I can't apologize, I just have to be away from here, do you understand?"

His shoulders slumped, and she could see the fight go out of him. "Damn it, yes, I under*stand,* all right? Can we reach you at home?"

"I don't know. You can try."

As she passed the nurses' station, someone called out to her; Jenn kept going, stopping only when she heard footsteps running after her. It took all she had to turn and wait. Rainie Smith, one of the nicer veteran nurses on the ward, hurried up. She hasn't done anything to you, Jenn thought. Be polite. Rainie gave her an apologetic grimace. "Sorry, Doctor, I can see you're in a hurry, but we're getting an urgent request from MHU. Brad Dietz is pretty agitated, saying some pretty strange stuff. He keeps asking for you. They've called twice now. Could you drop by and see him?"

Jenn fought off an overpowering urge to say no. *Saying some pretty strange stuff,* so she had to handle it somehow, when all she wanted was to *get away from this place.* It made her want to scream. Instead, she forced a smile. "No problem."

❦

The moment she stepped into his room, Brad started babbling: "I saw him, Jenn—I saw him. He was here!" His eyes were wide, almost wild. In contrast to the last time she'd been here, every light in the room was blazing. She was relieved to see he was still strapped down to his bed—whatever he'd been saying, they weren't ready to believe him and let him loose.

Yet.

"Who did you see?"

"The man who cut my wrists."

Jenn's heart sank.

"I told you I'd never do a thing like that, and I didn't. He was right here, only an hour ago." Brad's face was pale. He looked terrified, and well he might be if he had really seen Zane. But it made no sense. Why would Zane come here?

To find out if Brad remembers anything.

Jenn suppressed a groan. This was a disaster. By showing himself, Zane had jogged Brad's memory. . . .

And somehow Brad had mustered the presence of mind not to react. It seemed incredible he could have fooled Zane that way, but he must have, or he'd surely be dead. Maybe his memories had not broken through until after Zane was gone.

You have to kill him.

The thought was gone as soon as it came. Even if I could make myself do it, she thought, I don't dare. They'd know it was me.

"Do you believe me?" Brad asked.

The pleading in his voice pulled at her, but she resisted. He had brought this on himself—

No. Whatever his faults, surely he does not deserve this.

"You say you saw a man in here," she said. "Did anyone else see him?"

"No! That's what's so strange. I've been yelling my head off. The whole staff must've been in here at one point or another, and none of them saw this guy. But he was there, I'm telling you. I was dozing, and I opened my eyes and there he was. Tall, big shoulders—moves like a dancer, but those eyes. . . ." Brad shuddered. "I felt like the devil was looking at me."

"Brad, listen to yourself."

"All right. All *right.*" He made a visible effort, taking a deep breath and closing his eyes for a few seconds. "Jenn, if you tell them I'm right, they'll believe you."

"It was a nightmare, Brad. You said yourself you were sleeping. This is a locked ward. All visitors are logged in by whoever opens the door. No one could just walk in here to your bedside without being seen." *Except one of us.*

Brad gazed at her, and she could see calculation in his eyes. "Jenn, you know I saw him, because you saw him too, that night at your apartment."

She kept her face calm, though she was reeling inside. *He remembers everything!* "We weren't at my apartment, Brad. You called me, and I came over—"

"Bullshit. I was in my apartment all right, watching the playoffs, and suddenly there was this big gap, and the next thing I know I'm standing in your bathroom. I feel dopey and weak. I try to drop to my knees and I can't, because he's got hold of my arms. And then you step out of the shower and start screaming at him, and I see this big guy, just a shadow, and then he's running and I pass out." Brad stared at her with a bug-eyed intensity that would have been funny were this not so deadly serious. "Don't tell me you don't fucking remember this," he said, "because you saw it too. When he was holding onto my arms, I could feel his fingers, but I couldn't see them. He can make himself invisible. All right, it's nuts, but there it is, it happened. I'm no goddamned suicide. You've got to tell them. They think I'm head cheese right now but they know you're not."

"Brad, if I said what you just said to anyone in here, they'd put me in the next bed."

He stared at her. "But you do admit you saw him that night."

"No." She focused every effort on looking calm, reasonable.

"You're lying," he said, as if the idea amazed him. "Why are you lying?"

"Brad—"

"No, I mean it. Why would you lie about this? Are you really afraid they'll put you here too? Or is it something else? Do you maybe know more about this than I do? Do you know the man who did this to me?"

Jenn felt cold. This was it, the thing Merrick had warned her about. Brad was one short step from knowing about hemophages. All he had to do was remember Zane coaxing her to drink from Brad's wrists. Somehow, she had to convince him to forget, or at least let it go, or his blood might become only the first drops in a torrent. "Brad, listen to me. It doesn't matter what you believe about this. It doesn't even matter if you really did see a man, which I'm telling you you did not. The only thing that will get you out of here is to forget it. I know this seems very real to you, but you've got to stop saying it. Go ahead and believe it if you must, but tell them you realize it was a dream. Be sheepish. Apologize. And when they let you out, never say it to anyone again. That's it. That—and nothing else—is what will get you out of here and keep you out."

Brad stared at her, and there was real fear in his eyes now. "Why won't you help me? Are you one of them?"

Kill him. Kill him now.

She took a step toward the bed.

No—they know you're visiting him. You have to think about this!

"Try and get some sleep, Brad."

And don't make me come back here.

As Jenn left Brad's room, Zane watched from the far end of the ward. Unsure whether he could block himself from her vision without her detecting it, he held himself perfectly still, cloaked in a deep shadow thrown by the corner of the nurses' station. He felt a keen satisfaction as he watched an orderly let Jenn out the exit at the far end of the ward. *This is working out just as I planned it,* he thought. *Everyone knows she hates Dietz. And now she's killed him!*

With a little help from me.

Hurrying to finish it, Zane drew his knife at Brad's bedside, then hesitated. The stupid normal looked around the room constantly, blinking too much, his face a mask of fear. Zane had no pity for him. *If you hadn't* tried to hurt my daughter, he thought, none of this would be happening. You can repay her, help her understand she can't be one of you, never again.

Zane brought the blade to Brad's throat. When the honed edge, razor sharp, touched his Adam's apple, Brad flinched and started to cry out. Instead, blood sprayed silently from his new mouth. He jerked once and it was over.

With a supreme effort, Zane turned away and ran from the room, leaving all the blood behind.

20

Christiana was surprised to feel a nervous pang in her stomach as she knocked on Julius von Hoffman's door. How would he react? After all, she didn't know him that well—just from that one time they'd been on the "NewsHour with Jim Lehrer" together. The topic—the politics of abortion—had been potentially explosive, and he'd handled his end with thoughtful answers, not the inflammatory ones Jim had been fishing for. Julius won't laugh outright at me, Christiana thought, but if he thinks I'm nuts, I'll know, and I'd hate that. If only he'll take me seriously.

Shifting the box containing the video camera to her other arm, she rapped on the door again, this time using the knocker, a weighty but bland hinge of antique brass—no gargoyles or lion heads for Dr. Von Hoffman. That squared with what she'd remembered—and liked—about him. For having such a reputation for brilliance, he had not been a showy man. She knew he was quite rich with old family money and could have afforded as fine a home as Georgetown had to offer, a brownstone near Dumbarton Oaks for example, but instead he'd chosen this narrow-fronted row house, quietly fashionable at best—

The door opened and he peered out at her. The tan on his face told her he'd returned recently from a dig. He was lean—thinner than two years ago when they'd done the "NewsHour" together, but handsome still, with that square, Germanic jaw and the salt-and-pepper hair too thick to part. Then he'd worn a dark suit, but he looked better today in faded jeans and a blue pullover.

"Ms. Clark," he said. "How nice to see you again."

"Please, Christiana. It's nice to see you, too, Dr. Von Hoffman."

"Julius. Come in." She stepped into the dark, narrow foyer, which gave way to a long hall, bounded on both sides by sagging bookcases. The pleasant, musty scent of old paper pervaded the still air. She was surprised to find it so dark. The carpet runner underfoot felt plush, but its colors were lost in the dimness and the ceiling was so high she could barely make out the antique, finely molded tin. Maybe it was a relief to him, the low light—a dark, cool cavern to return to after months on his knees under the burning sun. At the back, he led her into a study, where there was more light, from a window which faced on to a garden. The room contained no crucifixes, no paintings of Christ. There was a pew and a wooden communion table, from his days as Father Julius von Hoffman, S.J., which might have remained because they looked too massive to move out.

Spinning the leather chair at his rolltop desk around, Julius sat and pointed her to the only other seat—the rough-hewn pew. It looked like the ones she'd seen in a little church in Palermo. Instead of sitting, she put the video camera down on the pew and took a moment to inspect the communion table, which he'd turned into a worktable, now covered with a litter of artifacts, presumably from his latest dig: small tiles from a mosaic, beads of what looked like amber strung together into a necklace, and a stunning gold bracelet with snake heads at either end. "Pompeii?" she asked.

"Very good," he said. "Herculaneum, but you were close."

"The bracelet is beautiful," she marveled. "The Smithsonian lets you keep this stuff here?"

"Just while I'm studying it. I made it a condition of signing on with them—all my reference books are here."

"Don't you worry someone will break in and steal something?"

"They installed a safe in the basement better than you'll find in most banks."

Christiana wanted to pick the bracelet up, put it on her wrist, for the thrill of feeling next to her skin something that had once graced the wrist of a Roman noblewoman, but a glance at Julius's watchful eyes told her he'd rather she didn't.

She sat down on the pew next to the video camera. "Thank you for seeing me. I know you must be busy."

"It's a pleasure. I've been enjoying your commentary on 'Dome-Watch.' In fact, I've been trying to imagine how I, of all people, could enlighten you in any way on politics."

"This isn't about politics," she said. "I need your opinion on something in . . . your former area of expertise."

"Catholicism?"

She leaned forward. "Actually, the opinion of an *ex*-priest is what I need."

"Please go on."

"First, I must have your promise that you won't repeat to anyone what I'm going to say to you."

He looked uncomfortable. "With the condition that my silence wouldn't harm someone who'd be saved if I broke confidence."

"Did that ever happen to you in the confessional?"

He smiled a bit sheepishly. "Actually, no, but I always worried it might."

"Well, this is nothing like that."

"Fine. Then I promise."

"Thank you. Do you believe in angels?"

The sun-wrinkles around his eyes deepened in a wince. "Oh, dear," he said softly.

"All right, let's start with an easier question: when you were a priest, *did* you believe in angels?"

He said nothing, gazing at her as if she were an artifact he might have dug up. "Why do you ask?"

"I think I may have seen one." She was glad when he didn't smile.

"Are you sure you wouldn't be better off asking a practicing priest?"

"No. I want to hear from an expert whose opinion will not be distorted by faith, or by any sense of spiritual obligation."

"I see." He sighed. "I guess I should be glad you didn't ask me if there is a God."

"This is not some theological discussion I'm trying to have here. I'm talking observable fact."

Julius got up and went to the table, staring down at the pieces of mosaic. "This came from the floor of a dwelling in Herculaneum," he said. "I would give anything to know its overall pattern, to see it with my mind's eye, but too many pieces were washed away by the initial blast of gases and the torrent of lava. Maybe we'll find more in future digs, maybe not. But with these few, all I can do is make small discoveries—how the pieces were cut; perhaps, if I'm lucky, where the marble was quarried." He turned back to her. "That is pretty much the scale of observable fact. I've learned to be content with that scale, small as it is—to prefer it to grander questions which may never be answered."

"So is that yes, you believe, or no you don't?"

He laughed, showing white, even teeth. "This angel you believe you saw. Why don't you tell me about it?"

She did, telling him she'd dropped by a friend's apartment after meeting her at a party and had sat in the parking lot a minute to hear the end of a news piece on her car radio. She did not want to confess to this near stranger how she'd been planning to break into a young doctor's apartment. And she couldn't very well mention the stolen diary, which, though maddeningly vague, added up, she was sure, to something beyond normal human experience—that strange hunger while Jenn was sick, for example. As she talked, Julius walked around his study, trailing a hand along the shelf of a bookcase, pulling a leatherbound volume out an inch, then pressing it back in. When she got to the part about the angel vanishing, he turned and gazed at her. Suddenly his eyes had a sheen.

"You remembered seeing the man fall after you regained consciousness."

"That's right, but it really happened. There was glass all around."

"But no blood."

"I didn't see any, but it was dark. If there was, there couldn't have been much."

He stared at her. "I'm sorry, but are you having me on, Christiana? Because if you are—"

"I'm not. I saw it. I'm a reporter, Julius, a professional skeptic."

He held her gaze, then raised a hand in an atavistic gesture he probably had once used in blessing. "What made you think it might be an angel?"

She hesitated. "The fact that he wasn't hurt. That he was able to vanish. Also his face, his build and height. I was too far away to see him clearly, but there was something compelling about him, an eerie grace about the way he sprang up. What I thought, actually, was that he was a dark angel—you know, an evil angel, but he didn't harm me when he had every chance."

Movement caught the corner of Christiana's eye, making her jump. Turning, she saw a tortoiseshell cat strolling over to jump into Julius's chair. He patted the cat's head absently and said, "So much has been written about angels—much more than is commonly known. The Old Testament called them messengers, powers, princes, and, interestingly, men. A number are mentioned by name—Lucifer, Gabriel—or Jibril—Uriel, Raphael, Michael. The basic story, of course, is that there was a war among angels, which ended with the evil ones cast down from heaven, whereupon good angels were dispatched to protect us. But, according to ancient writings, even 'good' angels have been sent to mankind not just to aid but to punish. People think of a beautiful being on Christmas cards, but the angel of death swooped down on the houses of the Egyptians, killing all their firstborn. Think what sort of being could do that."

Christiana felt a chill. "You said ancient writings, but you're really just talking about Christianity, right?"

"Not at all. Angels are also a feature of Islam, Judaism, and Zoroastrianism. The Kabbalah speaks of a powerful angel named Metatron who was called Prince of the Countenance because he was able to look at God's face and live."

Christiana was struck. How serious he sounded! Did it mean he believed? "I didn't know angels were part of so many separate writings. It kind of adds credence, don't you think?"

He shrugged. "More so than if it had been only Christianity, I suppose. But these religions didn't arise in isolation from each other, so it may not be significant if they agree on some things."

"I see," she said, disappointed.

"Mind you, I'm not saying there isn't something real here. We cannot say something does not exist simply because there is little or no evidence of it. But if there are such real beings, they, like God, are probably different than the popular, wishfulfilling conceptions of them."

"The reality behind the myth," Christiana murmured.

He nodded. "That's what is most convincing about your story. It fits no popular conception. You saw no wings on this . . . creature. Indeed, it fell to earth, which it would hardly do if it could fly. The reason it smashed through the window is unknown, its motives in apparently not wanting you to see it and yet not harming you are unclear. I like that a lot better than if you'd given me a story that conformed completely to popular expectations."

"Then you believe me."

"I believe you are convinced you saw this thing, yes." A sudden shadow clouded his eyes, and he gave a bitter laugh. "Christiana, skeptical reporter, who does not believe in God, sees a miracle. Why *you?*"

"Instead of you?" she said softly.

Julius picked up the cat and held it to his chest, stroking it, his eyes distant. "Once," he said, "it would have meant a great deal to me to see what you claim to have seen, whether it was an angel or something else. Just to have seen with my own eyes that there may be more in this world than just us . . ."

"You know what?" Christiana said. "I think it would still mean a great deal to you."

He gave her a tight smile.

"I *did* see it, Julius."

"And I didn't."

"If you had, what would you think?"

For a long moment, he didn't answer. Then he said, "That I'd found a few tiles no one for many centuries has seen."

"And you would be, as you say, 'content' with that?"

He grunted. "You contend like a Jesuit." Putting the cat down, he walked over to the pew and touched the carton beside her. "What's in here?"

"A video camera," she said. "It has a special lens and infrared tape. In the words of my friend, it can pick up a black bear in the woods on a moonless midnight."

"Your 'friend'?"

"Actually, more of a government contact."

He gazed with new interest at the camera. "You're going to try and film this thing."

"That's right."

"You think you'll ever get near it again?"

She couldn't explain—not without bringing Hrluska into it, so she said, "Call it a reporter's hunch."

He shook his head. "You're not telling me everything."

"But I am."

"Ms. Clark—Christiana—from what you've told me, you know *nothing* about this thing. You don't know what it is. Even *it* may not know what it is. From what you say, it didn't want you to see it, and it may think you did not. But if you come after it with a camera and you actually manage to get close . . ."

"I'll be careful. Julius, this is real. I saw something out there, and it means something to you, too, I know it does. Maybe you can be content with knowing nothing more, but I can't." She stood. "It was good of you to give me your time."

He took her offered hand and shook. She was pleased. She had what she'd come for. He had taken her seriously. He thought she was on to something.

And now, if anything did happen to her, he'd feel involved, and he might follow up.

But nothing was going to happen to her. She didn't have to get near the creature who had fallen. What mattered now was the woman who had pushed him out, or frightened him so that he'd jumped. What kind of woman could do that? The diary revealed an ordinary girl in many ways, but something had changed Jenn Hrluska. Was it her miraculous recovery from leukemia? That was when the diary stopped. Dying, and then quite suddenly well, with no more entries to explain that. What was it this twelve-year-old dared not write down? That she was no longer a normal girl, but something different, something that could survive ten minutes without air, with superhuman strength, that could herself maybe fall seven stories, rise up unhurt, and vanish?

I'll watch her, Christiana thought, follow her at a safe distance, and next time there's something impossible, I'm going to get it on film.

And then Christiana Clark, who was going out of her skull with boredom, might just break the biggest story since the dawn of man.

Julius walked her to the door and shook her hand again. "Be careful," he said.

***

Upset by her visit to Brad, Jenn slipped into the front seat of her MG, desperate, now, finally to escape the hospital—

But something was wrong—the car was listing toward the passenger side. Had one of the shock absorbers failed? That's all right, she could still drive it, get it fixed later. She just wanted to be back home, safe inside her apartment. Her smashed window should be reglazed by now. She'd shut herself away in the sanctuary of her bedroom and think. She had big decisions to make.

She put the car in gear. As it started to roll from the parking place, she heard the sickening thunk-thunk of the flat tire. "Damn!" she yelled.

She popped the trunk and tore the spare from its bolt, stripping the threads and sending the nut skittering across the pavement. For an insane second, she considered tipping the car on its side rather than taking the time to fool with the jack. Then she got to work.

Twenty minutes later, she was rolling again. She found a parking place in a far corner of her apartment lot and loped through the lobby to the staircase.

When she entered her apartment, she caught the smell of blood again, very faint, but enough to raise her hackles. Must be the floorboards of the foyer still airing out. In her bedroom, she pulled off her white slacks and shirt and threw them into a corner. The act, so out of character for her, unsettled her. Retrieving them, she hung them in the closet, two pieces of her medical armor, so essential only a week ago.

Can I still be a doctor? she wondered.

What is happening to me?

Someone knocked at her door, a loud, continuous rapping. Annoyed, she pulled on her robe and stalked to the door, yanking it open.

A huge man in a suit and two uniformed cops stood in the doorway. A cold tendril of alarm slipped through her.

"Dr. Jenn Hrluska?" said the big man.

"That's right."

"I'm Detective Price. May we come in?"

"What's this about?"

"An associate of yours, Dr. Brad Dietz, is dead. It seems you were the last person to see him alive. I'd just like to ask you some questions."

She stared at him, stunned. *Zane! What in hell have you done!*

21

Christ—poor Brad! Staring at the huge detective standing in her doorway, Jenn blinked away a surprising pressure of tears. She had disliked Brad intensely, feared what he could do to her, but suddenly she saw the hollow-eyed young man, battling drug addiction to help himself so he could save children only a few years younger than he was.

Damn you, Zane, *why?*

But she knew why. Still, Zane's timing couldn't have been worse. He must have missed me by seconds, she thought. I was there only an hour ago. Half the staff must have seen me, but he didn't, or he'd never have put me in this mess.

"Dr. Hrluska?"

"I'm sorry, Detective. Come in." Stepping back, she made room for the big man to get past her. One of the uniformed cops stepped in with him. The other, a muscular man with a pleasant but unsmiling face, remained outside. To catch her if she tried to run out?

Jenn's heart began to pound. Maybe she *should* run. She got a terrifying flash of herself lying in a locked cell, starving for blood. No needles, no transfusion equipment, and if she killed another inmate, they'd put her in solitary. Slowly, she'd weaken and wither, turning old before their baffled eyes. She'd die in their cage while they studied her like a rat in a lab—one from which they'd learn far, far too much.

Dread brought Detective Price into a sharp, adrenaline focus: Six six, and broad as a door, with smooth ebony skin. Don't let that baby face fool you—but she could take him, and the other two with him. No prison, but her life would be destroyed. Worse, a young woman taking out three cops would be studied, too—especially if they got off some shots at her. *I swear to God I hit her, but she kept right on running, didn't even stagger.*

And if they managed to get a bullet into my brain, I'd fall, and then they'd get to see me recover. . . .

Jenn fought a trapped, helpless feeling. Stay calm, she told herself. If he'd meant to arrest you, he'd have done it already. He said 'questions,' so just give him the right answers and maybe you can get out of this.

Letting the tension bleed from her shoulders, she watched Price scan her apartment like a prospective buyer trying to see termites behind the wallpaper. The other cop who had come inside, a stocky man with the red face of a drinker, took off his uniform cap, revealing a matted tangle of dark brown hair. "Uh, Doctor, would you mind if I used your bathroom?"

"Through there, in the back."

"While you're at it, Jankow, do something about that hat hair," Price growled.

Jenn wondered if she should have let the cop out of her sight. But she could hardly have said no. And weren't they required to have a warrant to search? Anyway, there was nothing to find. Still, she did not like the way they were moving in on her, subtly boxing her in.

"How did Brad die?" Jenn asked.

"He bled out. Someone slashed a six-inch gap in his throat."

An image of white sheets soaked in blood hit her, raising both horror and the hunger. Backing up, she grabbed the arm of her recliner and sat down hard.

"Can I get you some water?" Price asked, mistaking it for shock.

"I'm all right."

Price lowered himself onto the camelbacked sofa with the slow care of a man who had caved in more than one piece of furniture. "Can you think of any reason," he said, "why someone would want to murder Dr. Dietz?"

"I have no idea."

"They told me you worked with him."

"That's right."

"What did you think of him?"

Jenn hesitated. If he hadn't yet learned she didn't like Brad, all he had to do was talk to her co-workers on pediatrics. "He could be hard to like," she said.

"In what way?"

"Brash, obnoxious—you know."

Price leaned forward with obvious interest. "You had some run-ins with him?"

"Not really. He hit on me a few times, but he did that to other women, too." Jenn felt the tension returning to her neck. He was trying to hem her in. He'll find out Brad turned me in for using drugs, she thought. Better I should tell him.

"He hit on you," Price said. "Did he ever try to force himself on you?"

"Never. It was just schoolboy stuff. Brad needed to grow up."

"I guess that's out, now." Price gazed blandly at her, but she could almost feel what he was thinking: *you killed him, Doctor, and we both know it.*

"There's something else," she said. "I'm quite sure Brad was using drugs. I confronted him on it in private. After that, he put some amphetamines in my locker and turned me in. It wasn't that big a deal—I was cleared right away."

"But it didn't exactly endear him to you."

"No." She forced a smile, and Price smiled, too, but without warmth. I have to do something, quick! she thought. "Detective, I didn't much like Brad, but I did feel sorry for him, and I tried to help him all I could. When he cut his wrists, I'm the one he called. I drove over to his place in the middle of the night and kept him from bleeding to death, then took him to the hospital."

Price stared at her with obvious surprise, and she thought she could see disappointment as well. "I wonder why no one at the hospital thought to tell me that."

"I imagine they're as shocked as I am. But it should be on the chart."

Price rose with a fluid, easy grace, all pose of weariness gone. "Sorry to have troubled you, Doctor. You'll be around, right, in case I come up with more questions?"

"Of course." Jenn stood, too, relieved. *I made it!* "I hope you find who did it." But she knew that good luck for this cop would be never getting a step closer to Zane.

"Jankow," Price shouted. "For crying out loud, let's go."

The cop stepped into the living room. In his hand was a handkerchief. It took Jenn a shocked second to see what dangled from his pinched thumb and forefinger—a big, long-bladed hunting knife. It glistened with water, dripping now on her floor. The droplets seemed to fall in slow motion. When they splashed, she could smell the blood in them.

Run! she thought.

NO!

A world-weary expression crossed Price's face. "Toilet tank?"

"Where else?" Jankow said. "Why does everyone think that's such a good hiding place?"

"I never saw that before in my life," Jenn said desperately.

Price turned toward her, reaching into the back of his coat for what she knew were handcuffs.

"I'm being framed," she said.

As if she hadn't spoken, he said, "Dr. Hrluska, you are under arrest for the murder of Brad Dietz. You have the right to remain silent . . ."

Still staring at the knife, seeing suddenly what had happened, she felt a crushing betrayal, a pain greater than she could have imagined. Zane *had* known she was there with Brad. In fact, he'd shown himself to

Brad purposely to jog his memory, knowing Brad would then demand to see her. She'd walked right into the trap, and as soon as she'd left, he'd slit Brad's throat. The flat tire—that was to give him time to get here and plant the knife.

The handcuffs felt cold and tight on her wrists. I will *not* cry! she thought, but the tears came anyway, pouring suddenly down her face. I wanted him to love me, she thought. All my life I dreamed of it. But he doesn't. He never did.

Jenn ached with humiliation and suppressed fury as she waited in the holding cell for Merrick to come. Spurning the sagging cot, she crouched on her haunches in a rear corner, pressing her back into the angle of the walls. From here she could keep an eye on the whole cell. It was a loathsome place, ten by ten, with three cinderblock walls and a fourth of bars, a floor of filthy gray concrete and not much else. The sink and toilet in the opposite corner reeked of lye and she could smell urine and mildew in the cot.

A cage.

She closed her eyes, but a white-on-black afterimage of prison bars continued to burn in her brain. Zoos were too enlightened to put higher primates in a place like this. But she was a higher primate no longer. She was a murder suspect, subhuman. Her skin burned with the memory of the matron's rough hands probing her during the strip search. The orange jumpsuit was coarse and clownish, without the laughs. Her fingers felt greasy with fingerprint ink. The voice behind the harsh lights, telling her which way to turn during the mug shots, had been empty of all human warmth. They had transformed her from Dr. Jenn Hrluska, pediatric intern, into Hrluska, J., prisoner number 10654F, letting her keep nothing of her former self.

Zane's name turned in her throat, sharp as broken glass. Zane, why? *Zane, why?* She remembered him only yesterday in her dining room, professing his love. How unreal! Well, no different from the foolish fantasies she'd harbored all the years she'd thought him dead. She'd imagined she could help him—that, unconsciously, he might want her to pull him in from the dark. But what he'd wanted was to pull her out with him, to destroy everything good she'd tried to build in herself.

I wish he *were* dead!

And then her fury faded. How? How could this have happened? Only a few hours ago she'd learned that one of her colleagues had been murdered—all right, she hadn't liked Brad, but she should have been horrified all the same. But an hour before that, she'd been thinking of killing him herself. Could she have sunk so low? I even was longing for Hugh to be a phage, she thought, a *killer*—my dear, good, tormented Hugh, who is terrified it might be true and would be destroyed if it is. She shuddered. Zane somehow had mesmerized her, deadening her to everything she held dear. She had never lacked for love. Why then had his meant so much?

Why did it hurt so, even now, to know she didn't have it, could never have it?

Pushing up, Jenn went to the filthy basin and splashed water on her face. It was tepid and smelled of chemicals. She became aware of the distant racket of other cellblocks, women shouting to each other—thin, desperate peals of laughter that sent a pulse of dread through her. I have to get out of here, she thought. *Where is Merrick?* She glanced at her wrist, but they'd taken her watch, another humiliation. At least they'd let her talk to Merrick—her one phone call. "Don't do *anything*," he'd told her. She'd known what he meant.

But he'd said he'd be right there, and that had been forty minutes ago, at least.

Turning from the basin, Jenn looked up at the single window, high in the back wall, out of reach of any normal human, but an easy jump for her. The bars didn't look that thick, and if they were, maybe the mortar would be loose. What was outside? This cellblock seemed empty except for her; if she could get through that window, find the courtyard, and then the outer wall—

No. Merrick said not to do anything. Wait for him.

Returning to the corner, she slid down the wall into a crouch again and tried to empty her mind. Instead, she remembered herself thrusting the leave slip at Dave Bledsoe, arrogantly telling him to take it—or fire her. She groaned. She'd give anything to be back on the ward, taking abuse from Fortis Wayne or showing Lila how to thread a catheter. That's where she belonged, not in this stinking cell—

There! Footsteps!

Springing to the front of the cell, she tried to see down the corridor, a kennel run of featureless gray cement. The angle was too sharp, but she recognized the duck-footed tread of the guard who'd brought her here, and then the much fainter signature of Merrick's feet. She nearly wept with relief. But by the time they stood outside, she had herself under control.

Merrick said nothing as the guard unlocked the door. Stepping into the cell, he embraced her. The guard, a thick-legged man with a bland, sleepy expression, stepped back against the wall opposite the bars and watched them. Looking over Merrick's shoulder, she held the man's gaze as she probed his racing blood. He was much more alert than he seemed.

"Are you all right?" Merrick asked softly.

"No."

Releasing her, he turned to the guard. "Patrick, I need a few minutes alone with her, all right?"

At once, the guard moved away.

Her surprise must have showed, because Merrick said, "I know him from my days on the force. He's all right—or as all right as they get in here."

She gave a ragged laugh. "Oh, that cheers me up a lot."

"Sorry." He took her by the arms. "Jenn, they can't hurt you. Remember that."

"Can't hurt me?" she whispered. "What about when I begin to need blood?"

Merrick said, "That won't be for a while yet. We'll face that. In the meantime, you must be calm. Maybe we can get you out of here. They have to bring charges. There'll be a preliminary hearing. Should be tonight, but tomorrow morning at the latest. I've gotten you a lawyer—

Morris Redmund, probably the best criminal defense attorney in Washington. There isn't a homicide cop in the city who hasn't lost a collar because of him, and that includes me. He'll be in after we're done and he'll go into the preliminary hearing and request bail. If we can get the judge to agree—"

"If?"

Merrick hesitated. "I understand they found the knife in your apartment."

"Where Zane planted it," she said in a low voice.

"That does make it difficult. From what you told me, you did have a possible motive for killing Brad."

"So he tried to get me in trouble with the clinical director. That doesn't mean I'd cut his throat." She gave her head a furious shake, trying to discharge some of her tension. "This is so stupid! How could they imagine me being dumb enough to openly visit Brad, slash his throat, and then keep the knife?"

Merrick put a calming hand on her shoulder. "If this ever goes to trial, Redmund will hammer that point home to the jury. But, Jenn, I've investigated thousands of murders over the years, and I can't tell you how many times brilliant people do stupid things after killing someone. The heat of it, the emotional upheaval, can wipe out reason, leaving the killer almost in a daze."

All at once Jenn felt even more scared than when she'd been waiting for Merrick to show up. In the back of her mind, she'd believed he could somehow fix things, but now there was no quick fix—maybe no fix at all. . . .

And then she remembered something. "They never showed me a search warrant!"

"I'm sure they didn't have one. There wouldn't have been time. But it might not matter. On the way in, I talked with Price—"

"Did you work with him?"

"He transferred in from the Chicago PD about the time I retired. I knew him by reputation, and he knew I had been in the department, so he told me more than he normally would. It's not good, Jenn. Price is a bulldog, and he's not above cutting corners to get a conviction if he thinks someone's guilty. Jankow, the cop who actually found the knife, claims he was just using the toilet and it started to overflow, so he took the top off to pull up the float."

"He's lying!"

"Probably, but it sounds credible, and if the judge agrees, it's not a search so the knife will be admissible. Or they might argue they were in hot pursuit of a viable suspect—the last person to see Brad alive." Merrick hesitated. "But we have maybe a bigger problem. This was very bloody. In a knife murder like this, one thing the prosecutor always wants to know is whether the killer cut himself. To look for your blood on Brad or around the crime scene, they have to have a sample of it first."

"Damn it!" Jenn felt suddenly as if the cell was narrowing, closing in on her. "Can I refuse?"

"We can have Redmund try and block it, but in my experience, despite self-incrimination and privacy issues, judges usually give the order."

Jenn stalked to the rear of the cell and slapped the concrete wall. "If they come to take my blood, I could handle them and escape, but that would raise bloody hell. Then they'd be obsessed with how I could have managed it. And I'd be on the run from then on. My life as a doctor would be over. You and I would be separated. Zane will have beaten us, damn him. . . ."

Struck by an idea, she turned back to Merrick. "Wait a minute. If you could slip back in here, using Influence so you're not seen, then intercept the blood sample after they've taken it . . ." His grim expression caused her to stop.

"I'm sorry, Jenn, but I've lost it. What little I had left disappeared a couple of months ago. That's why, when we feed, I don't come in until you've made them unconscious."

Her heart sank.

"If I stopped taking Fraction Eight," he said, "the ability might come back, but I just had another injection a few days ago. It might be months—if ever—before I showed any recovery, and that will be far too late."

Zane's trap, she realized, had closed perfectly, leaving her no way out except toward darkness. Her stomach twisted with dread. "Escape or stay," she said, "either way is disaster. Merrick, what do I do?"

"You have to choose. I can't make that decision for you. But whatever you do decide, I'll back you up every way I can."

She pulled him to her, hugging him tight. Dear Merrick—Grandfather. She'd always depended on him, and he'd never let her down. But now there was nothing he could do.

"There is one possibility, but he's a real long shot."

The reluctance in Merrick's voice cautioned her, but right now she'd grasp even the slimmest hope. Stepping back, she tried to read his face. "Who?"

"Hugh—if he *is* a phage."

22

Hugh McCall's stomach churned with worry and frustration. He jumped the three steps up from his living room and paced through the dining room to the kitchen phone, knowing it had only been ten minutes since his last call but unable to help himself. Pushing redial, he listened to the cold, indifferent buzz repeat itself on the other end of the line. *Click:* "Hello, I can't come to the phone right now, but leave a message and I'll get back to you."

Jenn's voice, smooth and confident, radiating that wonderful energy of hers. He didn't leave a message. What would he say that he hadn't put in the three previous recordings?

Jenn, where are you?

He hung up and was almost to the foyer closet for his jacket when he made himself stop. He'd never be able to persuade the super at her apartment to let him in a second time. And an hour ago, everything had been in order, no Jenn lying on the floor, no lamps tipped over. Her suitcase had been in the closet, and so were her clothes. So where was she? Her chief at the hospital would say only that she'd taken leave and he had no idea when she'd return. It was scary.

Why didn't she at least call me?

Misery swept him like a fever, making his face hot. I should never have confronted her, he thought. First she's afraid her biological father might be a killer, and now maybe me too. No wonder she's run off somewhere. Could she be trying to decide if she ever wants to see me again?

Picking up the phone again, Hugh dialed Merrick Chapman's number and once more got his machine, too. "Jenn," Hugh said, "if you're there, please pick up!" He repeated it several times to keep the tape going. After a minute, the machine clicked off anyway.

She's got to be there, he thought. When she's not here or home or at the hospital, that's where she goes.

He pulled on his leather jacket, then stood, rooted. What was he going to do at Merrick's, break the door down? He'd already stood ringing the bell for five minutes, until a neighbor came out and stared at him—

His own doorbell rang.

Hugh's heart leapt. *Jenn! Please God.*

He jerked the door open. For a wonder-struck second, it seemed Sean Connery had stepped out of one of the early James Bond movies onto his front stoop—the young Connery, but with the older Connery's silvery movie hair—and then Hugh realized who it was. The nape of his neck prickled, but he kept all recognition from his face. "Yes?"

"My name is Merrick Chapman. I'm a friend of Jenn Hrluska's. I'm sorry to intrude, but I wonder if I might have a word with you." A deep voice, cultured, and—despite the lack of Scots or any other accent, the impression of Connery deepened.

"Please, come in," Hugh said.

"But you were going out."

"It can wait." Pulling the jacket off, he threw it over the newel post and led the way to the sunken living room, feeling Merrick's eyes on his back. He motioned to the couch across from the fireplace, but Merrick waited until he'd seated himself in the sling chair before perching on the edge of the couch.

"Something to drink? A beer?"

"Thank you, no," Merrick said.

Hugh felt incredibly nervous. He'd planned and schemed for a chance to meet this man, who might have the answers he needed. And all the while, he'd managed to avoid actually coming face to face with him because he was so afraid of what he might learn. Now the moment had come, and he still wasn't ready. In a few days, soon, he'd try to find out what Merrick knew about the killings ten years ago. I've met him now, Hugh thought. That's a step. "Speaking of Jenn," he said, "have you heard from her lately?"

"Yes," Merrick said. "I just saw her."

Hugh felt a momentary, vast relief, which faded when Merrick did not go on. "Is she all right?"

"Certainly, why do you ask?"

"I've been calling her apartment, the hospital, trying to reach her, and no one seems to know where she is."

Merrick nodded.

Hugh felt a surge of frustration. "Look—"

"I'll tell you where she is, but first I have a few questions of my own, if you don't mind."

Hugh's scalp prickled. She told him, he realized with a shock. She told him everything I said to her. She *is* at his place, and the reason he doesn't want to tell me is because he's afraid I might be the killer he was after ten years ago.

But who made him Jenn's protector?

Hugh felt a stab of jealousy. Until now, he'd seen Merrick only from a distance, and the silver hair had fooled him. This guy was young— young enough to be in love with Jenn. If he *wasn't* in love with her, he was a fool.

But the only thing that mattered now was that Jenn was safe.

"How about it?" Merrick asked.

Curiously, Hugh felt himself relaxing into a fatalistic calm. If it was the price for knowing Jenn was all right, let Merrick ask his questions.

"Go ahead."

"Do you really think you may have killed one or more women ten years ago?"

The man's directness brought back Hugh's fear. "And if I said yes?"

"This is not going to become a police matter, if that's what you're asking. This is just between you and me, all right?"

He still wants to catch the killer, Hugh thought. Those rumors that he deliberately let him slip away aren't true. And then it flashed through Hugh's mind that if Merrick decided he *was* the murderer, that one of them might not leave here alive. But this was his chance, and no matter how much he feared the answer, it was time to know it—if he could. "All right," he said.

"You have a recurrent dream about killing a woman."

"Sometimes a dream, sometimes it's more like a flashback, a memory, very vivid, but broken up, incoherent." Hugh felt a fierce tightness in his chest. Merrick, the cop who had chased a vicious killer ten years ago and never caught him, had, at last, become his confessor.

"Do you specifically remember the act of killing them?"

"Actually, no. It starts with me waking up with a knife in my hand. I'm very confused, can't remember where I've been or what I've been doing. I'm in the backseat of a car. Then I . . . find the woman's body on the floor."

"Naked," Merrick said.

"No. She has all her clothes on. Her throat has been cut." Hugh felt the first tendrils of headache reaching up from the base of his skull.

Merrick leaned forward. "How old is this woman?"

"Mid-twenties."

"What is her appearance?"

"She is—was—pretty."

"What color is her hair?"

"Brown, just like the victims in those killings ten years ago. I've read all the articles, Mr. Chapman. I know everything written about the murders, and the women in my . . . nightmare fit the description." Hugh raised both hands, clamping his head briefly, trying to stop the pounding there.

"Headache?" Merrick asked.

"Always, when I think about this."

Merrick sat back, studying him. "You say the woman is always in a car. Does your dream ever include auto accidents?"

Hugh shook his head. He wanted to ask what Merrick was getting at, but before he could, Merrick said, "Ever have trouble sleeping?"

"I don't seem to need as much as most people," Hugh said. "I write at night until about 3 A.M. Then I knock off for a while. I usually get a few hours then, but sometimes I watch TV, old movies, whatever's on cable."

"Are there times when you don't sleep at all?"

"After I've had one of the nightmares. Scared to, I guess."

"How long?"

"A couple of days, sometimes more."

"You must get very tired."

"You'd think I would, but if I am, I'm not aware of it. I push it with the writing, get a lot of work done. It's an escape, I guess."

Merrick nodded. His face held a grim fascination. "So you have more energy after these dreams."

"If you can call suppressed panic energy."

"How about your sense of smell?"

Again, Hugh felt the presence of a deeper, hidden agenda. "What are you getting at? Epilepsy?"

"Epileptics are no more violent on the whole than anyone else, but they do have fugue states, so it's a possibility. What about it—any changes in your sense of smell?"

"Not that I'm aware."

A light frown creased Merrick's forehead.

"So what do you think?"

"Ten years ago," Merrick said, "the killer left some of his blood on one of the victims."

Hugh's stomach tightened. "That was never in the papers."

"No. Would you be willing to give me a sample of your blood? I can compare it to the killer's and I might be able to rule you out."

"Or in."

Merrick said nothing, gazing at him.

Hugh felt his body stiffen with dread. *I have to know.* "Let's do it."

Merrick took three paper packets from the pocket of his sport coat, one small and the other two larger. He tore the paper off one of the larger ones, revealing a scalpel. The small one held a glass slide. "I'm going to make a small cut just above the elbow," he said.

"Fewer nerve endings."

"Right."

Hugh rolled up his sleeve as Merrick tore open the third packet, revealing a square of sterile gauze. The blade stung as it passed over the tight skin above his elbow, then he felt the cool slide of glass as Merrick took the smear. Merrick seemed to fumble with the gauze, then searched his pockets, finally producing a roll of white surgical tape. Tearing off a piece, he taped the gauze into place.

"All right," he said.

"You can do the typing yourself?"

"I'll have my wife do it. She's a hematologist. I won't tell her what it's about, of course."

"How soon will you know?"

"She's out of town, due back in tonight. We'll do it as quickly as possible. How about that beer now?"

It seemed an odd request, but Hugh said, "Sure. And then will you tell me what's up with Jenn?"

Merrick nodded.

Hugh poured two Dominion lagers into his best glasses and brought them back to the living room. Instead of drinking, Merrick set his on the coffee table. "Let me take a look at that cut."

"It's fine. I barely felt it."

But Merrick had stood, so Hugh rolled up his sleeve again and felt the slight pull of the tape tearing loose. Merrick's expression was intent as he looked at the cut, and then his face relaxed. "Still bleeding a little," Merrick said. "You might want to keep a little pressure on it." He stuck the gauze back into place, then sat and held up the beer toward Hugh. There was a strange hint of disappointment in his face, but he said, "To innocence."

"Amen," Hugh said fervently, taking a deep pull at his own glass. "Now, about Jenn. You said she was all right."

"Yes."

"Where is she?"

Suddenly, Merrick's face, for all its youth, looked old. "A holding cell at the D.C. jail."

Hugh seethed with impatience as the guard put him through the metal detector and patted him down. At last, the man keyed him through into the visitation room. Jenn was already sitting behind the glass, gazing toward the door. As he hurried to her, he could see that she was trying to smile, but the torment in her eyes struck him with fear for her. He slid into the chair on the other side of the glass, frustrated that he could not take her in his arms.

"Jenn . . ." His throat closed.

"Oh, Hugh," she said.

All those prison movies, where the lovers pressed hands against the glass, but what he wanted was to smash it and crawl inside with her. "Are you all right?"

She nodded, finally managing an unconvincing smile. "Merrick called a few minutes ago. They let me take it. He told me about your blood test."

He forced a laugh. "He's really something, your friend Merrick."

"Isn't he."

"Jenn, for God's sake, why didn't you call me?" At once he was angry at himself—he'd resolved not to bring that up.

"I'm sorry, Hugh. I should have. Things just got so crazy."

"I was afraid you'd gone into hiding because of the scene I made at the cathedral."

"I wish I *had* gone into hiding. Hugh . . ." She swallowed. "I'm terrified."

He put a hand against the glass and she placed her palm opposite his. "I know."

"This is where they put you," she said, "that time you wouldn't testify against your friend and the judge found you in contempt."

He nodded. "I was pretty scared, even though I figured it would only be a few weeks. It *will* get easier."

"Hugh, I can't stay here."

"When they set bail—"

"The judge already turned it down."

His heart sank. "This is insane. They can't really think you would murder anyone—I don't care how many knives they found."

"But they do."

"Do you have any idea who framed you?"

For a moment, she held his gaze. "No," she said.

"Your father, that's it, isn't it?"

"Sh-h-h-h." She pushed against his hand, so hard he could feel the glass bend against him.

"Damn it, why protect him? He's nothing to you—"

"It wasn't my father. Forget him."

He stared at her, trying to understand. "Don't close me out, Jenn. I love you."

Jenn bit her lip. "I'm sorry. Just remember, whatever happens, I love you, too."

Whatever happens. What was she planning to do, commit suicide? He leaned toward her, feeling a sudden choking anxiety. "Jenn, listen to me, don't do anything rash. It will be all right. We'll get another bail hearing, and if that fails, they'll find you not guilty, I'm sure of it—"

"There isn't time."

All of a sudden, he understood that she had meant it literally when she'd said she couldn't stay here. He made his decision instantly. "I know this place," he said in a low voice. "The guards, the layout, the weak spots. All the time I was in here, I thought about escape—as a fictional exercise and to keep myself together. Just hold on and be ready."

"Hugh, no—"

"Yes," he said. "I'm going to break you out of here. Just you and me, baby, Bonnie and Clyde."

After they'd taken her back to her cell, Jenn made her decision. Actually, Hugh, with his quixotic talk, had made her decision for her. She'd done her best to make him drop the idea of breaking her out, but he'd refused. It was her fault, for letting him see how upset and terrified she was. But she could not let him get hurt or killed in some doomed jailbreak attempt. The guards all had guns, and Hugh, it turned out, was only a man after all, fragile, mortal.

And she could not believe how happy that made her. If Hugh had been a phage, he might have saved her from what was coming.

And lost himself.

The world needed the Hugh McCall she'd fallen in love with, a novelist who stirred people's blood, not a phage who shed it. And I need him, too, she thought, the kind, loving man who's still there after he's poured his demons into the word processor. But now—now I have to let him go.

Grief welled up, overwhelming her. What wouldn't she give for just twenty years with him—for one year?

But it couldn't be. Even if Hugh were not determined to risk his neck, she'd have to go. She couldn't put the slim chance of regaining the life she'd had here above the lives of all those who might die if, because of her, normals discovered phages. If she stayed, the normals would get a close look at her blood. What they could not learn from that, they'd begin to comprehend as they watched her weaken and age, her slow agonized death trapped in their cage, cut off from the blood she must have to survive.

Hugh promised he wouldn't do anything until tomorrow, Jenn thought. And he'll keep that promise, because it would take him at least that long to plan something. And by tomorrow, I'll be hundreds of miles from here—and Hugh won't be the only one wondering how I did it.

Sitting on the cot, Jenn composed herself. When she'd left the visitation room, it had been three o'clock. The guard, Patrick, perhaps out of deference for Merrick, had told her a tech would be coming between three-thirty and four to draw blood.

She felt her teeth clenching. Zane, she thought, you bastard. You never wanted me, all you wanted was to tear me away from Merrick. And in a few more minutes you'll have done it. She let the anger fill her and held on to it. It felt better than the grief. Getting up, she paced the cell, trying to visualize what lay ahead. She had to avoid using Influence except where she must, and keep physical force to a minimum, too. So easy to go too far, hit too hard. She was not a murderer and she was determined not to turn into one. If she was able to escape, afterward it must seem possible to those who'd be investigating it. It had to be an escape that, with determination and luck, a normal could have pulled off.

The door at the end of the corridor clanged, making her heart flutter. She took a deep breath and eased the air out. Closing her eyes, she listened: two of them—the guard, Patrick, and the other would be the technician. Yes, she could smell the anticoagulant in the test tubes. Her stomach went hollow with fear. A fierce tension gripped her. So much could go wrong, *don't let them shoot you, here they are—get ready!* Opening her eyes, she saw Patrick and a burly man in a white coat, with the standard kit. She waited until Patrick unlocked the door, then sprang at him, dilating his jugulars as she hit him in the nerve center just below his ribs. As Patrick went down, the tech gave a surprised grunt. Time seemed to slow; her body took over, her mind skidding as she kicked out the way she'd seen it done in a kung-fu movie once, slamming the tech against the bars. His head snapped back and his eyes went vacant, then closed as he fell.

The keys! she thought. Terrified someone had heard the crash of the tech hitting the bars, she dropped to her knees beside Patrick, ripping his belt from the loops to get the keys off. *Christ, hurry!* Shoving both bodies into her cell, she locked it. At the end of the corridor, she had to stop. Which key for this door? She had no idea. Controlling her panic, she slid one after another into the lock, trying to focus on what she'd find when she got through—a guard at a table, sitting there ogling her each time they'd brought her back and forth. *Got it!* The lock yielded, and she rushed through, sucking a quick breath. The guard pushed back from the table as he reached for his gun—*Damn you, no!* In a fury of fear, she lunged, knocking him against the concrete wall. He fell hard, heels rattling, and then she was past him, up another corridor, another brief but frantic key search, and she made it into the exercise yard. She could feel her heart hammering in a frenzy of fear and anticipation as she checked the two towers. A guard manned each, rifles on their shoulders. They'd see her the instant she ran into the courtyard, *got to use Influence now—no choice.* Her chest tight with anxiety, she blinded both men to her, then raced to the high wall and went straight up, finding plenty of purchase in the uneven slurry of cement. Concertina wire waited at the top, and she grabbed it, ignoring the searing pain, the slashes in her hands, fighting it, worming through as the knife edges raked her back and flayed her jumpsuit into strips, and then she was through. She heard a terrified gasping and realized distantly it was her. Clinging to the top of the wall with one arm, she tore loose a clean patch of cloth from her pant leg and took a moment to wipe all traces of her blood from the concertina wire. By the time she finished, the wounds in her hands and back had healed over.

Exhilaration filled her as she realized she was almost free. She let go of the wall and pushed off. Sailing down and down, turning like a cat, she landed in a crouch facing the road and sprang up again, registering the car that was parked there, and then the door opened and Zane stepped out.

She stared at him, stunned.

"Hello, daughter," he said with a smile. "What took you so long?"

23

Jenn was too astonished to speak.

Pulling open the passenger door, Zane said, "Hop in."

The hurt, the anger she felt at him blazed through her. "Go to hell!"

A siren on top of the prison wall gave an ear-splitting blast, then cycled through a slow, up-and-down wail that raised the hackles on her neck.

"I know you're upset with me," Zane said, "but right now, you need a ride."

Upset? Jenn stared at him, incredulous—Zane standing there, all this his fault, but saying I'll help you get away. How had the damned alarm sounded so fast? *Can I make it without him?*

The siren wailed on and on, beating at her eardrums, flooding her with panic. *Stop it, I can't think!* She felt herself lunge at the car, dive into the front seat. Zane disappeared, then reappeared on the driver's side, and she realized dimly that he'd vaulted over the roof. Sliding behind the wheel, he shifted into drive and pulled forward as he yanked the door shut. Instead of gunning the engine, he glided away from the prison with nightmare slowness. Jenn stared out the rear window at the prison gate. Any second, it would open. Cars would speed out to catch them. A choking dread filled her. "Hurry!" she cried.

"Don't you think you'd better leave this to me?" Zane said calmly. "I've had a lot more experience at escaping."

"You were in prison?"

He laughed lightly. "I should think not."

She looked out the rear window again, feeling some relief as they rounded a corner and the D.C. jail disappeared from view. All at once, she realized what Zane had meant. "Merrick."

His smile faded. "When the old bastard got close, he was a shark. And he has all the mercy of a shark, your grandfather—"

"Shut up," she said, and then felt a new spurt of fear. *Don't make him mad. He could bury you—maybe that's why he was waiting, to twist the knife into Merrick by putting you in the ground.* "Please," she said, "I can't listen right now, can't think—just get us out of here."

"Of course. Don't worry." She felt his hand on her shoulder for a second, light as a bird. He wheeled the car suddenly, making her gasp as he accelerated down a side street lined with run-down row houses. Dimly, she realized they were in Anacostia in southeast Washington, one of the poorest neighborhoods. As he sped down the street, she got blurred impressions of boarded-up windows, a trash-choked alley beside a grimy market. The light seemed dim and gray, the sky heavy as lead, and she realized twilight was coming. Zane wheeled around another corner and another, speeding now, doubling back so skillfully the tires did not squeal. A group of young men lounging on the corner watched them zip past.

"What are you doing?" Jenn asked.

"I think it's a motorcycle cop—no, don't turn around."

Her stomach tightened. She became aware of the throaty growl of the bike's engine several blocks behind. "Can you lose him?"

"Of course."

A moment later, Zane slowed. He drove south through the stark neighborhoods until a bridge took them across the Anacostia River and out of the city. He stayed on the highway for a few miles, then took a feeder road that meandered through the southern Maryland countryside. Seeing his hands relax on top of the wheel, she felt some of the tension leave her, too.

"We lost him," Zane said. "Normals are amateurs compared to Merrick. They can still be dangerous, especially in numbers, but I won't let them get you."

"You already let them," she said. "You ruined my life."

"You think that now," he said, "but it's not true, you'll see."

"It *is* true, you bastard." Unable to help herself, she whispered it again, *"Bastard,"* feeling a burn in her throat, a sudden pressure of tears. Look at him—her eyes, her mouth, her affliction, he *was* her father. Without him, she'd never have been born, and he'd risked Merrick to give her a second life. For years, thinking him dead, all she'd wanted was to believe he had saved her because he loved her, and then he'd come back, and she had seen it in his eyes—he *did* love her.

But he didn't—how could he, and do what he'd done?

"Ten years ago," she said, "you told me you were a king and I was your princess. That you had come back for me."

Zane's head snapped around and he gazed, wide-eyed at her.

"Watch out," she cried, "you'll wreck the car!"

He looked back just in time to swerve away from the shoulder. "You *remember,"* he said with wonder. "I thought you were almost unconscious when I said that."

"Of course I remembered. I made a vow that I'd never forget you. I clung to those few snippets of memory I had, even though I knew you did terrible things. I also knew it was you who saved me, and so I dreamed about you, made up stories in my head. Dreams were all I had because I thought you were dead. And then you come back, and make it all a lie. Upset?" She gave a bitter laugh. "Upset doesn't begin to describe it. You have no idea how you've made me feel, how angry, how hurt, how . . . *betrayed.* I wanted so much to believe you these past few days—in the woods, and then at my apartment, but it was all a lie, wasn't it! Merrick was right, damn him, all you cared about was *him,* all you wanted was to get back at *him.* You never cared about me." Tears began to roll down her cheeks, and she was furious with herself. You shouldn't be talking to him. Just get away from him as fast as you can.

Zane's mouth opened and closed, as if he couldn't find his voice. "I *do* love you," he said hoarsely. "I hadn't loved anyone for hundreds of years, and then I found you, and it was like I hadn't breathed in all that time, and now, suddenly, I could. It was so wonderful, the day I discovered you and realized who you were. I went to your house because I had once . . . felt something for your mother. Then I overheard her and her husband talking about you, about the leukemia, and I thought, 'No, it can't be,' but then I found your picture beside your mother's bed and saw myself in your face. I wanted to weep with joy, but I had forgotten how to cry. I went straight to the hospital. Every night, I sat by your bed, not daring to let you see me, but I kept grinning. Even deathly sick, you were so beautiful, my daughter—"

"Stop it!"

He fell silent.

She was furious at him again. Her emotions were on a roller coaster—fear, then anger at him, then the horrible sadness again. "How could you do this to me?"

"Why did you jump into that lake and pull out that child?"

"He was drowning!"

"Exactly."

"I was *not* drowning. I was doing what I loved."

"Were you? Were you really? It seems impossible." He seemed perplexed.

"How could you know?" she said. "You don't know me at all."

"But I know what it is to be one of us."

"Stop the car," she said.

To her surprise, he did. She sat looking at him, uncertain. Was he really going to let her go now? Would it be the last time she ever saw him? Despite everything, the thought panged her.

"I wish you would come with me," he said. There was such pain in his voice that she realized he might, after all, believe he loved her. But what use was that?

"Stay with me," Zane pleaded. "You need my help, and I want to help you."

"How sweet. You slaughtered poor Brad just to ruin me, and now you're going to help me."

"Yes, yes, all my fault, but that's why you have to let me help you now, get you out of this."

"I'll get out of it without you."

"You're sure?"

"I know how to use Influence."

"But do you know *when* to use it—and when not to? Are you sure you can manage it if they come upon you suddenly and you panic? Do you know how to alter your appearance so even your grandfather might not recognize you, how to get food without arousing suspicion, which roads are heavily patrolled, how and when to switch cars, where to settle so that no one will find you, but you can find everything you need?"

Jenn felt a rising anxiety. She'd had no time to think about any of these things. But, damn it, she was not going to let him intimidate her. "Thanks to you," she said, "I'll now have to learn all that."

"Thanks to my father, you couldn't have a better teacher."

"Stop trying to blame him for everything," she snapped.

Zane groaned, and she saw a vast frustration on his face. It gratified her. She wanted to hurt him, badly, the way he had hurt her.

"Maybe I *was* wrong to do this," he said. "I agonized over it, you don't know."

"You should have agonized over it some more." Jenn felt her firm expression crumbling toward tears. With an effort, she held the tears in check.

"You said I don't know you, and you're right, but how could I? I haven't been allowed. It's what I want more than anything." Zane looked both downcast and frustrated now. "You can't imagine how I've longed to sit down with you and talk—not just about what I want for you, but about your life, all I was forced to miss. What you like and dislike, all the little things I imagine a father loving to know about his daughter. That's what I came back for, and we were starting to get there the other night, and then

Father drove me off. That filled me with despair. I realized that as long as he was hovering over you, we would be lost to each other. Believe me, I'd never have done anything so drastic if anything less could have worked. I want to be a father to you, Jenn." He glanced at her, his eyes wide with hope—and something else, perhaps. Uncertainty?

"I have a father, a good, kind man who loved me and provided what I needed, and earned my love in return. I've done everything I could to make that man proud of me."

Zane looked stung. "I gave you all the love I could in the little time that was given to me. How can I persuade you, that despite all my blunders, all my unworthiness, I love you?"

Against her will, her heart began to thaw. She hardened it again. "There is no statute of limitations on murder," she said. "If I hadn't run, maybe I could have cleared my name, gotten my life back. But I had to run, because they were going to take a sample of my blood. You know all this, it's why you did it. So now I have to be on the run, I have to hide. In the eyes of everyone, I *am* a murderer, the very thing I have fought tooth and nail from the day I first took blood, and felt my first urge to kill. I spent years training to be a doctor, it was all I wanted, but now even if I manage to find someplace where I can settle down, where no one knows me, I can never practice medicine. For that you need licenses, a paper record of med school and internship, and my record, everything written on paper about me from the time I was born, is now a millstone around my neck, useful only to those who will be hunting me."

"Yes," Zane said. "But think: you became a doctor because my Father made you hate what you were born to be, to feel ashamed of yourself. He put you at war with yourself, tooth and nail, as you said. He never let you see how beautiful you are inside, how much a proper part of nature you are just as you were made. All I want is to help you love your true self, as you deserve to do."

Jenn couldn't help but feel the dark seductive power of his words. How skillfully he'd touched upon her deepest pain. She did hate a part of herself, he was right; she loathed the lust to kill that reared up in her every time she fed. When she thought about the Jenn who drank blood she wanted to shudder, to throw up. It was a terrible weight; how she longed to lay it down. But not his way, by deciding it was all right to kill. If there was no other way than Zane's, then she would carry her self-hatred always.

"In five hundred years," Zane said, "I never knew any of my children. You are the first. If I've made mistakes with you, it was not from malice, it was from not knowing. I've been alone so long, Jenn, and I don't want that anymore. I want to be with you, be a proper father to you, to give you back something that was taken away from you—something very precious. If you would just give me a chance."

"Don't you see? You're a killer, and I can never accept that, much less do it."

"We don't have to think about that now," he said urgently. "We can just be together awhile. I can get to know you, and you me. That other we will deal with when we have to—"

He stopped, cocking his head. A moment later, she heard it too, a distant siren growing slowly closer. Zane put the car back in gear and, keeping just within the speed limit, drove about a quarter of a mile through the countryside before turning off into a long gravel driveway. The house at the far end needed a coat of paint. Despite the overcast, no lights were on in the windows. He pulled around in back of the house and parked the car beside a rusted hulk that sat in the backyard.

"What if someone's home?" she asked.

"No one lives here. The place is abandoned."

She got a sudden, poignant sense of his life—always on the run from Merrick, consumed with watchfulness, attending constantly to details that normal men rarely think about. In a race glimpsed only in myths—the vampire, incubi and succubi—Zane was the ultimate hidden creature, a loner whose shadow never fell alone, but always among other shadows. So alone—he was right, and, despite her anger, she felt sad for him.

Listening to the distant siren, Jenn watched a pair of doves bob through a sparser patch in the overgrown grass, cooing to each other. Wind rattled the tattered remains of the convertible top on the rust-eaten car. Something nagged at the edge of consciousness. That motorcycle earlier, the way it had sounded—too loud, as if it needed a new muffler. Hugh's bike sounded just like that. Could he have been watching the prison, working on his escape plan maybe, and seen her come over the wall and get into Zane's car? When she'd heard the bike, Zane had said it was a motorcycle cop. *And he told me not to look back!* Jenn's heart twisted as she realized how near Hugh might have been. But if he'd caught up, Zane would have killed him.

She listened to the fading siren—this time a cop for sure, but he was getting colder every second. A desolate feeling came over her. There was no help for her—she was completely on her own now. And the first thing she had to do was get away from Zane. When she could no longer hear the siren, she said, "It's time I—"

He cut her off with a raised hand, and she realized he could still hear it. A moment later, he said, "All right, it's gone."

"It's time for me to go."

"Is there nothing I can say to persuade you?"

"No. I want you to leave me alone. That's what I need. If you feel anything for me, do it. Good-bye." Her heart strained to say more, but what was the use? She put her hand on the door latch . . .

And then she was with Hugh, sitting on the boardwalk at Ocean City, legs dangling over the edge as they watched a skinny young man with long hair, a full beard, and a deep tan sculpt the crucifixion in the sand. The man worked feverishly on one of Christ's outstretched arms, wetting a section of sand and then shaping it with his hands, his bare back glistening with sweat. Gulls wheeled and called overhead in an infinite blue sky, swooping down to peck around the edges of the man's fantastical domain. The smell of caramel corn started her mouth watering, and then she thought of the Dumser's dairy only a few blocks down, a vanilla cone, dipped, of course, which she would try to eat before the chocolate coating began dripping down on the boardwalk. Hugh put his arm around her, and she knew they would make love for the first time tonight, in the hot, close motel room over the amusement arcade, to the merry racket of pinball machines and speedway video games, and that it would be wonderful—

And then she was in Zane's car again, only now she lay along the backseat. She blinked, disoriented. What was that around her, cutting into her arms? She realized it was wire cable, very thick, wrapped around her from the top of her shoulders to her ankles. Panic burst in her and she fought the strands, but they were too thick, too strong. She succeeded only in bucking to the edge of the seat and almost falling over. A hand steadied her, eased her back. Twisting, she saw Zane's face above her.

"Untie me," she snapped.

"I'm sorry, but I can't do that. You have to stay with me, at least for a while. You have no idea how to run or hide. If they lock you up again, this time they'll make sure you don't get away."

"Let . . . me . . . *go!*"

He turned back to the wheel.

"Zane! Listen to me. I'll scream, as soon as we get near anyone."

"And then what? If someone tries to help you, and I decide to let them live, they'll see the face that will soon be on television and in the newspapers, if it isn't already. An escaped murderess. I could simply say I had caught you and was taking you back. I won't, of course, but your rescuers would. Prison, Jenn. Think: six months without blood and you'll be very weak. A year and you'll have trouble moving. It will take you another year to lose consciousness permanently, and even then you will not die. You are one of us now, whether you like it or not, and I am going to protect you. We'll go to Mexico. I know the area down south. It's quite beautiful."

"I'll never stay with you. I'll get away the first chance I get."

"Maybe. We'll see."

She fought the cable again, bucking and writhing in a fury of frustration, but she was helpless. A cold aftershock went through her as she realized what he'd done. This was the thing Merrick had told her about, his ability to extend Influence into blood vessels that served the memory cortex of the brain. She had been lost in a memory, which had seemed absolutely real. While in it, she couldn't see Zane or feel the cable snaking around her—she'd had no awareness of present reality at all. How could she fight something like that?

As Jenn felt the car start up and grind back down the gravel drive-way to the road, an abject hopelessness swept her, bringing a flood of tears. She made no sound as she wept, determined that Zane would not know. She grieved for everything she was leaving. Gregory, so bright and sweet, making me call him uncle even though he's only twelve. And Katie. She showed me how to be a doctor. Katie would have given a piece of her heart to Caroline, too—I wasn't wrong to do that, no matter how it hurt. I want my patients back. I want to see Lila again, hear her laugh. . . .

Letting herself think, finally, of Merrick, Jenn felt a choking pres-sure in her throat. God, I can't go two days without talking to him. My best friend, the only one who really understands me. How can I stand to lose him?

After about an hour, the car bumped suddenly onto the shoulder and stopped. It was nearly dark now, but she could see Zane's face clearly above her. It held a quizzical expression. His eyes shone with a strange, inner light. "Why didn't you threaten me with Father?" he asked.

She said nothing, but felt a sudden, fresh stab of fear.

"I know he won't leave Katie and his son," Zane mused, "not perma-nently, but surely he must have seen what I was up to when you were arrested. He should have anticipated my helping you break out. He should have been outside the prison, waiting for me. I was afraid of it—I looked for him, but he wasn't there. And now I tie you up, kidnap you, and all you can think to say is that you'll escape when you get a chance. No 'Merrick will find you and bury you.' How curious."

"He will find you," she said.

"I wonder. That night at your apartment, after I jumped, I never heard him behind me. I assumed he was there, but I never heard a foot-step. Is it possible he didn't chase me?"

"Of course he did."

Zane studied her face, and she remembered what Merrick had said about the ability of old, seasoned phages to read expression, to winnow through the smallest nuance of voice. She prayed he would not read the lie in her voice now. His eyes widened, and then a terrible, fierce grin transformed his face. "The gray hair," he murmured. "It's real."

"Oh, right—"

But he was outside the car now, and then the rear door opened and he lifted her out, slinging her over his shoulder and carrying her down an embankment and into a grove of trees. He laid her gently on the ground and, with another short piece of cable, padlocked her to the trunk of a maple.

"Where are you going?" she asked.

"I won't be long," he said. "The good news is that we won't have to go to Mexico after all."

"You think you can take him?" she said. "Go ahead, you fool—go on! He'll kill you. Good, that's good."

Struggling desperately against the cable, she heard a distant laugh, the rapturous cry of a man whose life's dream had come true.

"Father!" she screamed. The word felt strange, traitorous in her mouth, but she screamed it again. For a moment she heard nothing, and then his footsteps approached again, whispering through the weeds, and he stood over her once more.

"You say you love me," she said. "You ask how you can persuade me. This is how—show me this isn't about Merrick, that it hasn't been about him all along. Forget him."

Zane's eyes glittered. "Then he *is* weak."

"No." Her mind churned, trying to find the right words. "I don't want him to bury you."

Zane stared down at her with a mixture of hope and suspicion. "No," he said. "You're furious with me. You think I destroyed your life—you just said it would be good if he killed me."

"I didn't mean it."

"You're afraid I'll bury him. You are!"

"No. Can't you see? Even if you were right, which you're not, I want you to prove to me that you didn't come back to hurt him. That you came back for *me*."

"I can do both."

"No you can't."

"He deserves it, Jenn, for what he did to me. You saw that cell."

An image flashed in her mind, the marks his fingernails had left as he clawed at the steel door. She shivered in the cold of his hatred. "If you go back now," she said, "you'll be proving you don't love me, and I will never love you."

He stared at her, pressing a fist to his mouth. "And if I stay, you *will* love me?"

Say it, she thought. You must, to save Merrick. "Yes."

He stared at her. "Oh, Jenn. You are lying, don't you think I can tell?"

"No!"

But his face disappeared from above her and she heard him running away, and then the car door slammed and he was gone, gone to kill his father, and she cried out in despair, wishing more than anything that she could have just one more minute with Merrick to tell him how much she loved him.

24

For the second time in a hundred years, Merrick wanted to punch a man in the nose. As Detective Price tried to see past him into the house, the first time flitted through Merrick's mind: ten years ago, a cop that time, too—Lieutenant Cooke, demanding to know where he'd hidden Katie and Gregory a day after Zane had attacked them. Cooke he'd put on sick leave, not with a punch but with a few mental touches to major veins.

Now his fists were about all he had left.

Merrick slid both hands into his pockets. "What did you say, Detective?"

Price focused on him, hesitating, clearing his throat. "I said, you'd better not be hiding her here."

Merrick felt revulsion for the man. Look at him—big, cocky, trying to use his hard stare as a weapon of intimidation. Most detectives would maintain a certain courtesy with a retired cop, but not this bullying hulk of a man. You are not angry at him, Merrick told himself. Anger is not really what you're feeling. But you don't want to let this lout see your pain. "I may be retired," Merrick said, "but I'm still a cop."

"Meaning?"

"I respect the law."

Price looked amused. "Cut the bullshit, Chapman. You're not talking to some ladies' aid society."

I'm going to punch him anyway, Merrick thought. But he said, "Maybe you'd like a look around." *Not that you'd see her if she were standing right there beside you.*

"You heard him, boys."

The two uniformed cops who were with Price stepped past him into the house. One of them, a sergeant, touched the bill of his cap to Merrick.

"Digget?"

"That's right," the cop said with a smile. "I was just a patrolman when you left."

"And a good one."

"Thank you, sir."

The other cop, Jankow, had the fiery complexion of a boozer. As he passed, Merrick caught his arm. "Don't touch anything but doorknobs," he said softly. "Mess up my house and I'll mess you up."

Jankow raised both hands away from his body in a parody of fear. Still holding his arm, Merrick squeezed and Jankow's face blanched. "All *right!*" he gasped.

Turning back to Price, Merrick said, "Bullshit is claiming Dr. Hrluska's toilet was overflowing so you could look in the tank."

Price shrugged, his thick, hard face impassive. "That's for a judge to decide. And your friend Hrluska apparently wasn't at all confident she could beat the rap."

"That knife was planted."

"Was it?"

"That's what you should be asking yourself, not me. But you just want the collar, don't you? She *looks* good for it, so cash her in."

"Don't tell me you were any different," Price said, his eyes glittering suddenly with scorn.

"A lot of us are. Ask around."

"I did. The old-timers either worship your ground, or believe you had some kind of deal with the devil. Don't expect me to believe you ran up your count by being squeaky clean."

"I don't care what you think about me. But by arresting Dr. Hrluska, you took a skilled and caring young doctor away from children who need her."

"Hey, if she wasn't guilty, why'd she break out of jail?"

"Because she didn't belong there."

"What makes you so sure? Like maybe you did Dietz yourself?"

"At least now you're thinking outside the box," Merrick said. "But not very well. I'd never met Dietz in my life, and if you can find an attendant who let me in, I'll go to jail with you right now."

Price studied him. "I believe you would, just to get her off the hook. What is she to you, anyway?"

"A friend."

"Yeah, right. She gets one phone call, and she doesn't blow it on a lawyer, or her mom or dad, or her chief resident. Nope, she calls you. Her *friend*. Quite a looker, your friend. Was she as good in bed as she looked out of it?"

Without feeling himself move, Merrick had him by the jaw, lifting him up and back until his flailing heels, a foot off the ground, battered the wall. Merrick held him there a few seconds, savoring the fear in his eyes, then disgust at himself made him let go. Price dropped heavily to his hands and knees, gasping, then reached inside his jacket, pulling out his gun, seeming to move in slow motion. Merrick snatched the gun from his hand, surprised he could still move so fast, glad to know he hadn't lost everything yet.

Price gaped at his empty gun hand, then lurched to his feet. "That's assault on a police officer," he gasped.

"You come to my house," Merrick said softly, "and accuse me of harboring a fugitive, then of cheating on my wife," *with my own grand-daughter*, "and when I object, you try to shoot me, and I take your gun away. That would make a nice report, wouldn't it? How about it—would your captain and our mutual acquaintances in homicide believe me or you?"

"Fuck you."

Merrick took a step toward him and he backed up hastily, then stopped when he saw Merrick was handing him his gun back. He held it a second, then stuffed it into his shoulder holster as Sergeant Digget appeared from the kitchen. "I heard some noise. Everything all right in here?"

"Fine," Price grunted. "You find anything?"

"No. She's not here. I told you she wouldn't be."

Jankow appeared from the living room and gave a slight shake of his head.

"Let's go," Price said.

"Thanks for your cooperation, Lieutenant Merrick," Digget said with a sidelong glance at Price.

Merrick nodded. "Detective, a word with you."

Stiffly, Price turned. When the other two were outside, Merrick said, "Detective Price, I lost my temper. I apologize to you."

Price's shoulders sagged a little. He gave Merrick a look of wary curiosity. "You are more than a little strange, Chapman. Do you know that?"

"I know it."

"Maybe I was out of line, too."

Merrick nodded. "I appreciate it."

His hand on the doorknob, Price turned back. "I'm six foot six and I weigh two-eighty. That's fifty pounds on you, Merrick. I'd sure like to know how a retired cop, even a big lug like you, could lift me a foot off the ground with one hand."

"Yoga," Merrick said. "I can introduce you to my guru—"

"Forget it."

When he was gone, Merrick went into the living room and sat in front of the TV. His arm was trembling now, from holding Price up, and he rubbed at the sore muscle. Stupid, stupid.

Merrick thought of Jenn, out in the night alone, running, with no one to help her. Bending forward, he pressed his face into his hands, stricken for her, and for himself, wishing there was a damn thing in the world he could do about it. Somehow, it hurt that she had not told him her decision, even though he knew she'd done it to protect him, to keep him away so he wouldn't be suspected of helping her. But he at least could have helped her think it through. Had she considered that Zane might have been hanging around the jail, waiting for her to break out?

If so, she might not be alone.

And she would now be in the greatest danger of all.

Driven by a sudden fierce agitation, Merrick got up and paced around the living room. *Had* Zane been there? The more he thought about it, the less a question it became, the more an ugly likelihood. Zane might be content with seeing Jenn in prison, her life ruined, but wouldn't he find it even more satisfying to turn her to killing? If so, he'd have been waiting outside the wall when she came over, full of apologies, ready to help her escape—and then to go on "helping" her. Anguished, Merrick drove a fist into his palm. *If she'd told me she was breaking out, I could have been outside. With me there, Zane would be too scared to move in on her.*

And if he were not too scared?

I'd be dead now.

Demoralized, Merrick sank down on the edge of the couch again. If Zane *had* been lying in wait for her, how had she handled it? Had she gotten free of him, or would he be able to hang on, then begin to break her down, turn her?

Surely not.

And when he couldn't? Would he finally let her go, or bury her?

The phone at the end of the couch rang, and he snatched it up. "Merrick."

"Hiya, handsome."

"Katie!" Just hearing her voice sent a warm thrill through him. "Where are you?"

"I'm back."

"The airport?"

"No, I cabbed straight to the hospital. I'm in my lab. I got it, Merrick, a big sample."

His mind raced. What if Price had put a tap on his phone? Quickly, he said, "Great, Katie. Now all you have to do is find a cure and you'll be famous."

For a second, she said nothing. Then she gave a little laugh, and he knew with relief that she understood. "Right," she said. "I did some preliminary extraction and concentrating at the lab in St. Louis. I just have a bit more work to get the sample in . . . useful shape for . . . study. I thought I'd do that here in my lab, and then I'll come straight home."

"Fine," he said. Not sure who might be listening in, he could not tell her there'd be no use in making Fraction Eight to bring Zane down; that Jenn was gone, and Zane with her. "I miss you terribly," he said.

"Well then, we'll just have to teach you how to miss me properly."

He managed a laugh.

"Where's the Greg-meister?"

"Shooting Zombies on the neighbor's PowerMac."

"I can see I've been away too long."

"That you have."

"I'll be home soon. Love you."

"I love you too—properly."

"Oh dear," she said. "We'll have to fix that, too."

He hung up and, before his mood could sink again, switched on the TV news. It was five minutes before they got to the top story—Jenn. The anchor's eyes lit with an interest in the story that did not seem faked: "Earlier today," she said, "officials at D.C. jail were stunned by the daring and mysterious escape of Dr. Jenn Hrluska, who had been jailed yesterday on suspicion of murder."

The prison photo of Jenn appeared on the screen. Merrick's heart compressed. There was no sign of fear on her face, but he could read the desolation in her eyes. He cursed softly—the earlier report had not carried a photo. Now Jenn would have to hide herself. She wouldn't dare sit down in a roadside restaurant, drive through a tollbooth. Whatever she needed, she'd have to steal. Whether Zane turned her or not, she'd gone from children's doctor to outlaw. The simplest acts would now be dangerous.

Merrick listened carefully to the newswoman's account, weighing each expression of amazement by prison officials and the anchor herself, trying to judge the level of peril. "Prison officials still have no idea," the woman said, "how young Dr. Hrluska, twenty-two, managed to escape. In fact, they have not ruled out that she may still be in the prison somewhere, hiding out in some ductwork, perhaps, or maybe in a space behind some wall. Original blueprints of the prison are being studied in the chance she is still inside. Guards in the tower saw nothing suspicious and the sheer walls of the exercise yard are topped by razor-sharp concertina wire, impassable unless cut, which it was not. But the prevailing opinion is that Dr. Hrluska indeed escaped, possibly by clinging to the underside of a service vehicle. She would apparently be strong and athletic enough, since she was able to overpower three men, two of them guards, in her initial escape from her cell. But after that, she vanished, and, despite an area-wide alert and search, there has thus far been no sign of her."

Merrick switched the set off, relieved at least of one fear. At this point, no one was attributing Jenn's escape to superhuman abilities. She had used ingenuity, avoiding any clearly impossible moves. He felt a perverse pride at how cool she'd been under enormous stress. But the broader danger wasn't over. For the next few weeks or months, there would be a tireless pursuit—

A smell, very faint, made Merrick's scalp prickle. Leaping from the couch, he turned, appalled at how close Zane had gotten. His heart hammered with a sudden, deathly fear.

"Hello, Father."

Standing there in the living room doorway, Zane, only twelve feet away, a hand poised on the arch to give him an extra push if he had to run, and Merrick realized he wasn't quite sure yet.

"Hello, son." Suddenly, looking death in the face, Merrick felt a strange calm. He weighed his few options. Rush him now, and hope he would run? But if he didn't run, all bluffing would be over.

"I thought you had bleached your hair," Zane said. "To convince the normals around here you were getting older."

"You *thought*?"

Zane flicked a hand in negation. "It's too late, Father. If I was wrong you would have charged me the minute you saw me. You've lost it. Somehow, some way, you've lost it. I thought we were supposed to live fourteen or fifteen hundred years, but something's cutting you down. All that clean living?"

The cold hatred, the dawning triumph in his son's eyes, chilled Merrick, but he forced himself to meet the hard gaze. "Has it occurred to you that I have not 'charged' you, because I want to know what you've done with Jenn? If you have me at any disadvantage, that's it."

"Oh, really? Then I'll tell you. Jenn is with me now."

"That is certainly a lie."

"You think you're the only one she could care about? If she can love the grandfather who was willing to let her die, she can love the father who saved her."

"I didn't know then that she was ours," Merrick said. "But you were right to save her, and I was wrong."

Zane's face lost its harsh focus for a second, then hardened again. "And how about putting your own son in the ground? Was that a mistake, too?"

"No. It was the most difficult thing I have ever done, but it was not a mistake."

Zane shook his head. "Even now you're in my face. You've got guts, old man. I'll say that for you."

"I don't need guts," Merrick said, "to handle you. Now tell me what you know about Jenn. Tell me the truth, and I may let you go."

Zane gave a harsh laugh.

Had there, Merrick wondered, been just the slightest uncertainty in it?

"Your granddaughter is lying in a ravine, trussed up in cable—a trick I learned from you, Father. But the time will come when the blinders you put on her will fall off and she'll understand that, in fact, I have liberated her."

"Will that be before or after you untie her?"

"We'll go hunting together, Father, I guarantee it."

"She saved children, Zane."

"And nothing could be more wrongheaded."

"Have you no heart at all?"

Zane's eyes flashed. "You know nothing. Why do you think I keep myself apart from normals? Because I don't care about them? You've got it backward. I manage not to care about them because I keep myself apart. You have no idea what that's like, do you, you sentimental old fool—to be alone? You think your love of them is an act of nobility. It's a monstrous self-indulgence! Merrick doesn't want to be alone, so he isn't. How very simple. But you're the one who is perverted, not me. We are the lions, Father. And they are the zebras. Nature made us to thin the herd, and the herd *needs* to be thinned, but you—"

"Zane the moralist," Merrick said, disgusted. "You don't give a damn about any of that, but you still try and justify yourself."

"Thanks to you, old man. Because I loved you, you had the power to make me hate myself, and you did your best at that, you did. I may have run from you for five hundred years, but I'm the stronger one now, because I've managed to undo what my father did to me. You're right. I don't give a damn about thinning the herd. I love to kill, and Jenn is going to love it, too. I just wish you could live to see it."

Merrick looked him in the eyes and said, "You think you can take me? Come and get me."

The green eyes glittered with a sudden sheen. Fear, or rage?

And then Zane sprang.

As Zane sailed over the couch at him, Merrick knew an instant of bitter resignation. Running was useless. Crouching, he raised both hands to ward off the first blow—

And then he was sitting with Sandeman on a bench in Gorky Park. After six days in the dark, sooty train compartment with only a stopover in St. Petersburg to relieve the cramped monotony, it felt wonderful to sit in the open on a bright cold day. Sandeman had bought them beers, from a kiosk near the park entrance. Merrick took a long swallow, fragrant with malt.

"*Pazhalsta,*" said a stoop-shouldered babushka with a broom, and Merrick lifted his feet so she could sweep beneath them. Spring, but three inches of fresh, powdery snow covered the park, obviously a personal affront to the old woman. She clicked her tongue irritably at the way his and Sandeman's boots had compressed the snow into foot-shaped pancakes that resisted her broom. A girl and three boys skated by on one of the paths, scarves trailing, warming the morning with their laughter. Beyond the skating path, the gray-brown Moscow River, skirted in ice, rolled sluggishly up toward the Kremlin. Merrick inhaled deeply of the raw air, glad to be alive in an intriguing and alien city. When the old woman had moved on out of earshot, he said, "What do you think of Khrushchev?"

"A thug like all the rest, but worse because he has imagination."

Sandeman looked thin, as always, even in his black greatcoat. At the station, Merrick had almost failed to recognize him because of the glasses. Being a phage, Sandeman could only have perfect eyesight, especially at long range, but maybe the lenses helped him stay focused on his precious books. The horn-rimmed spectacles and the neatly trimmed black beard made him look like a professor who'd wandered up from nearby Moscow University.

"So how have you been faring, Sandeman?"

"I believe I had a dream yesterday."

Surprised, Merrick turned toward him on the bench. "You've been sleeping? How long since you've fed?"

"I forget."

Merrick laughed along with him, a good joke. "Seriously."

Sandeman's smile faded. "Two months, three weeks, five days and . . . six hours, rounding off to the nearest hour. An NKVD captain who liked to arrest young men and take them to Lubyanka, never to be seen again." He spat in the snow.

Merrick nodded. Always, Sandeman took the sadists, the murderers. He hated the Communists, especially the secret police, and he'd found plenty of the Tsar's regime equally deserving of his attention. Yet, he could never forgive himself for condemning even such vile bastards to summary execution. Any more than I could, Merrick thought. He said, "I brought transfusion equipment along."

Sandeman nodded. "I'll try it again. But when I see the blood . . ."

"I know. Tell me about the dream."

"I was in my flat, reading over some letters from Schopenhauer I'd kept from my years as a German. I must have dozed off, because I heard a sound at the window and when I looked, I saw a man there, outside the glass."

Puzzled, Merrick said, "You're still in that place on Kutuzovsky Prospekt?"

"Right—ten stories up, if you recall. For a second, I thought he was one of us and had climbed the wall, but no, he was floating, hands and feet free. It startled me, I can tell you. I was about to run when the man— or whatever it was—smiled at me. Merrick, you can't imagine the beauty of that smile, the goodness." Paradoxically, Sandeman shuddered. "He was striking, a bronze face that glowed with its own light, perfect, masculine features. I found myself moving toward the window. As I got closer, I saw arching lines of light around the man's shoulders, almost like wings, but not wings. Some peculiar field of energy, it seemed. The window was still closed, but I heard him speak. His voice was musical, like an organ. I didn't see his lips move. It was as if he had directly stimulated my auditory nerves. What he said was, 'Sandeman, you are trying to be righteous on your own strength, and you can't.' And then he was gone, vanished. Next thing I knew, I was back in my chair, awake, but sitting as if poleaxed. A dream—it had to be—but so real."

"You've gone too long without blood, that's all."

Two more boys raced along the skating path. The one behind caught the leader and pushed him off the path into the snow. The fallen boy laughed up at the sky, and began swinging his arms and legs, making a snow angel—

And then the boy was gone, and Merrick found himself in the front seat of a car, staring at Zane, who sat at the wheel. The intense reality of the memory clung, and Merrick found himself checking the backseat for Sandeman, wanting to ask him if he was the one who'd let Zane out of the vault. Then his head cleared fully and he realized Zane had attacked him with Influence, triggering a memory so sharp it had obliterated reality. While he was submerged in the memory, Zane had led him like a sheep into the car. If he tried to get away now, Zane would just shackle him inside some other memory.

Regret passed through Merrick, burning in his chest like a smoky breath. Sandeman was dead, except in memory.

As I will soon be.

Curiously, he was only a little afraid. Looking out the window, he saw that Zane had driven them into the woods near the vault, as far as the path would allow.

Zane stared at him with interest. "What did I make you remember?"

Merrick remained silent.

Zane laughed. "None of my business, eh?"

"My memories are my own."

"May they comfort you as you die."

Merrick felt a lacerating sorrow, a pain he had not felt since ten years ago, in this same place, their roles reversed. "It's such a shame we couldn't have been together."

"And now he tries to soften me up," Zane said with derision. "Why don't you try begging, like I begged you? Maybe *I'd* be more merciful." Zane gazed expectantly at him, then made an impatient sound, low in his throat. "Too stubborn to beg. All right, let's get this over with. Are you going to make me carry you?"

Merrick got out of the car. As he walked ahead of Zane toward the vault, the fear began to come, not for himself but for Katie and Gregory. Katie was here, he thought, when I put Zane in the vault, and he can't have forgotten that. To keep her from letting me out, he'll have to kill her. Merrick's heart twisted inside him. Blinded by sudden tears, he stumbled as a vine caught his ankle and he went down, sprawling in the musty leaves.

Zane stood above him, eyes pitiless. "Get up."

"Katie doesn't remember where this place is," Merrick said.

"Please."

"She doesn't know the combination."

"You'd shout it up to her."

"Through a foot of concrete, tons of dirt?"

Zane shook his head impatiently. "The cell I'm putting you in—the one you put me in—has a half-inch crack, as you'll discover, hidden in the angle of one back corner of the wall. There must have been an earthquake at some point, because there's also a small gap between the outside of the wall and the dirt that was once packed against it. It's only an inch, and there's no way to enlarge it—believe me, I tried—but it's enough of a vent to the surface that even a normal could make himself heard to someone in the immediate area above. All you'd have to do is put your mouth against that crack in the corner and shout. Katie's sharp enough to come out here, and if she starts yelling, you'll hear her and shout up the combination."

Merrick's desperation deepened. "Then take me somewhere else, damn it. Dig a hole and bury me in the dirt where she'll never find me."

"Are you begging me?"

"Yes!"

"Sorry. It has to be here, where you put me."

"Zane, she has a son who needs her. Think how it hurt you to lose your mother. Gregory's your brother, nearly the same age you were then. Do you really want him to suffer as you did?"

Zane's face softened, but only for an instant. "No. You are going into my cell, old man. But I promise Katie will never see me coming. She'll feel no fear, no pain, which is more kindness than you deserve."

"But my son—"

"What do you care about your son?" Zane screamed.

Merrick stared at him, shocked by the sudden, maniacal rage in his face. This was useless, maybe worse. Even if Zane could muster feelings for anyone else, they'd be so stunted and deformed that he might decide to kill Gregory too, so he wouldn't have to miss his mother.

"Get up," Zane growled, "or I'll carry you."

Merrick found it hard to rise, as though the air had turned to lead, pressing him down. Struggling to his feet, he stumbled forward into the clearing. Tears streamed down his face. *Katie, I'm sorry.*

Zane pulled up the trap and dialed open the door beneath, and Merrick realized dimly he'd been right about Zane memorizing the combination from the sound of the tumblers.

Zane pointed to the hole. Merrick started for it, then lunged at Zane's legs, hoping to tumble him in, but Zane kicked him away. He lay, stunned, feeling a distant pain in his ribs. He was dimly aware of Zane picking him up, of the light fading as Zane carried him down the ladder, and then it was pitch black. Merrick couldn't see the withered bodies as

Zane carried him between the cots, but his skin crawled from their closeness. The door to a cell creaked open and Zane dropped him on the cot inside. Blinking back his tears, Merrick could just make him out, a lighter shadow against the black rectangle of the cell doorway.

"If you had loved me," Zane said softly, "it would never have come to this."

"I always loved you," Merrick said. "Even on the day I put you here."

Zane made a sound too bleak to be laughter. "Then I must love you too, because I'm returning the favor. Good-bye."

The door clanged shut, and the bolt slid home. Merrick lay paralyzed for a second, then pushed up and groped his way to the door, pounding on it in terror and frustration. He had to get out, get to Katie before Zane did. He groped his way to the back corner and found the crack Zane had talked about. Screaming in the darkness, he begged Zane to let him out.

Finally, he realized Zane was gone.

Merrick sank to the floor, lying on his side on the cold floor. Jenn, he thought. Maybe she'll get free of him and come to let me out.

But he knew it was a vain hope. Jenn was under Zane's power now. Even if eventually she could break away, Katie would be dead by then.

For the first time in a thousand years Merrick felt the horror of total helplessness. Let me die, he thought. But he knew he could not even do that, not for a long time.

***

Jenn tried again to break free of the cable, bucking and squirming, but it was too tight, unbreakable, and at last she fell still again. Galled, she lay back. The weeds, beaten down by her repeated struggles, made a tangled mat beneath her. The shadow of the tree to which she was chained darkened then melted away again as clouds flowed across the moon. How long had she been here? Several hours—more than enough time for Zane to return to Washington and kill Merrick. Almost enough time for him to get back here. She had to break free soon, or it would be too late.

Maybe Zane hasn't killed him yet, she told herself. He'd want him to suffer. Maybe he'd toy with him, make him dig his own grave. . . .

No! He'll put Merrick in the vault—the same cell he was in!

Sudden hope buoyed her, and then she shuddered as she thought of the horrible, lingering death Merrick would still be facing. But not right away. There was time to save him, if she could just get free now.

She rolled around the base of the tree again, feeling the cable twist tight below her ankles as she groped the mat of weeds with her cheek for a stone, anything sharp. As before, there was nothing. A fierce frustration gripped her. She tried to calm herself. Even if she couldn't get loose now, surely Zane wouldn't keep her chained up. If she could give him the slip in the next few weeks, there'd still be time to go back and free Merrick.

And then she realized the rest of it and her heart sank. As soon as Zane had put Merrick in the vault, he'd go after Katie, because Katie knew where the vault was. A sick horror filled Jenn. Zane won't toy with Katie, she thought. He'll kill her the instant he finds her, so he can come back and get me.

She twisted, straining to pull an arm free, but she remained as tightly bound as before. Zane had left no slack at all in the cable, knowing her circulation could be restricted for days without doing any permanent harm.

Would Zane kill Gregory too? Jenn's dread deepened . . .

Listen!

A faint buzz from the roadbed above grew slowly louder, turning into the growl of an approaching motorcycle. She gathered herself without much hope. Several cars had passed earlier and she'd screamed each time, hoping a window might be down. She'd have to really yell to penetrate a cyclist's helmet and the noise of his bike—

The muffler—it sounds like the Harley!

Jenn started screaming Hugh's name. The roar of the bike swelled, then began to fade down the road. Her screams turned to sobs, and then she realized the bike had stopped and was idling up the road. She screamed again: *"Hugh! Hugh!"*

The engine cut off.

"Help! Come back! I'm down here!"

The engine revved up again and the sound swelled, then shut off above her, but she kept on screaming, until she saw him scrambling down the bank. He knelt beside her, looking horrified, then furious. She was so glad to see him she forgot the cable for a second and tried to hug him.

"My God, Jenn. Who did this to you?"

"Hugh, we don't have much time. We need a saw, anything sharp."

His face lit and he scrambled back up the bank, returning in seconds with a set of long-handled bolt cutters and a skewed grin. "Will this do?"

"Hurry—he might come back."

"Your father?"

She hesitated, *the hell with it,* then nodded. Slipping one blade of the cutters under the wire where it crossed from her arm to her chest, Hugh grimaced as he bore down on the handles.

"You just happen to have bolt cutters on your motorcycle?"

"I can explain, but only if you tell me how you got over that prison wall."

"Later."

The blades slipped and he cursed. "Wait a minute . . . there." He tried again, his face darkening with effort, and she heard the cable snap and felt it loosen; twisting, she fought and shimmied her way loose, scrambling to her feet as the cable unraveled and fell away.

She hugged Hugh so hard he wheezed. "Sorry," she said, stepping back. "How did you find me?"

"After you and I talked, I knew you wouldn't wait, so I went home and got the sawed-off Uncle Tydus gave me and drove back. I parked my bike out of sight of the guard towers and walked to the gate with the shotgun under my jacket. I don't know what I planned to do, but I didn't get a chance to find out because the alarm went off as I reached the gate. I hid inside the archway there, and kept sticking my head out to look down the wall. I saw a car down a ways, and then I saw you getting into it and this big guy jumped over the top and got in the driver's side. I ran to get my bike, and managed to follow you to Anacostia, then you lost me."

Jenn nodded. So it *had* been Hugh behind them, and not a motorcycle cop, as Zane had told her. In the panic of the moment, the bad muffler hadn't registered—not that it would have made any difference.

"I picked you up again south of the city," Hugh said, "and stayed way back, but he lost me again. I've been crisscrossing the back roads ever since."

She kissed him, then kissed him again. "We've got to get out of here before he comes back."

"Let him. I've still got the shotgun."

"No!" she said.

"I wouldn't shoot him—just scare him off."

"It's better if we run, believe me." She sprinted up the bank, pulling him up after her, then settling on the rear of the saddle. "Let's go!"

He hopped on in front of her. "Anyplace special? Remember, you're pretty hot right now."

Katie—too late to warn her? Maybe not. "The nearest phone," she said.

"There's a gas station about two miles back," he said.

She clung close to him as he drove, filled with love and gratitude and an agony of fear for Merrick and Katie. After about a mile, he pulled off on a side road and idled the bike.

"What are you doing?"

"When I went to the prison, I brought some clothes you'd left at my place. They're in the saddlebag."

She realized she was still in the prison jumpsuit, half shredded by the concertina wire, still damp with her clotless blood. While Hugh watched the road, she changed hurriedly into the jeans, blouse, and light jacket he had brought, burying the bloody jumpsuit beside the road.

The gas station phone was around the side, away from the attendant. Getting off the bike, she told Hugh to stay on it, she'd be right back.

"You'll need this." He pressed a quarter into her hand.

She ran to the phone and dialed Merrick's number, then realized the phone might be tapped. Never mind—even if they traced the call here, she'd be long gone in minutes.

"Hello?"

Katie's voice, tight with strain, sent a sympathetic shock along Jenn's nerves.

"Katie, it's me—"

"Jenn, Merrick's gone. He knew I was coming home, but he's gone, no note, nothing. He wouldn't do that. I'm scared."

Jenn heard Hugh coming up behind her. Dismayed, she tried to wave him away, but he kept coming.

"Jenn?" Katie said.

"I think I might know where Merrick is—"

"Where? You've got to tell me."

Jenn hesitated, not wanting to terrify Katie, then realizing she was right. *If I can't save Merrick, maybe she'll be able to.* "Katie, I think Zane has taken him to the vault."

"Oh, God!"

"Katie?"

"I'm all right, I'm all right."

"Good. I'm on my way there now—"

"I'll meet you there."

"No! You've got to look after Gregory. Zane will be coming for you both."

"Shit. You're right. God damn it!"

For a second Jenn was shocked. Katie never swore. "Take Gregory, and get out of the house, right now. Go to the most public place you can find, where there are lots of people. I'll get Merrick out, I promise you."

"You'll need the Fraction Eight," Katie said. "It's in a syringe."

Fraction Eight? After a second, Jenn understood. Katie must have extracted a concentrated dose to use as a weapon against Zane. But why hadn't Merrick told her?

He was afraid I might not go along with it. "All right, just leave it there and go—you and Gregory."

"Jenn, if he comes here, and I've got the Fraction Eight—"

"No. He's much too fast for you, you know that. Just leave the syringe." Jenn thought quickly. "Leave it in the piano bench and go. If I get Merrick out, I'll leave you a message at the hospital. Keep calling in. If you don't hear anything in a day, then go to the vault. But whatever you do, get out of the house now, and stay out."

There was a pause. "All right."

Hanging up, Jenn turned. Hugh was standing right behind her, his face pale.

"What is it?" she asked.

He touched his temple. "Nothing. One of my headaches."

"Maybe they have aspirin in the station. I'll wait for you on the bike."

"What did you mean about the vault?" Hugh asked.

"Go get some aspirin. Then we'll talk." She gave him a little push toward the station and walked away toward the bike, praying he'd left the key in the ignition.

He had.

"I'm sorry, Hugh," she said softly, "but you're no match for Zane, shotgun or no. I have to do the next part alone, and I need your Harley."

She turned the ignition. Putting the bike in gear, she roared off down the road, hearing Hugh's faint shout behind her, making herself ignore it. If Merrick was in the vault, he'd be safe for now, but Katie was another matter. I have to go there first, Jenn thought. Make sure she got Gregory out—and didn't come back.

And pick up the Fraction Eight, because I'm no match for Zane either.

2 6

Christiana sat in her car, watching Merrick Chapman's house and worrying. If Dr. Hrluska showed up, would the video camera really catch it from this far away?

Was a block and a half far *enough* away?

The other night in the parking lot, she'd been half this far away when the man-thing had sprung up and looked straight at her. Christiana shivered. If Dr. Hrluska was cut from the same eerie cloth, how far was "out of range"?

She tried to put it from her mind—there wasn't another parking space to be had on this street anyway. She'd been lucky to find this one so late at night in Georgetown. If she could have gotten here an hour sooner . . . but no, Officer Jankow would have to be a slow drunk. And, naturally, his favorite bar would have to be all the way out in Fairfax, a terrible black-painted dive with a sticky floor and so much smoke the skinny topless dancers looked like ghosts. Christiana shivered again, remembering the creepy way Jankow had kept looking at her mouth and chest instead of her eyes. But mostly he'd looked at the Red Dogs she'd kept buying him, until finally he'd loosened up enough to talk about the investigation. Even then it had taken two more beers to get this lead. Thank goodness beer was a greater weakness for him than women.

Steadying the camera on the dash, Christiana bent over the eyepiece. The night-vision optics lent a greenish tinge to the tree-lined street, restoring a summery, chlorophyll brightness to the canopy of autumn leaves and painting the stately house fronts a garish chartreuse. Streetlights made bright smears in the roof of leaves. A five-foot bank raised the houses on Merrick's side of the street into view above an unbroken line of parked cars.

Christiana found the zoom button and held it down. The street rushed forward, giving her a swooping sensation as the houses flowed past and vanished on either side. At high magnification, the picture jittered as she inched the camera over to take in the front of Merrick's house. A maple shaded the small yard. A lush, untrimmed hedge of azaleas hid the foundation, and the house itself was covered to the eaves by shags of ivy. As she centered the camera on the door, the autofocus fine-tuned itself, giving her a sharp-edged view of the mail slot. Panning down to the parked cars, she zoomed out to maximum range to pick up the windshield of the unmarked police cruiser at the far end of Merrick's block. The autofocus hung on the windshield for a moment, and then movement behind the glass drew it through as the man in the driver's seat raised a thermos cup to his mouth. Christiana studied his face. He had that cop hardness around the eyes, and the expression of weary boredom that would come with long hours of watching. She read his lips as he said something to his partner in the passenger seat: "[Something] out of my skull. I'd give my [something] for one of [something] back rubs."

A stakeout, yes, confirming Jankow's boozy hints about something fishy between Dr. Hrluska and her "close" friend Merrick Chapman. With the D.C. budget in ruins, the police wouldn't expend two men here unless they thought the fugitive doctor might try and link up with Chapman. If Hrluska did show up here, it would be fascinating to see how a woman who had thrown a mugger thirty feet handled two cops trying to arrest her.

Not just see it, get it on videotape.

The cop drained his cup and screwed it back onto the top of his thermos, staring at Merrick's house again, then his gaze roamed down the street toward her. All at once he was looking straight at her. Spooked, Christiana jerked back from the eyepiece, then gave a nervous laugh. There was no chance he'd actually seen her. Without the camera, she could barely pick out the distant, unmarked car.

She tore open a packet of the orange crackers stuck together with peanut butter. Their oily, *eau de vending machine* fragrance gave her a déjà vu thrill low in her gut, the way excitement had felt to her years ago. Raising the cracker to her mouth, she found she just couldn't—her palate had become coddled by years of stone-grounds and Brie on the political circuit. So she poured herself a cup of iced Darjeeling from her own thermos and drank a few sips, not too much, or she'd have to go to the bathroom.

Bending over the camera again, she focused on the glowing window of Merrick's front door. A silhouette flowed across it, and she sucked a sharp breath. Someone *was* in there! Merrick, watching for Dr. Hrluska?

Come on, Doctor, Christiana thought. I don't know if you're a killer or not, but I *do* know you're not quite human. Give me just one more chance, and I'll make us both stars.

⁂

Zane stalked past the front window, burning with frustration and a restless, chafing fury. Where was Katie? Surely she wouldn't be working this late at the hospital. He needed to kill her and get out of here, back to his daughter. Not that Jenn could escape, but he hated the thought of her lying bound in that ravine, uncomfortable, terrified for her grandfather and furious at him. Returning here to settle with Merrick had set him back with her, no question. Would she forgive him? That she might not terrified him.

Zane cursed softly. Nothing was working out as it was supposed to. This should be the happiest day of his life, Jenn with him at last, and Merrick sealed away in his own cell—how many times had he dreamed of this, knowing it was impossible, but longing for it anyway, imagining the look on the old bastard's face, the way he would beg for his life. I did it, Zane thought. I actually did it!

So why am I not happy?

It was too easy. The old man is nothing now, not much stronger than a normal. And he didn't beg for his life, only Katie's and his son's.

And even if I hadn't put him away, he's dying.

Zane paced into the living room and sat on the couch, then pushed up again. It was a mystery. Phages were still strong and vigorous at a thousand years—in many ways just hitting the full peak of their powers. Merrick should not be dying. What had happened to him?

Or did he do it to himself!

Zane stopped pacing and stared at an ornate grandfather clock in the corner of the living room. The pendulum hung straight down, motionless. Merrick, committing suicide? The idea had a crazy rightness to it. Maybe, worn down at last by his long indulgence in guilt, he'd found a way to age himself so he could die and be done with it.

Or maybe he was tired of leaving his women. Could he really be such a romantic fool? He'd fallen head over heels for many other women before Katie, one after another down through the centuries, and he'd never tried to grow old and die with any of them.

But Katie *was* a remarkable woman.

Memories of ten years ago flooded Zane. She fought me like a tigress, he thought. When I went to her son's bedroom, she grabbed a baseball bat and swung it all around in a frenzy, trying to hit me even though she couldn't see me. Her mother had collapsed in panic, but Katie was fearless. She is the only one of Merrick's wives to know what he is, the only normal in the world who knows we exist, and yet she has never let it slip. She's beautiful, intelligent, loyal, and fierce. If any woman could be worth dying for, she is.

An oppressive heaviness settled over Zane, blunting his anger. He would not enjoy killing Katie. How very odd.

Where was she anyway?

She probably came home, Zane thought, found Father gone, and rounded up her son and went out to eat. They'll be back. Just be patient.

An agitated tension drove him into motion again, upstairs to the den Katie had used as an office ten years ago. The rolltop desk was still there; a photograph on one corner—Katie and her son standing together in front of a brilliant yellow hedge of forsythia. He'd grown tall, Gregory; a handsome kid with dark hair. Katie's hug had pulled him off-balance against her; his pained grin could not entirely conceal the adoration in his face. He'd be twelve now, Gregory.

Almost the same age I was when Mam died.

Zane grimaced. An embarrassing moment, Father trying to move him with that old sadness. Losing Mam had hurt terribly—he could remember that. But after five hundred years, the pain was long gone, broken away like a plaster mold.

Turning away from the photo, Zane saw another desk, probably Merrick's. Curious, he tested the drawers. One resisted and he jerked it open, splintering the wood away from the lock. A ball rolled into sight, and then his heart skipped a beat. Astonished and shaken, he picked up the small, wooden sphere. It had used to be blue, but the last bit of paint must have flaked off centuries ago. He could remember Father working on this by the fire evening after evening while Mam joked with him that it was getting too small and there would be nothing left if he didn't give up his mania to make it perfectly round. "I've almost got it," he'd tell her. He'd roll it along the table, and when some tiny flaw nudged it off course, he'd go back to work until, inevitably, he'd cut a bit too deep and another entire layer had to come off. I watched him, Zane thought, night after night, until I became obsessed too. I was ten years old, and I called him Da then. Each time he'd cut too deep, he'd howl and stalk around in mock despair, then go back to work. I knew that if he ever got it perfect, he'd never part with the ball. Then one night, he rolled it and it went perfectly straight. He rolled it again, a dozen times, while Mam and I clapped. The next night, he painted it.

And when the paint was dry, he gave it to me.

Zane's eyes stung suddenly, as if smoke from those evening fires long ago had seeped through the wall of time. I loved this ball more than anything I had ever seen, he thought. Da and I must have thrown it back and forth a thousand times. At night, I'd take it to bed with me, roll it in my hand and feel its perfect smoothness. I vowed to make one just like it if I ever had a son.

Then Mam died. After a few months, Da tried to get me to play catch again, but I would remember how Mam watched him make the ball, her laughter that I'd never hear again, and finally I threw it into the woods. Da looked sad, but he didn't go after it. I thought it was lost. He must have gone back out to find it.

Rolling the ball between his palms, Zane felt its perfect, mesmerizing smoothness, still there in the ancient wood. He wanted it, and could not imagine why. Father hunted me the same way he made this ball, Zane thought bitterly, year after year, never giving up, no matter how many times I got away. I should hate this thing.

Zane tossed it in the air and caught it, tossed it, caught it.

He held it to his nose, smelling the faint traces of oil from Da's hands, and then he understood. This had been made by Da, not by Father. That was why he wanted it.

But why hadn't Father given it to one of his other sons, even to Gregory, whose mother he was willing to die for?

Because it was ours, from when we loved each other.

A lump rose to Zane's throat. Ridiculous, absurd.

He put the ball in his pocket.

Fleeing downstairs again, he sat on the couch and thought about whether he should wait any longer for Katie to come home. What was he thinking? If he didn't wait and kill her, sooner or later, she'd figure out where Merrick was and go free him.

Maybe it would be later.

A month would be about right, Zane thought. That's how long I was down there.

Can he last a month the way he is now?

Incredibly, Zane felt a touch of worry. Katie's smart for a normal, he thought. It would probably be only a day or two—forty-eight hours in the death cell he made for me. Every minute of that time, he'll suffer as I did. He'll think his dear Katie is dead. He'll mourn the sunrises he'll never see again.

Zane stood, slipping a hand into the pocket, feeling the perfect, painstaking smoothness of the ball. Father can't hurt me anymore, he thought. I never need to be afraid of him again. Let Katie live. Let her go and get her Merrick out of the vault. Do it, and maybe your daughter will love you after all.

The weight dropped from Zane's shoulders. I've gone crazy, he thought. But he smiled as he started for the door.

Christiana almost missed Jenn. There was no sound to warn her, no movement or sound of a car coming down the street. Fiddling with the radio dial, trying to find some political news, she just happened to glance up, and there Jenn was, walking down the sidewalk, right past the unmarked police car.

With a gasp, Christiana picked up the video camera—quickly, quickly, before the cops jumped Jenn and it was all over! Steadying the camera on the dash, Christiana found her, the image jittering as her hands trembled. Hrluska was almost to Merrick's front walk now—any second, the cops would hurry into the picture. Holding her breath, Christiana watched Dr. Hrluska mount the three steps, then move up the sidewalk to the front stoop.

Now, Christiana thought. *Now!*

But neither man from the unmarked police car appeared in the close frame of the viewfinder, and she was afraid to move the camera for fear she'd miss something the doctor might do.

You're not taping!

Gasping in dismay, Christiana found the "record" button and thumbed it. *Stupid!*—she was blundering like a cub reporter. Too long since she'd tried anything like this. Never mind, it was taping now, and she'd missed nothing important. The doctor, green in the viewfinder, bent and removed a key from under the doormat. She slipped it into the lock—where were the stupid cops? They had to have seen her!

Jenn slipped inside the house, freeing Christiana to pan the camera toward the unmarked car. The cop at the wheel was rubbing at his neck, gazing at Merrick's front door, eyes still glazed with boredom. His partner was eating a candy bar.

Christiana's teeth chattered in a spasm of fear and excitement. They hadn't seen Jenn! She'd strolled right past them and somehow she'd made it so they'd never seen her! Hrluska did it to them, Christiana thought, just like that thing the other night did it to me!

What in God's name *is* she?

⁘

With a mixture of hope and dread, Jenn slipped into Merrick's foyer, then froze as she saw Zane coming toward her. He stopped, too, his face shocked. Her heart sank—*I'm too late.* The ominous stillness of the house deepened her fear. The shock faded from Zane's face and he gazed at her with the oddest expression—pride, she realized suddenly.

"Incredible!" he said.

"Where are they?"

"Where are who?"

"Stop it! I *know* why you're here." Despite her fear, she wanted to rush at him, pound him with her fists.

"Take it easy," Zane said mildly. "If you mean Father, he is now enjoying my old view in the vault. I don't know where Katie and Gregory are. How did you get away? And don't expect me to believe you broke the cable."

"You put Merrick in the vault," Jenn said, "then you came here to kill Katie and Gregory. Do you still think I could love you?" For a moment, fury made her bold; she pushed past him, through the living room and into the music room, dreading what she might see, knowing Zane could stun her at any second with another memory, then tie her up again.

Instead, he followed her.

Turning, she sat on the piano bench and let her elbows settle on the keyboard lid. Beneath her, in the bench, was Merrick's music, the Bach inventions he loved, the Rachmaninoff, the Scott Joplin . . . and a syringe of Fraction Eight—if Katie had got out in time. There was no smell of blood in the house, but Zane could have strangled or smothered her and Gregory, or given them a fatal stroke. Thinking about it made Jenn so tense she wanted to scream, but she knew she must stay calm, wait her chance to try for the syringe.

Zane perched on a corner of the love seat that faced the piano. "I'm curious," he said. "How is it that Father is dying?"

Suddenly Jenn could feel her heart pounding through her elbows against the lid of the keyboard. Did Zane suspect Fraction Eight? *Careful—he'll be trying to read you.*

"Merrick is dying," she said, "because he no longer wants to live. From the day he put you in the vault, he has wanted to die." *And that is the truth, or near enough.*

Zane gave a bitter laugh. "He could have pulled me out any time."

"And condemn how many hundreds of your future victims to death? No."

"Do you seriously expect me to believe Father has been dying of grief over me?"

"He never stopped loving you."

Zane stared at her. He cleared his throat. "If it's any comfort, I felt no pleasure at what I did. I expected to, deserved to, but I didn't."

"Then let him out. He's your father."

"And I was his son." Zane sprang up from the couch. "You know what's really crazy? I never stopped *wanting* his love, hoping for it, but he wouldn't give it—not unless I did everything—*everything*—by his rules."

"All he wanted was for you to stop killing."

"But that *is* everything. That's what I am."

She saw with alarm that he was getting angry again. She mustn't argue with him. She had only one goal now, to save Merrick, Katie, and Gregory. What would it take?

You know what.

Jenn felt heavy with despair. Zane wanted her with him. It was her only bargaining chip. "Let Merrick out of the vault, and I'll go with you."

Zane studied her. "And stay with me?"

"For a month."

He grunted. "I can see you aren't serious."

"Six months, then."

"Two years," he said flatly.

She felt sick to her stomach. "A year—*at least* a year. Whether it goes beyond that will be up to you."

He gazed at her with open longing. "Your word?"

She felt a joyless triumph. "You really haven't harmed Katie or Gregory?"

"I already told you I haven't. You have to learn to trust me."

"That's exactly right—I have to *learn*."

"Search the house if you like."

"And Merrick is unhurt? You locked him away, and that's all?"

"Yes."

"Then you have my word. We go to the vault now and let Merrick free, and then I'll stay with you."

He closed his eyes, as if in prayer, then reached hesitantly for her hand. She forced herself to let him take it. His eyes were shiny with tears. "You won't be sorry," he said softly. His face was alight, but his joy deadened her. She pushed up from the bench. As he turned away toward the door, she eased up the lid beneath her, and there was the loaded syringe, just as Katie had promised. Jenn slipped it into her pocket. Zane would keep his word now, or one of them would die.

27

Hugh stood at the high-test pump of the Old Dominion gas station, rubbing his temples, trying to ease the throbbing tension of his headache. At the same time he watched the dark country road, thinking: come back, Jenn, *please* come back. But he knew she wouldn't.

He had the sickening sense that doom was rushing at him and he could do nothing to stop it. Time was slipping away, like his blood that time on the Shenandoah trail when he'd taken a stray slug in the leg from some distant deer poacher and couldn't get the bleeding stopped. If only he knew where she had gone. To track her father down at some vault, that was clear, but *where*? It was insane—how could she willingly give the bastard another crack at her? This time he might not settle for tying her up.

I have to find her, Hugh thought.

He sucked a lungful of cool October air, but it was laced with gasoline fumes, bringing a spike of nausea up his throat. That phone call: *I think I might know where Merrick is . . . Zane has taken him to the vault . . . I'm on my way there now.* Apparently Jenn's father had tied her up and left her in a ditch in order to return to Washington and deal with Merrick by taking him to a vault . . .

Vault. Why did that strike such a deep, gut unease into him? The headache had begun the moment she'd said it, an instant drumbeat of tension, and he never had the headaches except when he was thinking about that blank period ten years ago, trying to penetrate the fog of that lost week.

Feeling a needle of pain behind the left eye, Hugh pushed a hand against his forehead. Suddenly, a series of vivid mental images spilled past his mind's eye—a bed of dry leaves, his own hand reaching down, grasping the handle of a trap door and pulling it up, and then another door, like a safe—

—a room full of cots, an ancient corpse, long white hair framing a mummified face—

Not a room, a vault!

Hugh gasped at another fierce jab behind his eye. As he tried to concentrate, to remember more, the pain sharpened, making him thick-headed. A vault, lying under a trap door, hidden by a thick bed of fallen leaves—

The woods!

A grenade of pain exploded inside Hugh's head. Stumbling to the roadside, he fell to his hands and knees and threw up. His head cleared a little. The woods, yes, after his book party—the place where he'd gone ten years ago to scout for a moonshine still that had been the last thing he'd remembered for a week.

With a ragged shout, Hugh pushed to his feet. The gas station seemed very far away. He started for the lighted window, dimly aware of the attendant in the center, a thin kid staring out at him, what was his name—*Buzz*. Hugh pushed through into the station, and Buzz shrank back behind the counter. "Hey, buddy, you all right? I saw you throw up out there. What's the matter? Stay back!"

Hugh halted. "Aspirin," he gasped.

"Sure, sure." Buzz plopped a small bottle on the counter.

"Open it."

Buzz fumbled with it. When he'd slit the seal and worked the cotton out, Hugh snatched it away, shook four tablets into his hand and gulped them down dry.

"Want some Coke? That's good for throwing up."

Hugh had the insane urge to laugh at the fractured syntax, then saw the bodies again, withered rows of bodies, just a flash of them, making his scalp crawl.

"Here, I'll get you that Coke," Buzz said.

"You have a car?" Hugh asked.

"Uh . . . nope."

"How do you get to work? We're in the middle of nowhere."

"Look, you cain't have my car."

"I'll pay. Just to rent it."

"No way." Buzz stared at him. "How much?"

Hugh pulled his wallet out and threw everything he had on the counter, four twenties, a ten, and three ones. Buzz stared at them but did not pick them up. "How'd I know you'd bring it back?"

"I'll leave you this, too." Hugh shucked his VISA onto the counter. "There's a ten-thousand-dollar limit on that card. If I'm not back with your car by tomorrow, go on a shopping spree, my compliments."

Buzz snatched up the card and bills and put some keys on the counter. "That Chevette out back. She's full up, but don't push her over sixty."

Hugh grabbed the keys and ran out. The Chevette started up with a dry cough, and he forced himself not to gun it until he was down the road. It began to shimmy at sixty-five, and he eased back, thinking about the roads between here and the big woods in Fairfax County, seeing each turn in his mind. The aspirin began to work, dulling the pounding in his head. He did not try again to think of that night ten years ago. He would go to the woods, just go to the woods, and if they weren't there, then he'd start over, but if they were there, he prayed he'd be in time to help her—

Looking for a good site for a still, and then he'd heard faint screams, and he followed them, the screams getting louder, and then the screaming stopped and a voice came up from the ground, telling him what to do. . . .

Hugh came back to himself jockeying the Chevette down the weed-choked lane to the edge of the woods. He could not remember what he'd been thinking about, some dark reverie too dangerous to allow into the front of his mind where the pain was waiting. But he'd gotten here, and that was what counted, right where he'd taken his bike after the book party. The trees forced him to slow to a crawl. Branches scratched the Chevette on either side, thank God Buzz didn't favor Lincoln Town Cars. The headlights picked up the flank of another car ahead, a white Nissan pulled off between two trees, and just beyond it, blocking the road, the car he'd seen Jenn get into with her father. Hugh felt feverish with fear and excitement. *They're here!*

An image seemed to flash on the dark screen of the windshield, *a yawning door, a dark form illuminated suddenly in the beam of his flashlight, hands reaching out to him with bloody fingernails—*

He braked the Chevette to a shuddering halt and gripped the wheel, frozen in dread. *I can't do this. I have to get out of here. Now.*

Switching the engine off, he sat, gulping deep breaths of air. All right, he thought. All right, all right. Then he got out and walked through the trees, following the thin sheen of moonlight between them, making himself take each step toward the clearing. Something moved off to his left, and he froze, peering through the darkness. He could see nothing at first, and then, through a gap in the trees, he made out a shadowy human shape, someone holding a video camera, pointing it toward the clearing. But that made no sense, no sense at all, and he decided it was an optical illusion, an oddly shaped bush, his mind playing tricks with the shadows. He took another few steps toward the clearing, and then he heard a faint, deep voice ahead.

It's him!

Panic flooded him. Turning to run, instead Hugh grabbed the trunk of a tree and held on.

⁂

Zane could not take his eyes off Jenn as she groped through the leaves for the trap door above the vault. He felt an incredible joy, and at the same time a fear that if he looked away, she might disappear. I'll be able to see her all the time now, he told himself. Watch everything she does, how she talks to people, when she smiles and why.

He watched her hands, her fine, graceful hands, go clumsy with haste as she yanked the trap door up, spilling leaves away to reveal the safe door beneath. How much she loves Merrick, he thought, pained. If she could love me half so much, I'd be happy, at last.

And now I have my chance.

He felt an airy lightness in his chest and shoulders. I've won! he thought.

And I've changed.

He shook his head, dumbfounded at himself. Even a week ago, he'd not have believed that, were he able to destroy Merrick, he would instead let him go. He felt guilty at the way he'd used it to bargain with Jenn, even though he'd already made the decision before she'd walked in. Maybe he should have offered to release Merrick with no strings. It would have proved to her that he was not the monster Merrick had said.

But would she have stayed with him of her own free will?

Jenn turned to him. "I don't know the combination."

He bent over the dial, rotating it this way and that, feeling the tumblers click. Was Merrick hearing it down below, and feeling the first bright surge of hope? Zane found that he didn't care one way or the other.

"How did you get away," Jenn asked, "ten years ago?"

Unnerved, Zane missed a turn and had to start over. It wasn't safe to talk about that, not until they were well away from here. "I'll tell you later," he said. "It's not important now."

The safe door clicked open and descended on its hydraulic hinges into the darkness.

"After you," he said.

She did not move, waiting for him to go first, driving home to him once again that she did not trust him. Pained, he descended the ladder into the anteroom, then through the commons to the door of his cell, the proud hunters around him now only a dusty smell in his nostrils. Sliding back the bolt, he pulled open the door to Father's cell.

Merrick was standing beside his cot, a look of dread on his face. Instead of rushing out, he sniffed the air.

He's smelling for blood. He's afraid I brought Katie's body back to him.

Zane shook his head. "You're free to go."

Still, Merrick did not move. "Katie?"

"I have no idea where your wife or son are. I haven't hurt them."

And then Merrick reached out for him, grabbing hold of his coat, sagging against him with a muffled sob. Zane wanted to push him away, but another impulse, old and unfamiliar, but not unwelcome, stopped him.

"Merrick?" Jenn called down from above.

"Get out of here, old man. Before I change my mind."

Merrick stood back and grinned in his general direction. "I'd love to, but I can't see."

Exasperated, Zane brushed Merrick's hands from his coat, took his arm, and led him to the antechamber, where enough moonlight fell through to show the way. The old man scrambled up the ladder and into his granddaughter's arms. Zane pulled the safe door shut, restoring the trap door and its covering of leaves.

"You made a deal with him?" Merrick asked.

Zane turned in time to see Jenn nod. The pain in the old man's face gave him no satisfaction. He just wanted to be out of here, quickly, to have the deal done.

Merrick gazed at him. "Don't let them catch her."

"I won't."

"And don't try to change her. Let her be."

"The way you let me be?"

"Is that what you want? To be like me?"

Zane stared back, stunned. "I'm not like you, old man. That's absurd. How could you say it?" He turned to Jenn. "Come on, it's time to go."

She nodded, and his fear dropped away as he realized she was really going to do it, come with him.

"You!" said a voice at the edge of the clearing.

Startled, Zane whirled. It was Hugh McCall, stepping from the trees. Zane groaned in horror as he felt everything he had won sliding away from him.

28

Seeing Hugh step from the woods, Jenn stared in shock. *How did he find us?*

Zane will kill him!

Terror gave her chest a sudden, cold squeeze. Turning to Zane, she saw his eyes narrow into the fierce squint of a cornered animal. She slipped a hand into her jacket pocket and gripped the loaded syringe with trembling fingers. Her mouth was dry and she could feel her heart hammering in her throat. *I'll only have one chance. If I don't make it, he'll kill us all.*

Hugh advanced into the clearing, legs stiff, face terrified, yet he kept coming. "I was exploring these woods ten years ago," he said, staring at Zane. "When I got to this clearing, I heard screams coming from the ground. I yelled down to you and you shouted back, told me what to do—"

His mouth distorted suddenly and he pressed the heel of his hand against his forehead. For a terrified instant, Jenn thought Zane was striking into his brain, then realized she would pick up such a burst of Influence, and there was none—not yet. This was one of Hugh's headaches.

What should she do? If Zane could hold back from hurting Hugh, she'd have to keep her part of the bargain. But if she waited and Zane struck, she'd be too late. She looked to Merrick, hoping for some signal in his eyes, but he seemed unaware of her, gazing at Zane with a relieved expression. He said, "Then it wasn't Sandeman who let you out!"

Merrick can't help me, she realized with dismay. This is up to me.

Ignoring Merrick, Zane stared at Hugh. "You should never have come here."

"You made me come with you," Hugh said accusingly, "after I'd let you out. You must have drugged me or something. You kept me in the car, driving west. I remember now—Denver, Salt Lake City. You killed women and put them in the car with me. You . . . you drank their blood!"

Zane seemed frozen; Jenn tried to guess what was in his mind, to decide if he was about to strike. Hugh had remembered too much—and now, seen too much. He could bring them all down with what he knew. Why hadn't Zane killed him already?

And then she saw the answer, so obvious for anyone but Zane: he's *grateful.*

Ten years ago, scrambling up from hell into the light, he must have been ready to give Hugh anything, but all he dared give him was his life—and a hole in his memory.

Now that hole has healed, and it's come down to this.

Oh, Hugh, I can't lose you, we've only just begun.

"Don't touch him." The growl, coming out of her own mouth, surprised her.

Zane gave her an imploring look. "He has to die, surely you see that."

"I love him."

"I warned you—"

"I *love* him," Jenn repeated urgently. "Can't you please understand what that means? If you kill him, we're finished forever, you and I."

"Think, Jenn. He knows what you are now, or he'll quickly figure it out. He'll be as horrified of you as he is of me. He'll go to the police, the press—"

"No. Katie has kept Merrick's secret, and Hugh will keep mine." But she felt a tremor of dread. How *could* Hugh love her, knowing what she was? And if he could not, then Zane was right, and hundreds of thousands would die.

The backs of her eyes prickled, and she realized with horror that Zane had started to strike mentally at Hugh. Pulling the syringe from her pocket, she plunged the needle between Zane's ribs and shoved the plunger down. With a shout of surprise, he lashed out sideways. His arm caught her across the shoulder, knocking her sprawling. Before she could rise, he leapt on her, and now there was a knife in his hand. Jenn screamed with panic, and then Zane lurched forward, dropping the knife as Merrick bowled into him from behind. He swatted Merrick aside easily, and she realized with dismay how strong he still was. *Did I get any of the Fraction Eight into him?* Pinned beneath him, she hammered at his face, but he ignored her and, reaching into his coat, pulled out a short piece of wire cable. He grabbed one of her flailing hands; with a fierce effort, she bucked him to the side and scrambled up breathless with fear. He sprang toward her and she leapt high over his head, landing in a crouch behind him.

She glimpsed Hugh running at them, his face red with fury. Her heart compressed with dread for him. "No!" she screamed. "Keep away!"

Zane lunged at her, and she dodged, then bolted for the edge of the clearing, determined to draw him off from Hugh. Zane came after her— *so fast!*—but she reached the trees first, then reversed and dived under him as he lunged high. Scrambling away, she crashed straight into a small maple, snapping it off at the trunk. Grabbing the splintered end, she swung the tree at him, catching him across the chest and sending him staggering away.

"Jenn!"

She glimpsed Merrick, holding Hugh by the collar with one hand. With the other, he tossed her the knife. Catching it by the blade, she felt a distant pain before the cuts closed. She flipped the knife to its haft as a dark shape filled her vision. Instinctively, she jammed the knife forward. Zane staggered back with a shocked look, his chest spouting blood. She leapt at him, slashing and cutting in a frenzy, sobbing in anguish with each thrust. *You will not take Hugh!* Blood sprayed around them, spattering her eyes, making it hard to see. Zane reeled away, his eyes bright with pain and, as he continued to bleed, she realized the Fraction Eight *was* having an effect.

He sank to his knees and stared at her with horrified incomprehension. "What have you done to me?"

A rush of tears cleared his blood from her eyes. She raised the knife and took a step toward him.

"No!" Merrick cried.

"I have to finish him," she sobbed.

Zane lurched up and ran into the woods, and she knew she must follow, must end it now while he was weakened, while he could bleed out, or Hugh would never be safe again.

<hr />

Watching through the telephoto lens, Christiana gasped, unable to believe what she was seeing. Jenn had jumped ten feet into the air—no human could do that. She'd uprooted a small tree and swung it as easily as a broomstick. And the creature who'd fallen from her window—Jenn had stabbed him in the heart, buried the knife four inches into him, slashed him all over the chest, and yet he'd gotten up and run. Through her horror, Christiana felt a rush of elation. She'd got it, got it all on tape. All she had to do now was keep her head down until they all were gone, and then she'd take the camera over and film that hole in the ground. And then on to the networks—

The footsteps crashing to her left veered her way. Terrified, she looked up from the camera's eyepiece and saw the big man-creature running past, saw in a splash of moonlight, his head turn toward her, felt a stab of terror as his beautiful, wounded eyes looked straight into hers.

Pain exploded inside Christiana's skull; she felt a cool gush inside her brain, and cried out as the dark trees tilted around her and the woods began to fade . . .

⟡

Torn between the woman's cry of pain and the need to catch Zane, Jenn swore and broke off the chase. She could still hear Zane's footsteps faltering ahead, and she was faster than he was now, but she had only seconds to spare. She stopped in shock, looking down at the fallen woman. "Christiana!" she said.

Christiana's eyes flickered, searching for her, failing to find her, and Jenn saw with daylight clarity the expanding left pupil, and knew the woman was doomed. Zane had found a weak spot in a major cerebral artery, an aneurysm now hemorrhaging into her brain, and she had only seconds of consciousness left before the torrent of blood choked off all higher function, then squeezed down the brain stem as well.

"Dr. Hrluska?"

Jenn realized Christiana must have recognized her voice. "Yes, it's me."

"Help me."

Jenn saw the camera lying beside her and realized with horror that Christiana had somehow managed to follow them here and film everything, and that was why Zane had struck her down. Kneeling beside Christiana, she took her hand, feeling the tide of death sweep through the woman's brain. Her helplessness infuriated her. Even if they were at a hospital this second, there was no chance she could save Christiana.

"Are you there?" Christiana whispered.

"I'm here. It's all right." But it was not all right. Jenn felt bitter despair, knowing that, even if she and Christiana *were* in the ER this second, she'd be given no chance to fight for her life. Another doctor would do it as they arrested her.

"I see light." Christiana's voice was no longer afraid.

Jenn gazed with wonder into Christiana's eyes, wishing she could see through them for just a second.

Christiana's hand tightened on hers. "What *are* you?" she asked.

"I don't know," Jenn said. "I'm sorry. I don't know."

"The light. Beautiful. This time it's *real.*"

Jenn, her senses swept by the river of blood, felt Christiana die. "I'm sorry," she whispered. Releasing the limp hand, she took the videocassette from the camera and put it inside her jacket.

She could no longer hear Zane's movement through the woods, only footsteps hurrying up from behind her, the direction of the clearing. Then a car started up with a distant rasp. Before she could move toward the sound, Merrick appeared beside her, and then Hugh, too, catching her arm. "Jenn—"

"Your car—the keys, quickly."

He gave them to her; she gazed at him a second longer, wanting his love so much, but dreading what he must feel toward her now.

Then he grabbed her and kissed her, and her heart overflowed.

"Let me come with you," he said. "Don't shut me out."

"Oh, Hugh, I won't—never again. But you've got to stay with Merrick. I'll come back, I promise."

"Wait!" he said, but she broke away and ran toward the sound of the car engine, sailing through the woods on a tide of adrenaline and fear, because she must catch Zane now—if he got away and had time to recover, she'd never have another chance.

She reached the path just in time to see Zane smash his car into the Chevette, back up and smash it again, squeezing past, then speeding away. Racing to Hugh's car, she saw with a sinking feeling that it would never drive—even weakened, Zane had managed to pull one of the tires off the rim.

Christiana! She must have driven here, too.

Through the trees, Jenn saw the little Nissan. Running to it, she threw the door open, but the keys were not in the ignition. In her mind, she saw Merrick's hands working the wires of Emmy Rittenhouse's car, the dead woman Zane had left in her foyer, his ghastly gift. Willing her hands to do what Merrick's had done, she crossed the wires, and felt a rush of hope as the engine stuttered and coughed to life. Zane had smashed Hugh's Chevette far enough to the side that she could just slip past. Hitting the twin ruts of the car path, she pushed the accelerator down. She could not see Zane ahead; then he topped a rise in the field and there he was, bouncing up onto the road. Come on, come *on!* she thought. Christiana's Nissan leapt forward as she flattened the accelerator to the floor. Gunning the car up the bank and onto the main road, she saw Zane's car weave, then find its lane. He's badly hurt, she thought. If he dies, I have to be there, take care of his body, make sure no one finds it.

Suddenly she was weeping. She gritted her teeth, determined to do what she must, bury Zane or kill him, whichever it came to be. Zane held the road ahead of her, driving just at the speed limit. She could catch him easily, but as she started to speed up, she saw a state police car just ahead of him and slowed again, frustrated. The cop could not hurt her, but she did not want to hurt the cop either. Forcing herself to relax, she settled back. As long as Zane didn't try to lose her, she'd just follow him until he stopped.

The police car headed toward Washington and Zane followed. She kept him in sight, her worry deepening as the traffic thickened. Even after midnight, there was plenty of activity on Route 50, people with things to do, but none as awful as hers.

Zane drove into the city, probably hoping to get lost among the normals, surround himself with the prey he so closely resembled, and hope she would either lose him or be unable to get a clear shot at him. But she was determined not to let him out of her sight. He headed across the Potomac into Georgetown, and from there up Wisconsin Avenue, finally turning in at the grounds of the Washington National Cathedral. She followed, surprised, wondering what was in his mind. Defiance, because this was where he'd flung down the gauntlet to Merrick ten years ago? Or did he hope she would not kill him in a holy place?

Zane pulled into a parking space beside the cathedral. Jenn saw a man in a dark security uniform step from a small stone house across the south drive and head toward Zane. She dropped the guard to the grass, leaving him in a deep sleep.

By the time she had parked beside Zane's car, she could see him on the wall of one of the great towers, clearly laboring as he scaled the big blocks of granite toward the ramparts. She felt a horrid heaviness in her own arms and legs as she climbed up behind him. In seconds, she was close enough to hear his gasps, to feel the fine shower of mortar kicked down by his feet.

At the crest of the tower, he shrank back under the stony lip of the summit, cornered. She stopped a yard from him. If he were whole, he could jump down past her now, but he was not whole. She gazed at his face. It was pale with blood loss and pain. The wounds in his chest were still oozing; the Fraction Eight was not out of his system. A deep enough stroke to the throat should kill him now, and that would be the end of it.

Closing the last few feet between them, she put the blade to his throat. He gazed at her, his eyes strangely calm, but said nothing. Wind sprang up, blowing her hair to the side, moaning through the arches of the flying buttresses far below, a colder wind than she had ever known. She could feel the soft resistance of his throat through the knife. One deep stroke. *Do it now. You must!*

But her arm would not move.

"Hugh loves me," she said, "and I love him. We're going to be together always."

"Always?" he said.

For a moment, she thought he was mocking her, and then she saw the sadness in his eyes. "Hugh will never betray us."

"You won't know that until the day he dies."

Suddenly Jenn realized something. *He was able to kill Christiana. He could have killed Hugh, too.* She stared at him, mystified, and he gazed calmly back. How brave he was. Her heart clenched.

"If I let you live, will you promise never to touch Hugh?"

Zane's eyes widened. "Why would you let me live?"

"Because you are my father, damn you!" Grief and love twisted together in her throat. With an anguished groan, Zane covered his face. She realized he was weeping, that he did not want her to see. She pulled the knife away, wanting to touch him, but not knowing if he would want it, too. He looked away, out over the city. She saw it beyond him, a spill of pinpoint lights trying to beat back the darkness.

"I'm going to give you back your life," he said.

"How?"

"I'll confess to Brad's murder." A smile touched his mouth. "After all, I *did* kill him."

Jenn refused to let herself hope—not yet. "Why would they believe you?"

"Because in those last hours before I killed him, he gave everyone who would listen my description. The doctors and nurses thought he was crazy, but when I show up, the police will know he wasn't. I'll tell them I was Brad's drug supplier and he refused to pay up. So I killed him and framed you because everyone knew you and he had clashed. They'll believe me."

"But no one let you into MHU."

Zane flipped a hand in dismissal. "I stole a key so I wouldn't have to bother picking the lock. I'll give it to them and that will seal it."

Jenn realized he might be right. He *was* right . . .

And then her heart sank as she grasped the rest of it. "You can't go to prison," she said. "How will you get blood? You'll die."

"Who said anything about going to prison? I'll be on my way before the arraignment is over."

Of course! Jenn thought. If I can break out of jail, he can surely break out of a courtroom. A tremendous weight dropped away from her. She wanted to stand up, shout with ecstasy. Joy rippled through the muscles of her shoulders, as if the memory of wings were coming to life there, and she could spring away from the stone and soar out over the city. *I can go back, be a doctor again!*

"You could have killed Hugh," she said, "when you were running from me. Why didn't you?"

"I don't know." He looked baffled.

"You came back to change me," she said. "Is it possible I changed you?"

She watched him ponder this, as though it were a great mystery, and realized how alone he'd always been, how little he knew about the effect people could have on each other. It made her heart ache for him. How many centuries had he held himself away from human contact, using Influence, but *influencing* no one, feeling no sweet pulls on his own heart?

"How could I not have seen it?" Zane murmured. "I hated what my father did to me, then tried to do the same thing to my daughter. I've been a fool."

"It's not uncommon," Jenn said, "among us humans."

Zane drew a deep breath, as if nerving himself. "When all this dies down," he said, "I *would* like to see you from time to time."

"Do you think you could ever stop killing?"

He looked away, and she caught a flash of teeth, the killer cat in him making an instinctive protest. But when he looked back at her, his eyes were the tormented eyes of a man. "If anyone could persuade me to be other than I was born, it would be you. I *do* love you, daughter. And I have not loved anything or anyone in a very long time. Help me."

"I will." Gently, Jenn touched his face. Then, before he could respond, she leapt down from the ramparts, leaving her father high among the gargoyles.